Entwined Publishing books by K.E. Turner

The Wolves of Langeias
Wolf's Keep
Wolf's Prize
Wolf's Redemption

I0662165

The Wolves of Langeias

WOLF'S REDEMPTION

K.E. TURNER

ENTWINED PUBLISHING

Wolf's Redemption
ISBN # 978-1-80250-707-2
©Copyright K.E. Turner 2024
Cover Art by Erin Dameron-Hill ©Copyright November 2024
Interior text design by Entwined Publishing
Published by Eternal name, an Entwined Publishing imprint

Published in 2024 by Entwined Publishing, United Kingdom.

Entwined Publishing is a division of Totally Entwined Group Limited.

WOLF'S REDEMPTION

Dedication

To all those who need a little extra time to get
your shit together — this book is for you.
You've got this.

Acknowledgements

Though I may sit at my desk alone and write, bringing a story to life and publishing it is never a solo effort. Thank you to the team at TEG for all the work that goes on behind the scenes. A special thank-you to my editor Rebecca Scott, who tirelessly explains why a certain word belongs here and not there, fixes my grammar lapses and never complains about how many commas she has to add or delete, or how many questions I ask. To my cover designer Erin Dameron-Hill, for your amazing covers. As someone who lacks any real skill in graphic design, I am in awe of what you continue to create for me. To my beta readers Danni Line and Victoria Brown, I am so grateful for the time you spend reading and critiquing my stories. Your encouragement keeps me going even on the days when writing is a struggle and the characters won't behave. To the amazing RWAus Aspirers group for creating such a supportive space and for cheering me on. You guys rock! To my family for your never-ending support, which is beyond value. And to my readers — thank you for choosing to go on this journey with me. Special mention to Annette and Georgina who, on their holiday in Europe, took a detour to Langeais Keep and sent me some amazing photos. You're the best.

Author's Note

Dear Reader,

When I encounter foreign words I do not know the meaning of in a book, it causes me to pause each time I see them in the text, taking me out of the story. Here is a brief list of foreign words and meanings I have used in this book.

Anglo-Saxonne — English

Bretaigne — Britain

Aumonier Chaplain

Archeveque Archbishop

Chevalier knight

Comte — Count

Comtesse — Countess

Donjon keep (in Old French)

eveque — Bishop

Fougueuse Fiery

Franceis — French (in Old French)

Dame — Lady (title), i.e., La Dame Adeline — Lady Adeline

L'enfer — hell

Lundenburg — (or Lunden) London (as known in the tenth century)

Ludenwic — the port area of London (as known in the tenth century)

Petite Cracheuse de Feu — Little Fire Breather

Ma Dame — My Lady

Mademoiselle — Miss

merde — shit/fuck

Mon Dieu — My God

Monsieur — Sir

Mon Seigneur — My Lord

Mon Seigneur Comte — My Lord Count

As Old French is, well, an old language, there are many variations. I've chosen the terms I think best apply. In some instances, when I've not been able to confirm a word or phrase in Old French, I have taken the liberty of using modern French.

I have also chosen to use some modern words instead of tenth-century terms—especially French terms—for ease of readability. Many archaic words have survived to be used in modern language; however, the meaning has subtly changed over time. Using such terms could be confusing. For example, the word *Donjon* in Old French means keep or stronghold, and includes a hall and chambers for sleeping as part of that definition. *Donjon* in modern French translates as dungeon.

If you've made it this far in the series, then you've read *Wolf's Keep* and you'll know (from Erin's chat with the intern in Chapter One) that dungeons weren't really a thing back in the tenth century. Prisoners were political hostages and kept in chambers, often at the top of the tower.

An oubliette is little more than a shaft with an iron grate for access and a rope ladder to descend. While there are some similarities with Lothair's horrid underground chamber, it doesn't quite fit the definition. Also, there are now challenges within the archeological community as to the actual use of oubliettes. There are suggestions they may have been used for storage, to secure valuables or as part of a garderobe/latrine/cesspit system and not for prisoners. But the latter makes for a far more interesting story.

Langeais Keep and Langeais are real places. However, they have been used in a fictitious manner. There isn't, and has never thought to have been, an underground chamber or oubliette in the ruins of Langeais Keep.(If you head on over to my Facebook page, you'll see a picture of Langeais Keep, taken by one of my readers.) There were many Comtes de Anjou over the centuries (none named Lothair that I am aware of, although Lothair was a popular name at the time). One of them, Comte Foulques de Noir, built Langeais Keep to guard the crossing point of the Loire River.

Comte Foulques de Noir, The Black Falcon, was notorious for his wars with other comtes—as were many comtes of that era. His power base was in Tours, and Langeais Keep, one of the first stone keeps built, was just one stronghold for him. An important one. It is, to this day, one of the oldest, still standing (partly) stone keeps in France.

He did, however, dress his wife up in her wedding gown and burn her at the stake. She was also his cousin. They did things a little differently back then. Burning people at the stake was a popular way of ridding yourself of your enemies while making a statement to the masses at the same time. He wasn't the only one to use such methods.

My Comte Lothair is a fictitious Comte de Anjou, created from a compilation of many comtes of that era. And, as much as there were myths and legends of the *Loup Garou* (werewolf) in medieval France, there are no documented instances of werewolves in tenth-century Langeais. In case you were wondering.

We are all like the bright moon,
we all have our darker side.
Khalil Gibran

Chapter One

Langeais, Frankia
999

The clang of the grate above had Ulrik Voclain on his feet. His chains rattled and the silver shackles around his wrists and neck shifted, brushing over red and blistered skin. He hissed, steeling himself against the pain. Footsteps descended the steep steps cut into stone—confident and purposeful. He faced the stairs, tilted his nose and sampled the air, his visitor closer than he would have liked when he finally caught his scent.

Lothair, Comte de Anjou.

Ulrik's lips curled in a snarl and anger burned a fiery trail from his gut to his throat. He drew himself up to his full height but repressed the growl threatening to form. The man who had taken everything from him, who had thrown him in this dank, godforsaken hole, would not see him cowering. But to unleash his rage would serve neither him nor his pack.

"Ulrik Voclain."

Lothair stepped into the tight space, a candle held aloft, its meager flame doing little to stave off the darkness. Ulrik smirked. The lack of light did not make *him* uneasy.

Anger flashed in his comte's eyes, the air tainted with its sharpness, but it was gone as quickly as it had appeared. "Laugh all you like, Ulrik. I may not have your ability to see in the dark, but *I* am not the one chained to the wall."

This time, Ulrik could not suppress his growl.

Lothair set the candle on the bottom step and surveyed the small, airless space, one hand resting on the pommel of his sword. Ulrik rolled his lips, quashing his grin. Even now, chained and bound in silver as he was, Lothair saw him as a threat.

"How do you like my little underground chamber, Ulrik? It is impressive, is it not?" Lothair brushed a hand over the rough stone wall. "Secure, unpleasant and hidden beneath the bowels of my keep. I never imagined I would use it to contain a werewolf." Lothair's gaze settled on him. "Ironic, you should be the one to end up secured in here after what your family sacrificed to save you from this very thing."

Ulrik roared and lunged for Lothair. His chains snapped tight, keeping him well beyond the reach of his comte. He howled, filling the chamber with his anguish and his loss. Nervous shuffles and anxious whispers from the guards above filtered down the stairs, along with the heavy stench of fear so strong he could scent it even in his weakened state.

Amusement flashed across Lothair's face, but he took a cautious step back. "Tsk, tsk, tsk. Always the hothead." He shook his head. "Calm yourself, Ulrik. We do not want rumors of a beast beneath my keep spreading now, do we?"

He wanted to howl, but the silver of his shackles kept his wolf repressed. He had never felt such loneliness within his own thoughts. Where once the comforting and familiar presence of his wolf had filled his mind, a constant since birth, now only a deep silence remained.

Damn the silver. Damn Archeveque Renaud and his wolfsbane trap.

If there had been any other choice... If he could have saved Gaharet, his alpha, without stepping into that ring of wolfsbane... Had his alpha's mate's life not hung in the balance... He breathed through his rage until it settled into a calm acceptance. There had been no other choice. If not him, Gaharet would have stepped into the trap. Ulrik could never have allowed the unholy alliance between Lothair and the scheming archeveque to imprison their alpha. Not while he still breathed. The pack needed Gaharet more than it needed him.

Lothair paced in front of him, close but not close enough. "Archeveque Renaud came to see you." Lothair's lips twisted in a sardonic grin. "Did you think I would not know? That my men would not inform me of his visit? Ha! Renaud is a fool if he thinks I would not suspect his game." Lothair cocked his head. "What did he offer you? Freedom? Vengeance?"

Ulrik glanced away.

"Ahh. Both. Very free with his promises, is our archeveque. And what, pray tell, was the archeveque's price? No." Lothair held up his hand, halting words Ulrik had no intention of speaking. "Let me guess. He wanted you to bite me. Turn *me* into a werewolf, rather than I choose a sacrificial keep guard or some lowly chevalier to turn. The perfect excuse for him to use all his newfound skills at binding werewolves. The church to the rescue of the people of Langeais, saving them from the wicked and now cursed Comte de Anjou. What a coup for Archeveque Renaud."

Lothair took a step toward him. Ulrik met his stare. "Renaud may see you as an easy target, Ulrik. An open festering wound he could poke a few times and stir into action. I know you are too smart to fall for his promises."

Ulrik's nostrils flared, and his hands clenched into fists. Renaud's offer had tempted him. He could not deny it, not to himself, but he had not given his life freely for his alpha, only to turn on him now. Not again. He stepped back and let the tension ease from his chains, if not his body.

The knowing smugness that settled across Lothair's face rankled, but Ulrik held it in. For all the rumors of his loose grip on sanity, the comte had an uncanny ability to be one step ahead of any scheme or plot against him.

"I always win, Ulrik. You know that."

Ulrik gritted his teeth, but he kept his expression neutral.

"And I always get what I want."

Ulrik stared down his comte. "Do what you will, but I will not bite you or anyone else. I will not help *Renaud*" —he spat the name out—"and I will not help you create an army of werewolves."

Lothair shrugged. "We shall see."

Ulrik steeled himself. From the moment he had thrown himself into Renaud's wolfsbane trap, putting himself at the mercy of his comte, it had always been going to come to this. Lothair would use whatever methods necessary to achieve his goal, and that promised Ulrik pain and suffering. "I will *die* before I give you what you want. You may be the Comte de

Anjou, but I will never kneel before you again. I *renounce* you. I rescind my oath to serve you."

"You think to taunt me into killing you swiftly?" Lothair hummed his amusement. "In the end, you may wish for death, but I assure you, it will not come anytime soon. You are too valuable a commodity, and you possess knowledge I require."

Defiance stiffened Ulrik's spine. "I will tell you nothing."

Dark eyes turned flinty, a steely determination dancing in their depths. "Oh, you will. Renaud has an informant. One of your own. I"—Lothair pointed at Ulrik's chest—"have you. The days of drowning your sorrows in wine and women are over. It is time to get your head in the game. Work with me and you may be one of the few members of your pack to survive."

Ulrik's breath caught in his throat. Confirmation they had a traitor amongst them. Who? Lance, their oldest and most experienced surviving wolf? He had stood by his alpha and supported Gaharet's leadership of the pack. The twins, Aubert and Edmond, big and brutish? He had always thought them steadfastly loyal. Aimon? The newest member of their pack turned after the battle of Montsoreau had left him mortally wounded. Could he have designed to infiltrate their pack at the behest of Renaud? It seemed a risky move. If not for Gaharet turning him, Aimon would have died. Or Godfrey? Quiet, scholarly and ever the strategist? He had his own secret. Did he know Ulrik had uncovered his predilections? Did he suspect the others had knowledge of them, too?

"Is Renaud not forthcoming with all you need to know?" Ulrik sneered. "He is not much of an ally for you, is he, if he keeps things from you?" Or was it the traitor to their pack that had been less than forthcoming? Either way, Ulrik would sow whatever seeds of discontent and distrust he could. Lothair was enemy enough. It would only aid them if he could break up his alliance with Renaud. "Why should *I* tell you anything?"

Lothair grinned. From beneath his tunic, he removed a small gold disc on a gold chain. He dangled it in front of Ulrik, the disc spinning. A howling wolf's head on one side and a blood-red stone on the other. The binding amulet. The one Gaharet had given to him in exchange for his own. Their hastily planned deception rested on his possession of it.

"Remember this? Renaud tells me it is the alpha's amulet. That you killing Gaharet, *as you claim*, makes you the new alpha. Only problem is..." Lothair stepped closer, lowering his voice to a conspiratorial whisper. "I know Gaharet is not dead."

Ulrik kept his breathing even. Lothair was baiting him.

"You may have duped Renaud with your little ruse. It appears to have also fooled your pack. But not me. Gaharet is not dead, and *you* are no alpha." Lothair stepped back and resumed his pacing. "Since only the alpha can turn men into werewolves, your usefulness extends as far as the information you can provide. For everything else, I must hunt Gaharet down."

Ulrik rasped out a laugh. "You question my claim, yet you believe every word out of that treacherous archeveque's mouth."

Lothair paused, an eyebrow raised. "And which piece of information of Renaud's should I discard?"

Ulrik met Lothair's stare, letting his comte see the truth of his words. A truth he had never thought to reveal but was now the one thing that could keep his alpha safe. "Any of us could have helped you turn men into werewolves, helped you create your werewolf army. Even the one who betrayed us. All it takes is a bite—our saliva mixed with another's blood. It need not come from Gaharet."

Lothair's lack of surprise at his revelation fanned the sparks of unease in Ulrik's gut. *L'enfer.* How had he once thought he could best Lothair? Risked his pack, challenged his alpha—the man he had, in times past, called his friend—determined to have his vengeance against the comte. He would not make that mistake again.

"And the turning itself?" asked Lothair. "What does it entail? How does it affect the one being turned?"

Ulrik glanced about the small room, not taking anything in, his mind racing. He had said enough, and only then, to keep Gaharet safe. He shifted on his feet, wincing as the silver of his manacles touched unblemished skin and raised fresh welts. He would say no more.

"I see." Lothair grunted and turned to leave. "Then I must hunt and trap Gaharet."

Ulrik filled his lungs with the stale air of the chamber, exhaling slowly. That he was even considering revealing the secrets of his pack turned his blood cold, but... Though he may not survive this, Ulrik would see that Gaharet lived. He owed him that. He swallowed, his throat dry from his days of confinement as much as from what he was about to reveal. "Wait."

Lothair turned. Silence hung heavy between them. Lothair gave him a hard stare. "I am waiting."

Ulrik gritted his teeth, the words clogging his throat. "Pain. The turning is agony," he said, forcing the words out.

"How much? For how long?"

"Three days. Or more."

Lothair grunted. "Three days, you say? Bearable."

Ulrik barked out a laugh. "Bearable?" He fixed his gaze on Lothair. "Let me save you your delusions. Many do not survive. Some go mad." If he could guarantee Lothair would die during a turning, he would bite the comte himself. "You should ask Aimon about his turning. He was not born like the rest of us."

Lothair blinked, the only hint of his surprise a flicker of a frown as he made the connection. "The battle of Montsoreau?"

Ulrik inclined his head. "Ask Aimon how he *screamed* for days on end, strapped to a cot to protect him. To protect us. I can still remember his torment. How he begged us to end it. To end him. Ask him how many months it took to learn how to control his wolf." Ulrik paused, letting his words sink in. "Aimon was lucky. He had us to shield him, to train him. When he was at his most vulnerable, we were there." Ulrik allowed himself a vicious grin. "I imagine Renaud is eagerly awaiting an opportunity to catch you at your weakest."

Lothair stilled. What little air there was in the chamber seemed to be sucked into the silence.

"You think you have it figured out?" Ulrik scoffed. "That you have outsmarted us all. But you know nothing. About us, or what you are asking for."

Lothair fixed him with an impenetrable stare, the corner of his lip curled in a sardonic half-smile. He tossed the amulet and caught it in his hand. Palm out, he revealed the reverse side, the blood-red stone glinting in the candlelight. "I know this amulet, with its red stone that reeks of blood magic, denotes more than the alpha."

Ulrik's heart stalled.

With a flick of his wrist, Lothair tossed the amulet and Ulrik followed its arc across the room until it landed in the dirt at his feet. "I also know if I try to kill or capture another werewolf, if they recite the inscriptions on *their* amulets, if they disappear..." He jerked his chin at the gold disc on the floor. "I need only be near that one, with its red jewel instead of an inscription, to find them. That it will draw them in like a beacon for lost souls."

Ulrik tried to keep his emotions under control and his breathing even. How had Lothair known of the true purpose of the amulet? The inscription? The bloodstone? Had the traitor told Renaud? He did not think so, for Renaud would have used that information to good effect. And he had not.

Lothair chuckled. "I always win, Ulrik." His smile vanished. "Never forget that." He turned on his heel, grabbed the candle and climbed the stairs.

The grate above screeched open, then clanged shut and the comte's footsteps receded. Ulrik eyed his surroundings. He must escape this hole in the ground. Staying, holding out as long as he could, was no longer an option. With only seven of them left, not a single female among them, and one of them confirmed as a traitor, things had never been more dire for the pack. Or his alpha. Gaharet had to be warned. But how in God's name would he get free of this silver?

Chapter Two

Deptford, London
2022

Rebekah Clarke stepped off the bus into the rain and dashed under an awning. She dug into her bag, rummaging through unused tissues, a pen, old receipts, a paperback shifter romance she'd gotten from the book exchange, stray mints, her purse and whatever other unmentionables she'd thrown in there at one time or another. What a crap day. Her fingers closed over her keys. A glass of cheap red wine and a meal of two-minute noodles were all she had to look forward to, but at least she could enjoy them in the privacy of her flat. No more dealing with her boss Charlie's lecherous looks and grabby hands.

"Your rent is late."

Bek looked up and groaned. In the doorway of The Spicy Dragon, beneath the stuttering neon sign, stood a tiny woman, arms folded across her chest, her skin as wrinkled as a long-forgotten apple in Bek's fruit bowl.

"Mrs. Wu."

Mouth-watering smells emanated from the restaurant. A damn sight better than her intended meal, but Mrs. Wu would as soon extend her credit, or comp her free food, as she'd cut off her right arm. The woman might be four feet nothing, but she was a tyrant of epic proportions. It wouldn't surprise Bek if the restaurant was a front for the Chinese Triad, and Mrs. Wu the Dragon Master.

"You're two weeks late with rent." She waggled a bony finger at Bek. "You don't pay, I evict you."

She bloody well would, too. "I got paid today, Mrs. Wu."

She hadn't. She was supposed to be, but her boss had stiffed her again. While propositioning her. Charlie knew there were few employers who would take her on. The bastard also worked on the assumption if he didn't pay her, she wouldn't have money for rent, and she'd have to give up her flat. With nowhere to live, but desperately needing to keep her job, she'd be at his mercy. Bek would peddle her firstborn before she slept with that cretin. "I'll go down to the bank first thing tomorrow."

Mrs. Wu narrowed her eyes and pursed her lips. "You better. I be waiting for it. Many people are interested in renting your place."

Bek plastered a smile on her face. As if. This wasn't Mayfair, and The Spicy Dragon was *not* the Michelin starred Hakkasan. Nope. Her flat was a cockroach-infested dump, and the restaurant wasn't much better. One phone call to the health board and they'd shut it down. *And then I'll be back to having nowhere to live.* "Tomorrow, I promise."

Mrs. Wu scowled, then retreated inside.

Bek huffed, unlocked the door and climbed the narrow stairs to her bedsit above the restaurant. She dropped her rucksack on the worn and wonky table and kicked off her shoes. Then she flicked on the heat, removed her sodden jacket and shoved her cold feet into her slippers. Her neighbor, a skeevy tweaker, was already in, the pounding beat of Black Sabbath loud enough to penetrate the thin walls of her flat, but not so loud as to piss off Mrs. Wu. She'd bang on the wall if she thought it'd make any difference.

She plonked a glass and a half-empty bottle of cheap wine on the coffee table, and threw herself on the sofa and checked her phone for messages. Four from her parole officer. She screwed up her face. Charlie had probably phoned him after she'd stormed out, swearing her head off and telling him he could stick it where the sun didn't shine.

Bek poured herself a glass of wine and gulped it down like water. Like she needed it to survive. She did. Her parole officer was a hard-ass. And a friend of Charlie's. *Lucky me.* She rubbed her temple, the hint of a headache already forming. *How has my life come to this?* At thirty-two, she should have her shit together by now.

Bek poured more wine. She'd gotten herself into this mess, she'd get herself out of it. She slipped her hand into her pocket and retrieved her find. A little gold disc about the size of a fifty pence piece. On one side was a howling wolf's head. She flipped it over. On the other, four lines of strange, curling script.

She'd found it on the floor of the bar. With the patrons who frequented Charlie's, chances were the owner hadn't come by it through honest means. Charlie would've kept it for himself. So, instead of handing it over as lost property, Bek had slipped it into her pocket.

Now it was hers. If she could figure out its value, it might be her ticket to a Charlie-free future. And better living quarters. Ignoring her messages, she thumbed up Google.

* * * *

Three glasses of wine and an hour later, Bek found a match for the script on the disc. Something called Theban, from the fifteen hundreds. She slumped against the faded and torn upholstery. *Bollocks.* She couldn't hock an artifact. Whether it came from a museum or a private collection, someone would be looking for it. Most likely the cops. Wouldn't her parole officer just *love* that?

Her phone beeped a low battery warning, and she groaned. Another thing she couldn't afford—a new phone with a battery that lasted more than a few hours. She poured the last dregs of the wine into her glass, took the two steps to her kitchenette and tossed the bottle in the rubbish. She missed. It hit the corner of the bench-top with a sharp crack and shattered. Bek let her head fall back and stared at the peeling paint on the ceiling.

Could this day get any worse?

Kneeling, she picked up the pieces of glass, slicing her finger.

Why? Why does the universe have it in for me today?

With more care, she cleaned up the mess. Stemming the blood from her finger, she searched through her rucksack for her phone charger. She dug beneath her purse and the paperback novel, scrounging amongst the useless crap she kept in her bag. No charger. She checked her jacket pockets. No luck. She pawed through her bag again. Seriously, it was like a mini version of the Bermuda Triangle. Things went in there and were never seen or heard of again.

Bek tipped the contents out onto the table. Beside the book, her purse, a pen, tissues and a lollipop that had seen better days, she found a lipstick she'd thought lost months ago and a condom, expired last week. But no phone charger. *Bollocks.*

She slapped her forehead with her palm. Bloody Charlie. He'd grabbed her ass as she was unplugging her phone. She must have forgotten her charger as she'd stormed out of the bar. *Great. Just great.* She'd have to make do with whatever battery she had left.

Bek returned to the sofa and the disc. Clicking out of Wikipedia, her eyes caught on another link.

"Diary of a Madman."

Below it, in amongst the text, the word Theban. Bek looked at the wall, beyond which her neighbor's music still reverberated. Wasn't *Diary of a Madman* an Ozzy Osbourne album? She clicked on the link. Yes. And there, the explanation she'd been hoping for. Ozzy Osbourne had used the Theban script on the inside cover of the album.

Excitement buzzed in her veins. Maybe it wasn't an artifact. If she could link this to Ozzy, it could be worth something. Hunting around for a piece of paper, she scrolled through Google until she found the Theban alphabet and set about translating.

Bek stared at the four lines she'd written. *WTF?* A bunch of gobbledygook. No wait. It kind of looked like... Could it be... *Latin?* And she was back again to it being an artifact. Maybe. Ozzy had once bitten the head off a live bat. Who knew what weirdness he was capable of? Another search through Google for Latin to English, then she transcribed the translation.

Bek threw her pen down on the coffee table. Four lines. A rhyme. She rubbed the little gold disc between her fingers, blood from her cut sinking into its grooves. She stared at the words again. Not a single mention of Ozzy, though it had an occult-like ring to it. She went back to her phone, clicking on links relating to Ozzy, Black Sabbath, *Diary of a Madman.*

Nothing.

Would her neighbor have any ideas?

Halfway to the door, Bek halted, the disc in one hand, her translation and her phone in the other. *Am I crazy? I can't trust him.* He'd take it and hock it himself. Nope. She'd figure this out on her own.

Bek stared at the rhyme. What did it mean? She read the words out loud.

"Vanish from all human sight,
Those who favor moonlit night.
To bloodstone shall they return,
So no man of their secret learns."

Darkness hit like a solid wall, sucking away her breath and making her ears ring. Bek reeled, lost her balance, lost all sense of up or down, and fell. Like a slow-motion video, she hung suspended in the air, arms flailing for what seemed like an eternity. Then she hit the floor with a thud.

"Oof!" That'd leave a bruise. Or two. Thank God she hadn't dropped her phone.

"Damn it, Mrs. Wu. I said I'd pay rent tomorrow. You didn't have to cut off my electricity."

Bek closed her eyes and rested her forehead on the floor, the damp earth cooling her wine-flushed face.

Wait. *Dirt?* Her eyes snapped open.

She scrambled to her knees and turned on her phone, lighting up the surrounding space. Yes, *dirt.* And stone walls. No faded sofa, no peeling linoleum and no seventies-style kitchenette. The pervading smell of dampness replaced sweet and sour pork, and the guitar riffs of Black Sabbath were noticeably absent.

I haven't drunk that much wine. Have I?

Maybe. And she'd not eaten since lunch. Was this some weird, alcohol-induced dream? Would she wake up in the morning with a pounding headache, a crick in her neck and a hideous floral pattern imprinted on her cheek because she'd passed out on the sofa?

Bek got to her feet, the cold seeping through the thin soles of her slippers and chilling her toes. Goosebumps erupted across her bare arms. A little too much realism to be a dream.

She swung her phone around. *Where the hell am I?* Some kind of…basement? Below The Spicy Dragon? A sinkhole, maybe?

It'd rained for two weeks straight. Pipes had burst all over the city, flooding streets, houses and office buildings. One had opened up down the street and swallowed a car.

Wide-eyed, she took in her surroundings. Mrs. Wu would be pissed.

But… *If I've fallen in a sinkhole…* Bek patted her body. *Why am I still alive?* Where were the signs of a collapse? The mud, the water and half a restaurant? The room was whole, devoid of anything but her.

A low chuckle broke the silence, and the hairs on the back of her neck stood on end. She swallowed, her fingers clenching around her phone. Slowly she turned, holding it out in front of her and lighting up the small space. Her heartbeat fluttered in her chest, and her hand shook, bouncing the light around like a strobe. Not an empty room. Not only her. There was a man.

A man chained to the *freaking wall.*

He stared at her through strands of long, blond hair, his bearded face dirty, and reflected light from her phone glittering in his eyes. Shackles encased his wrists and neck, and the surrounding skin was blistered and raw. A torn shirt hung from his broad shoulders, and Bek's gaze skipped across muscled pecs and ripped abs.

He pushed himself off the wall, standing tall, his chains clinking and black pants stretching over powerful thighs. Footballer's thighs. Keen eyes studied her with a burning intensity. His gaze raked over her from head to toe before returning to her face, then dipping and lingering on her cleavage. Heat bloomed, and her nipples pebbled.

God Almighty.

She took a step back. Then another.

He advanced on her, stalking her with an animal-like grace surprising for such a large man, until his chains snapped tight, halting his progress. Her panties dampened. What was it about dangerous men that had her ovaries going off like it was midnight on New Year's Eve?

He inhaled deeply through his nose and closed his eyes. A low rumble emanated from his chest, and a wicked smile tilted the corner of his mouth. He licked his lips, and she followed the progress of his tongue with a hungry gaze.

Down, girl.

He opened his eyes, his gaze locking with hers, full of heated promises. Bek sucked in a breath and backed away until she hit the wall.

Fuck me.

"Mrs. Wu, you really are a Dragon Master."

Chapter Three

Frankia
999

The scent of woman and wine—his two favorite things—hit Ulrik hard, and he drank it in. At his feet, the binding stone glowed, signaling its activation. Before him, a woman. A woman like he had never seen before. She stood, staring at him, her bare arms adorned with intricate markings like the Picts of old and her ears and nose decorated with silver pierced through her skin. In her hand, she clutched an amulet.

Gaharet had sent him aid. He licked his lips. *And in the most delightful form.* The woman had the curves of the most buxom maid, soft and full. Curves a man could hold on to, could sink into. If his nose did not lie, an aroused woman, and one who shared his affinity for wine.

Where Gaharet had found her, Ulrik did not know. Nor did he care. He would escape Lothair's underground chamber with her help and erase the memory of his days in this hellhole by bedding this beauty. Her reward for helping him. Perhaps the very reason she had volunteered. His cock twitched and his gaze dipped to her generous bosom. He would see her well compensated.

A light in her hand flashed white and bright, like lightning contained, as it bounced around the chamber. Witchcraft? The last he had seen of Gaharet was his retreating back as he had headed east, seeking the witch in the forest, his wounded mate in his arms. It stood to reason he had sent someone with knowledge of magic. Ulrik would need every advantage to escape Langeais Keep.

His gaze skimmed over her body. Tight breeches hugged womanly hips and her short, fitted tunic clung to her luscious bosom. His mouth watered at the thought of his lips and tongue on her skin, on her nipples—licking, sucking and nipping. He would feast on her body and wring every last cry, whimper and moan from her delectable lips. For helping him escape, he would pleasure her with the dedication of a man starved of female succor.

He grinned. It would be no hardship.

Her light flared in his face, blinding him and he flinched, averting his gaze. She lowered the light a little.

"*Merci.*"

"You're...French?" She did not conceal the surprise in her voice. "How the hell did you end up here? Do you speak English?"

Awareness tingled up his spine. The language of Bretaigne. Not the familiar form he remembered from his youth spent there. But he *had* heard it before. Once. And with a similar cadence. From Erin, Gaharet's mate.

Erin who had come from a world so different from theirs. From the future.

This woman came not from Langeais. Gaharet had not sent her.

"Look." Her gaze darted about the chamber, lighting on the steps. "I don't know if you understand me or not, but I'm going to try to get out of here. When I do, I'll send someone back to help you." Concern flickered in warm brown eyes lined with kohl. "If you're lucky, it won't be one of Mrs. Wu's goons." She moved toward the steps.

"Wait."

She turned back to him. "So you do speak English. Good." She nodded, her dark hair, strangely streaked with green, dancing about her face. Short hair, shorter than he had ever seen on a woman before, but more than enough to fist his hand in. "That'll make things easier when I send someone to help you."

He shook his head and his chains rattled. "Alerting the guards to your presence is not wise."

"If they're still standing. It's bound to be absolute chaos up there. The fire brigade, ambulance, the boys in blue — all the emergency services are going to be up there. And I dare say, The Spicy Dragon is going to look like a disaster zone. Chances are, anyone who survived the sinkhole is going to be more worried about saving their own skin and not getting linked to" — she swung her hand around indicating her surroundings — "this. Or you."

"The...Spicy Dragon? A *sinkhole*? Emergency... services?" With each word she spoke, he became more convinced she came from a similar place as Erin. Not the same, though. Her accent was different, more clipped.

"Yeah. You know. Mrs. Wu's restaurant. The people who dragged you down here and chained you to the wall."

Amusement danced on his tongue. "Where is it you think you are, sweetness?"

She rounded on him. "*Sweetness*? *Really*? I'm trying to help you here. Could you possibly be more condescending?"

She crossed her arms over her bosom, pushing up her already ample cleavage. His gaze fixed on the inviting creamy skin revealed by the low neckline of her tunic and his cock thickened. *Merde*, he could not wait to get his hands on those. His mouth watered.

"Hey." She pointed to her face. "Eyes up here." She threw her hands in the air. "What did I expect? You're chained to a *wall*. That doesn't happen to nice, respectful, help-grandma-cross-the-street kind of guys."

Ulrik swallowed his indignation at her slight to his character. He wanted out of this place and he would need her help. Having her in the clutches of the guards would serve neither of them. If there was one thing Ulrik knew a lot about, it was women. And getting them to do what he wanted was something he excelled at.

He stepped as close to her as his chains would allow. Though she stood her ground, the catch in her breath gave her away. She was not as unaffected by him as she would like him to believe. She broke eye contact, and her gaze strayed to his biceps. Ulrik repressed a smile and shifted his body so the torn remnants of his tunic hung loose at his sides, leaving his chest bare. She rewarded him with the heat of her gaze burning across his abdomen. Lower still, it slipped to his groin. His cock hardened. He angled his hips forward, showing her what he had to offer her.

Her mouth parted and her breathing quickened. Then she scrunched her face up in a frown and shook her head. "Get a hold of yourself," she muttered, then turned from him and moved toward the steps.

Ulrik gaped at her. Had his intentions not been clear? Was seduction so different in the future she had not recognized his signals? It must be so, for no woman had *ever* turned him away. Not in his inexperienced youth. Not in his time in Bretaigne. Not when he had returned to Frankia. Not *ever*.

She climbed the first step.

L'enfer. He had to stop her. *Whatever it takes.* "My name is Ulrik Voclain." He searched around for the right words in Anglo-Saxonne. "*Sir* Ulrik Voclain."

She halted, turning to take him in. Good. He bit back his grin. He had recaptured her attention. Then she arched her eyebrows, threw back her head and laughed. At him.

"Knighted by the Queen." She snorted. "Right. And I'm a princess, heir to the throne of England. Huh!"

She climbed another two steps.

Stubborn, obtuse woman.

Oh, how he had laughed when Erin had challenged Gaharet, refusing to do his bidding. He was *not* laughing now.

He bit down on his frustration. "Listen to me, *sweetness*. We are not below this...*Spicy Dragon*. You are in an underground chamber beneath Langeais Keep. In Frankia. It is the year of our lord, nine hundred and ninety-nine. Lothair de Anjou is the Comte—Count— of Anjou. And if you reveal yourself to the guards above, you will be in more danger from them than you are with me."

Pity glimmered in her dark eyes. "Oh, my God. How long have you been down here?"

He threw his head back and let out an explosive breath. "Long enough," he said through gritted teeth. "But I have not lost my wits, as you are suggesting."

A stream of rapid Franceis split the air from above. She gaped up the stairs. The jingle of keys proceeded the screech of the grate hinges. Her eyes darted to him. The guards had heard them and were coming to investigate.

"*L'enfer.*"

Any moment now, a guard would appear. Shackled to the wall, he could do nothing but watch. Dressed like she was, he had no doubt what the guards would do with her.

"Come stand behind me and I will keep you safe. Trust me, woman."

More Franceis — a heated debate over who would descend the stairs first — cautious steps and a flicker of candlelight. Indecision warred across her features.

"I give you my oath. I will not hurt you. They will."

A muttered curse from above, and she made her choice, retreating from the steps. And from him.

Merde.

Her light winked out, and she pressed herself into the corner as a guard stepped into the chamber, a candle thrust out and his sword brandished in front of him. Ulrik snarled and rattled his chains. If he could keep the focus on him, she might escape detection.

A second guard stepped into the chamber, also armed, and holding a bunch of keys. The glint of silver caught Ulrik's attention. The key to his shackles.

"There is no way anyone could have gotten in here, Clement," said one guard to the other. "Not without us opening the grate. I think I would have noticed a woman."

"I know what I heard, Gael," said Clement, his gaze darting about.

Gael snorted. "You have taken leave of your senses." He waved his sword at Ulrik, his grip loose and his stance relaxed. "There is only him and he is going nowhere." He leered at Ulrik. "Not so intimidating now, are you, Voclain?"

Ulrik's lip curled in a snarl. If the guard stepped closer, he could disarm him in a heartbeat. Take his sword *and* those keys. Even shackled to the wall, he was more than a match for this fool.

"But—"

"Look around you, Clement. Can you see anyone else in here? Maybe his reputation with the ladies has preceded him and a succubus has come to visit." Gael chortled. "Your imagination has run away with you, boy. First a man turning into a beast and howling like a wolf, and now you are hearing voices."

"Bastien heard the beast, too," Clement mumbled.

Gael snorted. "Give me that." He snatched the candle from Clement's hand. "I'll show you there is nothing here but him."

If Gael turned but a little, he would see her. Ulrik roared and lunged for Gael.

Both guards stumbled back and raised their weapons. The candle faltered but did not go out.

Ulrik fought hard, but the iron chains held him fast.

Gael chuckled and lowered his sword. "Is that what you heard, boy? No more than a berserker on the battlefield. Just stay out of his reach." Gael held the candle aloft. "And there is no woman here, despite what you think you heard."

He shoved light into every corner. Into *her* corner.

Gael stumbled back a step. "Well, well, well. What have we here?"

She stood, her kohl-lined eyes wide and her magic light clutched in her white-knuckled hand. Ulrik swallowed. He could do nothing but watch.

Gael shoved the candle at Clement. "It is our lucky day, Clement. Seems you did hear something, after all."

Chapter Four

Bek stared. Two men in *chain mail*? Brandishing *swords*? What had he said, the so-called knight? The year of our lord nine hundred and something or other? She'd thought him delusional.

She blinked. Blinked again. Had her neighbor spiked her wine?

The younger guard gaped at her. The older one moved toward her with an oily grin and a glint in his eye she recognized all too well.

Oh, hell to the no.

She didn't put up with this crap from Charlie. Some guy dressed like an extra from Medieval Mayhem stood no chance.

Bek pushed herself out from the corner and shoved the little disc and her phone into the pockets of her jeans, freeing up her hands. She'd learned a few things from her ex, Spider, and his crew. The life she'd once led was not for the fainthearted, and Bek was no princess. At least these guys held swords, not guns. They wouldn't be expecting her to fight back, but there *were* two of them, and her only help was a guy chained to the wall. A guy who had already made it clear he wanted in her knickers.

Grandpa thrust the candle at the other guard, who was barely more than a teenager. The kid's rapid-fire French spat bullets at Grandpa. Grandpa turned on him, snarling. The kid said no more and stepped back.

It was down to her and Grandpa.

He turned back to her, his hand reaching beneath his mail and grabbing at his crotch. Her stomach roiled and her tongue did a stellar impression of sandpaper, dry and raspy. He set his sword against the wall.

Yes.

Things still weren't in her favor—he was bigger and stronger—but the odds had evened out a little.

He stalked toward her. Behind him, shackled Thor roared and strained against his chains. She cast a glance at him. If she could force Grandpa within his reach, would he deal with him? He had to want out of those chains, and this guy must have had something to do with his imprisonment. *The enemy of my enemy is my friend and all that guff.* It was worth a shot.

Bek steadied herself. She'd only get one chance at this. If she ballsed it up, he'd have her in his grasp. She took a deep breath, clenched her fist and went on the attack.

Lunging at her would-be rapist, she struck out and punched him square on the nose. Pain exploded across her knuckles, but she forced down the impulse to clutch her hand to her side. Too stunned by her assault, Grandpa had yet to react, and she couldn't waste the opportunity. She followed through with a solid kick to his groin.

He bellowed a spray of blood and spittle and raised his fist to retaliate. She wouldn't get a chance for another hit. Bek tucked her shoulder in and launched herself at Grandpa, throwing her whole body into the move and hitting him square in the chest. He stumbled back, right into the path of the man he'd been guarding.

A chain snapped around Grandpa's neck and pulled tight, cutting off his air.

She stepped back, clutching her injured hand to her chest. Had she broken her knuckle? It sure felt like it.

Wide-eyed, the kid brandished his sword at her, his attention flicking between her and the prisoner. More rapid French. A few curses she recognized, but the rest she could only guess at. It didn't take a genius to figure it out.

Grandpa's life for hers.

Bek snatched up Grandpa's sword with her good hand. The thing had a solid weight to it. Good. Worst case, she could swing it at him like a sharp-edged cricket bat. She gripped the handle with both hands, wincing as pain flared across her injured knuckles. She widened her stance, holding the sword out in front of her. The tip wobbled a little, and she fought to still the trembling of her hands and keep it steady.

Grandpa's eyes bulged, his face turning a motley purple and his hands clawing at the chain. Her manacled fantasy sneered as he wrenched on the chain. A loud crack reverberated off the walls.

When he released the chain, Grandpa crashed to the floor. Dead.

Holy fu— He'd killed— How strong was this guy? Didn't that sort of shit only happen in Hollywood?

The kid's gaze darted about wildly, from Bek, to the chained up so-called knight, to dead Grandpa, to the steps.

The knight grinned. In his hand, he held a ring of keys.

Bollocks.

Before either she or the kid could move, he had unlocked the shackles, and they fell from his wrists and his neck with a clatter. He tracked the guard, all predatory vengeance. Death on two legs.

"Don't kill him. He's just a kid." Her words were out before she could stop them.

The knight turned his intense stare on her for a split second, and Bek blanched.

The kid took advantage of the brief reprieve and swung his sword, but he was no match for medieval Thor. He disarmed the kid in seconds, and hit him on the back of the head with the butt of his own sword. The kid slid to the ground, and with him went the candle, plunging them into darkness.

Oh crap, oh crap, oh crap.

With trembling fingers, Bek reached for her phone. She turned on the torch, lighting up the room. The now free knight, if that's what he really was, stood over the unmoving guard. His attention turned to her, his hand shielding his eyes from the glare of her phone torch.

Bek edged toward the steps, keeping the sword pointing in his direction, her eyes never leaving him. Two down, one to go.

Then her phone battery died.

Fuck.

She made for the stairs with as much speed as she dared. And slammed into something solid, something warm, and landed on her ass. Bek screamed and scrambled back. Her heart pounding, she kept a tight grip on the sword and got to her feet. She raised the weapon, waving it blindly in front of her.

A large hand clasped over her wrist.

"No, no, no, no, no."

In a heartbeat, he'd disarmed her. Now he had two swords, and she had none. She scuttled back, her heels connecting with...*something* and she fell. She landed on...

Oh God. Is that the dead guy?

She whimpered, scrabbling backward until she hit a wall, two walls. She leaned into the corner, trembling, her eyes straining, but unable to make out anything in the pitch-black.

"It is not safe for you out there alone."

His voice was close, homing in on her. Bek froze, her ears pricked for any sound.

Nothing.

She swallowed. Was he still or stealthy?

"It's not safe for me here either," she said.

It was a risk, speaking again, but if he answered her, she could pinpoint his location.

"You think I would hurt you?" He sounded affronted. Bek didn't care. "I would never hurt you."

His voice floated out of the darkness. Close. Too close. *Shit*. Stealthy it was.

Her fingers clenched around... She still had her phone. With a flat battery, it had but one use now. As a distraction.

Bek threw it away from her. It hit the floor off to the right with a satisfying thunk. Easing to her feet, she took a silent step to the left. Then another, and another, feeling her way along the wall with shaking fingers. She'd follow it to the stairway.

"I gave you my oath. I would not hurt you."

His voice sounded off to the right, near where her phone had landed. *Yes!* She pumped her fist in silent celebration and kept following the wall. The stairs had to be close.

"You think I would try to force myself on you like that *filth*?"

His disembodied voice moved closer and the hairs on the back of her neck stood on end. She took another step.

Where are those damn stairs?

She kept moving, placing each foot with care, though she wanted nothing more than to bolt.

"I would only ever give you what you ask for."

Her thighs clenched, his raspy voice sending shivers down her spine, and heat straight to her clit. She closed her eyes against the suffocating darkness and focused on calming her racing heart. The darkness was doing a number on her. That and the erotic image of him, bare chested and wielding a sword, like an actor in some period drama or action flick. Chris Hemsworth, eat your heart out.

Get a grip, Bek, and get the fuck out of here.

She took a steadying breath, opened her eyes and inched her way forward, cautious in her movements. Her questing fingers hit the cold stone wall. The corner. *Thank God.* She turned, trailing one hand along the wall. Was she close to the steps? Did she have the right wall?

A prickle of awareness skipped up her spine. Her heart stuttered and her muscles locked. He was right behind her. She just knew it. She could feel it.

Oh, shit.

The press of his chest against her shoulder blades and the heat from his body seeping through her cotton blouse made her tremble. His scent, deep and musky, swirled around her and his long hair brushed her shoulder.

"And you will ask," he whispered, his breath hot on the side of her face. "Nay, you will beg for my attention."

Bek ran. She bolted for where she hoped the stairs would be, colliding with a solid wall of muscle.

She screamed. He laughed.

Then she was in the air, flung over his shoulder like she weighed little more than an empty sack, his arm banding about her thighs.

"Put me down, you overgrown oaf!" She pummeled his back with her fists, wincing as pain flared in her injured hand. He didn't even have the decency to grunt at her efforts.

She tried harder, kicking her feet, hoping to connect with something soft and sensitive. "As if I'd ask for it, *beg* for it… In your dreams, asshole!"

He chuckled. "My, you are a sassy wench."

His palm shifted, sliding up between her thighs. Bek shrieked. "Touch me like that again and I'll rip off your balls."

He threw back his head and laughed. "You can try, sweetness. And I shall very much enjoy the trying." He slapped her on the ass. "Now duck."

"What?"

"Duck, or you will hit your head."

Bek fumed, as the sting of his slap heated her cheek and dampened her knickers. She had little choice except to do as he asked as they climbed the steps. She'd bide her time. He'd have to put her down at some point. Then she'd show him what sassy really was.

Chapter Five

"Be a good girl now, while I get us out of here," Ulrik cajoled, his hand still carrying the memory of her lush ass beneath his palm.

"Be a good... Oooh! Go to hell."

Ulrik halted on the stairs, grinning at her indignation, and slapped her hard on the ass. Again.

"Stop doing that."

He did it once more, wishing he had the time to strip her bare right here, right now. Would her ass be nice and pink? He stifled a groan at the erotic image that flashed through his mind.

"I *swear* you're going to pay for that."

He chuckled. "Oh, sweetness, I will hold you to your vow. And I think I shall much enjoy paying your price."

She punched him in the kidney, one handed this time, and he grunted. She had a surprisingly good arm on her. Gael had found that out to his detriment. But it had not come without cost, if the scent of her blood and the way she favored her right hand were any indication. He would see to her injury once they were clear of the keep.

"Careful, little one. You do not want to hurt your other hand."

On impulse, and because it was beyond him to resist taunting her, he turned his head and bit down on her hip.

She stiffened against him, the bitter scent of her fear lacing the air.

He froze. *L'enfer*. He was such a fool. Only moments ago she had faced down Gael, prepared to fight as he had never before seen from a human woman, rather than have the guard's base intentions forced on her. Now, here *he* was, taking liberties and touching her in ways that could only constitute sexual interest. He was behaving no better than the dead guard. Were his mother alive, she would have strung him up by his innards.

He heaved in a breath and released it on a heavy sigh. "My apologies. It was uncouth of me to touch you as I have. You have every right to protest. I am sorry. I vow to you it will not happen again."

Silence weighed heavily between them. He could only imagine the confusion on her face. She shifted uneasily, her thighs clamping together.

Ulrik suppressed a grin. "Unless you ask it of me."

"Dream on," she muttered.

Ulrik chuckled. No matter her words, her body did not lie. He continued his ascent, amused by her curses. Curses inventive and crude enough to make even the coarsest of brigands blush.

He paused at the top of the stairs and reached out with his senses, his wolf's familiar presence once again filling his mind. The skin on his wrists and neck tingled as they healed, the welts on his fingers from handling the silver key already gone. Around his neck hung the familiar weight of an amulet. Not his, but the binding amulet he had scooped up from the floor. Lothair might come to regret throwing it at his feet.

Tilting his nose up, he scented the room above. Empty. He had doubted there were more guards. If there had been, the ruckus they had made below would have drawn them, but it never hurt to be cautious.

Ulrik pushed on the grate, its hinges screeching in protest, and stepped into the lit room. He breathed in deeply, filling his lungs with fresh, if pungent, air and the intoxicating scent of the woman over his shoulder. It felt good to be out of that hole, no longer bound in silver. Even better with his present company. He rubbed his hand against the back of her leg, careful to keep it low, near her knee and away from the enticing aroma wafting from between her thighs. She rewarded him with another shriek all the same.

He grinned. He was beginning to see the appeal of a woman with attitude. This one breathed fire.

He glanced about the room. An interrupted game of dice lay spread on the table with a few coins and a wineskin. In the corner sat his sword and scabbard, his mail, his surcoat and his daggers. It had taken four men, even in his weakened state, to wrest him from his armor. He may have chosen to step into the wolfsbane trap, but he had not been willing to go down without a fight.

He hastened over, exchanging the guard's sword for his own of far superior quality, and palmed his best dagger. As an afterthought, he grabbed his surcoat. Barely dressed, it would keep her warm. His hauberk, gambeson, greaves and vambraces, he left behind.

Taking them would mean putting her down, and they did not have the time for the struggle that would most definitely ensue.

He slung his surcoat over his shoulder, over her.

She wriggled about. "What the —"

"Grab the coins." He swung around and dipped at the knees so she could reach them. "We may need them. And the wineskin."

He definitely needed that. She may, too, when she truly appreciated where she was. From what he remembered of the things Erin had said, future living was a very different affair.

"Geez, when did your last slave die?" But she scooped up the coins, and the weight of the wineskin thumped against his back as she grabbed that, too. "What the hell place is this? Who uses *wineskins* anymore?"

He huffed out an impatient breath. "As I told you before, you are in Frankia. In the keep of Lothair, Count of Anjou."

There was little point in saying more. She would have no choice but to believe him soon enough. She went strangely quiet. Had the reality of his words, and her surroundings, finally sunk in?

He exited the room and made his way down the corridor. Getting out of the keep would not be easy. He did not know if his imprisonment was common knowledge, but he must assume it was. If he tried to leave by the gate, he risked being recognized. He also suspected the spirited woman over his shoulder, though quiet for the moment, would not be so for long.

She had proved herself defiant and smart, using him to dispatch the lecherous guard. She had made use of her failed magic light to her advantage, too, throwing it away from her as a distraction, and trying to escape him in the darkness. Had he been an ordinary man, it might well have worked. It now sat tucked snuggly in the band of his breeches, a hard shape against his skin. Was she quiet because she was biding her time, looking for a way to escape him? He would not put it past her.

He paused at the end of the corridor. Left or right?

A familiar scent caught his nose — older and overlaid by the more recent passing of servants and chevaliers. Gaharet's. He sniffed again. And Erin's. Gaharet had fled the keep with Erin not so long ago. Had he known of another exit? A secret one? Ulrik would trust his nose. And his alpha. Turning left, he followed the scent.

The hour was late, and they passed no one in the corridors. Gaharet's trail led him to a storage room and ended at a stack of chests. He frowned, taking in the room. No second doorway.

He sniffed again. Gaharet and Erin *had* come this way. He eyed the chests. Did they hide a passageway under the walls?

Ulrik tucked his shoulder against the side of the stack and pushed. The chests shifted as one and a cool draft of air hit his face. He pushed a little harder, revealing a narrow tunnel. If his sense of direction did not lead him astray — and it never did — it should bring them out underneath the keep wall close to the postern gate. Ulrik grinned.

He set her down and his surcoat slid to the floor. The moment her feet touched the floor, she lunged away from him.

"Not so fast, sweetness."

With an arm around her waist, he slammed her back into his chest. She shrieked and kicked out at him, but her small feet and soft shoes were ineffective weapons, barely enough to raise a bruise on his shins. He kept a grip on her wrist and turned her around to face him.

He picked up his surcoat and draped it around her shoulders. "Put this on. It will warm you and go some way to conceal you."

She gaped at him as if he were the village idiot. "You're insane if you think I'll just go along quietly."

He chuckled, backing her up against the wall and crowding her with his body. "I do not expect you to go quietly at all, *petite cracheuse de feu*."

She stared at him, eyes wide but flashing defiance.

"Scream all you like. Down here, the chance that anyone will hear you is negligible. And if they did, they would be unlikely to come to your aid. But screaming or no, come with me, you will."

"You're just saying that to keep me quiet." The look she gave him was all scorn. "As if I would believe you?"

That she did not take his word as truth rankled, but he would add it to the long list of slights slung his way over the years. He had a tarnished reputation, and he was well aware he could lay much of that at his own feet.

"I am many things, but I assure you, a liar is not one of them. Test my word if it pleases you."

She scowled and clamped her mouth shut, but she did not make it easy for him. He guided her struggling arms into his surcoat, buttoning it up at the front, covering up her delectable bosom. Warmth was not the only benefit to be gained by her wearing it. Ulrik needed all his wits about him, and those bountiful attributes he longed to have bare and cupped with his hands were quite the distraction.

"Why don't you just leave me here?" Dark eyes challenged him. "I can make my own way out, and then you won't have to worry about me giving you away or attracting attention."

Leave her here? At Lothair's mercy? Lord, no.

He tilted his head to the side, regarding her. "What do you think the lord of this keep will do when he finds one guard dead, another unconscious and his prisoner missing?"

She stopped struggling and her gaze grew wary.

"And that unconscious guard will not be so for long. Once he wakes, he will tell Count Lothair of the woman he saw. The woman who appeared to be working with the prisoner and helped him kill that guard."

Her breathing stuttered and her face paled.

He shook his head. "No. I cannot, in good conscience, leave you behind."

Taking her from the keep against her will was for her own good. She would not fare so well in the hands of Lothair. No matter what she believed about him, he was doing it for her. And also for himself. He wanted this woman in his bed.

Ulrik crowded her in, the wall at her back and her way forward barred by his body, giving her nowhere to go. She let him, going limp, her worry reflected in her expressive brown eyes. He released her hand to buckle his scabbard and sword around his hips and she made no attempt to move. He did not like the acrid scent of her fear, but he would use it if it meant he had her obedience, even if it was only temporary.

"You have saved me, sweetness, from Lothair's underground chamber. Now *I* will keep *you* safe." He stepped away from her. "Come. We need to leave. Once they discover my escape, we will have the entire keep guard to contend with."

Her eyes widened further.

Good. Perhaps she would see him as the lesser of two evils. "Keep your head low."

He took her arm and guided her into the tunnel. She did not protest. He pulled the stack of chests back into place behind them, plunging them into darkness. This hidden passageway had served their pack well, twice now. They could not afford to reveal this advantage, nor lose it.

Ulrik pushed past her, crouching low and taking the lead. Each brush of his shoulders against the damp walls released the musty smell of moss and algae. He traversed the short distance, following the tunnel as it took a turn first to the left then the right. He kept a firm, but gentle, grip on her arm. The darkness was no hindrance to his enhanced vision, but it would all but blind her. He halted at a second door and pushed it open. His sword at the ready, they exited into the clutches of a prickly bush.

Ulrik surveyed their surroundings, getting his bearings. As he suspected, they weren't far from the postern gate. Had Lothair thought to post a guard there after Gaharet's escape? Their kind were stronger, faster, and had all the enhanced senses their wolf gave them, but they could not climb the ramparts unaided. With the concealed entrance the only other access to the bailey, other than the main gate, Lothair would have reasoned this was how Gaharet had evaded him.

His ears pricked at the shuffled movements from above—the keep guard on patrol. They did not walk the ramparts as they should, rather they stood, huddled together. One yawned. Another muttered about the chill in the air, wishing to be at home in bed. *Imbeciles.* Lothair would have them flogged for their inattention, but it suited his purpose well.

He pulled the woman against him, banding his arm about her waist. She barely reached his chin, and she tilted her head back to look at him.

"We are going to run. You are going to keep quiet. No screaming. Agreed?"

The brief flash of defiance in her eyes faded and she pressed her lips together in a thin line.

She gave him an abrupt nod. "Let's do this. I'm not going to be held accountable for something I didn't do. Not this time."

There was hurt and betrayal beneath the squaring of her shoulders and the determined thrust of her chin. Her pain clung to her, as visible to him as the pinched expression on her face.

Something shifted within his heart. He wanted to... *What? Take it away? Wrap her up in my arms and protect her so she would never feel such pain again? Kill the one who had betrayed her?*

His wolf pushed to the surface, and he tightened his grip, pressing their bodies together, her lush curves soft against the hardened planes of his chest. She swallowed, and an unexpected scent caught his nose, sending a pulse of heat straight to his cock. Arousal. He leaned in and ran his nose along the curve of her throat. She trembled. A growl rumbled in his chest. Her scent deepened. Oh, he would definitely have her in his bed soon. Or any bed. Or on the forest floor. He did not care where, but he would have her.

A muffled laugh from above broke the spell. Right now, he needed to get them beyond the grounds of Langeais Keep and into the forest.

He touched a finger to her lips. "Not a sound."

She nodded. He released her from his embrace and grabbed her uninjured hand.

"*Mon Dieu*. Would you look at that?" A guard's voice rang out.

Ulrik stilled.

"*L'enfer*. The moon."

Ulrik's spine tingled. What about the moon? From their position flush against the keep, he could not see it. He could feel it, though, and sense its fullness. Was that what had caught their attention? It mattered not. With the guards focusing on the moon, this was their chance.

Keeping low and hugging the wall for as long as possible, he ran down the slope, her hand clenched in his. He only slowed as they approached the postern gate, the scent of two men, and steel, coming from mere feet beyond the entrance.

Merde.

If Lothair had informed the keep guard of his confinement, he would need to kill them, too.

He slipped through the opening with the woman in tow. These two guards were more alert, but fortune favored him again. He recognized them. Two recently invested chevaliers. They were no match for him, though he had not the desire to kill them unless they gave him no choice. They were mere boys.

He pulled the woman in behind him, keeping his sword arm free.

The guards snapped to attention, eyeing his torn shirt and the woman behind him, draped in his surcoat. "Seigneur Ulrik."

One boy peered around him and grinned. "And Ma Dame." He nudged his fellow guard.

"Looking for somewhere quiet?" asked the other guard, grinning.

It seemed Lothair had kept knowledge of his imprisonment to a trusted few.

Ulrik pulled the woman against him, snaking his arm around her waist and giving the boys a smirk and a wink. "And somewhere a little private."

It would not be the first time his reputation with the ladies would come in handy.

Ulrik pressed his fingers against her side in warning. She may not understand Franceis, but his meaning was clear, and it was reason enough for her to want to run.

He leaned down, and kissed her cheek, like a lover. "Play along," he whispered in her ear. "I do not want to have to kill these boys."

She shivered, but she leaned into him and placed her hand on his naked chest. At her touch, Ulrik almost forgot his purpose. A snigger from the boys snapped him out of his lust-filled daze.

"Take care in the forest, Seigneur Ulrik," said one lad. "There have been wolves prowling about of late."

"Thank you for the warning."

It was a timely reminder. The keep guards were not the only threat. Wolves could mean actual wolves. They would be of little hindrance to him. But if members of his pack were roaming the forests, he would do well to be cautious. With a traitor in their midst, he could not risk trusting any of them.

With a cheeky grin at the boys and a firm grip on the woman, he cleared the entrance, not stopping until he had them well concealed within the trees. He looked back at the keep. No one had raised the alarm. No one had followed them, but now he could see what had the guards on the ramparts so transfixed.

The full moon hung above Langeais Keep, and it glowed a deep, dark red.

Chapter Six

Bek's breathing slowed, but her heart still raced, and heat still pooled in areas she would much rather ignore. The moment he'd pulled her into his embrace... She shivered. If not for the thick leather of his coat, he'd have felt her hardened nipples against his bare chest. And oh, what a chest it was. And on full display, too, between the remnants of his torn shirt.

Following on the heels of his heartfelt apology, her traitorous body had melted at his touch and her brain had gone on the fritz. Her hands had itched to touch him, and she'd quivered with an almost uncontrollable desire to wrap her legs around those lean hips of his and rub herself all over him.

So what if he'd apologized? He'd killed that guard. There was no mistaking she was in the presence of an apex predator. And if the way he touched her was anything to go by, she was his next prey. Then he'd growled... And she'd been all but his for the taking.

What the hell is it with me and dangerous men?

She pulled out of his grip and eyed the darkened forest, unease trickling up her spine. "Where are you taking me?"

"Somewhere safe."

She planted her hands on her hips, wincing at the tenderness of her knuckles. "Safe for who?"

His hands firm on her shoulders, he spun her around. "Tell me what you see?"

She blinked at the vision before her. Blinked again.

No way.

A stone tower. Ancient. Medieval. It loomed out of the darkness, a stronghold against invading armies sitting atop the hill. The blood-red moon hung low behind it, staining its walls and giving it a macabre hue. She shivered. It wouldn't have surprised her to see a horde of bats flying free from the top. What had he called it? Lonjay Keep?

Tower, my ass. It's a freakin' castle.

Like Rochester, only all that remained of Rochester was a hollowed-out shell, a remnant of the past and a tick box on a history tour of England. From what she'd seen — from her upside-down hazy vision of rough stone walls and antique-looking furniture — this *Lonjay Keep* was anything but a ruin.

She opened her hand, palm out, and stared at the coins she'd grabbed from the table. Silver and irregular. She'd seen similar ones as a kid on a school trip to the Museum of London. Slung over her shoulder was a worn leather wineskin. Not standard issue in the modern world either. Maybe medieval Thor wasn't so delusional after all. Bek suddenly needed a long drink of the wineskin's contents.

She pulled her arms out of his grip and turned to face him. "I don't know what the hell is going on here, but you need to start talking." She fisted her hands around the coins, widening her stance. "I'm not going a single step further until you explain" — she waved her hand behind her toward the keep—"that."

He huffed, shaking his head. "We do not have time for this now."

Bek held her ground. Maybe poking the beast wasn't a wise idea, but now, clear of the keep, she could afford to be a little braver. A little bolder. She was not moving. Not until he gave her an explanation of how she'd wound up down Alice's rabbit hole and in the middle some kind of medieval drama. Not until she could rationalize heading off into the woods with a complete stranger. One who, until recently, had been chained to a wall.

"*Merde.*" He tossed his arms up in the air, heaving out an exasperated sigh. "Fine. What can you remember from before you ended up here?"

Bek frowned. *What* do *I remember?*

"I'd been drinking." Her hand slipped to her pocket and fingered the little gold disc. "I...ah..."

No way was she admitting she'd basically stolen it and had planned to hock it. The last thing she needed was some sort of bond with this guy based on a morally questionable decision she'd made.

"I found this." She pulled the disc from her pocket and held it out in her palm, its tarnished gold stark against the silver coins. "I translated the strange writing on it. It's some sort of rhyme or verse. Totally weird. Then everything went black. I fell. Next thing I knew, I was here. Well... in that basement...cellar... room...with you."

"Were you bleeding?"

"No... Wait. Yes. What's that got to do with anyth — Oh, come *on*. Blood magic? Really?" *What is this? An episode of* Supernatural? Although... She cast her gaze over his bare torso again. Nah, Dean didn't hold a candle to *this* guy.

"Yes. Truly." The man was deadly serious. He pointed to his chest. "See this amulet?"

Her gaze followed his finger. There, hanging from a chain around his neck between the shreds of his shirt, was a gold disc. It looked just like the one she had in her hand. No, wait, not the same. His had a red stone in it. How had she missed it before? Her gaze flicked over his exposed chest, tinged red by the moon. She rolled her eyes. *Yeah, that was how.*

He picked up the amulet, showing her the stone. "This is a binding amulet."

She screwed up her nose. *Binding* amulet? Binding what?

"Before my time, someone, most likely a powerful witch, created a lot of amulets and bound them to this one with magic." He pointed to the one in her hand. "That is one of those amulets. With blood and the words spoken, you activated the spell and the binding amulet drew you to it. Call it blood magic, call it sorcery, call it whatever you will, but that is how it works. That is how you came to be here."

She snorted. "Sure."

"You do not believe me? Very well. Then explain how you came to be in that underground chamber with me. A room with one entry point — a locked grate — that you never opened. To a place far from your home soil where everyone speaks a language you do not speak. To a year, I would wager, that is long in your past, centuries even."

He held her gaze, the challenge in his eyes unmistakable. Her stomach did a little flip-flop. She ignored her body's call to action. "I don't know how to explain it, but…"

A muscle ticked in his jaw. "The guards, did they behave like these *emergency services*, these *boys in blue* you were expecting?"

Bek remained silent, his logic irrefutable.

"Is seeing a man bound in silver shackles and chained to a wall, something you have encountered before? Is it *normal* in your world?"

'Well…no, but… I wouldn't put it past Mrs. Wu.'

"*Merde*, woman. Open your eyes."

The rasp of his voice, the lilt of French and his accent… *God Almighty*. Even when he swore at her, it sounded sexy. It spoke to her of smoky, dimly lit bars, of black leather stretched across broad shoulders. Of the burn of whiskey shots down the back of the throat, and God help her, it spoke of sex. Down and dirty sex. Just the way she liked it.

For fuck's sake, Bek. Get a grip. "Okay, let's for a moment assume you're right—"

"I am right."

"Let's *assume* you're right. Why should I go with *you*? Why should I trust *you*? They chained you to a *wall!* What awful thing did you do to end up down there?"

Geez, that was rich coming from her.

She brushed aside the twinge of guilt. "Maybe I would be better off with… Who did you say owned this castle? A count? Maybe I should take my chances with him. Tell him you… I don't know…witchcrafted me here."

"Oh, trust me, sweetheart, that is the last thing you would want to do. You are not safe with the count. *Nobody* is safe with Lothair de Anjou."

She flicked her gaze to the castle. "I still only have your word on that."

"Enough." He sliced his hand through the air. "You are coming with me. For your own good. You can walk on your own or you can go over my shoulder again. Make your choice."

Bek glanced back at the keep and shivered. Yeah, she'd only been bluffing about returning there. She wasn't stupid enough to head back to the scene of the crime. Her swollen knuckles were enough evidence she had somehow been involved in that guard's demise. Testimony from the kid when he regained consciousness would only corroborate that.

She regarded the man standing before her. She knew little of history, even less about French history, but what she did know wasn't comforting. As a woman, dressed as she was, and with her poor grasp of the French language, she didn't much like her chances on her own. That left going with him. For now.

He raised an eyebrow. She took an involuntary step backward. He moved toward her, ducking his shoulder.

"Wait." She held out her hands, holding him at bay. "I'll walk."

He straightened.

"But"—she wagged her finger at him—"if you so much as look at me the wrong way, that sword of yours is going to go somewhere *really* unpleasant."

He chuckled. Bek scowled.

She might be half his size, but she was no wilting wallflower. "Try me, buddy."

"Though it would amuse me to see you attempt to shove my sword up my ass, now is not the time. Come." He grabbed her arm. "The guards will think something amiss when we do not return."

Bek cast one last glance at the castle behind her as he propelled her along with him, taking her deeper into the gloom the forest. Had she made the right decision? It wouldn't be the first time she'd put her trust in the wrong man.

Chapter Seven

Ulrik moved through the forest, his senses alert to his surroundings. He would not lead Lothair to the witch's hut east of them. Gaharet and Erin might still be there. He could not make for his own demesne, or Gaharet's, to the west. Chances were Lothair had reclaimed those lands, or at the very least had men watching them. To the south lay the River Loire.

He headed north, skirting villages and farms, angling toward the county of Blois. He would change course in a day or two. If Lothair tracked him somehow, let him think Ulrik had fled the county. Only then would he return and seek the witch. He hoped she would have news of Gaharet.

He slowed his pace, matching it with the woman's. Her boots, a pale washed-out shade of gules and absurdly fluffy, were no good for traversing the forest. He had no clue what function the sewn-on ears and button nose performed, or if they were merely fashionable. Women's customs in the future must be strange indeed.

"What is your name?" he asked.

"Bek."

"Beck?"

What sort of name was that? Maybe she came not from the same place as Erin. Erin, with her strange accent, though unusually defiant, had passed easily as a woman of their time. Beck, with her green-streaked hair, colorful and intricate markings on her arms and her ears and nose decorated with silver, would not.

"It's short for Rebekah. Rebekah Clarke."

"Rebekah." The name rolled off his tongue. He liked it.

"Only my parents call me that."

A familiar dull ache pressed against his sternum. His own family was lost to him. Chances were, hers were now, too. If Gaharet had not found a way to reverse the spell to send Erin back to her time, there was not one to be found. That Gaharet had been willing to search for one to help his mate leave confounded Ulrik. If he were ever to meet his mate, under no circumstances would he ever let her go.

"Family is sacred. I shall call you Rebekah."

She gave an indelicate snort. "My sleaze bag of a boss calls me Rebekah, too."

What a sleaze bag was, Ulrik could only guess. From her tone, it was nothing good.

"It irritates the hell out of me," she said. "That's why he persists in doing it."

Ulrik smirked. Oh, he would definitely call her Rebekah now.

"So, Ulrik," she said, as she trudged along beside him. "You're really a knight?"

"I am a chevalier, yes."

Perhaps not in name anymore. Lothair would be sure to relieve him of that title, along with his family estate and its title as well. A sobering thought. Gaharet's father had fought hard to have it reinstated to him when he had returned from Bretaigne. Once again, his actions had been the cause for its removal.

"So then, if you're a knight, what were you doing in the dungeon?"

"What was I doing in the keep?"

"Well, you weren't just in the keep, you were locked in the dungeon."

Ulrik stopped walking, his hand on her elbow jerking her to a stop with him. "Dun jen?" The word was unfamiliar to him. Something from her world, perhaps? "You mean *donjon,* as in the keep?"

She screwed up her face at him. "No, the dungeon. The oubliette. The tiny little room beneath the keep. Where you were a prisoner."

"Ah." Understanding dawned. "You call that an oubliette?"

"Yeah. Oubliette. Like from the movie *Labyrinth.* It means a place of forgetting."

Movie? Labyrinth? He knew naught of these things, but a place of forgetting was an apt description of it. Only, Lothair would not forget about him, nor stop hunting him. He would not let Ulrik get away easily. Ulrik grunted and continued walking, her soft footfalls in those ridiculous boots forced to keep pace with him.

"Why *were* you in the oubliette?"

Because Archeveque Renaud had set a trap to bind a werewolf. Because one of his pack had betrayed them. And because Lothair, Comte de Anjou, wanted a werewolf army and, perhaps, wanted to be one himself. None of which he could tell her.

"Did you kill someone? Commit treason? Are you a thief?"

He huffed. She was not going to let this lie. He had to give her something. "Because I had something the comte wanted."

"And you wouldn't give it to him? To get yourself out of there?"

"No."

"Must've been something really important. Or valuable. Or precious."

Yes, to all three.

"What was it?"

Defiant *and* tenacious. "Nothing you need concern yourself about."

"Hey!" She poked him in the arm. "I'm trusting you here. Following you to God knows where. I think I have a right to know exactly what type of person I've hitched my wagon to."

Hitched her wagon to?

Ulrik kept walking, but she pulled against his hold, digging her heels in. He turned. She stood her ground, her free hand on her hip, feet planted apart and her chin thrust out.

Stubborn woman. Glorious woman. He could not wait to get her beneath him. She promised to be all fire, and he wanted to feel the heat of her flames, but right now he needed to get her moving. He could throw her over his shoulder again.

As if sensing his intent, she scowled at him. He bit back a grin.

"My...lord has fled with his...wife." He chose his words with care. "Lothair demanded something he had no right to ask for, and now Lothair wants him found. He wanted me to betray my lord." All truths.

"Huh."

He raised his eyebrows at her. "Can we continue on now?"

She gave a small nod and fell into step beside him. "Were they newly married? Your lord and his wife?"

Newly mated? "Yes."

He had scented the truth of it the moment he had approached them in the clearing that fateful night. The night he had succumbed to wolfsbane and Renaud had bound him in silver. But Gaharet had not told Erin everything. She had known Gaharet was a werewolf, but little else. And she had not accepted Gaharet as her mate. Not fully. She had wanted to return to her world. A world Ulrik had not known she'd come from until that moment. Would she still want to return home? Even now that Gaharet had initiated her turning? Had bitten her to save her life?

"He was protecting her, then? Like William Wallace in *Braveheart*?"

Brave heart? "I know naught of this William Wallace, but of course he would protect her. She is his...wife."

Gaharet would do anything for Erin. Had Ulrik not intervened, Gaharet would have risked his life and the pack's future for her.

"I don't blame them for fleeing," she said. "That first night rule thing is...ugh! I mean, what woman would want to have sex with some random lord on her wedding night? What man would stand for it? Would just let his wife be taken away?"

Ulrik peered at her through the darkness. What nonsense did she speak of? What first night rule?

"This lord of yours, he's a good man then?" she asked.

He brushed her ramblings aside. "Yes, he is a good man."

Another truth. One he had not been able to see for so long, his vision clouded by grief, anger and shame. He touched a hand to the scars on his neck. The welts from the silver shackles were gone, leaving nothing to show they had ever been there. These scars, years old now, would always remain. The wound inflicted too deep to heal fully, they were a constant reminder of that day. Of what he had done.

"And you're loyal to your lord?"

"Yes." Though Gaharet had doubted him. As had the others, he suspected.

"Does that make you a good man, too?"

Ulrik's step faltered. Was he a good man? He was trying to be. To make amends.

He shook his head. Enough of her questions. He turned, ran his gaze over her from head to toe. Ulrik liked seeing her draped in his surcoat, though it covered all her curves. He would like her better naked.

He smiled down at her, letting his desire for her show. "Oh, I am good, Rebekah. You will not regret *'hitching your wagon'* to me. That I promise you."

Bek's breath stuttered, and she stared up at him. Bearded, rugged and strong. God, the man was her own personal wet dream. And he'd made his intentions clear. Thrown down the gauntlet. She gritted her teeth and forcibly ignored the fluttering in her stomach and the dampening of her knickers.

Not. Going. To. Happen.

Even if chevalier did sound sexier than knight. Biker had a nice ring to it, too. *Better than outlaw gang member.* Look where that'd gotten her. A stint in jail, that's what. A victim of her own naivety. Unlike his lord, who'd defied this Comte Lothair for his wife, her man had used her, betrayed her, and thrown her to the wolves.

Ulrik might sound like a loyal, chivalrous knight. As Vice President of the Demons, Spider had shown a devotion almost religious to his crew. But self-preservation, and his crew, had proved more important to him than any connection he'd had with her. He'd walked away from her without a second thought. Left her to wallow in jail while he'd moved on with someone new. Bek had sworn never to be in that position again. That she'd get her shit together. Live a better life.

Ulrik tugged on her arm, and they started walking again. Getting her life back on track meant making good, responsible decisions. Sir Ulrik Voclain didn't feel like a good decision. More like a feel-good decision. She'd made enough of those to last a lifetime. And she would never trust, nor give herself, to a man like him again.

Chapter Eight

Lothair paced the floor of his underground chamber. One dead guard. One living. No werewolf. Ulrik Voclain had escaped. The silver shackles and a ring of keys lay beside the body. The surviving guard trembled before him, his face ashen and a bloody gash on the back of his head. Free, Ulrik would have easily overpowered the inexperienced guard. And the battle-hardened veteran. But how had he gotten free? How had he gotten the key to the shackles?

"How did this" — he waved his hand over the scene before him — "happen?"

"Mon Seigneur Comte, there was —"

Archeveque Renaud stepped into the room, the candle in his hand casting shadows over his gaunt face, making him seem more like a walking corpse than usual. "After all the trouble I went to, to catch him alive, you let him go?"

Lothair leveled a glare at the clergyman. "You are treading on dangerous ground, Renaud. The hour is early, and I am not in the mood for your disrespect."

He shifted his hand to the grip of his sword. If the threat perturbed Renaud, he did not show it. Lothair gritted his teeth. The hour *was* early, not yet dawn, though he had not been sleeping. Neither, it seemed, had Renaud, but his appearance so quickly after the change of guard had raised the alarm suggested only one thing. Renaud had an informant in his keep guard. Maybe more than one. His grip on his sword tightened, and he itched to draw it from its scabbard.

He would not stand for spies in his own guard. He would rout them out and hang their entrails from the ramparts as a warning. Or place their severed heads on pikes at the gate. He would like nothing more than to place Renaud's head on a pike and be done with it, but the repercussions for killing an archeveque were more churchmen in his county. *That* he did not need. Not when he had plans involving werewolves.

I wonder... Could he sniff the spies out if he were a werewolf? Would his sense of smell be that strong?

Renaud retrieved the ring of keys from the floor. The archeveque was almost salivating at the prospect he would take the risk of being turned into one. Baiting him to take it. The archeveque played a dangerous game. Lothair relaxed his hand, releasing his grip on his sword, finger by finger. Best to avoid temptation.

He returned his attention to the quaking guard. "Explain."

The guard's lip trembled and his hands shook. "I heard voices. We came to investigate. I... I do not know how it was possible, Mon Seigneur. No one passed by us. We did not open the grate for anyone, but..."

The pack had used the amulet. A risky move that could have resulted in two werewolves trapped. Lothair had not taken Gaharet, or any of Gaharet's vassals, for fools.

"But?" demanded Renaud.

Lothair bit back a snarl. The guard's eyes bulged, his gaze shifting between Renaud and him, settling on him. As it should.

The young man's throat convulsed. "There was a woman in here."

A *woman*? Lothair's eyes narrowed. One like Kathryn Beauchene? One of *them*?

"I swear, Mon Seigneur Comte, I do not know how she got in here, but she was *in here*. Hiding in the corner."

Renaud snorted in disgust. "It is obvious how she got in. One of you let her in, fooled by the charms of the flesh."

"Renaud." This time Lothair did not hold back his snarl.

"Did she ply you with wine, flaunt her bosom at you? Smile prettily and ask to the see the chevalier chained beneath the keep?" Renaud's thin, bloodless lips pressed into a straight line. The guard trembled. "Fools. I will see you punished for this. It is fortunate for your fellow guard he is dead. In time, you may wish your fate had been the same."

Fury surged through Lothair, his blood pounding in his ears. "Renaud! You overstep yourself!"

Renaud turned to him, red splotches on his cheekbones and his eyes blazing with barely contained rage.

Lothair narrowed his gaze on the archeveque, his hand tapping against the pommel of his sword. "Careful, Renaud. The church may have appointed you archeveque, but you are in my county, at my pleasure."

Indeed, the archeveque remained living only so long as he deemed it inconvenient to kill him. The time was fast approaching when Lothair would not care about the consequences of dispatching such a high-ranking member of the church.

Renaud opened his mouth to respond.

Lothair slid his sword partially from its scabbard with a scrape of steel. "Do not tempt me."

Renaud's mouth snapped shut, and he gave a perfunctory bow of his head. "My apologies, Mon Seigneur Comte. The incompetence of these men made me forget my place for but a moment. I am grateful for the considerations you allow me while in your county."

Lothair masked his revulsion as Renaud's sudden obsequiousness settled over him, thicker than pitch. "Speaking of, when are you leaving, Renaud? Surely you have duties elsewhere that need attending to. I would not want the spiritual health of your other jurisdictions to suffer on account of the time you are spending in Langeais."

A muscle ticked in Renaud's jaw, and the archeveque's hand clenched around the ring of keys.

"If you are uncertain if your chaplains are saving enough souls and damning enough sinners, Renaud, I would be happy to keep them in line for you. In fact, I will send a message to your cardinal and suggest that very thing."

Renaud smiled, the grotesque grin of a corpse. "Thank you, Mon Seigneur Comte. I appreciate the offer, but it will not be necessary. What I have come here to accomplish is almost complete. Once it is, I doubt I will have any need to return to your county."

"And what is it exactly you are trying to accomplish? Perhaps I can be of some assistance."

"Church business, Mon Seigneur Comte. Nothing you need be aware of."

Lothair's nostrils flared. Anything happening in his county he needed to be aware of, especially if Renaud was involved. He grunted. This conversation was getting him nowhere.

He turned to the guard. "Dispose of this body. Tomorrow you will report for cesspit duty."

The guard's obvious relief disturbed him. Had he been too kind?

He slammed his sword back into his scabbard and turned to Renaud. "I believe you were to arrange for your informant to meet me. Do not keep me waiting too long." He turned to his capitaine. "Assemble the guard. We have an escaped prisoner to hunt down. And check with the guards at the postern gate."

Lothair swept past the scowling archeveque and climbed the stairs. He would waste no more time with Renaud. He had an escaped werewolf to find.

* * * *

Renaud gritted his teeth as several guards maneuvered the body up the narrow stairs. *Damn* Voclain. *Damn* the useless keep guards. And *damn* this unknown woman. He had spent many moons working on his plan, using the information his informant had given him. It had not been easy capturing a werewolf. Indeed, many had willingly chosen death over capture.

Renaud wiped a hand across his brow. He had thought himself so clever, targeting the women, but he had killed them all through his own ignorance. Before he had found the balance between making them weak and making them dead. Before his informant had approached him with the knowledge of wolfsbane and its effect on werewolves. And still, they had fought to the death. And they had those damned amulets. They would disappear before he could bind any of them.

He glared at the silver shackles glinting in the candlelight. He had finally captured one. Finally had one at his mercy. He had poked the wounded beast that was Ulrik Voclain, certain the man's lust for revenge against Lothair would aid his plan. Now, all because of a *woman* and the idiot guards who had let her in, Voclain was gone.

He turned away from the shackles. He would have to start again. Only now, Lothair knew how to control the werewolves, too. His usefulness to the comte was ending. That would not do. He needed another werewolf, chained and bound. As for arranging for his informant to meet with Lothair... No. That must never happen. His informant was as likely to turn on him. Renaud suspected he already had. It could only have been he who had contacted that pretentious git, Eveque Faucher.

A flicker of white in corner caught his eye and he knelt to retrieve it. A piece of white parchment. Thinner, whiter than any parchment he had seen before. And smooth. He turned it over and held the candle up to it.

Lines of writing flowed across the page. Twelve of them. Four in the now familiar script found only on the beast's amulets. Another four in what appeared to be some strange form of the language of Bretaigne. Not at all like the example he had seen of Caedmon's hymn. He lifted his gaze from the parchment.

Had not d'Louncrais' betrothed hailed from Bretaigne? Coincidence? I think not.

He returned his attention to the writing. The final four lines he recognized. Latin. The language of the church. His lips curled into a semblance of a smile, and he slipped the parchment into the folds of his robes. Even that wretched Eveque Faucher did not have what he now possessed — the key to the amulets, to the werewolves' disappearances. The translation of the spell. With this, he no longer had need of his informant. Time to sever his alliance. And he knew exactly how to do it.

With a smile hovering on his lips, Renaud climbed the steps and left the dark, little chamber.

Chapter Nine

Bek stumbled along, the flimsy soles of her fluffy, pink bunny slippers providing little protection from stones and exposed tree roots. Her feet felt like two enormous bruises, her legs lumps of wood, and her injured hand throbbed. She'd done a ten-hour shift at Charlie's, and now they'd walked for... How far had they walked? Miles? Too damn far. Any effects of the wine had long since worn off. It felt like forever since she'd sat on her couch, drinking a few glasses of cheap red, looking forward to a meal of two-minute noodles. Her stomach rumbled.

Again, she attempted to wrest her arm free from Ulrik's grip — not tight enough to give her bruises, but not an inch of give.

"How much further?" She cringed at the whine in her tone.

"They will be out hunting us. Once they discover we left via the postern gate..."

His pace didn't slow at all as he answered her. The man was a veritable machine. Not a single stumble or misstep, his pace measured and even. Perhaps slower than he would normally walk because of her. Chained up for God knows how long and he could still walk the pants off an Olympic triathlete.

"Can we take a break? Just for a moment?"

"No."

Bek groaned. She eyed the wineskin hanging over her shoulder, bumping against her hip as she walked. Getting drunk on ancient wine wouldn't help them any, but it sure would make her feel better right now and blot out the misery of her aching muscles.

"We need to get as far ahead of them as we can. They will be on horseback. Need I point out the obvious?"

Bek grunted and forced herself to keep walking.

After what felt like another mile, the sound of running water reached her ears. Would they stop now? Even if he let go of her, she doubted she'd have the energy to run from him. At least, not fast enough or far enough that he wouldn't be on her like white on rice. He wasn't even puffed.

She stumbled, her tired legs buckling. He was there, strong arms catching her and holding her upright.

"We will stop here for a few moments, *petite cracheuse de feu.*"

Pettie crashooze de fer? What the hell did that mean? Did she even want to know? She'd been called many things by the patrons at Charlie's, by Charlie, by the prison wardens. Many of them unpleasant. None of them in French. *Probably something like pain in my ass, or mouthy bitch.*

Whatever it was, to her tired mind it sounded much nicer in French than English. And she wanted him to say it again. Whisper it against her hair as he held her in his arms, the warmth of his body soaking into her fatigued muscles. Bek let out a contented murmur and relaxed into his hold. Her eyelids fluttered closed, her reasons for escaping, for keeping him at arm's length drifting away. If she could just stay here for a moment…

She snuggled into him, rubbing her cheek against his bare chest.

"Begging for my attention already?"

Bek's eyes snapped open, and she wrenched herself from his arms. He chuckled, the smugness of the sound leeching through the darkness.

"Sit for a moment, Rebekah. I will tend to your hand, then I will remove my boots and roll up my breeches and we will wade upstream."

Seriously? He was going to make them walk *farther?* In *water?* She looked down at her slippers, trying to summon the energy to remove them and roll up her jeans.

He snagged her chin, forcing her to look at him. "You are exhausted. I will carry you."

Bek stumbled back. *Oh, hell no.* "I can walk."

"Rebekah, sit."

She balked at the command, but when his hand pressed on her shoulder, she slumped to the ground. Just for a minute or two. Until she got her second wind. Then, once he was barefoot, she would take the opportunity and run. Good plan.

Ulrik ripped a strip from his torn shirt and dipped it into the stream. Then he knelt beside her and gently wrapped it around her bruised hand. The cool cloth was a balm for the throbbing of her knuckles. She leaned her back against a large tree, the leaf litter on the forest floor providing a surprisingly soft seat, and she stretched out her legs. The breeze whispered in the trees and the water in the stream bubbled over rocks. Moonlight filtered through the canopy — the reddish glow gone with the ending of the eclipse — and Bek closed her eyes.

* * * *

When she next opened them with a start, they were moving upstream, she nestled in his arms, her face flush with his bare chest, as he picked his way through the shallow water. In her lap lay the wineskin and his boots.

"Go back to sleep," he said, his voice a mere rasp of sound. "We have a ways to go yet."

She wanted to protest, demand he put her down so she could walk on her own, but her eyes closed of their own volition, and she slipped back into blessed darkness.

She awoke again as he lay her down on the ground.

"We are safe here for the moment, Rebekah. Rest up while you can."

She blinked at him through sleep-laden eyes. Standing over her, he looked every bit a medieval warrior. She had a moment to appreciate what a truly magnificent looking man he was, to try to remember the reasons she must stay awake, before she succumbed to fatigue once again.

* * * *

Bek's stomach grumbled. She groaned. Another few minutes of sleep. She rolled over. Birds tweeted, warmth bathed her face and a hint of cooking meat and smoke tantalized her nostrils. She sat bolt upright.

Shit.

How long had she slept? She brushed leaves from her hair and looked around, taking in the grassy clearing, the early morning sunlight filtering through the trees and the creek bubbling along, emptying into a pond. A small fire crackled, cooking some kind of dead animal, skinned, gutted and suspended over the flames. Bek's mouth watered. It should repulse her, but she hadn't eaten since a rushed, soggy tuna sandwich at lunch yesterday. And it sure beat two-minute noodles.

But where was Ulrik?

Ripples in the pond drew her gaze. On the bank sat his sword and scabbard, his clothes and boots. His head appeared, and he tossed it back, his long hair flinging water about. He stood, and her gaze followed the rivulets of water running down his back, past narrow hips and across tight buns. Bek strangled a gasp and flopped back down, watching him through slitted lids, and pretending to sleep as he turned his head in her direction. She dare not move. She just lay there staring and imagined running her hands over that very fine ass.

He spun around.

Bek's breath stalled in her throat, and her eyelids twitched with the strain of keeping them slitted. It would take a better person than her to turn away, to not look, to not take the opportunity to see what he was packing in those tight trousers of his. And it was a lot. Thick and long, and not at all affected by the cold of the water, and his ball sac hanging heavy between his muscular thighs. Bek's fingers curled. He had a nice cock. She salivated. A very nice-looking cock. It was all she could do to not move or make a sound. To not rise from her position and join him in the pond.

What the hell am I thinking? Haven't I learned not to play with fire?

Escape. That's what she needed to do. Run as far away from this damn man as she possibly could. Before she did something really stupid. *Like jump his bones.*

She could find a village. Peasants would help her, wouldn't they? Or a farmer? Farmers were supposed to be good people.

Then he took himself in hand, and his long, slender fingers stroked his length.

Oh, dear God. This guy was trouble with a capital T. In bold. In italics. Highlighted *and* underlined.

He continued to work himself, water lapping at his upper thighs.

I'd like to lap at his upper thighs.

Bek squeezed her eyes shut, blocking out the debauched vision before her, and took deep breaths. When she opened them again, he'd turned away from her and was sliding back under the water.

Forget what he's doing with his hand. Get up. Go. Now.

Bek leaped to her feet. If their trek through the forest last night had proved anything, she had no hope of outrunning him. She had to outsmart him. An idea formed in her mind, and she grinned. That'd slow him down.

She crept toward his pile of belongings and scooped up his boots, pants, dagger and sword and backed away into the tree line. Once she was out of sight, she turned and ran.

She didn't have a lot of time. More if he finished what he'd started, believing her asleep. She stumbled, her mind catching on the erotic image. She squeezed her thighs together, gritted her teeth and pushed on.

Yes. Get away from him as fast as you can.

She glanced over her shoulder. He was still underwater. Good. She paused, and grabbed one of his boots, drew her arm back, and threw it as far as she could. She started off again before it had hit the ground, running as fast as her useless bunny slippers would allow.

Why couldn't I still be wearing my work boots?

She halted again by a dense, prickly bush and tossed his pants into the thick of it. If she was lucky, it would have some sort of toxic leaf. A rash on his balls would certainly cool his ardor for her and was no less than he deserved.

Bek raced on, stopping only to hide his torn shirt behind a rock by the stream, and his sword in a crevasse under an overhang. Breathless, her sides heaving, she stopped one last time, and shoved his other boot into the hollow of a fallen tree. No matter how strong he was, he wouldn't get far without his boots or pants. The chances of him risking a confrontation with villagers while starkers was low. His dagger she held onto. It might come in handy.

She set off again, slowing her pace as she followed the stream. Logic told her water was as relevant now as it was in her century. Only here, they wouldn't have it plumbed into houses, so it stood to reason any village would be near a convenient water source. Like the stream.

Bek didn't have to go far to be proved right. She skidded to a halt as the forest gave way to an open meadow and farmers' fields. Beyond them stood a ramshackle collection of small huts. Villagers — farmers by their clothes — men and women, dotted the fields.

She tucked the dagger beneath the surcoat, securing it handle down, in the waistband of her jeans. It settled in the small of her back, along her spine. If she was careful, it would be fine. The last thing she needed was to injure herself. She had enough things to worry about. Like how she was going to communicate when her school-girl French was rusty at best. And how would she make them understand she needed to get back to the twenty-first century? Without sounding like a lunatic?

If she'd thought her life was a mess before, her current situation took things to a whole new level of disaster. Dealing with Charlie and his unwanted attentions, checking in with her dick of a parole officer and facing the wrath of Mrs. Wu when she didn't pay her rent on time wasn't so bad. Better than being stuck in a barbaric medieval world, hunted by keep guards and escaping the dubious safety of the sexy-as-sin warrior who was on the run from what passed as the law in this place. A man who put her darkest fantasies to shame and had her ovaries, her own damn cheer-leading squad, urging her to play big, play hard and score.

She was *so* screwed.

Bek took a deep breath, planted a smile on her face, and stepped out from the shadows of the forest. Time to go chat up the natives.

* * * *

The wolf crouched, concealed, his one good eye fixed on the woman as she made her way down to the village. About her clung a scent. Male. Wolf. Tantalizingly familiar. Something from his past, perhaps, yet he could not place it. Nor did he care to. He had no business with her, nor the male. The one he sought was close by. The one who had tried to kill him.

The scars across his back itched, the cut of betrayal as fresh as the day one of his own pack had cut him down. He had come too close to the truth of his mother's death. As had his father. He had known it then, seen it in the traitor's eyes. Luck, and a dogged determination to survive, was all that had kept him from being another casualty of his attacker's scheming.

But survive he had, and the time would soon come when he would have his vengeance. When this man, this wolf, would pay for his sins. Unlike his betrayer, who had made the mistake of leaving him to die, he would make certain his prey did not survive.

Chapter Ten

Ulrik rose out of the water. It felt good to be clean again and to be free of the silver that had burned his skin and subdued his wolf. He looked down at his erect cock, the cold water doing little to tame his desire for the woman he had rescued. Ulrik grinned. He had heard her muffled gasp. As if she could hide her reaction to him. As if he had not known she only pretended to sleep.

Ulrik suppressed a chuckle. He had enjoyed goading her, stroking himself while she watched, but it left him throbbing and wanting. Should he take himself to completion while she lay there listening? His hand brushed against his cock, and it jerked, happy for any attention. He would prefer it to be her hand, not his. Better still, her mouth.

A noise behind him cut off his moan. He stilled.

Merde.

She was no longer by the fire but fleeing through the forest. He spun, surging out of the water, only to find his breeches, his boots, his sword and his dagger, gone. Clever wench. She could not hide from him, nor could she escape him, but if she made it to the nearby village before he caught her, she could bring the keep guard down on them. Worse still, the village belonged to the Vautour estate. To Lance.

L'enfer.

Until they routed the traitor, he could trust none of his pack save Gaharet. Not even Lance, whose council Gaharet had often sought. Nor could he guess how any of his pack would view him, given what they must believe he had done. They could accept him as their new alpha, or they could want his blood for supposedly killing Gaharet.

He kicked dirt on the fire, threw the partly cooked hare carcass into the forest, and called forth his wolf. He took off at a run, sandy hair exploding across his body, his fangs elongating in his mouth and his bones cracking as he shifted mid stride. With his nose to the ground and his ears pricked, he followed her trail.

That she had thought to delay her escape, stopping to throw his boot away from her path and into the forest, caught him by surprise. She was wily, more like the she-wolves he remembered from his younger years. Not canny enough, though, to notice her magic light hidden inside. With his boot and its precious cargo in his jaws, he set off again, hunting for the rest of his clothes.

Ulrik found his breeches in the prickly grasp of a thick gorse shrub. He shifted back to human, his snout too sensitive to brave its needle-like foliage, and carefully extracted them. He donned his breeches and secured her magic light against his hip, tightening the laces to hold it in place. Pulling on his boot, he set off again. There was no time to waste. Lord knew where she had hidden the rest of his clothing.

He found his tunic beneath a rock near the stream and slipped it on. Its torn remnants did little to hide his torso, but he would attract more attention bare chested. Attention he did not need. He tracked her scent to a crevasse beneath an overhang. There, he reached in and retrieved his sword. He strapped it around his hips and continued on.

He found his other boot inside the trunk of a fallen tree. A colony of ants had made the rotting hollow their home, and his boot was crawling with them. He snarled, tipping this boot upside down and giving it a vigorous shake. He doubted she had known of the trunk's occupants when she stuffed it in its hollow, but it had benefited her. Yet another delay.

Shoving his foot into his boot, he ignored the bites of the few ants he had failed to remove and stomped through the forest after her. Had she known to follow the stream? That it would lead her to the village? Or was it luck she headed directly for it? Given she had had the presence of mind to take *and* discard his clothing, in five separate locations, no less, he suspected it was the former. Ulrik grinned. He liked a challenge. This woman was by the far the most intriguing he had come across in a very long time.

An unexpected scent caught his nostrils, banishing his smile. He froze, all his enhanced senses alert. Wolf. Not a real one. A werewolf. Familiar and yet... He raised his nose to the air, inhaling deeply, searching for the scent again. Nothing. The hairs on the back of his neck rose. Wolfsbane? His last encounter with that foul herb had seen him confined beneath Langeais Keep. He snarled. Not this time.

With a cautious tread, he circled back the way he had come, peering into the forest and sniffing the air. Not wolfsbane. The scents of the forest, of oak, beech and pine, were sharp. And the sounds — insects scurrying, the hint of a breeze through the canopy, the distant braying of animals in farmers' fields — were clear. But the twitter of birds and the scurrying of rodents and game were absent. A predator lay in wait. The sense of being watched crawled up his spine.

Ulrik allowed his wolf to hover close, should he need to shift. It was not Lance. He would have recognized him, or any other member of his pack. A wolf from another pack, maybe? From across the continent? From Rus? Werewolves did not range far from their pack. Could it be a rogue? A wolf banished for misdeeds too vile to forgive. If so, Gaharet would need to know. Another reason to find his alpha. And fast.

He turned full circle, his gaze darting about. If he could catch sight of it, scent it again... But he could not. This wolf was clever, experienced. Not young then, or newly turned. Definitely male. But there was something about this wolf that triggered a feeling of familiarity. Had he met him during his banishment in Bretaigne?

As suddenly as the scent had caught his attention, the sense of the other presence dissipated and Ulrik was left standing alone in the forest. He let his wolf retreat, but he did not relax his vigilance. Should he try to track it? Perhaps this wolf was Renaud's informant. Perhaps it was not one of their own who had betrayed them. Or mayhap it was tracking Rebekah. A cold fist of steel gripped his entrails. *Rebekah.*

Ulrik set off after her, his pace faster now. He reached the edge of the forest and paused. The small mud-brick huts of the village lay beyond. Curls of smoke rose from chimney holes and the heavy scent of meat and vegetables simmering in pots over fires filled the air. In the surrounding fields, villagers plowed the ground, tended their grazing animals and harvested their crops.

About to break the calm routine of their working day strode Rebekah. His dark umber surcoat flapping about her ankles and the stripes in her hair a vibrant green in the morning sun, she approached a man guiding a team of oxen pulling a large wooden plow. The farmer did not stop, nor did he acknowledge her, continuing with his task as though she were not there.

With a shrug of her shoulders, Rebekah crossed the field and waved a greeting to a woman harvesting vegetables. Without a word, the woman picked up her basket and walked away. Rebekah placed her hands on her hips and stared after her. Undeterred, she approached another woman. This time Rebekah retreated fast when a man, most likely the woman's husband, stepped toward her, shouting at her and waving a pitchfork.

Ulrik had always found those who lived and worked in the shadow of the Vautour Keep to be unwelcoming. Not that they had ever viewed him with hostility when he had visited, but rather they had a deep sense of distrust of strangers. Rebekah would seem stranger than most.

With a frustrated set to her shoulders, and warily skirting the man with the pitchfork, Rebekah made her way toward the huts. She would find no more help there than in the fields.

Ulrik kept to the edge of the forest, avoiding the farmers and their fields, and slipped up behind her. Before she could approach anyone else, he grasped her elbow, clamped a hand over her mouth and dragged her behind the tanner's hut. The smell of putrefying flesh and animal waste assaulted his nostrils. He would bear it, for it would hide their scents, and he planned to be gone before too long. A villager would, for certain, once finished with their chores, alert their lord to the strange woman in the village.

He stood her against the wall, blocking her escape, and removed his hand from her mouth. "Where do you think you were going, Rebekah?"

Her eyes were wide and her pulse raced at the base of her throat, but she met his stare, undaunted. "I see you found your clothes."

He grunted. "Yes. Thank you for that. By the time I retrieved my boot from the fallen tree you so kindly stowed it in, a colony of ants had taken up residence."

She laughed.

He scowled. "I am glad you find it amusing."

She gulped and licked her lips, and his gaze lingered on the gleam of moisture that clung to them.

"I…"

He held out his hand. "My dagger, if you will."

Without a word, she retrieved it from beneath his surcoat and handed it to him. She was lucky she had not cut herself with it. The blade was sharp.

"Now, we are going to walk out of this village together and return to the forest."

She scowled at him and opened her mouth to speak.

He pressed a finger to her lips. "You will go quietly."

She shoved his hand away.

His wolf surged forward, and a rumble rose in his throat. He placed a hand on the mud-brick hut on either side of her head and stepped closer, his lips a mere breath from hers. He stared into her eyes, so full of defiance. Any other time, he would take up her challenge. It tested his control not to, but he was no more an untried, inexperienced wolf than the one he had encountered in the forest. She would not best him that easily.

"Do not test me, Rebekah."

"Or what? You'll throw me over your shoulder? Mm, that'd make a scene. Believe me, I won't be quiet if you do. Not this time. I'll scream this whole damn village down."

The mutinous expression on her face told him she would, too. *Merde.* Could the woman not understand he was trying to help her?

He inhaled a calming breath. This close to her, his nostrils caught her scent above the stench of the tannery — an intoxicating mix of all that was Rebekah overlaid by his own scent from his surcoat. It lodged in his throat and stirred his darker half. His wolf prowled in his mind, urging him to… He shook his head, reining the beast in.

"I will do what needs must, whatever it takes, to get us from this village unseen."

Her scent deepened, tinged with her irritation and a little unease, but she did not flinch, and her expression revealed none of her apprehension. The woman had the heart of a lion. No. A she-wolf. Yet her scent did not lie. She was all human.

He pulled away from her and took her arm. "Come. None of these villagers will help you. No more so than they did in the fields."

But perhaps he knew someone who could. Gaharet may well have found a way to send Erin home, back to the future, as she had wanted. If she had survived the turning. At the very least, Gaharet would protect Rebekah, and if Erin had remained in this century, Rebekah might find comfort in her company. Another woman from her time. If he had to frighten her a little to get her to do what he wanted, to keep her safe, he was comfortable with that.

Ulrik rounded the corner of the tanner's hut, Rebekah in tow, and came to an abrupt halt.

Godfrey.

Seated on his horse and fully armed, the chevalier rode through the village, his yellow surcoat bright in the morning sun.

The stench of the tanning solutions had worked against him and had concealed Godfrey's approach. Ulrik ducked back behind the hut, dragging Rebekah with him. He held her against the wall with his body, his hand over her mouth, lest she scream or make a fuss. She squirmed, pulling at his hand. Her sumptuous curves rubbed against him, and turned his cock hard in an instant.

Lord, she would test the vows of a saint.

He groaned. She struggled harder, and the friction stole away his breath, his concentration and his control. His hold on her mouth loosened, and she ripped her face from his grasp, drew in a deep breath and opened her mouth wide.

Ulrik was no saint.

He took her mouth in his and swallowed her scream. With the wall at her back, she had no room to retreat as he tasted her, taking what he had wanted from the moment she had first appeared before him in Lothair's wretched underground chamber.

She fought him, and his blood soared. She pounded her fists on his chest. Ineffective against his strength, they were a powerful blow to his conscience.

What the fuck am I doing?

He released his hold on her and stepped back, her chest heaving and fury blazing in her eyes. And yet, back arched, pushing those beautiful breasts toward him. She wanted him. He smirked and cocked an eyebrow. She drew back her arm and slapped him across his face.

Ulrik gaped at her. She had slapped him. Hard. He held his hand to his stinging cheek. *L'enfer.* He did not like it. Not at all. But he had deserved it. His gut roiled and his cheek burned. He had promised her he would not touch her unless she asked, and he had forsaken his vow so quickly and so easily. *Merde.* His parents had raised him to be a better man. He would not sully their memory, no matter how much Rebekah tempted him.

He took another step back, reining in his prowling wolf, ignoring its demands to pounce, to take and to mate. Her dilated pupils tracked him. Oh, she wanted him. Her scent did not lie. She did not *want* to want him, but she did.

A strangled moan escaped her throat and she reached for him. She grasped the edges of his torn tunic, dragged his face down to hers and planted her lips on his. Ulrik's eyes widened, but he needed no second invitation. He wrapped his arms around her, pulled her in tight and ground against her. She quivered, a slight softening of her body, and he knew he had her. He licked the seam of her lips. She opened for him and he plunged his tongue into her mouth. She greeted him with a swipe of her own.

Yes.

Ulrik slipped his hand between the laces of his surcoat, settling it on her ribcage, a bare hair's breadth from her lush breast. *Mon Dieu,* he longed to cup her in his hand. He deepened the kiss, stroking her tongue with his.

Burning pain shot through his tongue, and he ripped his mouth from hers.

"*Merde!* What did you—"

She hauled her arm back and slapped him. He gaped at her. She had burned his tongue then she had hit him. Again.

"*L'enfer,* woman. Why did you—?"

"The first slap was for kissing me without my permission."

He glared at her, then gave her a reluctant nod. "I will accept that. I deserved it. But why did you hit me again?"

"The second one was for making me *want* to kiss you."

Triumph surged through him, and despite his stinging cheek and burning tongue, he smiled. She crossed her arms over her chest and scowled at him. He rubbed his cheek, his tongue tingling as it healed. A blister on his tongue he could withstand. Other parts of his anatomy... He winced, and his cock shriveled. Was it possible she had jewelry in her ears, nose *and* tongue? He grimaced at the idea. Whatever had burned him like the silver shackles had his wrists and throat, he would need to identify and remove. But he *would* kiss her again, were she to ask, no matter how painful.

Her cheeks flushed, her chest heaving and her lips moist and plump from his kiss, she was a delight. All fire and passion ripe for the plucking. Rebekah *would* come to him willingly, and it would be all the more sweet for the wait.

He raked his gaze over her. "You tempt me so, Rebekah. I make no apologies for that. But I am not in the habit of taking what is not given freely. When you are ready, *petite cracheuse de feu.* I can wait."

Chapter Eleven

Bek glared at Ulrik. As apologies went, it wasn't much of one. Nor was it an admission of guilt, but he had stepped back, and he wasn't forcing himself on her despite the lust swirling in his dark whiskey eyes. And he hadn't reciprocated in kind when she'd slapped him. At least that was something in his favor. That and, *damn it*, the man could kiss. She could still taste him on her tongue, feel the pressure of those lips on hers. Bek bit back a groan. She'd always been a sucker for a good kisser. It figured a Frenchman would know his way around a French kiss.

But what had made him stop? Had he caught himself on her tongue ring? Whatever it was, Bek was grateful for it. She closed her eyes, blocking out the vision of his drool-worthy chest and the evidence of his arousal straining in his trousers. Who knows how far she'd have let him go had he not pulled away.

All the damn way. Yep. That's what she was afraid of.

Ulrik's hand on her elbow had her eyes popping open.

"Come. We will find you some clothing so you can blend in." His gaze dipped to her feet. "And boots that are more functional."

Her stomach rumbled and his lip quirked, revealing a flash of white teeth. God, the man was gorgeous when he smiled.

"And food. But we must be gone from here before someone reports your presence to the lord of this village."

The lord of the village? Was that the man in the yellow coat? Would he be more helpful than the villagers themselves? They'd turned their backs on her when she'd approached them, refusing to acknowledge her. Not a single good Samaritan amongst them. One had threatened her with a pitchfork. She'd never had the chance to approach anyone inside the village, but would they have been any different?

She met his stare, his eyes swirling with shadows. "Why are you doing this? You'd travel much faster without me. You could have just let me run and continued on your merry way. Why didn't you?"

It seemed an awful lot of trouble, and risk, for a man to go to just to get into her knickers.

He shook his head. "You are not safe here on your own."

She wasn't necessarily safe with him, either. "But I'm not really your problem, am I? Why don't you just ditch me? Let the count or the lord of this village deal with me?"

He stared at her, those strange swirls in his irises intensifying. Then he looked away, inhaling a deep breath and releasing it on a long sigh before meeting her gaze once more.

"In truth, Rebekah, helping you reminds me of the man I used to be."

Oh. His words were a sucker punch to her lungs. She knew that sentiment. Felt it in the very marrow of her bones. Wanting to be the person you'd been, all bright and shiny, full of the promise of youth, before your choices had dragged you down and turned you into someone you no longer recognized. And didn't that burrow deep down into her chest and make her heart wrench for him.

Regret and pain shimmered in his eyes. Is that what people saw when they looked at her? Did her sense of shame hang over her like his? This man, this knight, was chasing his redemption as much as she was chasing hers.

She pressed her tongue ring against the roof of her mouth, mulling over his words. What were her choices here? She had no money, nowhere to go and she didn't speak the language. Other than him, she knew no one, and next to nothing about life in historical bloody France. She'd be lucky to last a day on her own. If the farmers she'd approached were any indication, the chances of her getting help from anyone else were slim. The only reason she'd made it this far was because of him.

Ulrik promised food and boots. Two items she desperately needed. Back in the forest, he'd had a fire going and food roasting over it. Pretty impressive since all he had was a sword, a dagger and his bare hands. The man knew how to survive, not only in this world but also in the forest. Bek was capable of neither.

He'd not hurt her. She squeezed her thighs together. No, that kiss hadn't hurt. Not at all. And that was the crux of things. For her survival, he was her best option. For her morally corrupt and irresponsible libido, he was like pouring gasoline on a fire, but survival came up trumps. It had to. She'd just have to lock her lust down, hold tight to her vow to fix her life and keep him at arm's length. No more carrying her, no more clinches against walls and absolutely no more kisses.

"Righto." She looked down at her pink bunny slippers. "Let's go get me some boots."

His eyebrow quirked, and a glimmer of confusion flashed in his beautiful eyes.

"I'm so hungry I could eat a horse." Bek pushed herself away from the wall. "Wait. You guys don't *actually* eat horse, do you? That's an urban myth, right?"

He looked offended by her question. "I would not eat my horse unless I were starving and had no other option."

"Phew. Good. Because if I had to eat Black Beauty, I think I might have to become a vegetarian."

He stared at her for a moment, and she swore she could see the cogs turning in his brain. "Black Beauty is a horse, yes?"

"Yeah."

"And by vegetarian, you mean you would abstain from eating the flesh of animals?"

"Yep."

"Hmm. I think I am beginning to grasp your use of your language, strange as it is. No horse flesh, I promise. Even if they wanted to, these villagers could not afford to buy a horse. Come."

His hand firmly on her elbow, Bek let him lead her from building to building. At each little hut, he paused and listened. Some he passed by, others he opened the single wooden shutter and peered in before moving on. Finally, he stopped at one of the little mud-brick huts, satisfied with what he had seen inside. He climbed in and offered her his arms to help her through. She brushed his hands away. *Nope. No more touching.* She climbed through the window under her own steam.

If the keep hadn't convinced her she was no longer in the twenty-first century, this would have. Standing in a one-room hut with a thatched roof and straw strewn across the dirt floor, she was as far from her London flat as she could get. In one corner sat a rough-hewn worn table with bench seats. In another, a collection of mattresses that looked like they were stuffed with straw, and storage chests stacked side by side. Rough-looking shelves held an assortment of bowls and cooking pots, with baskets of vegetables stored neatly beneath them. Near the door, a pen made from tree branches sectioned off a space. For a dog? A pet? Or did they bring their livestock inside at night?

In the middle of the hut, drawing her in, was a pot hung over a lit fire, its contents bubbling away. The smell of stewing meat filled the room. God, she was so hungry. Whatever it was, it smelled divine. She grabbed the ladle and scooped up the thick stew. Steam rose from the full ladle and her stomach rumbled. She blew on it, then tasted it.

"Mmm. S'good." She held the ladle out to Ulrik. "You want some?"

Ulrik shook his head. He moved about the hut with purpose, rifling through the chests and grabbing items.

He thrust an item of clothing at her. "Take your clothes off and put this on."

Bek dropped the ladle back into the stew with a plop. "Say what, now?"

"You need to blend in." He gave a cute quirk of his eyebrow. "As best as you can. So strip."

He tossed the clothing to her. It hit her in the chest, and she grabbed it before it slid to the floor. Damn that raspy voice of his. Combined with the words 'take your clothes off' and 'strip', she'd almost spontaneously combusted.

She glared at him and shifted away, holding up the clothing. It was an ankle-length dress of coarse wool in a dull gray with long sleeves. It looked to be all in one piece, with laces at the waist. Sure, she'd blend in, but if he thought she'd strip in front of him... *Not. Going. To. Happen.*

"No thanks. I think I'll stay in my own clothes. Your coat mostly hides everything."

He stopped rummaging and stared at her. "Women do not wear surcoats. Put the dress on, Rebekah."

She put a hand on her hip. "Or what?"

He raised an eyebrow. "Or I'll do it for you."

She stared at him, measuring how serious he was. He raked his gaze over her and heat flared in his eyes. Yeah, he'd like an excuse to get his hands on her again.

She glared at him. "Fine. Turn around."

"Oh, no, sweetheart." He crossed his arms over his chest and planted his feet firmly forward. "I fell for that once. You will not catch me off guard again."

Bek bared her teeth at him. She wrenched his surcoat off her shoulders and dumped it on the floor. He watched her with an intensity that unnerved her, dark swirls in his whiskey eyes. If he thought she would give him the satisfaction of seeing her strip down to her underwear... She raised her chin at him, daring him to stop her, and slipped the dress on over her clothes.

Her triumph was short-lived. The dress would've been a tight fit over her thirty-six double Ds. With the added material of her work shirt, it was an impossibility.

"Shit."

She glanced up at him. Amusement warred with heat in his gaze.

Fuck.

She wrangled the dress back over her head, scowled in his direction, and turned her back to him. She undid the buttons on her shirt, her neck and back tingling with awareness of him watching her, his gaze burning hotter than Superman's X-ray vision. Bek gritted her teeth. She just bet he was enjoying this. Best to get on with it and be done quick, rip off the proverbial sticking plaster.

Bek whipped off her shirt, goosebumps rising on her arms with the brush of cool air. He rumbled low in his chest, making her quiver and her nipples pebble. She snatched up the dress and drew it over her head, shoving her arms into the sleeves and quickly pulling it down to cover her naked flesh. Her jeans would stay right where they were, thank you very much. An extra layer against the cold of nighttime in the forest. An extra barrier against *him*.

She laced up the sides, drawing in the waist, and turned around. There it was again. That rumble. Primal. More animal than human. Her nerve endings danced along her skin and the hairs on the nape of her neck stood on end.

With a strangled growl, he tore his gaze off her, grabbed a sack and thrust it at her. "Put your tunic, your fluffy boots and my surcoat in this."

Eager to break the spell, Bek snatched the sack from him and stuffed her bunny slippers and her shirt inside. She picked up his surcoat, hesitating as she caught sight of the emblem on the front. In their trek through the darkened forest, and her hasty flight from him as he bathed, she hadn't noticed it before. In orange, stark against the dark brown of the leather, was a stylized bird emblazoned on the front left panel.

She ran her fingers over the design. "Is it a—"

"Phoenix? Yes."

The symbol of resurrection. A bird rising from the ashes. She turned to look at him. His fiery gaze focused on her, like a predator eyeing up his prey. He fisted his hands at his sides and a muscle ticked in his jaw. Something dark danced in the depths of his eyes and the air grew thicker and harder to breathe. A musky scent, stronger than the smoke from the fire and the stew cooking over it, swirled around them. Bek wasn't sure if she wanted to run from him or to him.

"I have a—"

His lips pursed in a thin line, he nodded. "I saw. On your shoulder. You have marked yourself with a phoenix."

An emotion flickered across his face. What exactly, she couldn't say.

A shiver raced up Bek's spine. Was it a sign? She didn't believe in signs, but... What were the chances? She stuffed his coat into the sack. "The phoenix on your coat? It's your family crest?"

He took a few deep breaths, then shook himself like a dog might shake off water. His hands unfurled, his shoulders relaxed and the air cleared, save for the smoke and the smell of cooking food. The dark shadows in his eyes were also gone. Had they even been there at all?

"Yes," he said, his voice softer, the guttural harshness gone.

Whatever darkness had risen in him had vanished as quickly as it had surfaced. The dampness in her knickers remained.

Damn it. Why couldn't the one man who wanted to help her be kind, sweet, and bland? She'd have friend-zoned him in a heartbeat. This guy, with his sword, his warrior's body and the threat of danger he wore like a comfortable, familiar coat, pushed all her buttons. She was all but panting for him like a bitch in heat.

Ugh. Get yourself together, Bek.

"A family crest, huh?" Nothing special. Something chosen by his family many years ago, perhaps centuries ago. "Passed down through the generations?"

He handed her a pair of boots, his long fingers curled around them sparking the memory of him in the pond, his hand wrapped around his girth as he'd stroked himself. Her cheeks heated, and she snatched the boots and slumped onto the bench seat.

"Usually."

She pulled on the fur-lined boots and laced them up. "Usually?"

"My family's crest was a rook. When they..." The corner of his mouth dipped and a look of intense sorrow, and something else gone too fast for her to identify, flashed in his eyes. "It no longer seemed adequate. The phoenix is more fitting for my circumstances now, more so than the rook."

She'd chosen the phoenix tattoo on her back because of what it represented. Her rising from the ashes of her mistakes and the mess she'd made of her life. Had he done the same?

His expression turned hard. "Enough talk. We have lingered too long."

He picked up the sack, adding what looked like a loaf of thick bread and a coil of rough-looking rope. He snatched a wineskin off a hook by the door and slung it over his shoulder.

Bek moved toward the basket of vegetables by the table. "Should I grab some more food?"

"No. These peasants have little enough to eat. I will not take more than is necessary. I can hunt for us once we're in the forest." He moved to the window. "Those coins you picked up at the keep... Leave them on the table."

Bek pulled the coins out of her jeans pocket. "Shouldn't we hang on to them in case we need them?"

His eyes narrowed. "You would take food, wine and clothing and not pay for them?"

Bek flushed. "When you put it that way..."

She dropped the coins on the table. An outlaw with a conscience. Wasn't he a regular Robin Hood?

Satisfied, he peered out of the window before climbing through. Bek followed, his hands firm on her waist not helping her libido any.

As they slipped away from the village, she studied the big knight. Sword strapped to his waist, his hair and beard wild and untrimmed, he moved with a fluid grace uncommon for a man of his size. Right out of the history books, he was as foreign to her as they came. Yet, after what he'd revealed about himself, she wondered if they weren't so different after all.

Chapter Twelve

Lance poured wine into two goblets, handed one to Godfrey, then settled back in his chair. Rarely did any of the pack visit him at his keep, and it should have delighted him. He had worked hard to gain his fortune and took pride in how far he had come from his humble beginnings. In the embroidered hangings adorning the walls, the ornate pewter goblets filled with expensive wine and the large table that rivaled the one in the d'Louncrais Keep. All the luxuries he had yearned for as a youth. Not today. Circumstances being what they were, he had little time for reveling in the comforts of his keep.

He raised the goblet to his lips and took a sip, studying the man across the table. When the pack had last met, Godfrey had behaved oddly — unusually argumentative and aggressive for the quietly spoken scholar. He had gone so far as to challenge Aimon for the newly discovered she-wolf, Kathryn Beauchene. Kathryn had chosen Aimon, as Lance had suspected she would the moment she had entered the clearing. No one could dispute a she-wolf's right to choose. Not Aimon, not Godfrey, not he. Pack law was inviolate. As the oldest wolf, and once Gaharet's closest counselor, it was up to him to ensure they all obeyed pack law in the alpha's absence.

"You had something you wished to speak to me about?" asked Godfrey. "Something you could not discuss in front of the others?"

There was an unfamiliar wariness about Godfrey. Because of the news about a traitor amongst them? Or something else?

Lance put aside his goblet and leaned his elbows on the table. "I have known you for a long time, Godfrey. Since we were children. Is there something bothering you? I have never seen you as agitated as you were the last time we met."

Godfrey's eyes narrowed. "We have lost our alpha, Ulrik is in Lothair's clutches and our pack is bordering on extinction. Does that not *bother* you?"

A non-answer. It reeked of things not said, though Lance scented nothing but truth in it. "Are you angry Kathryn chose Aimon?"

Godfrey took a sip from his goblet before carefully setting it down. "You are concerned I would disregard pack law."

"Should I be?"

Godfrey cocked an eyebrow. "I am not the only one who petitioned Lothair for Kathryn's hand in marriage, and by extension the d'Louncrais estate. Perhaps I should ask you the same question."

Anger flared, but Lance kept a tight rein on his emotions, even more certain now that Godfrey was hiding something. What other reason would he have for avoiding his questions?

Lance leaned back in his chair and rubbed his hand across his chin. "The d'Louncrais estate is in safe hands now. As is Kathryn. Do you agree?"

Godfrey gave a nonchalant shrug. "Aimon is young, but he is loyal. Through him, the estate has remained within the pack. As long as someone stronger does not challenge him for it."

Lance met Godfrey's stare. "And where would I find you standing if that were to happen?"

Godfrey did not flinch. "Where I should be." He took a slow sip of wine, holding his gaze across his goblet. "With Aimon."

The footfall of servants in the corridor and the scent of food stilled any further conversation. Unlike Gaharet, Lance had never trusted his people with his secret, and he wasn't about to start now.

He quietly studied the other chevalier as the serving maids slipped into the hall and set platters of cooked meat and fresh bread on the table. As they ate, both he and Godfrey skirted around polite pleasantries, conscious of the servants hovering—bringing more jugs of wine, a plate of freshly churned butter, more bread.

Annoyed, Lance waved them off, determined to get to the heart of Godfrey's behavior. "You have not answered my question, Godfrey. What is bothering you?"

"Pardon me, *Mon Seigneur*. Forgive the intrusion."

Lance turned, concealing his frustration at the interruption from his steward. "Yes?"

"The villagers have reported a strange woman in the vicinity."

"Strange?" Lance set down his knife. "How?"

"Unfamiliar to these parts, Mon Seigneur, but also...different. The villagers say she has unusual markings on her skin and in her hair, and she was wearing a chevalier's surcoat."

Lance glanced at Godfrey. The chevalier had straightened in his chair. What were the chances of two unknown women appearing in little over a month? First Erin, and now this one.

"What color was the surcoat?"

"Umber, Mon Seigneur, bearing the phoenix crest of the Voclains."

Lance was on his feet. "Ulrik."

He shared a glance with Godfrey.

Godfrey's eyes narrowed. "He has escaped?"

"Where is this woman now?" he barked.

"Farmer Pierre saw her disappear behind the tanner's hut. She was in the company of a man bearing a striking resemblance to Seigneur Ulrik."

Godfrey rose. "How is this possible?"

"Does it matter? Now? He is here." Lance slapped his hand on the table. "We must *find* him."

"I have prepared your horse for you, Mon Seigneur. And yours, Seigneur Godfrey. I suspected you would wish to investigate."

Lance was at the door with Godfrey close behind. In the keep courtyard, they mounted up and rode the short distance to the village.

They dismounted at the tanner's hut, and Lance grimaced. "We will find little trace of him beneath the stench of the tanning fluids and drying hides."

Godfrey nodded. "Truly. He may well have been here when I rode through your village, using the tanner's hut to camouflage his scent. For all his drunkenness and whoring, Ulrik is canny. It does not surprise me it is he who found a way to circumvent the effects of silver."

Lance stalked around the hut, looking for signs — a scuff in the dirt, the tread of boots. Ulrik may be cunning, and he would use all of his wolf abilities to avoid detection, but that did not mean the woman had not left some sign.

"There!"

He pointed at a fresh print, small and leading away from the hut.

They followed the footprints away from the tanner's hut, along the row to another, the scent of Ulrik and a female growing stronger. And something else, something familiar.

Godfrey snorted. "One of Ulrik's conquests? Even in escape, he can think of mating."

Lance sniffed the air, letting the scent roll across his tongue. "There is something strange about her scent. Something…unfamiliar. There is a foreignness to her scent." He paused. "Do you remember when we first scented Erin at Gaharet's keep?"

"Of course."

"This reminds me of her. There is that same underlying sharpness I cannot identify."

Godfrey turned his nose to the breeze. "You are right. And the villagers reported she had strange markings. Where are these women coming from?"

"I do not know." He turned his attention to the forest. "But I think it is time we found out."

"Agreed. Should we send word to the others?"

Lance returned to his horse, motioning over a villager. "Return our horses to my stable."

"Of course, Mon Seigneur."

The villager took the horses' reins and led them away. Tracking Ulrik was best done on foot. If need be, they could shift and hunt him as wolves, covering great distances with ease. Ulrik, hampered by a female who, though strange, was entirely human, could not. Horses would only give away their approach. Godfrey had the right of it. For all Ulrik's faults, he was shrewd. It was his impulsiveness, and his hot-headedness that usually got him into trouble.

Lance moved to stand beside Godfrey. "Let us not call the others in yet. We should track him in the forest. Find him. You know how the twins feel about Ulrik. Imagine if they were the ones to reach him first. They were baying for his blood the moment they learned he had killed Gaharet."

Godfrey's lip curled. "And Aimon will be busy with his new mate."

Lance chuckled. "That he will. And as well as Gaharet trained him and his wolf, he is young and lacks experience. He is no match for Ulrik."

Picking up the scent of Ulrik and the strange woman, Lance entered the forest with Godfrey close on his heels. He spared the other chevalier a glance. He had yet to unearth what was troubling him, what he was concealing.

"We still have much to discuss, Godfrey, but perhaps another time."

Godfrey shrugged. "Perhaps. Perhaps not. We all have our secrets, Lance. Even you." Lance's gaze snapped to Godfrey, but the chevalier's shuttered expression gave nothing away. "With any luck, this sorry business will all be over soon, but first we must find Ulrik."

Lance nodded, and Godfrey strode ahead into the forest, his words ringing in Lance's ears. What did the chevalier think he knew? What was he hiding? It was enough, as they hunted for Ulrik, that he would keep Godfrey firmly in his sight.

* * * *

The wolf slunk downwind, the scars on his body itching and his one good eye fixed on the men. Two chevaliers, two werewolves, stalking the woman and the blond wolf. Distrust lingered in the air. One of them was loyal to the pack. One of them was a traitor. On silent paws, he followed them.

Chapter Thirteen

The afternoon shadows were lengthening when Ulrik stopped in a small, sheltered clearing. Rebekah was tired and would be hungry, and from the slight limp in her step he guessed her boots chafed at least one of her heels. He could continue on much further. She could not. They had made good progress and had put a fair distance between them and the village, stopping only for a quick bite to eat as the sun had reached its zenith. He could risk stopping again for a few hours, to rest and to hunt for food.

The villagers would be certain to alert Lance to Rebekah's presence. Lance would investigate. It would not take long before Lance would catch his scent, and he would be sure to follow it. Tomorrow, Ulrik would need to push them hard. Wading through creeks and avoiding muddy ground would throw Lothair and his keep guards off his trail. It would not fool Lance, or any other of his kind. Lance would track him through his scent. The cooler nights of autumn, and the heavy dew of the morning would only aid Lance, not them. What Ulrik needed was a rainstorm. He could only hope the fates, and the weather, were on his side.

He dropped the sack to the ground and rummaged through it. "We will stop here for a few hours," he told her, grasping what he sought.

He needed to go hunt. That was best done in his other form, and could not risk her following him. Nor did he completely trust her to be here when he returned. Her sudden change of heart, her acceptance that he was her best chance, perplexed him. It could all be for pretense. Was she waiting till he dropped his guard? Again. It would not be altogether unexpected. She had proved herself a wily one.

"Oh, thank God." She slumped against a tree. "I swear you're like the Energizer Bunny. You just keep going and going and going. News flash. One of us is a mere mortal, not a supremely fit chevalier. And in case you didn't get the memo, that mere mortal is me."

Ulrik chuckled. *If only she knew.* He moved behind the tree, uncoiling the rope as he went.

"I am sorry, Rebekah."

"It's all right. Maybe remember it for tomorrow. That's if I can even move— Hey! What the *fuck!* What are you doing?" She tried to get to her feet, but he had already looped the rope around the tree and her. "Ulrik!"

He ignored her, circling the tree twice more before pulling the rope tight, but not too tight, and knotting it behind the tree beyond her reach.

He moved to crouch down in front of her. "I am sorry, but I must hunt us some food and I need to know you will be here when I return."

She stared at him, her mouth agape and her brown eyes stormy. "You could have just *asked* me to stay."

"Mm. Perhaps. But you have run from me once already, Rebekah. I will not be trusting you again so easily."

He retrieved the wineskin of mead and dropped it into her lap, before striding from the clearing and into the trees.

"What if I need the bathroom?" she called after him.

Bath room? She wanted to bathe? *Now?* He shook his head and kept walking.

"What if I need to pee?"

"Pee?"

"Pee. You know...wee. Visit the little girls' room, void my bladder, urinate."

Now *that* he understood. "Then do not drink all the mead and you should have no need to relieve yourself." He grinned at her disgusted huff behind him. "If the urge overcomes you, cross your legs. I will not be long."

A rock bounced harmlessly beside him in the forest. He chuckled, but did not turn back, the echo of her curses a delight to his ears. Not so long ago, he had marveled at the way Gaharet had interacted with Erin. How his alpha had found amusement in Erin's spirit. Erin was brave and strong minded, but Rebekah was all fire. At a particularly vile curse, he chuckled again. Ulrik could not resist poking the embers.

"Keep quiet, *petite cracheuse de feu*. We are not the only ones in the forest."

A sharp intake of breath, silence, then a muttered curse, much quieter this time. He suppressed the urge to laugh out loud. He would not be leaving her alone had his senses not told him there were no humans for leagues, save for her. No predators, but for him. He had not scented that wolf, unknown to him and yet so familiar, since that morning, but he would stay close all the same.

"What the hell does that even mean? Pettie crashooze de fer?" she muttered. "Humph. Go hunting then. Bring back food. I'll just wait here. Bloody Neanderthal. Next thing I know, he'll try to drag me about by my hair."

Ulrik's smile slipped, heat hitting with the force of a boulder slung from a trebuchet. He compelled himself to keep walking, the image of his hand fisted in her hair as he took her from behind almost enough to make him turn around.

With a concerted effort, he focused his attention to the task at hand. Stopping by a dense gorse shrub, he unbuckled his sword and slipped out of his boots and clothes. He had to force his breeches past his semi-erect cock, and it tested his determination to go hunting, to not turn around and stalk Rebekah instead of food.

Ulrik gritted his teeth and tucked his belongings beneath the shrub. He could not afford to waste time. He may have secured her well, but he would not underestimate her ingenuity. Ignoring his burgeoning erection, he allowed the change to flow through him. On large paws, he trotted away to hunt.

* * * *

He'd *tied* her to a *tree*. Bek fumed. That was why he'd grabbed the rope. He'd planned this all along, right from the moment they'd stood in that hut. While she'd been half naked in front of him and vulnerable. After she'd agreed to go along with him. Willingly.

Bek glared into the trees in the direction he'd departed. She'd followed him, kept pace with him in her stolen clothes, not once complaining about the rub of boots a size too big. She'd sat with him in companionable silence while they'd stopped for a break. They'd shared bread and wine, for Christ's sake. Hadn't that proved anything to him? That she was no longer a flight risk. That she'd decided to throw her lot in with him and hope for the best.

She tugged at the rope, a braid of woven fibers he'd tied firmly about her waist and the large tree she'd rested against. She eyed the wineskin in her lap. It would serve him right if she drank it all. As tempting as that was, she left the stopper in. Bek didn't want to have to pee before he came back. And she needed her wits about her. At the very least, so he didn't get the jump on her again. Not to mention whatever else was out there in the forest.

As if to confirm her concerns, a wolf howled in the distance. The mournful sound echoed before trailing off into silence. She shivered. *Great. Just great.* Her time in this century kept getting better and better. She'd spelled herself back in time, wound up in some kind of dungeon in medieval France, narrowly avoided being assaulted by a lecherous guard and was kidnapped by a rogue chevalier. And kissed by a rogue chevalier.

Yeah, that bit wasn't so bad.

She shook her head, banishing the memory. Now, as she was beginning to trust him, he'd left her alone. In a *freaking* forest. Tied to a damn tree. Unarmed. There was every possibility that a wolf would find her and want to eat her. *Fucking wonderful.* Good kiss, no, great kiss aside, medieval life sucked big, hairy balls. It made her life back home seem almost tame.

And that's saying something.

The wolf howled again, snapping Bek out of her pity party. Was it closer? She couldn't tell. She strained her ears and listened. Nothing. No more howls, no sounds of movement amongst the trees. Was that a good or a bad sign? Did it mean the wolf had moved on or that it was sneaking up on her?

Birds twittered in the canopy of trees. That was a good thing, right? The birds going on as usual. Either way, she wasn't about to sit here, trussed up like a Christmas turkey, and wait to be devoured. She had to get herself untied.

The tree was too wide for her to reach the knot, but perhaps she could slip free of the rope. She wiggled against the binding and got the rope as far down as her hips, but no further. Scrambling in the dirt, she got her feet beneath her, hoping the leverage would be enough. She pushed up, her back scraping against rough bark and the rope biting into her hips. It wouldn't budge. She gritted her teeth and pushed harder. It gave another inch, but no more. Kim Kardashian might have made booty fashionable again, but fat lot of good that did her now. She slumped against the tree, the pressure of the rope easing a little.

Maybe she could get the rope over her head. She slid lower in the bindings, the rub of the rope chaffing, but she didn't stop. She wiggled as far down as she could. This time, the rope caught on the underside of her breasts.

Shit.

The damn things had been nothing but a nuisance since she'd started wearing a training bra. Too big to run comfortably with, or to fit into many popular fashions, all they did was garner her unwanted attention. Now they were stopping her from slipping free of the rope. She eased back into a sitting position. When Ulrik got back, she was going to kill him. He'd regret ever taking her from the keep when she was through with him.

She tugged at the rope with her hands, trying to stretch it. All that did was give her rope burn on her palms.

Why did I give up his dagger so easily? She mentally gave herself a kick up the ass. She'd hidden the thing well. If she'd thought faster on her feet, she could've lied to him, and told him she'd ditched it along with his sword and his clothes.

But she wasn't going to give up. She might not have a knife, but perhaps she could saw at it with a sharp rock. She scanned the surrounding dirt, searching for something suitable. Her gaze settled on a small rock, smooth but with angled edges. A piece of flint? Wasn't that what they used to make arrowheads from? *I could be so lucky.* She palmed it and began to saw away. The rope was thick, braided and wrapped around her three times, and while the rock had an edge to it, it wasn't particularly sharp. It was worth a try.

How long she sat sawing away at the rope, her hand cramping and her progress slow, Bek couldn't be sure. She stopped, dropped the rock in her lap and stretched her fingers. This was a waste of time. Ulrik would be back long before she could cut through the first loop.

The wolf howled again. She went cold and her head snapped up. Was it closer? The sound echoed, making it difficult to tell. She searched around for a sharper rock or a weapon. Anything. Her gaze fell on a branch not far from her feet. If she could reach it…

A shadow flitted amongst the trees. Her lungs seized.

Shit. Shit. Shit.

She needed that branch. Now. She tossed the rock aside and wiggled her body down the rope, stretching her toes toward the branch. It wobbled at her touch, but she couldn't hook it with her foot. She slunk further down, as far as her breasts would allow. *If I get out of this experience alive, I'm seriously going to consider getting a breast reduction.* She stretched both legs out and snagged it between the toes of her boots.

Yes!

As quickly as she could without losing her hold, she dragged the branch toward her. As soon as it was within reach of her hands, she grabbed it. Solid and thick, it had a decent weight to it. Maneuvering herself back into a sitting position, she tucked her feet up against her body and faced the forest, brandishing her makeshift weapon.

Bring it on, wolf.

The shadow moved closer. She tracked its movements as it shifted to the left, the hairs on the nape of her neck rising when it disappeared beyond her line of sight, behind the tree. It appeared again on her right, circling her, a mere shadow making not a sound—not the crack of a branch or a footfall amongst the fallen leaves. The forest held its breath along with her, aware a predator lurked nearby. No birds twittered in the forest canopy now.

Bek tightened her grip on the branch, the tip quivering as she attempted to get the shaking of her arms and her body under control. She squinted at the dark shadow slinking through the trees, trying to see more than its shape. Was it a wolf? Or something else?

It paused. She strained, listening, as beads of sweat formed on her top lip. A sound, cracking and popping, loud against the stillness, had her cringing. Had it found a smaller animal to prey on? Were those noises the poor creature's bones crunching between strong jaws and vicious teeth? Bek wanted to close her eyes, drop the branch and block her ears, but she didn't. She couldn't. She remained resolute, facing the danger. If she was going to die now, she would go out fighting. Spider and the consequences of his betrayal had nearly broken her, but she had survived, was still surviving. She would not cower now.

The shape grew larger, taller. Her mouth went dry and nausea rose and hovered in the back of her throat.

Come on, wolf. Show yourself. Give me a look at you. Let me see what I'm dealing with.

With a rustle of dried leaves, the shadow moved into the light.

"Argh!"

She pitched her arm back and hurled the branch. It fell short, landing at Ulrik's feet, his torn shirt held loosely in one hand, a pair of dead hares in the other.

"Damn you, Ulrik. I thought you were a wolf. Now get over here and untie me before the real thing gets here. I heard it howling. It has to be close."

He dropped the hare carcasses at his feet and stalked toward her. "Do not fear, Rebekah. The wolf is long gone."

"Are you sure?" Her gaze flicked past him to the trees. The dark shadow could have been him. He could have circled the clearing to admire his handiwork. She wouldn't put it past him. That didn't mean they were alone out here. That the wolf, even now, wasn't watching them, stalking them.

"I am certain."

She considered him for a few moments. He seemed confident. He knew the forest far better than she. And he did have his sword.

"Okay," she said. "Now bloody well hurry up and untie me so I can kick your ass. I can't *believe* you tied me to a tree and left me here. I could've been eaten."

Ulrik tilted his head to the side and considered her.

She stared up at him. "What are you waiting for? Untie me."

"If you are going to kick my ass when I do, why should I not leave you as you are?"

"Are you kidding me? You can't leave me here."

"Oh, but I can."

Her eyes widened. "You wouldn't."

He chuckled, kneeling before her. "It is very tempting, *petite cracheuse de feu.*"

Even now, despite her anger, his raspy voice sent delicious shivers down her spine. That he'd most likely screamed himself hoarse in that dungeon should bother her. Arouse her sympathy, not her body. But Lord help her, she was all but melting into her knickers like a hot puddle of lava. His nostrils quivered, and a muscle ticked in his jaw.

He leaned in and brushed a hand against her cheek. Their gazes met, and for the life of her, she could not look away. A strong musky scent enveloped them.

"Why do you call me that?" She couldn't help the breathless quality of her voice. "What does it mean?"

"*Petite cracheuse de feu?*"

She nodded.

He swallowed, his Adam's apple jerking in his throat. "It means little fire breather."

"Oh."

She didn't know whether to be offended or not.

He leaned closer. He was going to kiss her again. Did she want this? Yes. Should she want this? Hell, no.

Abruptly he stood and disappeared from her line of sight, behind the tree. Bek leaned back against the rough bark and closed her eyes. Hadn't she vowed not to let him touch her again? She'd come so close to throwing all her promises to herself out the window. She thumped her head against the tree trunk.

Shit.

She couldn't afford to get caught up with this guy. It was a slippery slope to a hell she'd already visited. Every morning she'd woken up on the wrong side of the prison bars, the memory of Spider's betrayal had fueled her determination to never go down that path again. Burned it into the fabric of her soul so she'd never again repeat her mistake. Or so she'd thought.

Chapter Fourteen

The moment the rope around her waist loosened, Bek was on her feet and slipping from its loops. As tempted as she was to kick his taut ass as he squatted to assemble sticks into the makings of a small fire, she kept her distance. Distance was good. It kept her away from temptation. The last twelve hours had proved her willpower was sadly lacking when it came to men. Especially highly sexed men with a dark edge to them. Ulrik had that in spades.

Muscles flexed across his broad shoulders as his hands worked to create a spark. Bek curled her fingers into fists by her side, resisting the powerful urge to touch, to caress. She turned her back to him and unstoppered the wineskin. She needed fortification. Lots of it.

She took a sip and the sweet liquid slid easily down her throat. And another sip, then a big gulp. How much of this would she need to be pleasantly buzzed enough to drown out the urging of her lady parts that were all for a little fling in the forest? A quick shag on the carpet of pine needles beneath her feet? She took another swig. Then another.

By the time she'd turned around, confident she had herself under control, Ulrik had the fire lit, his knife in hand, and was skinning and gutting the hares. She seated herself across the fire from him and watched him work, those long fingers of his deftly wielding the knife as he prepared the hares for cooking.

She raised the wineskin to her lips, blocking her view of him.

What the actual fuck? A man gutting an animal is sexy? What is wrong *with me?*

She needed to put on her big girl panties and behave like a responsible adult. That giving in to her libido would feel good was never in doubt, but that he would be good for her was. Nope. This guy was getting nowhere near her knickers. By design or by default. *Hell to the no.* She'd keep her wayward desires under control. This time, she would look out for herself.

"So, do you have a plan?" She stoppered the wineskin and set it aside. "Or are we just going to wander aimlessly around in the forest for a while avoiding people, villages and wolves?"

He glanced up at her as he built a makeshift spit over the fire. "I will find my lord. There is a woman in the forest, east of the keep, who may know where he is."

"We're going east?"

He set a hare on the spit and the flames flickered over the carcass. "No."

"You're going east, and I'm going…home?"

"No. We are heading north, then turning northeast. Then we will make for the…woman in the woods. I will not be responsible for leading Lothair to my lord."

She'd noticed the pause, the hesitation before he said the word 'woman'. An ex-lover? As intriguing as it would be to meet her, hiking through the forest and sleeping in the dirt for however long it took to get there wasn't in her game plan.

"Here's an idea. Why don't you tell me how to use the amulet so I can go home? I'm only slowing you down, and there's no reason for me to stay." She hiked up her dress and retrieved the gold disc from her jeans pocket. "So what do I do? Say the words again? In reverse maybe?"

He stared at her over the fire. "You are eager to return home and to reunite with your family. I understand. Family is precious."

"Precious?" Bek snorted. "Not my family. I haven't seen them in years, and I have no desire to. A bigger bunch of crooks and con artists you'd ever find."

She hadn't looked back when she'd skipped out on them a day after her seventeenth birthday. Not a glance, not a fare-thee-well, and she'd made no promises to return. And, unless she was willing to join the family business, they couldn't give a toss that she'd gone either.

He frowned at her. Lucky him to have a family that cared.

"Then you must have a... What is it called... A career?"

She grimaced. "No."

No one would call working at Charlie's a career. It was a necessity. One she could avoid if she stayed here. Now there was a novel solution to her less-than-perfect life.

Firelight danced across his face and chest. It certainly had some appeal, but it wasn't a workable option. Not if she wanted to keep her resolution of not getting involved. She needed to return, preferably before her parole office put out an APB on her for skipping out of town. And being in the twenty-first century again was a surefire way to ensure she did nothing stupid with Mr. Sex-on-a-stick. If ever that term applied to anyone, it was him. Fuck, he was gorgeous and deliciously sinful.

She shoved away the smutty images. "I don't belong here, Ulrik. Though my life might be a crap-shoot back home, it's still mine, and it kind of beats living in a forest forever."

She'd miss her playlist, her favorite tattoo artist on the corner of Evelyn and Gosterwood. Hell, she'd miss running water, flushing toilets, instant heat and her bed. As old and lumpy as her mattress was, it trumped sleeping on the ground. "I have to go home."

He studied her across the fire. "I do not have the answer for you, Rebekah, but I know someone who may. The last time we spoke, my lord had intentions of searching for a reversal to the spell."

"Oh."

Damn it. Guess she wasn't leaving anytime soon, then. She tucked the little gold disc back into her jeans.

"If it gives you some comfort, my lord is with a woman who is also from the future."

"Another person got pulled back in time?" She leaned forward. "Really?"

Was this something that happened to people all the time? They found an amulet and *whoomph!* They're back in the tenth century? *There must be all sorts of modern people running around here.*

He set the second hare over the fire. "Yes, truly. Much the same as you, she found an amulet and deciphered the script." He shook his head. "It is uncanny. Two women, in such a brief period, traversing time, when I have never seen the likes of it in all my life."

Okay. So not an everyday occurrence. "Maybe it was the eclipse."

"The blood moon?"

She shrugged. "You're right. That's just superstitious guff. There's probably a scientific reason for it all far beyond my comprehension. I wasn't exactly the smartest kid in class."

He stood up, reached into the waistband of his trousers, and pulled out her phone. "You understand this, and it is clearly a scientific marvel. Not magic, as I first thought. And"—he gave her a rueful smile—"you almost outwitted me."

He moved to sit beside her, and Bek's gaze followed every lithe movement, every stretch of his trousers across his muscular thighs. He handed her the phone and took the wineskin, removing the stopper and raising it to his mouth. A drop trickled down into his beard. She tracked the droplet, itching to reach out and stop it. Or maybe lick it off with her tongue. She pulled her gaze away and stared at her phone, her body flushed. This man was killing her.

Her phone was dark and the screen cracked, a spiderweb of lines running across its face. "It's a communication device. Nothing special. An outdated model. It's not even an iPhone. Everyone in the twenty-first century has one of these."

He spat out his wine, and the fire flared with the splash of alcohol.

He wiped his face on his sleeve and stared at her, his eyes wide. "The *twenty-first* century?"

"Yeah." She shrugged. "Like you said, I'm from the future."

His Adam's apple jerked in his throat. "That is… That is more than a *thousand years* in the future."

"Yep. Modern girl here." And a city girl. "*Totally* unsuited for a place like this."

He took another swig from the wineskin. Then another. Then he handed it to her.

She gulped the sweet liquid down. "Mmhmm. I know the feeling."

Ulrik took the phone from her hands, his brow furrowed. He turned it over, running his fingers over it and tracing the cracks on the screen as though deciphering it might help him come to grips with how she'd come to be here.

"How does it work? How do you make the light shine?"

She shook her head. "You can't. The battery's flat. That's why the light went out in the dungeon. Without my charger…"

Bek frowned. How did one explain the concept of electricity and power sockets to a man who lived in a world where they cooked food over a fire? Where the sun and candles were the only sources of light, and the only modes of transport were on foot or horseback.

"It needs a power source. It's useless to me now, but essentially I could…connect with anyone who had one of these, as long as I knew the right set of numbers linked to their device. If they had their device turned on. Then I could talk to them, even if they were all the way back at the keep."

He nodded, still staring at her phone. What did he make of it all? He seemed to be taking it in his stride. Then again, he had a magical amulet. That couldn't be bog standard. She doubted every knight in the tenth century was wandering around with one. She eyed him, running her gaze over him from head to toe. So what made him so special? *Apart from the obvious.*

Ulrik handed her phone back and reached for the wineskin. He took a long drink and stared into the fire. He passed it back to her. Bek took a sip. It had been one of those days. One of those weeks, and it didn't look as though things were going to get any easier. Chances were, if she was going to figure this out, they were going to need a shit load more wine.

Chapter Fifteen

They sat in companionable silence, eating the first proper meal Ulrik had had in weeks. He should be savoring it, but he chewed with nary a thought, barely registering the tender flesh or the smoky flavor of the meat, so aware was he of the woman beside him. Watching her take delicate bites of hare and licking her fingers with a swish of pink tongue had aroused a hunger in him for something other than food.

He got to his feet, the flare of desire in her eyes as she caught sight of his cock straining at his breeches highly satisfying. He restrained the urge to pull her into his arms, the hint of her need rich and thick in the air. His body hummed with heat and his wolf prowled close. He had never been one to control his impulses, much to Gaharet and the pack's obvious disapproval. He did now.

Who knew how wide a circle Lothair would cast with the keep guard to recapture him. And they were still too close to the Vautour estate for his liking. When

Rebekah gave herself to him, and he did not doubt she would, he wanted to give her his full attention, and he wanted plenty of time. A rushed coupling, with his senses focused on the surrounding forest, was not what he had in mind.

Anticipation for the moment he would have her beneath him, his hands cupped around those voluptuous breasts, his hips between her luscious thighs, welled up within him and stole the breath from his lungs. When he took her, had her screaming his name as he brought her to release, the passion between them promised to burn hotter than any fire.

The feeling washed over him and he embraced it. His wolf panted within his mind, eager and hungry, all its enhanced senses fixed on her. It heightened the tension in his body, keeping him on the knife's edge of control. It was not an entirely unpleasant sensation. *Surprising.* He had never thought he would enjoy delayed gratification. It certainly wasn't what he was used to. Women never said no to him. Never made him wait, and he never had to pursue them. Perhaps that was what he had been missing. The chase. After all, he was a predator.

Ulrik kicked dirt onto the fire, putting it out. They had to keep walking. The light of a fire at night could be seen for leagues, and his fellow werewolves would catch the scent of smoke and cooked hare easily. It would be sure to draw them in. He had only lit it to cook the hares. In his wolf form, he would have eaten the hares raw, and not bothered with skinning, gutting, or cooking them. Not so Rebekah.

Rebekah from the twenty-first century. More than a *thousand* years into his future. It astounded him, confounded him. For one who could shed his clothes and shift his human body into another form, there was not much that surprised him. She had.

Now she sat there, blinking and waiting for her eyes to adjust. No demands he keep the fire lit, and no hysterics at being plunged into darkness. For all her concerns about her lack of intelligence, the woman was smart. And brave.

"I know you are tired, Rebekah, but we must continue on for at least another few hours. We need to put as much distance between ourselves and the remains of our fire as we can."

She got to her feet. Ulrik slung the sack over one shoulder and set the wineskin over hers. She flinched at his touch but did not move away.

"Okay. I understand." She held her hand out toward the forest. "Lead the way."

Instead, he took her hand in his. Without his enhanced vison, even with the light of the moon flickering through the leafy canopy, she would have difficulty seeing. "I will guide you."

Before she could protest, or think to pull her hand from his, he set off walking, giving her no choice but to follow.

* * * *

It was but a few hours before dawn when he stopped again. Rebekah's feet were dragging, and he was all but pulling her along with him.

"I think it is safe enough now for us to stop for a few hours' rest."

He let go of her hand and she slumped to the ground. She was exhausted, but she had not complained, nor demanded they stop. Not once. A woman out in the world alone, without the support of her family, would be no stranger to hardship.

Dropping the sack, he removed his surcoat and laid it out on the ground. It was not much, but it would provide some comfort against the cold earth. With the rope in his hand, he approached her and looped it around her waist.

She backed away from him. "What? No. You're not seriously thinking of tying me to a tree again, are you?"

She put her hands on her hips and glared at him.

"No. I am not tying you to a tree." He tugged on the rope, pulling her against him and leaned close to her ear. "I am tying you to me."

She gave a startled gasp and back-stepped hastily away from him until the rope played out and pulled her to a stop. "You know, I thought, after all we've been through together, you would trust me by now. I mean, I did follow you from the village of my own accord."

He paused, a knot in the rope half-formed. She had, and she had stayed with him all day, not once attempting to escape him. He took in the weary slump of her shoulders and the drooping of her eyelids. Her body was tired, more so than his.

"Are you going to run?"

She threw her arms into the air. "Where? The villagers would barely look at me and the forest has wolves that will eat me. You're the only one who's offered to help."

Ulrik considered her words. "Very well."

He loosened the incomplete knot and let the rope slip from around her waist, then coiled it and set it aside. He unbuckled his sword and it joined the rope, then he lay down, stretching himself out.

"Come. Lay beside me." He patted his surcoat. "Between this and my body heat, it will keep you warm."

She huffed and rolled her eyes. He rested his hands beneath his head and watched her debate what to do. She scoped out the surrounding ground, then settled herself in the dirt.

He rolled onto his side, observing her as she fussed about getting comfortable. "You will get a better night's sleep over here where you can be warm."

"That's debatable."

He allowed himself a grin, knowing she could not see well enough to catch his amusement. "Very well, then."

He rolled on to his back and stared up at the stars through the leafy canopy. She patted the dirt, brushed aside a few leaves and dislodged a few pebbles. He waited. Rebekah rolled over. She wiggled about, shifting position and tugging at her dress. She turned back over. With a muffled curse, she shifted closer. Ulrik continued to stare at the night sky. A wolf, a real wolf, howled in the distance.

She froze and her heart skipped, then beat a staccato rhythm loud in his ears.

"Fine. You win." She shuffled over to him. "But you keep to your side, and I'll keep to mine." She drew an imaginary line between them. "You stay over there. *Capisce*?"

Again, he patted the space beside him. "Come lie down, Rebekah. I am a man of my word. I have told you I will not touch you unless you ask."

"Yeah? I might have believed that if you hadn't already kissed me back at the village."

"A momentary lapse. For which I apologized. And you seemed to enjoy it."

"Ha. That is irrelevant."

Not to him. Nor was her lack of denial of her enjoyment. "All the same, it will not happen again. Not unless you ask."

She jutted her chin out at him. "Don't hold your breath, buddy. Those words will *not* pass these lips."

He released a chuckle, low and dirty. "Oh, how wrong you are, Rebekah. You *will* ask."

She snorted. "Don't bet on it." She turned her back to him and lay down, resting her head on her hands. "Arrogant asshole," she muttered, barely above a whisper. "I'll show you."

Ulrik suppressed his mirth, ensuring he kept on his side of her imaginary line. It was early autumn. The temperature would drop as the night progressed. As a betting man, he knew the odds were in his favor. Before long, she would be in his arms, seeking the warmth he could provide.

He would not deny her. No, he would pull her in close and hold her soft, lush curves tight against his body and imagine what it would be like to have her naked beside him, skin to skin. It was the closest he could get to having what he wanted, and it would be enough. For now.

He settled in to wait, as content as he could be given his current circumstances. Not so long ago, being captured by Renaud, confined by Lothair, his chances of living had narrowed significantly. Now, here he was, free in the forest with the most interesting woman he had met in a long time. He smiled, strangely content for the first time in years.

Chapter Sixteen

Bek's eyelids fluttered, and cold seeped into her back. She shivered, and snuggled deeper into the warmth of the mattress, her legs clenching around… Her eyes popped open.

Oh, God.

Beneath her cheek was a warm, naked chest. Wrapped around her, keeping her in place, were two muscular arms. Between her legs…

Fuck.

Bek swallowed hard. In the bleak light of pre-dawn, her situation clarified. She was on top of Ulrik. *Straddling* him. Her body heated and her core clenched. How had this happened? Had he… No, *he* hadn't moved. He lay flat on his back as he had when she'd finally succumbed to sleep.

She'd waited for what felt like hours, convinced the minute she closed her eyes he'd try to move closer. He hadn't. *She* had. Hell, she'd damn well climbed on top of him. While she'd been sleeping. Freud would have a thing or two to say about that, subliminal messages and all that jazz. She cringed. *How embarrassing.*

How the hell was she going to extricate herself from this? Before he woke up? The thud of her heart in her chest beat faster than the rhythm of his against her ear. She raised her head a little. The steady rise and fall of his chest continued unbroken. The bird's-eye view of his naked pecs, the soft brush of chest hair against her chin and his musky scent filling her nose with every breath, only added to the heat pooling between her thighs.

She blinked. Blinked again. The dark copper circle of his nipple lay mere inches from her mouth. She closed her eyes, resisting the urge to shift closer and take a swipe with her tongue, a brief taste. She bit back a moan.

Focus, Bek. On moving. Not on his lickable nipples.

She got her inclinations shakily in hand and opened her eyes, forcing her reluctant gaze past his pecs, up his throat, toward his... She paused, her attention caught on his throat.

Wtf?

No reddened or blistered skin. Any sign of the damage done by the shackles he'd worn was gone. How was that possible? They'd escaped the dungeon barely two days ago. Yet his skin was not smooth. Deep scars crisscrossed his throat. Old scars, long since healed, jagged and bracketed by puncture wounds, as though an animal had tried to tear out his throat. Could this be the reason for his raspy voice?

Incapable of stopping herself, she traced her fingers across the puckered skin. What had happened to him? Scars like these... It was a miracle he wasn't dead. The man sure lived life on the wild side, just like Spider.

Danger swirled around him, and it called her name with an ever-increasing urgency. All the more reason to keep her distance.

As she withdrew her hand, she nudged his arm. It slipped off her and fell hard against the ground. She winced and glanced at his face. Still sleeping. *Phew!* She placed her hand beside his shoulder and put her body weight onto it and her knee. If she could lever herself up, she could roll off...

Bek froze, her breath catching in her throat. Was that...?

Against the crux of her thighs, long and thick, and growing harder by the moment, was his cock. She raised her gaze to his face. Caramel eyes under heavy lids watched her, a satisfied smirk gracing his lips.

Busted.

Bek tried to get off him, but his arms, like two vices, snaked around her and held her firm. "I didn't intend... I must've... I was asleep, I have no control of..."

His grin widened at her spluttered protests.

"It was cold last night, all right. Now let me up."

His answer was to hold her firm and grind his hips against the vee of her thighs. Bek gasped, almost releasing a low moan of want, but catching herself in the nick of time. By his self-satisfied smirk, he knew the effect he had on her. She slapped her hand on his chest, intent on giving him a serve, when he rolled his hips again. Her fingers curled in his chest hair, and this time she couldn't stop the breathy moan from slipping from between her lips. His hands shifted from her waist to her hips, gripping tight, grinding against her again, the inseam of her jeans rubbing against her clit.

Bek wavered. Twelve months in prison, another eight months on parole, and she'd not even looked at a man. She'd contented herself with her own company and battery-powered relief. Here, now, she wanted. Wanted him. Wanted passion with another human being, not some empty release that tamed the sexual need of her body, but not the loneliness of her soul. To have him touch her and slide his hands across her skin. To lose herself in his kisses, wrap herself up in the moment and forget all her troubles.

She leaned over him. Her breasts, heavy with her need, pressed against his chest. Her mouth hovered a breath away from his. Heat flared in his eyes, and dark shapes swirled in their depths, making them seem more dark rum than golden.

Bek swallowed her pride. "You were right. I am asking. Kiss me, Ulrik."

He crashed his lips to hers. His hand shifted to her head, holding her firm, as though she might retreat from that which she'd demanded of him. Far from backing away, she opened for him, inviting him in. Like an experienced chevalier, he stormed the castle that was her mouth, evading any remaining defenses she may have thought to erect. Bek groaned and slipped her tongue into his mouth, her thighs tightening around his hips.

He hissed and withdrew. Her mewl of disappointment faded as his lips settled on her throat, nipping and sucking his way to the sensitive spot where her neck joined her shoulder. A wave of pleasure washed over her, and she shivered.

His large hand cupped her breast, heat from his palm searing her through the fabric of the dress. Her nipple hardened, and she arched into his hand.

"You have the most amazing breasts." He squeezed her gently. "I want to see them bare, kiss them, lick them, suck your nipples into my mouth and delve into your bosom with my face."

Bek threw her head back, her puckered nipples straining against the wool, begging him to do just that. Ulrik squeezed tighter, his face buried in her neck, the scratch of his beard heightening the sensation. He flipped them over and rolled her beneath him, bracketing her shoulders with his arms, and ground his hips against her. Bek locked her ankles around his hips. She was *so* close. The rub of his cock, the delicious friction and the heavy musk scent surrounding them — it drove her wild. She arched into him, thrusting her hips in rhythm with his.

"Oh, Rebekah, you are all flame and passion, just as I suspected."

He captured her mouth again, stealing her breath away, and she writhed beneath him. She thrust her tongue into his mouth.

He pulled back. "We should stop." Regret flashed in his hooded eyes. "The sun is rising."

He kissed her again, opened mouthed but with no tongue. Bek entwined her fingers in his hair and attempted to pull him closer.

"Rebekah." He groaned and dived in for another kiss, a brief one, before pulling away. "We must stop. We cannot afford to linger too long here. The guards —"

"I don't care." She was too close to the brink. She tightened her hold on his hair, dragging him back to her. "You can't stop. I need..."

A thrust of his hips, a pinch of fingers at her nipple, muted through her dress, and she tossed her head back.

"Yes. I need that. *Please*."

He growled, a deep rumble reverberating through his chest, shooting heat straight to her clit. She'd given into the craving, granted herself permission and proved him right. He couldn't leave her hanging.

"Please don't stop."

Determination flashed in his eyes. "I will take care of you, Rebekah. I will give you what you need."

He shifted his hips and hiked up her dress, fumbling with the button of her jeans. Once free, he tore at the fabric. Her zipper gave. Then his hand was where she wanted it, slipping beneath her knickers. He sought her clit and rubbed against it. She bucked beneath him, crying out. His fingers slipped lower, sliding through her slick folds.

"So wet for me," his raspy voice whispered in her ear.

He tugged her jeans down and slid one long finger inside her. Then another. With a sureness that spoke of years of practice, of experience, he found her G-spot. With a hoarse cry she shattered, clinging to him, his hand trapped between their bodies, slipping, sliding, rubbing and wringing out every last spasm of her orgasm.

Bek flopped back and lay limp, eyes closed and her chest heaving, residual spikes of pleasure pulsing through her body.

How am I ever going to move on from that? Top that?

The man not only knew where to find her clit *and* her G-spot, he also knew what to do with them. A man like that was as rare as rentals with air-conditioning. For all that sex had been good with Spider, it had never been like *that*. And she hadn't had sex with Ulrik. Yet.

She opened one eye to look at him.

He stared back at her, an eyebrow cocked. "Are you well sated, Rebekah?" He shifted his fingers inside her and she gasped. "Or do you need me to make you come again?"

He slipped his hand from her jeans, raised his fingers to his nose and inhaled. He licked his fingers. "Or perhaps I should use my mouth."

Bek sucked in a breath, her body quivering, more than on board with that idea.

Fuck. Imagine what this man could do with his tongue?

He rolled off her and got to his feet. "Alas, now is not the time."

He buckled his sword around his waist. Another *sword*, proud and ready for battle, begged for her attention. He ignored it as he sorted their meager belongings. Bek ignored it, too. As much as it was possible to ignore the elephant in the room. Or the forest.

She pulled up her jeans and buttoned them, her broken zipper a reminder of what they had done. What he had done. To her. What she had *asked* him to do.

She turned away from him, heat flushing her face. Not because he had given her one of the best orgasms in her life. She wasn't embarrassed about that. Or her need to feel the hands of a man on her. Or even that she'd asked for it. Nor did it bother her that she'd not reciprocated the favor. Too many men in her life had left *her* unsatisfied. One man would barely tip the scales in balance.

No. Her shame came because she'd let her weakness for dangerous men rule her once again. She'd given in to the attraction between them, when barely moments before, the evidence of his scars had convinced her he was a man to avoid at all costs. Bek turned away from him.

Lord Almighty. Why didn't anyone warn me being good would be so damn hard?

Chapter Seventeen

With a pounding of horse's hooves and the jingle of harnesses, Lothair swept into the bailey of the d'Louncrais keep, a score of keep guard at his back. Three days of searching and not a single trace of Ulrik Voclain or this mysterious woman. He was running out of patience. It was time to see if the wolves of Langeais knew of his whereabouts.

As the dust settled, he dismounted and stared up at the stone keep. It was not as large as his, or as fortified. Nor did it have the strategic location guarding the River Loire, but it was a symbol of power and wealth accumulated, nonetheless. They had always had influence, the d'Louncrais. In Lothair's father's and grandfather's time, too, but only he had allowed one of them into his inner circle. Gaharet. He had trusted him, relied on his steady presence and his wise council. Dare he say he had called him friend. For that, Gaharet had betrayed him and fled Langeais to God knew where.

So he had given the d'Louncrais estate to the Beauchenes. Used it and the unmarried Kathryn Beauchene to bait the pack. His plan had worked, though not quite as he had expected. It had not flushed out Renaud's informant, but Lothair could work with the end result.

Two figures appeared at the door, one a servant, the other the chevalier he had come to see. Aimon Proulx, his white-blond hair loose about his shoulders, smiled in greeting, but his gaze was wary.

"Mon Seigneur Comte. To what do we owe the pleasure of your company?"

"Come now, Aimon. Do not be obtuse." He turned to his keep guard. "*Capitaine,* secure the keep. You four" — he pointed to the guards on his left — "follow me." He planted his hand on Aimon's shoulder. "We have much to discuss. How fares things with Mademoiselle Kathryn?"

The young chevalier stiffened beneath his touch, sharing a look with the servant, who scurried away. To hide Kathryn from him? To warn Gaharet of his presence? The latter, he hoped. He would welcome Gaharet's counsel, though he doubted Gaharet would risk revealing himself with so many of the keep guard present. He was an alpha werewolf, not invincible.

Lothair swept through the keep and into the library. Aimon followed, and Lothair's four guards took position outside the door. Aimon was a werewolf. Kathryn, too. Lothair had not survived so long by taking unnecessary risks.

He poured himself some wine, chose a chair by the brazier and scanned the room as he sipped from his goblet. Chests of scrolls, parchments and books lined the walls. Never had he seen so many in one place. Not in his keep, nor in the cathedral at Tours he had once visited in his youth. Rumor had it there were works in here from as far off as Constantinople. What knowledge would he find were he to take the time to look? What secrets might it reveal? He drummed his fingers on his thigh. Perhaps he should take the vaunted d'Louncrais library for himself.

Aimon stood, waiting, his face revealing nothing of the emotions, the fear, Lothair was certain whirled inside him. He was learning. Ensnared in his trap for the informant, and unpracticed in the art of intrigue, Aimon had been too easy to play. Recent events had changed that, but Lothair had yet to meet a man he could not read.

"Tell me, Aimon, of your meeting with the pack. Did you uncover Renaud's informant?"

Uncertainty flashed in Aimon's bright blue eyes. Maybe he had been wrong to send in Aimon. He was no match for the experience of the others, Lance in particular.

"Tell me you have something. An impression. A feeling in your gut. Who fought hardest for Kathryn, apart from yourself?"

Aimon's gaze hardened. "Godfrey."

Mmm, interesting. He picked up the poker and stirred the coals in the brazier. Aimon ventured no further information. Well...*that* would not do.

"Aimon, I thought we had an understanding. In return for your assistance, I would let you have the girl, but..." He shrugged. "Perhaps I was wrong. Perhaps you do not wish for Kathryn as much as I believed."

A stillness came over Aimon, one Lothair recognized well. The readying of a predator before the attack. In the air a musky scent pervaded, and Aimon's intense blue stare fixed on him.

With a nonchalance that betrayed his own alertness, he set aside the poker and approached the young chevalier, casually draping his hand across the hilt of his sword. "Do you want to keep her?"

He stood toe to toe, eye to eye with Aimon. A man who could shift into a werewolf. The thrill of it zipped through his veins. Who would triumph in a match between them? The beast? Or the warrior whose precarious hold over his county, and at times, his life, had long since stripped away any conscience he may have been born with?

Aimon's lip curled back in a snarl, revealing an elongated canine. "Kathryn is mine."

His words were little more than a guttural growl as dark shapes shifted in his eyes. The musky scent intensified. How close was Aimon to shifting? Could he channel his inner wolf, the strength and the enhanced senses, without changing form? Lothair longed to know, to be on the other side of this standoff. To have what they had. He would have it. They *would* give him what he wanted. Eventually.

"I will ask you again. Do you want to keep her?"

He would not, could not, allow a challenge to go unchecked, not even in the privacy of this library. Aimon could still prove useful, but Lothair would not hesitate to cut him down. As a chevalier, Aimon was good, but not as practiced, nor as cunning as he. As a werewolf, he might think he could best him. But would a turning only a few years old give him the edge over an experienced warrior? One whose ruthlessness the pontiff had likened to that of the Devil? Had Lothair faced Gaharet, the outcome would be in question. But Aimon... Lothair was certain he had the advantage.

Aimon, it seemed, came to the same conclusion, for he backed away.

"It is time for you to earn your keep, Aimon." Lothair released his hold on his sword, pleased with the outcome of their little battle of wills, yet disappointed he had not the chance to test himself against a werewolf. "Tell me what happened at the pack meeting."

Aimon stared at the floor. "I could not discern who the traitor is. Godfrey was unusually angry, and he is hiding something."

Aimon's loyalty to his pack was strong. For one such as him, it would cut deep to give up their secrets. But his desire to protect Kathryn burned brighter, and Lothair would use that to get what he wanted.

"And?"

Aimon's face twisted into a grimace, as though telling him anything caused him physical pain. "Lance gave me a plausible excuse for why he lied about the night in the clearing, about where he was when Ulrik—"

"Yes, speaking of Ulrik. Where is he, Aimon?"

Aimon frowned, concern and confusion flickering across his face before it went as blank as un-scribed parchment.

Lothair considered the young chevalier. "Did you aid him in his escape?"

Aimon shot him an incredulous look. "How? You had him shackled in silver. I am no more immune to it than he is."

"And the woman?"

More confusion. "What woman?"

"The woman who helped him escape. The woman who, the guard swears, did not pass them, yet somehow got into a locked and guarded underground chamber."

Aimon shook his head. "How is that possible?"

"It is possible because I left the alpha's amulet with him."

Aimon's Adam's apple jerked as he swallowed.

Lothair smirked. "Yes, Aimon. I know how the amulets work. I understand the purpose of the alpha's amulet. What woman did you send to rescue Ulrik?"

Aimon again shook his head. "I did not..." He frowned. "Gaharet would not... Neither of us would risk our..." He swallowed again, his gaze darting about. "I do not know."

He did not know, but he had a suspicion. Lothair was certain of it. Could she have a connection with Gaharet's woman? None of his inquiries into this Erin Richardson had revealed a shred of information about her family or her past. Not even a whisper of a rumor. Not a single trace, as though she had appeared out of nowhere. He snatched up his goblet and threw back the remnants of his wine.

Lothair stood and wandered about the room, running his hand over tomes, picking up scrolls before setting them down again. "Where would Ulrik go? To Gaharet? Do I suspend my search for Ulrik and hunt, instead, for Gaharet?" He raised an eyebrow at Aimon's sharp intake of breath. "No?" His lips thinned, and he brushed past Aimon. "Then *find* me Ulrik."

He exited the library, his guards falling in step, passing a flustered Farren with a hand on Kathryn's arm, holding his daughter in check. Defiance glittered in the feisty she-wolf's eyes. Silly girl, if she thought to challenge him.

"*Capitaine.* Search this keep. From the ramparts to the storerooms." At the keep's entrance, he paused. "Remember, Aimon. What I give, I can easily take away." He stared pointedly at Kathryn, and Aimon drew her closer into the protection of his arms. "Never forget that."

Chapter Eighteen

Bek let the wineskin slip from her shoulder and she slumped to the ground. From the moment she'd straightened her clothing beneath dawn's early light, Ulrik had set a cracking pace. Any remaining buzz from her orgasm had faded faster than the blisters on her heels had appeared.

"I know, I know." She waved him off with a weary hand as he opened his mouth to speak. "We've got to keep moving. They're on horseback. Blah, blah, blah. I get it. Give me a moment to catch my breath and we can keep going."

He eyed the sun overhead. "We will stop to eat, but then we must move on." His restless gaze scanned the forest. "It is not only the keep guards we must concern ourselves about now."

She squinted up at him. "You mean the villagers? That we stole from?"

He handed her a chunk of bread, taking a piece for himself. "The lord of the village may well come looking for us."

"You think so?" She stretched her legs out in front of her. Her calf muscles hadn't received a workout like this since PE in high school. "Seems like a lot of trouble over a villager's stolen clothes and some bread and mead."

"I am...known to him."

"Right." She rolled her eyes at him. "Is there *anyone* in this century that isn't hunting you?"

He grinned. "Perhaps one. Or maybe two."

She chuckled. Who'd have thought? The man had a sense of humor.

"Well, someone didn't like you very much, if those scars on your throat are any sign." She'd been itching to ask about them all day.

A shadow slid over his expression, and he turned away.

"It's why your voice is so raspy, isn't it?"

He didn't answer, keeping his back to her, staring out at the forest.

"I thought you'd screamed yourself hoarse in that dungeon. Your skin was red raw from that shackle, so I didn't see them at first. But the redness has gone already, and this morning...well...they're pretty hard to miss."

"My body reacted to the metal in the shackles. It irritates my skin and makes it blister. It is a family trait. Once I removed the shackles, my skin was quick to heal."

Hmm. Like an allergy. Makes sense. She chewed on her piece of bread. Without butter or any condiment, it was dry, but as someone who'd once spent a week eating only packet noodles, she wasn't going to complain. It wasn't...

Wait a minute. An allergy? Was that what was happening every time he kissed her? He was reacting to the silver in her tongue ring? She swallowed the bread and pressed the silver bar against the roof of her mouth. It must be a pretty nasty allergy if his reaction to it was anything to go by.

"So, getting back to my original question. How did you get the scars?"

His shoulders stiffened.

Maybe she was pushing her luck. "I'm sorry. It's really none of my business."

Would knowing what had happened to him, where he'd come by those scars, change her decision to go along with him? Probably not. Was she curious? Hell, yeah. But everyone was entitled to their secrets. Lord knows, she had hers.

He regarded her for a few moments before shifting his sword aside and easing himself to the ground beside her. "Have you ever made a decision that you regretted? One that changed your life for the worst so that it was almost unrecognizable?"

Bek stared at him. Oh yeah, she'd been there, done that, all right. She had the parole papers to prove it. His eyes bored into hers and for a moment, it was as though he could see right through her, her soul was laid bare for him. Every black mark, every poor decision held up for his scrutiny. As if, for that split second, they'd connected, and he understood the shame, the regret and the anger she harbored at her own gullibility over the mistakes she'd made.

He broke the moment to stare out at the forest. "I let my emotions take control of me, and as a consequence,

I made an error in judgment. I…" He let out a resigned sigh. "I challenged someone I should not have. The wrong person, for all the wrong reasons, and it nearly cost me my life. It *should* have cost me my life."

"But you survived."

"He let me live. There is a difference." He stroked the skin of his throat, tracing the puckered scars. "He had every right to kill me for what I did." He hung his head. "Sometimes I wish he had."

Bek's heart squeezed at the emotion in his words. She laid a hand on his shoulder.

"Every time I look at him, I am reminded of the mistake I made. How I let my anger overrule my intellect."

He paused, and for a moment Bek thought he wasn't going to say any more.

"My actions cost me a lot that day. He was a good friend, like family. Had I succeeded, it would have cost many lives as well as my own. He saved me from myself."

By nearly killing him? Some friend.

"But… If he was your friend, why did you challenge him in the first place?"

He huffed. "Over a foolish notion."

She opened her mouth to ask for more details, but she didn't get the chance.

"My understanding is that things are very different in your century, Rebekah. Time changes many things. It changes our perspectives, our beliefs and our lives. Perhaps had I lived in your time, I would not have had the urge to do what I did. Perhaps there would have been no need."

Deep, but it did not answer her question. She cocked her head. "I've seen knife wounds before. Scars like those don't come from any blade. What did he do? Set his hounds on you?"

"Something like that." He regarded her, curiosity shining in his eyes. "What about you, Rebekah? You handled yourself remarkably well with that keep guard. One would almost think you had experience dealing with men like him." He snorted and shook his head. "Or men like me. And you certainly are not afraid to speak your mind. Now you mention a familiarity with knife wounds. I suspect you have made some mistakes in your life. That you have done things you regret."

Bek huffed out a breath. How would she even explain she'd been charged with drug possession? That the man she'd loved, the man she'd believed had loved her, had stashed the coke *he'd* been selling, and all the cash, in *her* purse when the cops had pulled them over. That the only reason she'd gotten off so lightly was because it was her first offense. That it'd quickly become clear Spider had used her as a scapegoat, and had abandoned her to her fate, moving on with another woman before the judge's gavel had descended. *Nope. Not going there.*

She got to her feet and brushed off her dress, his eyes tracking every move. "You forgot to mention the green streaks in my hair and my tongue ring." She poked her tongue at him, laughing at his astonished expression.

He was on his feet in a heartbeat. "You *do* have metal pierced through your tongue. Why?"

She shrugged and hooked the wineskin over her shoulder. Not an unusual reaction. Lord knows, she'd been asked that question many times before.

"Because I wanted to." Having successfully distracted him, she pushed past him and headed off in the direction they'd been walking. "We should keep going," she called back over her shoulder. "We can't have all those people chasing you catching up with us."

In a few quick strides, he was beside her. "What possible purpose could having metal pierced through your tongue serve?" He grunted. "Other than to burn my mouth when I kiss you?"

Bek suppressed a grin. "Well, there is another reason people get them."

"Oh?"

"Rumor has it, having a tongue ring adds to the sensation during oral sex. For both the giver and receiver."

Bek kept walking a few steps before she realized Ulrik was no longer beside her. She stopped and looked back.

He stood, staring at her, his eyes wide and his nostrils flaring. "You jest."

She laughed at his expression. "Nope." She started walking again. "Not that you'll ever know, given your reaction to it, for one," she muttered under her breath.

His dark chuckle followed her. He caught up with her and blocked her path, a wicked gleam in his eye. "Oh, Rebekah," he said, giving her a thorough eye-fucking. "Do not underestimate what I am willing to endure in order to have your pretty mouth wrapped around my cock."

She stiffened, her legs frozen in place, her whole body buzzing and flushed with heat. He cupped her chin and brushed his thumb across her lips, and it took every ounce of willpower not to take it into her mouth.

No, Bek. Just no.

The smugness in his gaze only inflamed her need and her frustration. He grinned, dropped his hand and walked off, continuing on their path. She stared at his retreating back and swallowed, the visual of his words replaying in her mind. She dropped her head back and stared up at the forest's leafy canopy. *Hell.*

"How long until we reach that woman in the woods?" she called after him, her voice a little on the breathy side.

"Another two days at least, from tomorrow."

Two days! That meant another two nights with him alone in the forest. At *least. Fuck.* How the hell was she going to resist this man? She unfroze her legs and set off after him, stomping her feet, following his broad shoulders, muscular thighs and taut ass as he strode through the forest.

Remind me again why I want to?

Chapter Nineteen

Ulrik glanced over his shoulder at Rebekah, her dark head down, her pace flagging and her feet dragging. He stopped, allowing her to catch up to him, and cocked his head and listened. Not a sound of pursuit on horseback or on foot. Nothing to indicate Lothair had picked up their trail. Nor was there any sign of Lance. Catching wind of his fellow wolf would be a greater reason for alarm than any keep guard. Lance would track them far more efficiently than any human.

For two days he had pushed them, changing direction often and keeping the breeze at their backs. They had walked all day, stopping only to eat and to take care of bodily functions. He had kept them walking on after night had fallen and had them rising before the dawn, lighting no fires and rationing out the remnants of the bread and mead, not willing to risk leaving her alone to hunt again.

Getting her to lie beside him on his surcoat to sleep had been a constant contest of wills, but logic, and the cold night air, had prevailed. Each night she had resolutely turned her back to him, insisting he turn his to her. He had complied, amused by her stubborn refusal to admit what her body told him she wanted. Had the sense of urgency to be gone from the area not pulled at him, had she not been overcome with exhaustion, he might have teased her and pushed at the boundaries she had so clearly set on their interactions.

At least now he knew what had burned his tongue. Even so, the mere thought of having her mouth on him had his cock responding. He tamped down on the growl forming in his throat. She'd use that piece of metal to keep him at bay. It would have to go.

She reached him, skidding to a halt and her head jerking up. "We've stopped. Oh, thank God."

She slid to the ground, lines of fatigue about her eyes. She pulled the stopper off the wineskin and took a sip.

A weary sigh escaped her lips. "Not that I don't like wine and all, but any chance we can swing by a creek and fill this up? I'm so thirsty."

He looked up at the dark clouds gathering. A big, fat rain drop splattered on his cheek. He smiled. *Thank the fates. Rain.*

"I think there will be water enough to appease you soon."

A gust of wind buffeted them, and a familiar musky scent teased at his nostrils. He stilled.

Lance.

A crack of thunder split the air, and the wind swirled clouds of leaves and dirt around them. His nostrils flared again.

And Godfrey.

He grabbed Rebekah's arm, pulling her to her feet.

"Give me a moment to catch my —"

"No. We leave now."

Her shoulders slumped.

"I know you are exhausted, Rebekah. I will carry you if needs be, but we must move now. They have found us."

Her eyes widened and she scanned the forest. "How do you know? I can't see anyone. Did you hear them? Where are they?"

"Close. Too close. Though I doubt you will see them until it is too late."

"Are you sure? We've not seen a single soul for days. It's like we're the only people in this whole damn forest."

He cupped her face in his hands. "Believe me when I tell you, we must move now. Trust me, Rebekah."

She threw her hands in the air. "Okay, fine, but I'm not a sack of potatoes. I can walk."

He grimaced, but dropped his hands to clasp her arm, tugging her along through the forest as fast as she could go. If he'd thought she would go quietly across his shoulder, he would have given her no option.

He eyed the darkened sky. More heavy raindrops fell as the heavens opened, dousing the landscape in water. His torn and sodden tunic whipped about in the bitter wind and the rain soon plastered his hair to his skull. He released her and spun around, his arms out and his head thrown back to the sky, laughing into the stinging rain. Any trace of their scent was now gone. All he had to do was stay ahead of them and get lost in the storm.

Rebekah stared at him. "Trust him, he says. We have to move *now*. They've found us. Then he stops to dance in the rain. The guy's not right in the head."

He laughed at her muttered words and grabbed hold of her hand. "Come, Rebekah. The rain has washed away our scent, but we must keep ahead of them lest they stumble across us by chance."

Ulrik forced her on through the rain-drenched forest, league after league, lightning slashing across the sky and the roll of thunder reverberating through the trees. He pushed against the wind, avoiding falling branches, each squelching, muddy step hard won. He dodged a falling limb, pulling Rebekah out of harm's way and clutching her to his side. She pressed her face against his chest, her woolen dress sodden and her body shivering. He pulled his surcoat from the sack and wrapped it around her shoulders.

"Let me carry you," he shouted over the driving rain.

She shook her head. "No!"

L'enfer. Stubborn woman.

She pushed out of his arms, took a few more steps and slipped, falling to her hands and knees in the mud. Ulrik cursed.

Before she could get to her feet, he scooped her up and cradled her in his arms. "Hold on, Rebekah. We are almost there." *I hope.*

This time, she did not fight him. Tucking her head into the crook of his shoulder and wrapping her arms around his neck, she let him carry her through the rain.

* * * *

The sight of the small hut huddling in the sheltered clearing, smoke curling from its thatched roof, nearly brought Ulrik to his knees. The rain had been a boon, but also a hindrance. He had worried he might not be able to locate it. With Rebekah shivering and pale, he had more than one reason to find it.

The door swung open and a glow from the fire inside illuminated the woman standing in the doorway. She beckoned them in, closing the door behind them, shutting out the bitter wind and muffling the sound of the rain. The room was small but cozy, with herbs hanging along the walls and crystals and jars of powder lining the shelves. Faint, but discernable to his sensitive nose, was the lingering scent of his alpha and his alpha's mate. It was all the confirmation Ulrik needed. He had found the right place.

"I am Ulrik. This is Rebekah."

"I am Constance."

She smiled, and Ulrik stared. The pretty young woman with the unusual eyes was not at all what he had expected.

"Put her over there." Constance directed him to a small cot on the far wall, and Ulrik eased Rebekah down. He raised an eyebrow at the pile of women's clothing laid out.

The witch met his gaze. "Your arrival is not unexpected."

Gaharet. "Erin? Did she…"

What state would Gaharet be in if Erin had died?

"Survive the turning? Yes."

A hint of sadness hung over Constance, teasing at Ulrik's nostrils. Perhaps Erin's determination to leave had resulted in success. And what did this witch know of the turning? Of them? Had Gaharet confided in her?

"She is well? They are well? Does Erin remain with Gaharet?"

Rebekah groaned and curled in on herself, her body wracked with shivers. He gently brushed a strand of wet hair from her face. She barely registered his touch. It would surprise him if she had caught the witch's words. He did not believe she spoke his language. That was a good thing. Some secrets were not meant to be shared.

"Yes." Again, the hint of Constance's sadness teased him. Ulrik frowned. Not sadness for Erin and Gaharet then. He brought his wolf forward, reaching out with his senses. A soul-deep loneliness wafted off her in thick waves. No. The sorrow was the woman's own. He reached out a hand to offer what little comfort he could.

"Go," she said, jerking her head toward the door. "Make sure we are safe. That the other two wolves have not followed you here. I will tend to your mate."

Ulrik shook his head. "She is not..."

Constance had turned away. She knew about his kind? She knew something, but now was not the time to question her. Not with Godfrey and Lance somewhere out there, searching for him.

He dropped the sack and the wineskin and stepped out into the storm, leaving Rebekah in the witch's care. He unbuckled his sword, stripped off his sodden clothing, and allowed the change to flow through him. On all fours, insulated against the cold and wet by sandy-colored fur, he disappeared into the forest. He had not escaped the keep and come this far to be brought down by his brothers.

* * * *

The cold wind and the relentless rain made his old injuries ache, but the one-eyed wolf kept still as the sandy wolf slunk off into the sodden forest. The sense that he knew this wolf, had known him, settled in his bones. Perhaps when he had lived as a man. When he had had a family and had lived in a stone keep. When he had had a brother. He shook the feeling off. It was of no consequence to him now.

His gaze shifted to the hut. A woman lived here. Alone. Slight in stature, her long hair twisted about her head in wheat-colored braids and her clothes patched and worn, she drew his attention away from the wolf. Had he known her before, too? He did not think so, and yet she drew him in a way that suggested he had.

Before she had closed the door, she had turned and stared out into the storm, scanning the trees where he lay. Her gaze had hovered over him. He had feared she had seen him. And yet he had wanted her to see him. Strange.

He resisted the urge to slink closer, to scent her. He had not come here for her. Nor for the big sandy wolf. He had lost his quarry in the storm, only to come across the sandy wolf and his woman by chance. He had followed them in the hopes he may reclaim the trail of his nemesis.

With the image of the woman in the hut haunting his thoughts, he slipped away into the forest. Avoiding the path of the sandy wolf, he continued his search. He would have his answers, and then he would have his vengeance.

Chapter Twenty

Bek lay curled into a ball, wet, cold and more miserable than the day the judge had sentenced her to twelve months in Bronzefield prison. The woolen dress clung to her, saturated and weighty. Her boots were a muddy mess and her feet were like two blocks of ice. She was so cold she couldn't move, though the warmth of the fire beckoned.

The woman spoke to her, words in French, gesturing to her wet dress, the fire and a pile of dry clothes. Bek nodded, her teeth clacking together, and let the woman help her peel off her wet garments and hang them up to dry, as Bek slipped into the dress provided. The woman, Constance she'd said her name was, eyed Bek's knickers and bra with curiosity, but said nothing as she draped them over a seat by the fire.

Constance handed her a mug, steam rising above the lip, and Bek gratefully wrapped her hands around it. She took a sip. Ginger. She took another sip and warmth spread through her chest and down to her stomach.

"Thank you. For helping us." Bek dredged up long-forgotten French words, hoping the basics hadn't changed too much over the centuries. "*Merci beaucoup.*"

Unlike the villagers who'd turned their backs on her, this woman had taken them in. Would she evict them, force them back out into the storm if she knew Ulrik was a fugitive from the local count?

The woman's two different colored eyes — one blue, one green — regarded her. Did she live all the way out here on her own? Had people shunned her, as the villagers had shunned Bek? Because she was a little different? Because she was born with a peculiar genetic feature? Or was there another reason for her isolation?

A woman in the woods, Ulrik had said, and he'd paused and Bek had wondered then, as they'd sat watching the hare carcasses cook over the fire, if she was a previous lover. What if... Her mind raced. What if he'd been going to say the *witch* in the woods?

Bek's narrowed gaze swept around the hut. The drying herbs, the bowls of powders, leaves and things she couldn't name and the cluster of colored rocks and crystals. The only thing missing was a Book of Shadows, a grimoire. And maybe a broomstick. Perhaps this woman was the last person who would turn them away.

Constance beckoned her to a seat by the fire, beside her drying undergarments. Bek dropped her saturated boots at her feet and sat, warming her frozen toes and sipping her ginger tea. Whatever Constance's reasons for taking them in, Bek was grateful. She hoped they could stay here for a little while. At least until she could thaw out and the storm had blown over.

The door swung open and a gust of wind swept in, buffeting the fire, before a bedraggled Ulrik closed the door behind him. He stood, dripping water, with several dead hares in one hand and his muddy boots in the other. Constance accepted the hares, and they exchanged a few words, too fast for Rebekah to catch any but *merci*. A few long strides took him to a pile of clothing Constance pointed at. More French. Whatever he'd said, Constance was pleased. He'd probably offered to hunt for her again.

Serving drinks in a dingy, noisy bar, Bek had learned pretty quick how to read people. It had served her well more times than she could count. With the language barrier, the skill would come in handy.

Constance arranged the hares on the table and grabbed a large cleaver. She raised it up and brought it down with a loud thunk, chopping off a hare's head. Bek jumped and nearly spilled her ginger tea. She looked away from the decapitated hare, her gaze sliding over Constance's shoulder to Ulrik. He'd turned his back to them and was peeling off his sopping shirt. It hit the floor with a wet plop.

The cleaver descended again. *Thunk.* Bek flinched, drawn back to the macabre scene unfolding on the table. Constance had removed the hare's front paws. Another chop and the back paws were off, too. Bek grimaced. It'd fascinated her when Ulrik had done this, watching his long fingers and those competent hands of his prep the hare, but now it made her a little queasy.

Her gaze lifted to Ulrik again. Muscles played across his naked shoulders as he dried his chest with a cloth. Broad shoulders that tapered down to lean hips. What would it be like to rake her fingernails across them? Or run her tongue down his spine. Would he arch his back? Would he growl?

The clunk of the cleaver against the table as Constance set it aside snapped Bek out of her smutty thoughts and drew her attention back to the hares. Now Constance held a wicked-sharp knife. With deft hands, she cut several slits in the skin. Then, gripping the fur tight in her fist, she stripped it away from the flesh. Behind Constance, Ulrik rubbed the cloth over his hair before dropping it at his feet.

The hare pelt set aside, Constance made a hole in the hare's stomach and slid the knife along its belly. Ulrik reached for his trousers. Constance gently eased out the slippery entrails. Ulrik peeled his trousers down.

Bek stared at the twin globes of Ulrik's bare ass, Constance and her hare preparation forgotten. The man had taut buns. You could bounce a penny off those things. And, God Almighty, wouldn't she love to get her hands on them?

He bent over to slide his trousers off his feet, treating Bek to a prime view of his heavy ball sack and the bulbous head of his cock. She bit her bottom lip, holding back her hum of approval. The sounds of Constance skinning and gutting hares continued — the thunk of the cleaver, the snick of the knife, the squelch of entrails being removed — but Bek only had eyes for Ulrik. She clenched her thighs, conscious she no longer wore her knickers.

Another hard chop. Another hare lost its head, and Ulrik turned around, hands on his lean hips. Bek's hands gripped her mug of tea so tight she thought it might crack. Her gaze skittered over his muscled abs, following the happy trail of sandy-blond hair down to his groin. Ulrik's casual nudity shouldn't surprise her.

The man was an exhibitionist at heart. He'd already proved that.

A soft chuckle had her cheeks heating. He raised an eyebrow, amusement and not a little heat dancing in his eyes. He dropped his hands from his hips and held them palm up, inviting her appraisal, daring her to look. Constance still worked diligently at prepping the hares. If she had any inkling of what was happening behind her, she gave no sign.

Bek met his gaze, refusing to drop it and look her fill. She wanted to. God, how she wanted to, but she refused to give him that satisfaction. She would content herself with her memory from the pond. Of seeing his long fingers stroking... Her breath hitched, and she turned her attention back to Constance and the bloody table with its hare carcasses. Even the sight of the severed heads and the wet pile of entrails couldn't shake the image of Ulrik with his hand fisted around his cock.

What would sex be like with a man like him? An expert with his fingers, he'd given her one of the best orgasms she'd ever had. Against her will, her gaze slid back to him. A wide grin split his face, and he folded his arms across his chest, widening his stance.

Bek's hackles rose. Oh, he thought they were a done deal, did he? She rubbed the barbell of her tongue ring against the roof of her mouth. Were they a done deal? Could she have sex with him and walk away? And make no mistake, he wasn't promising her anything except sex, but the sex promised to be *awesome*. She'd be leaving to return to the twenty-first century. Eventually. She hoped. There was no point in her catching feelings for him, but did she want to regret a missed opportunity?

She fiddled with her tongue ring again. *Should I, or shouldn't I?*

Her body hummed. Ulrik's nostrils flared and triumph glittered in his eyes.

Cocky bastard.

She turned away, sipping her tea and staring into the fire. In the periphery of her vision, she caught the roll of his eyes toward the thatched ceiling. With a frustrated snort, he gave her his back and dressed. She suppressed a laugh. The man wasn't used to being turned down. She was good for his ego. The women of the tenth century could thank her later.

She glanced up to catch Constance watching her. From the smothered grin and the amused side-eye Constance gave Ulrik, the woman understood more than she let on.

Bek set her mug on the table and held her hands out, motioning to the hares and the knife. "Can I...do anything to help?"

Constance handed Bek a knife and some vegetables and motioned to the pot. Bek focused on chopping up the vegetables, avoiding looking directly at Ulrik as he draped his clothes by the fire, but she was very aware of him. When he paused by her knickers, her stomach fluttered. When he fingered the lace of her bra, his brows drawn together in a frown, her breasts ached and her tongue stuck to the roof of her mouth.

She'd have to remove her tongue ring, given his allergy. *If* she were to take him up on his offer. Sex without kissing didn't bear thinking about. And the man could kiss. Magic fingers, a magic mouth. Would he also have a magic— His declaration in the forest, when she'd told him why some people had tongue rings, flashed through her mind and her body flushed with heat. There was that, too.

He left her bra and moved to sit beside her, his arms on the table and his thigh pressed against hers. As Constance filled a pot with hare and vegetables and set it over the fire, Ulrik conversed with her in rapid French.

Bek listened, her whole body tuned into the conversation, but all she could pick up was Ulrik's obvious relief.

"What did she say? Does she know where your lord is?"

Ulrik nodded. "She has given me a message from my lord. I know where to find him now. We shall set off first thing in the morn."

Bek groaned. More walking. "How far?"

"At the pace we have been setting, four, maybe five days."

Shit. Bek's shoulders slumped, and she leaned her head in her hands. "We should've stolen a bloody horse."

Chapter Twenty-One

They sat at the table, steaming bowls of hare pottage in front of them. As he ate, Ulrik mulled over what Constance had told him. Gaharet's mate, Erin, had survived the turning. With the mortal wound she had sustained, that information came as a relief. As did the fact she yet remained with Gaharet. Good tidings. The last time he had spoken with them, Erin had been determined to leave Gaharet, because leaving her career and her life in the future was too much of a sacrifice. Losing a mate could break a man. *Had* broken Gaharet's father.

But the witch knew more. How much more?

"Gaharet was searching for something when I last saw him? Did he speak to you of this?"

As he spoke, he reached out with his senses. He would catch her in a lie if she dared to offer him one.

Constance tore off a piece of bread and dipped it into her pottage. "You do not trust me. That is understandable. Know that Seigneur Gaharet did."

Ulrik could scent no deceit, but he remained cautious.

"He was searching for the reverse spell for the amulets. His mate had come from the future. She is not the first, nor will she be the last."

Erin was not the first? He glanced at Rebekah. And there would be more women like her appearing in this century?

As if sensing their regard, Rebekah stopped shoveling food into her mouth. "What?" She wiped at her mouth. "Do I have food on my face?" She ran her tongue over her teeth. "Is there hare stuck in my teeth?"

He kept his amusement in check. She was hungry. Lord knew they had eaten sparsely on their journey here. He would not deny the woman enjoyment in her food.

"All is well, Rebekah. Eat your food." Her eyes narrowed, but she complied, though he did not think for a moment she was not listening to their every word. To Constance, he said, "Did Gaharet find what he was looking for?"

She studied him, and he shifted a little in his seat. Her eyes had a depth to them, a wisdom uncommon for one so young, and the feeling she could see right through him and into his soul unnerved him. He knew what she would find there.

She gave him a smile, full of mystery and knowing. Had he come up wanting in her estimation? Unredeemable? He brushed the thought aside. *It is no matter what a lone witch in the woods thinks of me.*

"Sometimes," she said, "not finding that which we seek is what we are truly seeking."

Ulrik grunted. He could well imagine Gaharet not wishing to find the answers with Constance. But was she talking only of Gaharet? How much had his alpha told her?

"You know of the…"

Constance's gaze dropped to his chest where, beneath the tunic, lay the binding stone. "The amulets? Yes. It is many years since any of my family has seen one. It was my family, generations ago, who created them and the binding stone."

Ulrik dropped his chunk of bread into his bowl and stared at her. Her family had created… Did Gaharet know this?

"Hm. That shocks you. It surprised Seigneur Gaharet, too. We have long had a relationship with the d'Louncrais."

Ulrik had no recollection of any of the d'Louncrais having a connection with this woman. Or her family. Or any witch.

Constance regarded him with sad eyes. "We lost the connection upon the death of Seigneur Jacques. I have reaffirmed it with his son."

"Then you have the reverse spell? We can send Rebekah home?"

A strange twinge of…*something*…pinched at his heart. He rubbed his chest. Indigestion, perhaps?

She shook her head. "As I told Seigneur Gaharet, there is no reverse spell. We never thought there was a need for one. Nor can I create one. Not alone."

The tightness in his chest eased. *Strange.* "Why not?"

"The amulets and the binding stone required a full coven of witches for their creation. Thirteen witches. For a reversal spell, there would need to be the same. I am the last surviving member of my family and of my coven. You would need to find twelve more witches and trust them with your existence."

Ulrik rubbed his chin. Twelve more witches. Not an easy feat, when he knew of only her. Then they would need to entrust them with the knowledge of their kind. Gaharet would never sanction such a broad dissemination of their secret.

He glanced at Rebekah. Her dark eyes watched them, flicking between him and Constance. For all her self-deprecation about her lack of education and her inability to speak Franceis, she was smart. How much of their conversation could she understand? He refocused his attention on his food. No need to give her reason to suspect him of sharing something more than polite pleasantries with Constance.

They continued eating as the storm raged outside, Constance watching him with those strange eyes of hers.

Constance broke the silence. "You wear the binding amulet."

Ulrik stiffened. "For now." He pushed the remnants of his meal away, the rich, gamey taste of it turning to dust in his mouth. "I am not the alpha."

"I know."

There was no harshness or judgment in her words, but a mere statement of fact.

He dropped his head. "I am not worthy of it. Not after what I have done."

"And yet, in your alpha's eyes, you have redeemed yourself twofold."

His head snapped up. *I have?*

"You saved his mate. And him. You were willing to sacrifice your life for them and for the pack. He will not forget."

Ulrik swallowed, the enormity of her words crashing over him. He had not thrown himself at the mercy of Lothair and Renaud to regain Gaharet's good opinion, but knowing he was no longer viewed with suspicion lifted a weight from his shoulders.

"The white wolf also knows of your worth."

Aimon?

"Beware of the others. Some wish to kill you for what they think you have done. One wishes to kill you for what he knows you have not."

The traitor. Who was it? Could it be the other wolf he had scented in the forest? No. He had been alone. It had been the perfect opportunity to ambush him, yet the wolf had not taken it. He was not the traitor.

And what of Rebekah? Warm, dry and her hunger satiated, her eyelids drooped and her body sagged against the table. How would she react to the news she must remain here? Indefinitely. Erin had not reacted well at all. Best to leave the telling for when Rebekah would have the comfort of another who would understand her predicament.

Their meal finished, Constance cleared the table and stoked up the fire. "Rest now, Seigneur Ulrik. You have an arduous few days ahead of you. You will need to fortify your heart and mind to make the sacrifices required before you reach your journey's end."

She bid them goodnight and disappeared behind a heavy sack cloth to a bedding nook, leaving them alone. Ulrik stared after her. The woman spoke in riddles. Why did he get the feeling she spoke of more than their proposed walk ahead of them?

"What did she say?" Rebekah asked. "Anything that can help us?"

Ulrik shrugged. "Only to take care in the forest. She has seen many a keep guard of late." Rebekah narrowed her eyes at him. Had she caught him in his lie? "Come. Let us retire for the night."

He eyed the cot. It was narrow, but they both would fit if they pressed their bodies together. Not an unpleasant situation. It could only aid in furtherance of his goal to have her.

She objected when he picked her up, but when he placed her on the cot and wrapped her in a blanket, her protests died on her lips. Her eyelids fluttered, and she muttered a weary sigh, pulling the blanket tight around her shoulders. Instead of joining her, he gathered up his damp surcoat, laid it on the floor and lowered himself onto it. It would not be the most uncomfortable night he had spent in his life.

"What are you doing?" she mumbled, yawning.

He met her sleepy, puzzled stare. "Go to sleep, Rebekah. We have a long walk ahead of us."

"But...you'll be cold on the floor."

He smiled away her concern. "I will be fine."

She pouted. "But I'll be cold."

She pushed herself to the far side of the cot and raised the blanket. Was she inviting him in?

"Hurry up," she grumbled. "Before I change my mind."

Ulrik was on his feet in an instant, sliding beneath the blanket.

She snuggled into his side. "That's better."

Ulrik breathed in her scent and reveled in her soft body tucked in tight against him. Yes. Yes, it was. He stared up at the thatched ceiling, listening to the wind in the trees and the crackle of the fire, his beast within strangely content. When was the last time he had lain in bed with a woman? Just lay there, cuddling and sleeping. Not sex. He tried to recall. There must have been a time. His life had changed when his family had died, when Lothair had punished them for his crimes, but surely before then. Yet no such memory came to mind.

Rebekah's head nuzzled against his shoulder, the green streaks in her dark hair bringing a smile to his lips. His family would have liked her. His sisters especially. They would have delighted in the way she challenged him. How he could not intimidate her. How she fought his every command. They would have seen her as an ally. Another woman to rally to their aid, and to form a united front against him.

They had already had his mother on their side, leaving him and his father outnumbered. Debates in their home had been enthusiastic. His sisters were never ones to shy away from voicing their opinion or disputing his. They would have welcomed Rebekah, another strong female voice, with open arms.

His mood slipped as the familiar ache resurfaced. They would never have the chance to meet her, thanks to him. Yet, right now, the guilt and the shame, though present, did not clench in his entrails, or sour his gut as it was wont to do. The urge to grab for a wineskin and drown out his own bitter recriminations was a mere whisper in his mind. Perhaps he was tired. Perhaps his actions in helping to save Erin, and now Rebekah, were going some way to ease his conscience.

He closed his eyes, listening to Rebekah's soft breathing, the steady beat of her heart and the light fall of rain as the storm eased. They were safe for the night. He should sleep. They had several days' walk ahead of them, and though it would not tax him as much as it would Rebekah, his body was showing signs of fatigue. Too long in Lothair's wretched underground chamber, weakened by wolfsbane, silver and meager rations, and nights of sleeping light, conscious of pursuit from both

Lothair and Lance, had left him with little reserves. But his mind refused to rest.

Soon, he would reunite with his alpha. Despite Constance's assurances, after all that had come between them, he could not be assured of a welcome from Gaharet. Would Gaharet trust him to be so close to his new mate? After so much time, Ulrik could not imagine a reconciliation possible. Not after what he had done. Where would that leave Rebekah?

Rebekah shifted about on the cot beside him. She, too, was restless and unable to sleep. He loosened his grip on her a little and she settled against him. He was not about to let his little fire breather go. Not yet. Not when he had yet to know the pleasure of being between her silken thighs. His conscience may have eased a little, his need to drown out his sorrows receding, but if the state of his cock was any indication, one thing remained the same.

Her hand snaked across his stomach, perilously close to his hardened shaft. He could not prevent the rumble in his chest. His balls ached, the anticipation of being buried in her wet heat pounding through him. Soon. He would know this woman in the most intimate way possible and hear her scream his name on her release. He would sample her fire, and nothing Gaharet could say or do would stop him.

Bek shifted about on the cot. She was warm and snuggled up to Ulrik, and still sleep eluded her. The man brought the heat, and not the 'I'm cold, you'll keep me warm' type of heat. But as she enjoyed the feel of his hard body next to hers, there was more than sex on her mind.

It was disconcerting being on the outside of a conversation, not understanding what was being said.

With the glances they'd thrown her way, chances were Constance and Ulrik had been talking about her. Or something that concerned her.

Then, as she'd teetered on the verge of trusting him, seriously considering having sex with him, he'd lied to her. Told her some guff about Constance warning them about keep guards in the forest. She clacked her tongue ring against her teeth. Did he think she was stupid? That she'd missed the tenseness in his body and the worry in his eyes. Or his shock, hastily masked, at something Constance had said.

She might not be fluent in French, but she'd understood a *few* words. He'd mumbled something about an alpha. That couldn't be right. Or it meant something else in French. Then the words *loup blanc.* White…*wolf*? The words, cobbled together, made no sense to her outside of the shifter romance she'd been reading last week. Had she misheard? Mistranslated? Perhaps she had shifter on the brain. Whatever the case, if she was going to be stuck here for an indefinite period, then she was going to have to brush up on her French.

Chapter Twenty-Two

Ulrik trudged through the forest, Rebekah a few strides behind him. The afternoon sun filtered through the canopy of trees, a hint of the soon-to-come night on the air. Constance had bound Rebekah's feet with strips of fabric and given her salve for her blisters and, with each day, her pace increased. Four days they had walked, and they were almost there. Four days and not a scent, nor sound of pursuit. That he would head for the d'Louncrais estate, that Gaharet had chosen to hide there, would never have occurred to them.

Each afternoon Ulrik would call a halt, and he would slip into the forest to scout ahead, to ensure they were not being tracked and to hunt. He would light a small fire and a meal before night descended, then they would curl up together on his surcoat. By dawn, they would once again be on the move. His days were filled with her chatter, her attempts at Franceis as he set about teaching her his language, her observations about his world and, surprisingly, his laughter. His nights, as she snuggled in his arms for warmth, were filled with longing and a persistent throbbing in his groin.

Ulrik's hand strayed to the small, wrapped bundle secured in his scabbard. A tiny rod of silver with a ball on each end enfolded in a strip of his tunic. Giving his thanks to Constance, he had spied it on the table beside Rebekah's mug. The silver had burned his fingers as he had picked it up. Was this the tongue ring she had spoken of? He believed so. Knowing she had removed it, and what it meant that she had, did little to ease the constant tightness in his breeches.

Yet, she had not asked, and he would not break his vow to her. In truth, it was for the best. For if he had the chance to bury himself in her, he would not want to stop. Not for anything. With the keep guard and his own pack searching for him, they did not have that luxury. Not yet.

He paused. A splash of water tumbling over rocks told him they were close.

Rebekah turned to him, concern in her eyes. "Why have you stopped?"

"Why are you whispering?"

"Well, you're doing that stillness thing again. You know, where you just kind of freeze as though you hear something, and you're waiting to hear it again. Whenever you do that, I keep expecting a wolf or wild boar or something to come crashing through the trees. Or some of those keep guard."

Ulrik regarded her, his body tense.

"And you tilt your head, too, and sniff the air. Is that something they teach you in chevalier school or is it a tenth-century woodsman skill thing?" She scrunched up her nose. "Does it help at all? Because I tried it, and I still couldn't hear or smell anything different."

Lord, the woman was sharp. In mere days, she had noticed things other chevaliers had missed, or simply ignored, though he had spent most of his life amongst them. Given time, would she unravel the secret of his true nature?

"We are close."

"We are?" She scanned the forest. "There's nothing here. Just more forest. No village or castle. Obviously, your lord can't go back to his own castle, but don't people, wealthy people, seek refuge with friends? Other rich and titled folks?" She looked around her. "I can't imagine a lord and his wife, all decked out in their fancy clothes, sleeping on the forest floor."

A scent carried on the air, and Ulrik's nostrils flared.

He pressed a finger to his lips, motioning her to be quiet. She froze, poised to run. Ulrik tilted his nose to the air. Rebekah raised her eyebrows and pointed her finger at him. Yes, he was proving her observations right, but there was no help for it. He breathed in deeply, searching for the scent again. There. Aimon. And a *she-wolf*? Not Erin. Had Aimon turned a woman in his absence? Taken a mate. For there were no she-wolves left. Renaud had killed them all.

With Aimon and the she-wolf standing between them and their objective, there was no way for Ulrik to get past Aimon save going some distance out of their way. Even so, a slight shift in the breeze and Aimon would know of their presence. Constance had told him Aimon could be trusted, but could he trust the witch? She had not betrayed Gaharet, and had given them shelter from the storm and his enemies. He pushed forward, with Rebekah close behind him.

He trudged through the trees, down an embankment, and followed the trickling creek as it wound through the forest until they reached a sheltered, clear pool bordered by moss-covered rocks. Muted sunlight filtered through the canopy, giving the water an orange glow. At one end, water spilled from a rocky outcrop, creating a small waterfall that splashed into the pool.

"It's beau —"

Rebekah gripped his arm. She had spotted them. Two wolves. Across the pond. One white, and one a dark coppery red. Aimon and the unknown she-wolf.

"Ulrik."

Her voice wavered and she edged closer to him. He tucked her behind him. No matter Constance's assurances, Ulrik was taking no chances.

"Is that an...Arctic wolf?" Her words were a whisper of breath as she peered around him. "And the red one... I didn't know wolves came in that shade of red."

He dared not take his gaze off Aimon to look at her.

"Wow. They're so beautiful, so... I never thought I'd say this, but... You're not going to kill them, are you?"

Aimon settled into a crouch, curled his lips in a snarl and laid his ears flat against his head, his hackles bristling, guarding the she-wolf. His mate. Their scent did not lie. Aimon had mated, and he would protect the she-wolf. He would die for her if need be.

Ulrik held up his hands, keeping them away from his sword, but he called his wolf close. He stayed still, meeting Aimon's blue-eyed stare. Not in challenge, but he would not cower. He would protect Rebekah as Aimon did the red she-wolf.

The air bristled with the threat of violence as neither he nor Aimon moved. Then the white wolf dropped his snarl and shook his big head, raised his muzzle to the sky and howled. Then, keeping his body between them and his mate, he nudged her away from the pond. With one last look over his shoulder, Aimon herded the she-wolf away, and they disappeared into the trees.

Ulrik let the tension drain from his body. Gaharet now knew of his arrival.

"Phew." Rebekah stepped out from behind him. "That was a little freaky. For a moment there, I thought he might attack us."

Ulrik brushed a strand of green-streaked hair from Rebekah's face and smiled. "He would not have attacked us. Not unless I gave him cause."

"But…"

"He was protecting his mate, Rebekah. That is all. Ulrik turned to head around the pond. Come."

"Okay." She did not move. "But why are we now following them?"

"Because this is the way we need to go." He held out his hand to her. "Come, Rebekah. All will be well. My lord is not far."

She huffed and slipped her hand in his. "I've trusted you this far."

His heart warmed at her words. With her small hand in his, he led her along the old trail, overgrown from lack of use. They had often come here as boys—him, Gaharet and D'Artagnon. The old farmer who once lived here had been deaf, and the pond was the perfect secluded spot to bring young she-wolves.

The trees parted and he emerged into a clearing, skirting two grazing horses. Nestled in the center, the cottage wore its years of abandonment well. With the inhabitants long gone, most had forgotten this part of the d'Louncrais estate, making it the ideal place to hide from Lothair and his keep guard.

In front of the cottage stood Gaharet, Erin, Aimon and a woman with vibrant red hair. Memory teased at him, of a little girl with the same red hair as Gaharet's mother, skipping through the keep. Kathryn. Gaharet's cousin. Aimon had mated Kathryn Beauchene.

Erin's scent tickled his nose, drawing his attention. It had changed since he last saw her. Now the subtle musky scent of she-wolf surrounded her and…something else. It carried a fullness, as though… He met Gaharet's gaze and saw the truth of it there. Erin was pregnant.

"Ulrik. Good to see you alive and free." Gaharet's gaze slid to Rebekah. "And who is this woman you have brought with you?"

"Rebekah, this is my lord, Sir Gaharet d'Louncrais, and his wife Lady Erin." He spoke in the language of Bretaigne so Rebekah could easily understand. She did a wobbly little curtsy. "This is Sir Aimon and, if I am not mistaken, Lady Kathryn Beauchene."

Rebekah curtsied again, narrowing her eyes at Aimon and Kathryn, destroying any hope he had she would miss the similarities between them and the two wolves at the pond.

"Rebekah helped me escape Lothair. I could not leave her there. Not when she found herself in similar circumstances to Erin."

Gaharet quirked an eyebrow, and Erin's mouth dropped open.

"Indeed," said Gaharet. "An interesting state of affairs. Another woman from the future." He cast a glance at his mate. "Welcome, Rebekah. You have our gratitude for assisting Ulrik. Know that you are safe here with us."

Gaharet stepped forward, reaching for Rebekah's hand. Ulrik's wolf roared to the surface and he lunged between them, blocking her body with his. His canines filled his mouth and he pared back his lips to snarl at his alpha.

Lord help him.

He was challenging his alpha. Again. Yet he could not bring himself to back down, no matter the consequences.

"What the hell, Ulrik?" Rebekah jerked her hand from his. "You made me walk all this way to find this man, and now you have a problem with him?" She skirted around him, smiled at Gaharet and offered her hand. "My Lord —"

Ulrik grasped her around the waist and swiftly deposited her behind him. With a monumental effort, he forced his canines to retract, turned to face her and growled at her. It was all he could manage. Words were beyond him.

Hands on her hips, she glared up at him, not an ounce of fear in her eyes. "What is your problem? You said your lord could help me get home. He's not going to be so keen to do that if you piss him off by going all alpha male on his... Oh!"

Ulrik tensed. Her eyes widened, the light of understanding sparking in their depths. Her gaze slid past him to Aimon and Kathryn and the racing of her heartbeat pounded loud in his ears.

She raked her gaze over him and took a step back. "Your allergic reaction to my tongue ring. My *silver* tongue ring. And the silver shackles. Your inhuman strength when..." Her breath hitched. "When you killed that sleazy guard." Her eyes narrowed in on him. "You tracked me in that pitch-black dungeon and found me so fast in that village. You hear things I can't, and stand so still like..." Her face paled. "Like a predator stalking its prey."

Ulrik remained still, his gaze locked on hers. Would she react as Erin had? With curiosity? Or would she fear him now?

She dropped her gaze to his boots. "No, no, no. It can't be. I've read *way* too many shifter romances."

She inhaled deeply and lifted her head. Liquid brown eyes searched his.

"That time you went hunting for food, and I heard a wolf howl..." Her gaze darted past him. "And those two wolves by the pond, the red one and the white one..." She licked her lips, her gaze shifting and settling at his throat. "Those scars didn't come from a knife or a hound, did they? Tell me I'm wrong." Her eyes pleaded with him. "Tell me..."

He reached for her, and she stepped back.

"Are you? Oh, God." She covered her face with her hands. "If I'm wrong, you're all going to think I'm a loon." She clasped her hands together against her chin as though praying. "Do you... Are you..." Her gaze darted past him to the others. "Are they..." She threw her hands in the air. "Oh, hell. I'm just going to say it. Are you a werewolf?"

Behind him, Gaharet chuckled. "She's even bolder than you are, Erin."

"Yeah, and she figured it out much faster than I did," said Erin.

Ulrik blocked them out, his focus on Rebekah. He needed to know what she was thinking, what she was feeling. If things had changed between them.

He stepped into her space, crowding her, and took her hands in his so she could not retreat. She stared up at him, her lips parted and her breath held.

"What if I am?"

Rebekah stared into Ulrik's eyes. Dark shadows swirled in their depths and a strong musky scent enveloped her. He could shift from human to wolf?

Holy fuck!

He'd officially blown her mind. And intrigued her, and if she was completely honest with herself, turned her on.

His nostrils flared. Her cheeks heated. Good lord. If anything she'd read in shifter romances had an ounce of truth, then he'd know everything she was feeling through her scent.

She patted his arm. "Keep it under control, big guy. We're not alone in the forest anymore. Now's not the time."

She'd thought she'd spoken for his ears alone, but as they turned to the others, the smirks on their faces said differently.

Erin pointed to her ear. "Excellent hearing. And perfect eyesight. And a really, really good sense of smell."

Rebekah wrinkled up her nose. "Got it. Thanks."

Erin chuckled. "You're welcome. Is that a British accent I detect?"

"Yes. I'm from London. You?"

"Sydney, but I was working in France when the amulet zapped me into the tenth century."

"If France is Frankia and London is Lundenburg..." Lord Gaharet crossed his arms over his chest and regarded his wife. "Where is this Sidnee you speak of? And does this have any bearing on why your accent is so different to Rebekah's?"

Erin looked a little sheepish. "Yeah, about that. At the time, it was easier to let you think I was from Bretaigne rather than explain I was from a country that has yet to be discovered." She patted his arm. "I promise, I'll tell you all about it later. Right now"—she jerked her chin in Ulrik's direction—"we have more important things to think about." Erin slid her arm through Bek's. "Come on, Rebekah. Let's go inside and leave these men to talk. We can compare stories about how we both got here."

"Sure."

Her gaze slid to Ulrik. They were going to talk. Soon. She pressed her tongue to the roof of her mouth, the lack of her tongue ring unfamiliar. *Maybe more than talk.*

Erin turned to the other woman. "Kathryn?"

Kathryn shook her head, said something in French as Aimon helped her onto a horse, then mounted up. Werewolves, both of them. One white and one red. Would Ulrik's wolf be a sandy-blond like his hair? And Lord Gaharet a black wolf? Would Ulrik show her, shift into his wolf for her? What about Erin? Was she a wolf, too? No, she couldn't be. She'd come from the future.

"I hope they stay safe." Erin waved Kathryn and Aimon off. "It's a concern with the comte the way he is, and them not being hidden away like us."

"The comte? Is that the count guy at Langeais Keep? I can't believe he went all *Braveheart* on you and wanted to sleep with you on your wedding night. I can't believe that's really a thing."

"What? Is that what Ulrik told you?"

Had he told her that? Bek thought back to their conversation. No. Not really. But he hadn't refuted her assumption either.

"Because it's not," said Erin. "Really a thing, that is. Take it from me — as an archeologist — *Braveheart* would have to be one of the more historically inaccurate movies of all time. Scottish kilts weren't in vogue at the time William Wallace walked the earth. And *jus primae noctis*, the right of the first night that you're talking about, was a trope used to make England's kings look more evil and dastardly."

"Oh." Erin must think her dumb, believing everything in a movie. *An archeologist. Shit.* Bek hadn't finished high school. Going to college had never been an option. "Then what is it he wanted?"

Erin looped her arm through hers. "Come on. Let me catch you up on what's been happening. If you're going to be in this world, and Ulrik's world, you really need to know."

"Oh, I'm not staying, and Ulrik and I aren't…well, we're just…" She glanced over her shoulder at Ulrik, deep in conversation with Lord Gaharet. "Okay." She kept her voice low, hoping Ulrik wouldn't hear her. "Ulrik wants in my knickers. He's made that pretty clear. With the chemistry between us, sex with Ulrik promises to be off the charts hot. I figure, I'm stuck here for a bit so…" She shrugged. "I might as well have some fun. But that's all it'll be. For both of us. And then I'll go home."

The amusement in Erin's eyes as she led her into the hut was a little disconcerting, but Bek brushed it off. Sex and sex only. She'd already had one Spider. No way was she going to fall for another.

Chapter Twenty-Three

Ulrik stared after Aimon and Kathryn as they rode off into the forest. "There is a story there."

"There is," agreed Gaharet.

Erin and Rebekah disappeared into the cottage and the door closed behind them, leaving Ulrik alone with his alpha. "We need to talk."

Gaharet perched himself on a downed tree and folded his arms across his chest. "We do. Tell me, Ulrik, how did you get out of Langeais Keep?"

Ulrik stiffened. Constance was wrong. Gaharet had not forgiven him and did not trust him still. When last they had spoken, Gaharet had thought it was he who had betrayed the pack. Given their history, he could well understand Gaharet's suspicions. Despite Constance's assurances, one act did not atone for the many years between their broken friendship.

"I followed my nose. I tracked your path, yours and Erin's, to the storeroom and that passageway beneath the walls. Lothair had guards at the postern gate, but I knew the boys and I talked our way past them." He let the truth in his words ring clear. Gaharet could not fail to sense it. "I am glad for it. Had you not known of its existence, had you not used it to escape with Erin, I would have had a devil of a time getting out."

Gaharet's dark gaze bored into him, but Ulrik would not cower. He had nothing to hide.

"Very well." Gaharet unfolded his arms and leaned his elbows on his knees. "So, talk. I am listening."

Ulrik squared his shoulders. The information he had was too important to let their past conflict hold his tongue. "Lothair knows."

"That I am not dead?" Gaharet nodded. "I know."

Ulrik frowned at Gaharet's lack of concern. "I thought our plan was good. How did Lothair find out?"

Gaharet shrugged. "Our plan *was* good. I told him."

"What?" Gaharet's words hit him like a punch to his chest and he took a step back. "Why?" Had he spent all that time in that wretched hole, believing he was as good as dead, only to have *Gaharet* betray *him*? He snarled, his hand itching to reach for his sword. "Why would you do that? *When* did you do that?"

Gaharet remained seated, barely raising an eyebrow at his agitation. "I revealed myself to Lothair after they dragged you from the clearing. You and I both know Lothair is no fool. He already suspected it was a ruse. It is best we work with him, not against him."

"*Merde.*" Ulrik spun away.

"Do not let this dishearten you. Your time at Langeais Keep was not for naught. Lothair may know, but the others do not, save for Aimon."

Ulrik shook his head, restlessly pacing. Allying with Lothair? *No!* Not after all that had come before.

"You do not have to like it, Ulrik. Nor like the man himself. I am not asking that of you, but we cannot hope to combat both Renaud and the traitor, as well as

Lothair himself. We need to level the field." Gaharet rose and placed a hand on his shoulder, halting him.

Ulrik's emotions roiled inside him, the firm pressure of Gaharet's hand the only thing keeping his wolf in check and curtailing his rage. He longed to shake it off, but his alpha held firm.

Mon Dieu, I need a drink. Or to fuck.

The murmur of Rebekah's voice from inside the cottage called to him, tempted him. He could have neither. Not right now. He clenched and unclenched his fists, not willing to look at Gaharet. Not yet. Not until he had himself under control. To do so would invite a challenge, one his alpha could not let stand. One Ulrik did not want.

Gaharet squeezed his shoulder. "Think, Ulrik. Use your head and not your heart. We *need* Lothair."

Ulrik raked a hand through his hair and stared into the forest, seeing only the vague memories of his family. His mother's bright smile. The adoration on his father's face when he had looked at his mate. The defiance in his sisters' eyes. His memories of them had faded over time, but his anger and his thirst for revenge had burned brighter, stronger.

"You cannot win against Lothair, Ulrik." Gaharet moved to stand in front of him. "We cannot win. Your parents knew that. It is why they made the choice they did, and they would not want you to try. Do not let their sacrifice be for nothing."

A heavy weariness settled over him as all his rage drained away. Gaharet was right. He had known it when he faced Lothair in that godforsaken chamber. He knew it now. Ulrik let the tension slide from his shoulders. There was no point in fighting it.

"How can we survive this, Gaharet? Even allying with Lothair, the chances are slim. Renaud has an informant. One of our own. Lothair confirmed it when he came to taunt me."

Tension rolled over his alpha, and the low thrum of anger tainted the air.

"Yes. He does." There was an edge to Gaharet's voice. "And this traitor has wreaked havoc far longer than we had thought." Gaharet motioned in the direction Aimon and Kathryn had gone. "He attacked Kathryn the day he killed my mother."

Ulrik stilled. One of their own had... No, surely not?

"I thought... Aimon did not turn her? And your mother? Was that not bandits?"

The enormity of Gaharet's words sunk in. Kathryn had to have only been a child, and to kill Gaharet's mother... Which one of them would have done something so monstrous?

"And this..." Gaharet's lips curled in a snarl. "This *traitor* killed my father, too."

Ulrik's eyes widened. Gaharet's father *and* his mother? It made what *he* had done pale in comparison.

"Are you certain?"

The tightness around Gaharet's eyes, the thin line of his lips... *How did I forget I was not the only one grieving?* Gaharet had lost his family, too, and he, too consumed by his own grief and his thirst for vengeance, had failed to notice his friend's pain.

Gaharet nodded. "I found my father's journal. The way my mother died had never sat right with my father. I thought him lost in his grief, but..."

"His journal says otherwise?"

"It does. I can only surmise that he came too close to uncovering the truth, and that cost him his life. In the journal, he mentions confiding his suspicions to D'Artagnon."

"And now they are both dead." Ulrik's mind raced. Or were they? "But we never found D'Artagnon."

"No, we did not." Gaharet fixed him with an intense stare. "Do you have reason to believe D'Artagnon survived?"

Ulrik took a seat on the log, tugging at his bottom lip. That wolf in the forest near the Vautour estate... Could it be? Ulrik did not want to give Gaharet false hope. He could not be certain the wolf he had scented was Gaharet's brother, but the familiarity of the scent nagged at him. He had been many years in Bretaigne, and D'Artagnon was barely a man when he had left, but the scent had not belonged to any of the remaining wolves. Nor did it belong to any of Victor's pack from Bretaigne. A wolf from the pack in Rus, a rogue maybe, could have ventured this far, but there had been no contact with them for centuries. He had known this wolf's scent from somewhere.

"It may be nothing, but I caught a scent of a wolf near Lance's estate. I could not place it, though it was familiar. I have crossed paths with this wolf before. Could it have been D'Artagnon?"

Ulrik waited for Gaharet to ridicule his suggestion, but the dismissal never came.

Gaharet cast his gaze out into the forest as though searching for answers, or a glimpse of his long-lost brother. "I thought I caught his scent outside the walls of my keep less than a sennight ago. I believed it naught more than a memory."

"Perhaps not so much a memory at all." If D'Artagnon were alive... "If he came to your keep, why did he not reveal himself to you?"

"There was a gathering of the pack that night, not far from the keep. Perhaps he is after the one who tried to kill him. The one who killed our parents. There is an advantage in him being dead." Gaharet tugged at his beard. "You say he was near the Vautour estate? Could he be tracking Lance?"

"Or Godfrey. I saw him riding through the village on his way to the Vautour Keep."

"Godfrey and Lance. It keeps coming back to those two. Kathryn's memory of her attack rules out the twins. Too big, and Kathryn remembers a jewel on the pommel of the attacker's sword. Aubert and Edmond's swords are unadorned. As are yours and Aimon's. The timing rules out both you and Aimon as well. Aimon was not yet one of us when my mother died. You were in Bretaigne."

Ulrik huffed. "That is a relief."

Gaharet sat beside him. "I have not believed it could be you since that night in the clearing. I am sorry, Ulrik, that you suffered. Without your sacrifice, I would not have my freedom, perhaps my life. Nor would I have Erin." The horror at the thought of losing his mate shimmered in the depths of his eyes. "I cannot think of a worse fate than to lose her. I owe you everything. We both do. We are forever in your debt."

Tightness banded about Ulrik's chest. To be accepted, to be truly part of the pack once more and not viewed with distrust, with disgust, or as though he were a troublesome nick in a favorite blade to be honed out, was something he had longed for, but had never thought possible.

"It was nothing more than I owed you. For what I did." Ulrik reached beneath his tunic and drew out the binding amulet. He fingered the blood-red stone in its center. "I never wanted to be alpha. Not really. All I wanted was for Lothair to pay for what he had done and to avenge my family."

"I know."

Understanding glimmered in Gaharet's eyes. Had it always been there? Had he been so lost in his grief and anger he had not seen it?

"I am sorry, Gaharet. I was not thinking clearly."

"You were grieving, Ulrik. You had lost your entire family."

Guilt twinged in his chest. "So were you, and I gave it not a thought, too caught up in what was happening to me. What was happening because of me." He sighed and hung his head. "If not for my own stupidity, my arrogance…"

Gaharet hummed his agreement. "You always were impulsive and quick to temper."

Ulrik barked out a bitter laugh. He could not refute that. All his decisions, all his mistakes, had sprung from it.

He slipped the amulet over his head and held it out to Gaharet. "This belongs to you. You could have killed me that day. It was what I deserved for challenging you. But you did not. You make a far wiser alpha than I ever would have."

Gaharet's hand curled around the amulet. "Having this back will please Erin."

Ulrik quirked an eyebrow. "Your mate hungers for power?"

Gaharet removed the plain amulet from around his neck and handed it to him. "My mate is an archeologist. A studier of history and historical artifacts."

Ulrik slipped the familiar piece over his head and the comforting weight settled against his chest. The binding amulet had weighed far too heavily on him. It was a relief to have his own back where it belonged.

Gaharet slipped the binding amulet around his neck and tucked it beneath his tunic. "Erin found her amulet digging through the remains of Langeais Keep. In the underground chamber. With a headless skeleton and a wolf's skull."

"*Merde.*" The implications of *that…*

"Precisely. From the moment she realized I had swapped my amulet for yours, Erin has been beside herself with worry that the bones she found might belong to me."

"Especially now she is with young."

Pride and a fierce possessiveness glittered in Gaharet's eyes. "Yes. More so, now she carries my pup."

Ulrik shared a glance with Gaharet. "The bones belong to someone."

"That they do."

Ulrik leaned his elbows on his knees. "Some poor unfortunate sap Lothair sacrifices to get what he wanted?"

Gaharet cocked an eyebrow. "With an amulet?"

Ulrik grunted. "Could Renaud or Lothair have gotten their hands on one?"

Gaharet considered the idea. "The traitor could have handed over his."

"Possible. If so, we can always hope the bones belong to Lothair. Renaud wanted me to bite him. Offered me my freedom in return for the favor."

Gaharet's dark gaze fixed on him. "That must have been tempting."

Ulrik grimaced. "Oh, yes."

Satisfaction glinted in Gaharet's eyes and a knowing smile curved at the edges of his mouth. "But you did not."

"Give Renaud what he wanted?" Ulrik scowled. "I will not be a pawn for that wretched excuse for a priest. Nor would I trust he would hold up his part of any deal."

"I do not think it is Lothair who ends up in that chamber. Erin would have mentioned it as a possibility if there were a chance the bones belonged to him."

They sat in silence, staring into the forest, the chatter of the women a steady but muted hum. Rebekah's laughter rang out. Another burst of laughter, this time from Erin, dragged both his and Gaharet's attention to the little hut.

Gaharet's lips twitched. "I would wager Aimon is not the only one with a story to tell."

Ulrik shrugged. "Not much of one. Like Erin, Rebekah found an amulet. Circumstances coincided — she was bleeding, she translated the spell, then recited it."

Gaharet grunted. "On something called *Google*, I imagine."

"*Google?*" More laughter from the hut. "Their words are so strange."

"Truly. Erin tried to explain this *Google* to me. It is something called a…search engine. Not like something called an engine that powers a cart. Nor one that makes a carriage soar through the air like a bird. This engine can be anywhere and everywhere all at once." Gaharet puffed out a breath. "I cannot fathom it."

"A powered cart? A carriage that soars through the air?" Ulrik stared at the little cottage. "They are from our future. I suppose it stands to reason they would have things we could never imagine. Rebekah has a device that can create light and communicate across long distances."

"Interesting."

"It no longer works and the front of it has cracks in it. She says she needs a power source to make it work."

"If Rebekah is anything like Erin, and I imagine she is, I would guess throwing it at you is what broke it."

Ulrik grinned. It surprised him she had not, especially after he had tied her to a tree. "No. She used it as a decoy and threw it away from her in an attempt to elude me in the dark."

"Hmm. Clever. If you were human, it may well have worked."

"She is uncommonly canny," agreed Ulrik.

The rift between him and Gaharet was deep, a chasm he had never thought to bridge ever again. Could they find common ground because of two women from the future?

"You took a risk going to the Vautour Village," said Gaharet.

"It is not something I had planned. Rebekah…" He puffed out a breath, a little embarrassed to acknowledge the truth.

Gaharet chuckled. "She outsmarted you, did she not?"

"Yes." He scowled at the memory. "She ran off while I bathed in the creek. Took my clothes, my boots and my weapons. By the time I found all the separate places she had hidden them, she had made it to the village."

"She hid your clothes?" Gaharet threw back his head and laughed.

"She hid one of my boots in a log with an ant's nest. I got so many bites that my foot itched for hours."

Gaharet slapped his knee and laughed harder. Ulrik rejoiced at the sound. It had been a long time since he had conversed with Gaharet like this, laughed with him. Since before his parents had sent him away. He had missed it.

"She is smart," said Ulrik, defending himself. "*L'enfer*, how many people have been in our presence, how many centuries have gone by, and no one ever suspected what we are until one of our own betrayed us. She has been with me less than a sennight, and already she knows."

"Have you bedded her yet?"

His smile died on his lips and he glared at Gaharet. "No."

"But you want to?"

"Of course." He shrugged. "She is a beautiful woman."

"Mmm." Gaharet's amusement hummed between them. "How many days has she been in your care?"

He snorted. "With the keep guard hunting me, and shaking Lance and Godfrey off my trail, there was not the time."

Ulrik's protests sounded empty even to his own ears, his excuses thin.

Gaharet was openly grinning now. "She has refused you."

Ulrik huffed.

Gaharet slapped him on the back. "I think I will like this Rebekah of yours." He got to his feet. "Come. Let us join the women before they hatch a scheme between them both of us will live to regret."

Chapter Twenty-Four

The cottage, unfortunately, was not like the Tardis. A table, some bench seats, a fire pit beneath the hole in the thatched roof and a cot against the wall—it resembled Constance's hut in the forest. Cozy, but small. Erin, *Lady* Erin, resplendent in a burgundy gown, plonked a mug on the table.

"Take a seat." She fetched a wineskin and filled the mug to the brim, handing it to Bek. "I think you're going to need this." Erin settled herself across from her. "First up." Erin rubbed her hands together. "I need to know all the juicy details of how you ended up here."

Bek took a sip of wine, far richer and stronger than the mead they'd stolen from the village. Yeah, Gaharet and Erin had money. Even hidden away in this mud hut. She eyed Erin across her mug, the woman's expression open and curious. It'd been a long time since she'd sat down with another woman just to shoot the breeze. Two women chatting and gossiping, without a real agenda. In prison, she'd had to watch her back. She hadn't known who she could trust. With Spider back at the clubhouse, there was always some sweet butt angling to take her place.

Erin wagged a finger at her. "Don't think for a minute you can leave anything out. There has to be a story there, and I want *all* the goss. When I met Gaharet, he was running around the woods starkers."

Bek set her mug down. "Gaharet was naked when you" — she waved her hands around — "appeared out of thin air?"

Thank the Lord for small mercies that hadn't been the case with Ulrik.

Erin jiggled her eyebrows up and down. "Oh yeah. I thought he was a ghost. Or a hallucination. Then I thought he was practicing pagan rituals. Of course, *now* I know he'd been running through the forest in wolf form and had shifted back." Erin slapped her hand on the table. "Enough about me. Where did you find the amulet? I found mine on a dig site at Langeais Keep."

Bek rolled her lips together. "Um... I... A client left it behind at my work." No need to tell Erin everything. The woman was legit an archeologist. University educated, and now a Lady. Classy. Everything Bek wasn't, nor would she ever be. "One minute I was standing there translating the spell, then the next thing I'm in a dungeon with a man chained to the wall. Not naked."

"Oh." Erin poked out her bottom lip. "How disappointing for you. The not naked bit, I mean."

"I could see enough to rev my motors, don't you worry."

Erin grinned. "They're all pretty hot, aren't they? I mean, Gaharet, Ulrik, Aimon... Look at them. It's like a medieval Sexiest Man Alive spread."

She got that right. Ulrik, well… Chris Hemsworth eat your heart out. Gaharet was a walking, talking tall, dark and handsome, and Aimon had the body of a warrior and the face of an angel. All he needed was a set of wings.

"Okay. You're in Lothair's creepy underground cell. Ulrik's chained up. What happened next? How did you guys get out of there?" Erin straightened in her seat. "Wait a minute. Did Ulrik break the chains?"

"No. Um." Were they bonding? Over shared experiences?

Erin's eagerness shone bright and pure. All right. Bek might be a bit rusty at the whole making friends thing, but she could do this.

"I didn't believe I'd fallen through time. He insisted I had. Our arguing attracted the attention of the guards." Bek took in a breath and expelled it in a loud huff. "Yeah, that wasn't so good. Ulrik ended up saving me from the guards. That's how he got the key to his shackles."

"Mm. Sounds like Ulrik. He saved Gaharet and I, too."

"Yeah? Well, then he threw me over his shoulder, effectively kidnapping me. At one point, he tied me to a tree." The surprise on Erin's face was gratifying. Maybe the woman didn't know Ulrik as well as she thought she did. "But he *did* rescue me. That I'll grant him, though it didn't feel like it at the time."

Erin's eyes narrowed, then her face broke out into a beaming smile. "You really like him, don't you?"

Bek rolled her eyes. "Oh, please. I've known him all of a week and a half."

Erin smiled, but said nothing.

"And I've just found out he's a werewolf. That werewolves exist."

Did her protests sound forced? She avoided Erin's gaze.

"You're taking that rather well," said Erin. "The whole werewolf thing. I needed proof. I thought Gaharet had lost his marbles."

"It's kind of weirding me out a little." What about the last week or so hadn't? She was in tenth-century France, for fuck's sake. Bek took a long drink from her mug before setting it aside. She put her elbows on the table and leaned in. "You promised to fill me in."

"That I did."

Bek kept her expression neutral, sipping on her wine as she listened while Erin clued her in on all that had gone before. The count, Lothair, wanted Gaharet to turn chevaliers into werewolves to create a supernatural army. Yeah, turning humans into werewolves was a thing. Not one sanctioned every day, or something Gaharet would do for the count. *Not one mentioned in my shifter romance.*

Apparently, this Lothair was a piece of work. Gaharet's refusal to turn any of Lothair's chevaliers had pissed off the count, so Gaharet and Erin had fled Langeais. Ulrik, the guy so determined to get into her knickers, was the only reason both Gaharet and Erin were still alive. He'd sacrificed his freedom, and potentially his life, to save them.

Erin ran her hand over her rib cage and her expression turned somber. "We owe him everything."

Bek set down her mug and rubbed her face with her hands. Ulrik as a hero? The notion hit her libido like a punch of adrenaline, boosting it into overdrive. Heat burned in her chest, a shot of antifreeze to her determination to see him as nothing more than a night of hot, hot sex she could walk away from. It made her heart long for things it shouldn't. Like *more* than sex. Could Erin be right? *Did* she really like him?

We're going home soon, remember? Although...

She dropped her hands and stared at Erin. Going home wasn't the only option.

Bek took another sip of wine, forcefully tamping down on her thoughts of Ulrik. "Let me get this straight. Gaharet, Ulrik, Aimon and Kathryn are all werewolves."

Erin leaned her elbow on the table, her chin on her hand and nodded. "Mm-hm. And me. And all Gaharet's men."

All Gaharet's men? "How many of them are there?" *Wait.* Had Erin said —

"When I arrived here, there were only seven left." Erin ticked them off on her fingers. "Gaharet, Ulrik, Aimon, who you've met. Twins Edmond and Aubert. Godfrey and, the oldest, Lance."

Bek held up her hands. "Wait a minute. Just hold up a sec. You said *you* are a werewolf. How did that happen?"

There was no way Erin had been a werewolf before she came here. Having such a secret in the twenty-first century wouldn't be so easy to hide. Not with CCTV, cell phones and social media.

"Gaharet turned me."

And we're back to the whole turning people into werewolves thing. Like some sort of black and white horror flick and a part-man, part-wolf with slathering jaws biting down on a screaming human. Bek shivered and drained the contents of her mug.

Erin's hand strayed back to her rib cage. "He didn't have a choice, Rebekah. One of Renaud's mercenaries stabbed me. I would've died if he didn't." She rubbed at the spot on her side as though it still pained her. "Turning me saved my life."

Erin refilled her mug. Bek didn't stop her.

"And…who's this Renaud guy?"

"Archeveque — archbishop — Renaud." Erin screwed up her face. "How do I describe Renaud? Conniving, self-serving, corrupt, not above murdering people to get what he wants."

Had she seen the news of the Catholic church lately? Although murder was a new low for a priest.

"As I said, there were only seven werewolves left when I arrived, but there used to be a hundred or more. Men, women and children. Then a werewolf betrayed them and gave Renaud information on their weaknesses. He's been using that knowledge to hunt them. We believe his intent is to trap one. Ulrik is the first he hasn't killed."

"Weaknesses? Like silver."

Ulrik's allergy to silver was pretty intense. It was one heck of a weakness. *If* they could overpower him and get it close to his skin. She'd seen Ulrik's strength, his speed and his skill in a fight. He'd disarmed that kid guard between one blink and the next. It would take an awful lot to overpower him.

"You catch on fast," said Erin. "Silver is a weakness for werewolves. So is wolfsbane. Wolfsbane renders a werewolf unable to control their form. Shifting requires a lot of energy. If you're constantly shifting from human to wolf, it won't take long before you're exhausted and vulnerable."

Wolfsbane? *Bloody hell. I am stuck in a shifter romance.* Speaking of…

"What the hell was Ulrik's problem when we first arrived? I take it *Lord* Gaharet is the alpha. We trekked all this way to find him, then Ulrik gets all pissed at him. Was that some kind of challenge, or something?"

Did she really want to know the answer to that? She knew what it sounded like. The only thing missing was the guttural growling of the word 'mine'. No. That couldn't be right. She'd not read Ulrik as that kind of guy. She rarely got it wrong. Spider being the exception. Though as hurt as she'd been when Spider had betrayed her, she hadn't been all that surprised.

"It's a wolf thing."

Erin's knowing smile had Bek fidgeting in her seat.

"Gaharet did the same thing to Ulrik when he introduced me to him."

Before Bek could process the implications in that statement, the door opened and the two men entered. Men, and yet not only men. Werewolves. It was obvious now she knew their secret. The way they walked, prowled really, and the aura of danger about them. If Ulrik gave off bad-boy vibes, then Gaharet was all alpha. He oozed power and dominance, and though she found it difficult to look him directly in the eye, she stiffened her spine and resisted the urge to cower.

With a smile hovering on his lips, Lord Gaharet fetched two more mugs and set them on the table then poured mead from the wineskin. "Ulrik."

Ulrik ignored the mug in Gaharet's outstretched hand. He fixed his gaze on her, intent swirling in the depths of his eyes. Every wickedly delicious thing he wanted to do to her, with her, was reflected in those whiskey depths. Every nerve ending, every synapse, fired to life and heat spread through her body, the power of a thousand suns settling at the crux of her thighs. Her clit pounded out an urgent 'hell, yes!' Ulrik's nostrils flared and a strong, musky scent filled the room.

What had Erin said? *'Excellent hearing, perfect eyesight and a really, really good sense of smell.'* Bollocks. He could *smell* her arousal. *They* could, too. In the confined space of the little cottage, they couldn't miss it. Bek shifted in her seat. *Awkward.*

Ulrik held out his hand to her. "Rebekah, come. I will take you to the pond to freshen up. We can talk."

Her, Ulrik, a pond and a waterfall. There wouldn't be much talking going on. Bek eyed his outstretched hand. In her periphery, Erin and Gaharet shared an amused glance. Did she care what they thought? Nope. Not one iota.

She extricated herself from the table and took his hand. "Sounds like a plan."

They stepped out of the cottage and into the blessed cool air. In the time since they'd arrived, the sun had dipped from the sky and the forest was nothing but deep shadows with a hint of moonlight. Her hand clasped in his, they walked down the path to the pond.

"Rebekah," Ulrik began.

"You're a werewolf," she blurted out. "So are Aimon, Kathryn, Gaharet and Erin."

His grip tightened around her hand a little. "I am."

"Were you...born that way, or did someone turn you, like Gaharet turned Erin?"

"I was born a werewolf."

"Huh."

An owl hooted, and something scurried through the underbrush. She barely missed a beat. Ulrik would've reacted if it posed a problem—tilted his head to the side, nostrils flaring with that uncanny stillness settling over him. He kept walking.

"Field mouse," he said. "The owl is hunting her."

Damn. The man was good.

They stepped from the forest and stood at the edge of the pond. The serene water glimmered with reflected moonlight. The chirp of night insects and the gentle splash from the small waterfall broke the silence and the stillness of the night forest. Beautiful. Magical. But all her awareness centered on him. The man, the warrior, the supernatural being. She had to see it with her own eyes.

She dropped her hand from his. "I want to see you. What you look like in your wolf form."

He stiffened beside her.

"I want to see you shift."

He rubbed his hand across his face. Would he refuse? Claim some pack law dictated he couldn't? It wasn't as if he turned into some monstrous half-man, half-beast. The two wolves at the pond, Kathryn and Aimon, had looked no different to real wolves, though somewhat bigger.

"Are you certain?"

For a moment, the brash, overtly sexual man she'd come to know disappeared, and a streak of vulnerability flashed across his face. Did he expect her to run from him, screaming? He should know her better than that by now.

She fisted her hands on her hips and stared him down. "Yeah. I am."

He grinned. "You never fail to confront a challenge, do you?"

There was an element of pride in his voice. It warmed her and had her standing taller.

"Very well." He brushed a hand across her cheek. "No matter what form I am in, know I would never hurt you, Rebekah."

She cupped his hand against her face. "I know."

And she did. Deep down in the marrow of her bones, the certainty of it burned. Something shifted in her chest, a loosening of her control and a letting go of fear. In between one heartbeat and the next, Bek knew exactly what she wanted. Him. *All* of him.

She stepped away, giving him room. He unbuckled his sword and set it aside. His tunic followed. Every other time he'd been naked before her, he had taunted her, daring her to look. Not this time. With business-like efficiency, he shucked his boots and stripped away his breeches. Naked, he stood tall, shaking out his limbs, like a competitive swimmer waiting for their cue to step up to the blocks.

Bek waited, her hands clutched in the folds of her dress to hide her nervousness. He gave her a brief nod, then in one fluid movement and a crack and pop of bones, he shifted. For barely a second, she glimpsed his face, his body, as it contorted from human to wolf. Then it was gone. He was gone. In his place, a big sandy-colored wolf.

Fuck me.

Rebekah gaped, her eyes wide and her mouth open. She took a step backward. "Holy shit, that was fast." She raked her hands through her hair and clasped them at her neck. "One minute you were…well *you*, and now… Wow. Just. Wow."

She took a hesitant step toward him. "I mean… I knew what you were going to do. What you would look like, but…" She shoved her hands against her mouth to stop her babbling and tried to get her racing heart under control. "Can you… I mean… Oh, man, this is so freaky. Can you even understand what I'm saying?"

The wolf, Ulrik, sat on his haunches and nodded his shaggy head.

"Huh." She almost couldn't believe her eyes. She'd been expecting it, but the reality… "This is… This is so *awesome*."

Ulrik tilted his head to the side, his ears pricked forward.

"You're huge and…magnificent."

He chuffed at her. She curled her fingers into her palm, then uncurled them.

"Can I…" She took another step forward. "Can I touch you?"

Ulrik dropped to the ground in a classic dog sphinx pose.

"I'll take that as a yes."

Bek stepped forward. His tongue lolled out and the sides of his mouth curled up. Was that a grin?

"Are you laughing at me?"

His ears swiveled.

"Of course you are," she muttered.

Bek approached him slowly, holding out her hand. He tilted his head to the side, his ears cocked in her direction. Her hand dangled in front of his muzzle. She'd swear he quirked an eyebrow at her. He sniffed her hand, his cool, moist nose brushing against her skin. Then his long tongue shot out and licked her.

Bek yelped and snatched her hand back, then burst out laughing.

Ulrik's sandy-blond fur retreated as his bones shifted and reformed, all vestiges of the wolf disappearing. He unfolded himself from his crouching position until he stood before her, a man. A naked, fully aroused man.

She took in a deep breath, his musky scent filling her nostrils. Wetness soaked her panties. Any lingering thoughts of evil counts, scheming priests and the keep guard hunting them vanished, blasted from her mind as he stalked toward her. Chances were, a few hot kisses and a growl and she'd come. She'd never been so close to the edge so quickly, and without a single touch. Sex with a wolf shifter, sex with Ulrik, promised to rock her world.

Chapter Twenty-Five

Rebekah stepped away from him, and it took everything Ulrik had to not reach for her and drag her into his arms. To slake his need to have her pressed against him. Far from recoiling, his transition from man to wolf and back had enthralled her. More than. It had aroused her. This woman—bold, unapologetically defiant and fearless—she slayed him.

"My turn," she said, an impish grin on her lips. "You showed me yours. Now I'll show you mine."

Twice before, he had teased her, taunted her with his body. In the pond, stroking his length as she'd watched with slitted lids, pretending to sleep, and in the witch's cottage as Constance gutted and skinned the hares. He had not missed the burn of her gaze searing his bare back, the force of her attention on his naked ass. He had not forgotten. Neither, it seemed, had she.

She turned her back to him, unlaced her peasant's dress and slipped it over her head, tossing it aside. The red and yellow ink of her phoenix blazed across her shoulder, a mirror image of his crest on his surcoat. The subtle curve of her spine and the dips and shadows of her body called to him. He longed to trace his fingers, his tongue, over each one — nipping, sucking, caressing, licking. Seeking the places, the hollows, that would make her moan and tremble with desire.

Her hands went to her breeches. She threw a glance over her shoulder at him, full of challenge, as she wiggled them over her luscious ass. Inch by torturous inch, revealing a tiny strip of red fabric disappearing between her cheeks. His fingers curled, and his claws punched through the skin of his palms. Heat flared in her eyes, then she smiled and bent at the waist, giving him a glimpse of her red covered sex as she peeled her breeches from her legs.

Merde. His lungs seized, and his cock throbbed with a need to answer her challenge. To stride over to her, rip away that tiny piece of cloth, thrust inside her and pound against her willing flesh. Teach her what happened when she taunted the beast. He kept himself rooted to the ground. He had not spent a lifetime learning to control his darker half only to falter now. Rebekah would have the best of him. All his knowledge of how to please a woman. He would have her writhing in ecstasy, begging him to sate her, not some savage fucking in the mud.

She turned.

Ulrik almost spilled his seed right there and then. He searched desperately for some measure of calm. He was not some stripling lad, untried and inexperienced, but his cock was ready and willing. Had been since she'd first appeared in — what had she called it? — Lothair's oubliette. Nights of sleeping with her snuggled against him for warmth, and days of walking with throbbing testicles had done little to dampen his lust, his need for her.

She faced him, almost naked. Her pale skin, luminescent in the moonlight, emphasized the colorful etchings on her body. They snaked down her arms, across her shoulders, curled around her ankles and over her hip. Black straps over her shoulders attached to a dainty, open-weave black fabric cupped her breasts, thrusting them up in the most delectable way. Her dark nipples poked through the floral pattern, taunting him.

Ulrik had seen this garment drying in the witch's cottage and wondered at it. Now he saw it on her body, and he loved it and hated it in equal measure. He wanted to bury his face in the deep valley it created between those glorious mounds. He wanted to rip it off her. A man's hands and naught else should cup a bosom like hers. His hands.

That little scrap of red barely covered her pussy, with a hint of dampness at the crux of her thighs. Her scent floated to him on the still night air, and his eyes rolled back in his head. Heaven and all the temptation of hell rolled into one. All the wicked things he wanted to do with her, to her, flashed through his mind. Him inside her, watching his cock split her pink pussy lips, wet with her desire. Him behind her, gripping the creamy flesh of her soft, rounded ass. Rebekah on her knees, dark eyes focused on him as she sucked his cock with her defiant mouth. He salivated. His wolf pushed forward, forceful and eager.

She turned away from him and waded into the pond — the water caressing her calves, then her knees. Deeper still until it lapped at her thighs. It seemed ridiculous to be jealous of a pond, but Lord help him, he was.

She glanced over her shoulder. "What are you waiting for, Ulrik?" With a crook of her finger, she beckoned him. "Come join me."

Then she dove into the water and disappeared from view, only to resurface midway across the pond.

Ulrik strode into the water, his cock erect and pointing unerringly at the object of his desire. He dove in after her. Cold water surrounded him, chilling his skin, but it did little to temper the heat in his loins. By the time he had caught up with her, she had reached the waterfall, clambered up onto the rock ledge beneath it and stepped into the gentle flow. Rivulets streamed over her dark hair, down her shoulders, followed the curve of her spine and sluiced along the line of her hip.

Ulrik hoisted himself onto the ledge and clasped his arms about her waist, pulling her slick body back against his. His cock, harder than the tempered steel of his sword, crushed between them, pressed eagerly into the cleft of her ass. He groaned at the contact. She did not fight or twist away, rather ground her ass back into his groin.

He reveled in it, pulling her tighter against him, grinding his length into her sweet, soft curves. If he never found redemption, if heaven were to be denied him, right here, right now, he could not care. This, this glorious woman, naked in his arms, was all the redemption he needed. Heaven but a thrust away. Then he could die a satisfied man.

The red material covering her sex was soft, but it was an impediment to what he wanted. Her. All of her. Naked. He hooked his fingers in the material, prepared to tug it off, snap it, whatever gave him the access he wanted faster. She pulled away.

He gritted his teeth against the inner howl of his wolf and stepped back. He had never, would never, force his attentions on a woman. No matter how much he craved to lick and touch and suck every inch of her body. Or how much his cock begged, demanding he take what he wanted, what he craved with every fiber of his being. Every instinct in him screamed she wanted that, too, but he would not take what she did not offer freely.

She faced him, wet hair plastered to her forehead and her eyes glazed with lust. She stepped out of the flow of the waterfall. A bead of water trickled down her throat and carved a trail lower. He followed it as it slipped between the creamy skin of her breasts. *Merde*, he would love to get his hands on those. He sighed. Maybe not tonight. He swallowed his disappointment.

Ulrik raised his gaze to hers, prepared to retreat, to spend the night unsatisfied, with only the relief of his own hand. A poor substitute. He hesitated. Mischief danced in her brown eyes. Her tongue flicked out and she ran it across her top lip. He stared at it, tracked its progress as she repeated the motion. Now all he could think about was what he wanted her to do with her tongue. His cock leaked pre-cum. It needed little encouragement.

She stepped in close, her bottom lip clenched in her teeth and slowly, she sank to her knees.

Merde. By all that was holy. No woman had ever offered him this so boldly. The more jaded women of the court, the occasional bawdy serving wench, had taken his cock in their mouths. But only after he had pleasured them, and they lay sated and limp from his attentions. It was more an afterthought, or a duty, an expectation to be filled and reluctantly given. Yet Rebekah, gorgeous, lush Rebekah, kneeled before him, her mouth bare inches from his weeping cock with not a hint of hesitation. Little puffs of her breath teased his swollen head, and she stared at it with undisguised hunger.

She tilted her head up, locked her gaze on his, opened her mouth and placed her lips around the head of his cock.

Merde.

His knees all but buckled. *Have I ever seen a more beautiful sight?* He wanted to throw back his head and howl. To slide his fingers into her hair and shove his cock to the back of her throat and bury himself balls-deep in her warm, wet mouth. See how much of him she could take.

Her tongue worked his length, threatening to strip away the thin crust of his civility. He was more than the brutal chevalier who had killed the guard beneath Lothair's keep. More than a beast of myth and legend. His hands trembled with the need to touch her, but he kept them by his side, letting her have control. For now.

Chapter Twenty-Six

Ever since that moment in the forest, when she'd raised the topic of her tongue ring, when Ulrik had said he'd be willing to endure almost anything to have her mouth on him, Rebekah had been thinking about doing just that. Hell, she could have masturbated to that image for a thousand years and never tire of it. Now, wet from the waterfall and clad only in her underwear, she brought that fantasy to life. And it more than lived up to her expectations.

She lathed the crown of his cock with her tongue, tasting the saltiness of his pre-cum and reveling in the velvety feel of his length, his musky scent and the stretch of her lips around his girth. His gaze never wavered from hers, but he did not touch her, nor press himself deeper. Her hands gripped his thighs, all hard muscle and taut with tension. The man was holding back.

Bek growled her disappointment. His cock jerked in her mouth, and he puffed out a breath, almost a moan, but his hands remained resolutely by his side. She let his cock slip from her mouth with a slight pop and grinned up at him.

Challenge accepted.

Bek had never been one for sweet, under-the-covers, lights off, missionary position sex. Drawn to the darker side, to dominant men who could take control, she craved men who knew what they wanted and how to play a little dirty. Men who lived life hard and who fucked harder. It was probably why she'd fallen for Spider. Sexually, he had met her every need. Unfortunately, as a man, he had let her down.

There'd been many chances for Ulrik to ditch her. Numerous reasons why he should. As a man on the run, as a wolf, he would've made far quicker time without her. Unlike Spider, he'd chosen not to abandon her. Despite his bad-boy vibes, his dominance, and her antics when she'd escaped him, he'd stuck by her. Even chased her down, rather than leaving her to the mercy of the count, or the lord of that village. The cherry on top—the sexual tension between them had been off the charts from the instant they'd met.

Everything about him told her they'd be compatible between the sheets. Or under a waterfall. He could give her the darkness she craved. She knew it. Letting him cop out and be gentle and gentlemanly…well… Bek wasn't going to settle for that.

Releasing her grip on one of his thighs, she cupped his balls, stroking and teasing his heavy sac. Another moan and a tightening of his thigh muscle was all he gave her. She flicked her tongue across the tip of his cock, teasing the slit. She ran her lips along the thick vein all the way to the base and back again, nipping, sucking and grazing her teeth along the underside of his cock. His hands clenched and unclenched by his side and his chest heaved with each breath he took. What would it take to push him over the edge? Bek smirked.

What every man since the beginning of time had dreamed of.

With a deep breath, she sucked him in her mouth again, taking his length as far as she could. She suppressed her gag reflex until the tip of his cock pressed against the back of her throat. Then she swallowed. He groaned, and large hands darted to her head and fisted in her hair, holding her in place. The sting in her scalp brought goosebumps to her skin, and she moaned around his cock. She tried to pull back, but he held her tight and she quivered, her nails digging into the flesh of his thigh.

Yes.

He guided her head back, before sliding it forward again, gently, slowly. He did it again, faster this time and rougher. She let him. Mentally urged him to do it again. To give her what she needed.

"You like it when I take control," he rumbled, less of a question than an acknowledgment.

She did. Oh, how she did. She didn't like when a man tried to boss her around or treated her as less or stupid or as nothing more than an object, and she damned well told them when they crossed that line. But in the bedroom, she loved it when they took control. Instinctively, she'd known the moment she'd met him, Ulrik could give her what she craved.

"Oh, sweetness. It is like you were made for me."

His voice flowed over her, sparking a violent clenching of her pelvic floor. She let him guide her movements, her mouth, along his length. Her whole body thrummed with her need for him. With her need to get him off. She was so damned wet, and not from the waterfall.

She snaked a hand down beneath her red thong, moaning as her fingers brushed against her swollen clit.

His fingers tightened in her hair. "Yes," he hissed. "Take your pleasure." He thrust his cock deeper, and she nearly gagged, her eyes popping open. "Slide your finger in. Imagine it is mine."

She complied, slipping her finger inside her slick pussy, her muscles clenching. Her hand tightened on his thigh, using him for balance as she plunged her finger in and out, finger-fucking herself to the rhythm of the thrust of his cock into her mouth. Her body arched and tension sizzled up her spine, her peak dancing within reach.

He tugged on her hair and she looked up at him from beneath hooded lids. God, what a sight. Abs, covered in a fine dusting of blond hair, flexing with each thrust of his lean hips. His bearded face taut with lust, and his eyes locked on her. Her heart stuttered and her orgasm fluttered to life.

"Oh, baby. It would take a better man than me to stop now."

Then he stiffened, roaring his release as he exploded into her mouth. Thick ropes of hot, salty cum splashed the back of her throat. Her orgasm hit with a force of an exploding comet, burning her up until she wondered if there'd be nothing left of her but ash.

Suddenly, his hands were gone from her hair and grasping her under her arms, lifting her off his cock and pulling her to her feet. Then his tongue was in her mouth, and her mewl of disappointment turned into a moan. The scratch of his beard, the sweep of his tongue against hers, the lingering taste of his cum, and their hot breath mingling, undid her. Had her body lighting up all over again.

She'd wanted a tongue ring for a year before she'd gotten it. Never ever thought she'd take it out. Why on earth would she want to? Now, kissing Ulrik, Bek had no regrets she'd removed it. Hell, she'd remove it ten times over to have this.

He pulled back, sucking on her bottom lip as he did. Then he plunged in again, deep, as though with his kiss he could become part of her, touch her soul. Bek wasn't entirely sure he couldn't. She clung to him, their bodies wet and slick and her senses full of him. The hot press of his mouth. His scent. The heat of his body despite the chill of the water.

He drew back, spun her around and walked her through the waterfall, guiding her hands until they were flat against the rock. Beyond the steady fall of water, the deadening of sound heightened her senses and narrowed her focus to him and only him. The slide of his rough hands down her waist to her hips. His length, hot and hard, sandwiched between them. The man was insatiable, and Bek was right there with him.

He slipped a wet, muscular thigh between her legs and nudged them apart. He pulled on her hips, tilting them back, raising her up ready for him as he rubbed his shaft through the crease of her ass. The ache in her clit was almost painful. She pressed back against him, hard. God, she could almost come again. So soon.

A slap, his wet hand against her ass cheek, and she moaned out loud.

"Not yet. Wait. Greedy girl."

The command in his voice... *Oh, God.* It was killing her. *Death by orgasm. What a way to go.* And she was greedy. Bek wanted it, chased it. Him inside her. She wanted it all.

He hooked his fingers in her knickers and tugged. The sting as they snapped only heightened her arousal. Then he was on her, his hands, his body, his mouth — he surrounded her with his heat and his presence. His lips sucked and nibbled at her neck. One large hand cupped her breasts, teasing her granite-hard nipple until she thought it might shatter. His other hand cupped her mound, his fingers sliding through her slick folds and circling her swollen clit as his cock continued its grind against her ass. She was on sensation overload, a quivering mess. She dropped her head and moaned.

"Tell me no. Tell me to stop and I will."

His voice was little more than a growl, almost animal. Her legs trembled. If she turned around now, would she see the beast or the man? Her core clenched on nothing, and she whimpered. She wanted...she needed...

"Do you want me to stop, Rebekah?"

She shook her head, her hands clasping at the rough rock beneath her palms, incapable of speech. He slid one thick finger in her, then two, thrusting out a rhythm.

"Are you sure?" In answer, she bucked her hips against his fingers. "You want to come, baby? Again?"

She nodded.

"Words, baby. I need your words. Tell me you want to come."

Her mouth dropped open in a silent moan and she tilted her hips higher, chasing his fingers.

He smacked her ass again. "I will have your words, Rebekah."

If he thought smacking her and making demands in that raspy voice of his would chastise, wouldn't have her begging for more, he'd read her all wrong. He pulled out, and she whimpered at the loss.

"I'm going to make you come again, and then I am going to fuck you. Hard and fast. I will have you say you want it, too."

He thrust his fingers in again, scissoring them inside her.

"Yes, yes! Fuck me, Ulrik."

The words, ripped out of her on a guttural moan, hung between them for a moment.

He chuckled, his warm breath brushing against her ear. He thrust his fingers in deep, and pressed his thumb against her clit, hard. "Now, baby."

She obeyed. Bright, intense pleasure hurtled through her and she let go in a fierce rush of release, her hoarse cry mingling with the noise of the waterfall. Before she'd come down from her high, he slipped his fingers from her heated core. Without preamble, he lined up his cock and thrust into her, thick, hard and filling her as no man ever had.

How the hell am I going to leave this, leave him behind?

She trembled, her pussy fluttering around his cock.

Maybe I don't have to.

Chapter Twenty-Seven

He had his cock in her. Finally. Ulrik dropped his gaze to where they joined. Had he ever seen a more beautiful sight? His body flush against the rounded white globes of her ass. Her head tossed back, green-streaked hair teasing her shoulders. Water rivulets dripping down her arched spine, over the strap of the contraption that caged her breasts. Her heated channel gripped him tight, and it took all his control and considerable experience to not rush toward his release.

He held her still, his hands clasped firm on her hips, resisting the tingling of his testicles and the need crawling up his spine.

"Ulrik."

The word came out as a gasp, her chest heaving, the movement doing little to enhance the calm he was so desperately fighting for. He wanted to fuck her, savage her, like the animal he was, but he did not want to hurt her. Nor did he wish to frighten her, so he fought it. Never had a woman he had lain with made him want to let loose the beast inside as much as Rebekah did. Not even a she-wolf.

She thrust her hips back. "What are you waiting for?"

He sucked in a deep breath, inhaling the heady scent of her cum, her lust and the fragrance that was quintessentially Rebekah. Then he moved, sliding out and back into her with infinite slowness. She wiggled and he clasped her hips tighter, controlling everything—the motion, her and himself.

She growled, *growled,* at him. "Fuck me, Ulrik. Fuck me so hard and fast that I can't remember my own name. That's what I want. Give it to me. Or do I have to find another—"

He roared, the sound bouncing off the rock face and drowning out the waterfall. *No other. Just him.*

"Mine," he rasped.

Then he gave her what she wanted, thrusting into her with a mindless, ferocious need, the sounds of her pleasure echoing within their cocooned space. Senseless, broken words spilled from her lips every time he bottomed out, spurring him on. She took it all and begged for more. For harder, faster, and fuck if he did not give her everything she asked for. The slap of his thighs on hers and her breathy moans unspooled the last remnants of his control. *This woman...*

She convulsed around him, screamed out his name and squeezed his cock so tight he thought his heart might stop. Pleasure ripped up his spine and he spilled his seed inside her, plastering her clenching channel with his essence. Were he not a werewolf, he would have thought the violent clenching of her pussy had forever sucked him dry.

Her legs gave out and he caught her, sliding them both to the rocky ledge in a tangle of limbs. He cradled her against him, her chest heaving as much as his. Bloody hell. She still wore that blasted contraption covering her breasts.

"This," he said, in between panting breaths, his voice raspier than usual. "This needs to go."

She chuckled, even as she clung to him.

"From the moment I first saw you" — he slipped one strap off her shoulder and trailed his hand across her breast, swirling a finger around her peaked nipple — "I have wanted to touch these, cup them in my hands."

She sucked in a breath.

He slid the other strap down her shoulder and pulled the lace down, exposing her breast. "And take them in my mouth."

He groaned at the sight he had laid bare. *Merde, she is beautiful.* He leaned in and sucked one large, turgid nipple into his mouth.

She shuddered and languidly pushed at him. "Ulrik, I don't think I can—"

He released her nipple with a pop. "Just a little taste."

He dipped his head again and took the other nipple in his mouth, lathing it with his tongue and giving it a gentle nip with his teeth. It got impossibly hard beneath his ministrations.

She moaned, but then pushed at him harder. He released her nipple with a slow, reluctant slide of his mouth and a lingering glide of his tongue.

He eyed the frown that had settled across her brow and the wariness in her eyes. "Rebekah?"

She rubbed her face with her hands. "We didn't use a condom."

"Con-dom?"

He rolled the unfamiliar word across his tongue, trying to guess its meaning. *Con dom?* Was it some sort of device to enhance her experience of sex? He had pleasured her well. Fucked her till she had screamed out his name. He needed no *device* to aid him in bringing her to release. He pulled away from her, offended by her suggestion he did.

"Yeah, protection." She waved her hand at his cock, erect and instantly willing for another bout of sensational sex. "Like armor for your dick."

Armor for his dick?

She laughed at him. "You should see your expression. It's not real armor made of steel. God forbid. Wouldn't that be uncomfortable?"

She laughed again and the bouncing of her breasts drew his eye.

"Condoms are latex—a stretchy, waterproof material and it's shaped…well… It fits over your cock when we have sex and protects us both."

Ulrik stared down at his cock. It shriveled a little at the thought of covering it with anything, at the idea of a barrier between his cock and her warm, wet heat.

"I know this might seem like a foreign concept to you, but in the future we have things to protect against unwanted pregnancies and sexually transmitted diseases." She glanced down, the evidence of their union glistening on her thighs. "I have a contraceptive implant—something to stop me having babies—and it's good for another two months—but a condom helps stops any nasty diseases that can infect you through body fluids."

He grasped her by the hips, ignoring her squeal of protest, and lifted her onto his lap. "Do not fear,

Rebekah. You are safe with me. Regardless of this *implant*, or our lack of con-doms, there is no risk of either pregnancy or disease."

"Is that a shifter thing?"

Shifter? He thought for a moment. *Ah, yes. Someone who could shift forms.*

"It is a werewolf thing, yes. Werewolves can only procreate with other werewolves. As for disease, our werewolf blood destroys anything detrimental to our health and survival."

"That's handy."

Ulrik slid a hand up from her hip to her breast, certain the literal translation did not apply, but determined his hands would not be idle. Not when he had this beautiful woman in his lap. He slipped his other hand down to her inner thigh, but she pushed it away.

"I'm all sticky."

The evidence of their union, of his scent on her, pleased him, but he would forgo that delight to have her again. "Then before I feast myself on those wondrous breasts of yours, I shall wash you off."

He grinned, lifted her off his lap and tossed her through the waterfall and into the pond. She shrieked, hitting the water with a splash and sinking below the surface. Ulrik jumped in after her, landing beside her as she came up spluttering.

"You bastard."

She laughed, wiping water from her eyes and smoothing her hair back off her face.

From the tone of her words, and the splash of water she shot in his direction, she was not questioning the legitimacy of his birth, rather cursing him. She splashed him again, laughing, and dove away as he reached for her. She was not fast enough, and he scooped her up in his arms and pulled her into his embrace. Her legs wrapped around his hips, and her arms around his neck.

His gaze dipped to the black material still partially covering her breasts. He reached up and fingered it. "This thing has to go."

"My bra?"

She laughed again and he rejoiced at the sound. His life of late had held little laughter.

"You're such a boob man." She reached behind her, fiddling with the clasp and the garment fell away and she slipped the shoulder straps off her arms. "Happy now?"

Oh, yes. He snatched the offending garment from her and tossed out into the pond. It sank below the surface.

"Shit. I need that."

He slid his hand across her wet and slippery breast and thumbed her nipple. "No, sweetness. All you need is me." He walked her to the edge of the pond and laid her down in the shallows, water lapping at her sides as he nestled between her thighs. With a throaty moan, he buried his face in her lush bosom.

Chapter Twenty-Eight

Renaud paced the chamber beyond the sacristy, plotting his next move. He doubted he could lure his informant to another meeting. What would they have to discuss? With d'Louncrais dead, the chevalier had achieved his objective. He grimaced. With Ulrik Voclain now free, he was no closer to his. Even if it were possible to convince the chevalier to meet, the man would be leery after the successful capture of Voclain.

He paused by the window. One of the brutish twins leaned casually against the outer wall of the bailey, watching him. Aubert? Edmond? Did it really matter which? The twin tilted his chin at him, and Renaud scowled. The twin tipped his head back and laughed. Edmond. Aubert had but one facial expression—a perpetual snarl.

Renaud turned away from the window. A black-robed figure stood in the doorway. Renaud glared at the angelic face of the young eveque. Everywhere he went—the keep, the chapel, the village—Faucher followed, monitoring his every move. The mere sight of the man irritated him. When would he leave Langeais? He had thought to order the eveque to other duties far from here, but for certain Faucher had instructions that repealed any command of his. Renaud needed a distraction. If he could use one problem to rid himself of another...

He repressed the smile threatening to form on his lips. "Come in, Eveque Faucher. Your timing is impeccable. I believe I have some information that may interest you, given your proclivity for the dark arts."

The impudent git looked wary. "Less than a sennight ago, you ordered me to put aside such foolishness. What has changed?"

Faucher was wise to be suspicious. Renaud had a lifetime of scheming and manipulating people to his advantage. Faucher had not. He was young and overconfident in his abilities. To Renaud, he was merely an inconvenience and, perhaps now, a useful one.

Renaud touched his hand to his brow, allowing it to shake a little. "Forgive an old man his bad temper. I do not react as well to change as I used to. Come and take a seat. Perhaps I was a little hasty. It seems new information has come to me, and you may be the best to handle it."

* * * *

With his worn clothing and his feet bare, Remi crept through the sacristy, down the corridor, leaned against the wall outside the archeveque's chamber and listened. No one paid attention to a child. Less so to one from the streets such as him—a beggar, a street urchin.

His last three years alone on the streets had taught him how to move about unseen and unheard. Snatching a loaf of bread here, a piece of fruit there, a coin or two from the chapel's collection plate, or a fat purse picked from the folds of a merchant's tunic. It was that or starve. A few clips around the ears from irate stall holders, screeches from cooks in fancy homes calling for retribution, had soon taught him how to be stealthy. How to not get caught. Until the day the big chevalier had grabbed hold of his hand as he had slipped it beneath the warrior's hauberk.

Which was how he now found himself skulking through the chapel, spying for the big warrior by listening to the conversation of the highest-ranking churchman who had ever graced Langeais. Archeveque Renaud.

"There is a chevalier," said the archeveque, his voice clear through the open doorway. "He will tell you he and I have been working together."

Remi peered around the door frame. Archeveque Renaud sat hunched in his chair. The hint of silver thread spun through the black cloth of his cassock glinting in the weak autumn sun, Renaud stared out of the window with his hands clutched in front of him as though at prayer. Across from Renaud, with his back to Remi, sat Eveque Faucher. Young for an eveque, he had the hands and the countenance of one born to wealth and privilege, smooth and soft. Nothing so lowly as the son of a merchant or farmer. Luc glanced down at his own hands, grubby fingernails chipped and knuckles scraped. If not for the big chevalier, he would never have found himself near such illustrious persons.

"He claimed to be a werewolf," the archeveque said.

Werewolf? Interesting. Rumor had it Eveque Faucher hunted witches and all forms of ungodly creatures. Not that Remi believed in such things. He had seen many a monster in his short life, all of the human variety. But he had long ago learned the nobility often had strange ideas, and if it earned him a few extra coins from the big chevalier, he cared not what they believed in.

"I thought only to help a troubled man," continued the archeveque. "One whose grip on reality appeared to be fading. Now..." A deep inhale, a large exhale and a downturn of his thin lips.

Remi almost snorted. The archeveque should take a part in the next church playlet. *Did the eveque truly believe this? Trust this?* He had seen the young eveque arrive, had heard the confrontation between the two men. The old archeveque had been unhappy at the younger man's arrival. Yet, now, Renaud wanted to work with Faucher?

And the villagers think I am crooked?

Eveque Faucher leaned forward in his seat. "You suspect this man is exactly what he claims to be? Of telling the truth?"

The archeveque's shoulders slumped, and his gaze shifted from the window. Luc ducked back into the shadows of the corridor. "I fear...yes. I... It troubles me to break the sanctity of the confessional, but..."

There was the sound of a quill scratching across paper, and Luc screwed up his nose. The big chevalier would have paid more handsomely for a name, but he would not get it today. Perhaps he could pick the pocket of this visiting eveque. Remi had never learned how to read. Perhaps the chevalier had.

At the scrape of a chair and footsteps moving toward the door, Remi slunk away, slipping past

Aumonier Touissant with his head bowed in prayer, out of the chapel and into the bailey. He pulled up short at the two men standing by the wall.

Two of them? Twins?

He smirked as he made his way to the two hulking men. Maybe he could make them pay double.

* * * *

Archeveque Renaud hid a smile as Faucher departed, the name of Renaud's informant on the parchment clasped in his hands. Faucher would be relentless in tracking down the informant, but the chevalier was a wily one. The task should keep Faucher preoccupied *and* solve his problem of the chevalier.

He swiveled to stare out of the window. The little beggar boy he had spied eavesdropping on his conversation had joined the Montagne twins by the bailey wall. Edmond dropped two coins into the boy's grubby outstretched hand, and the boy slipped away, trailing along behind the unsuspecting Faucher. Renaud rubbed his hands together. Things were working out rather well.

* * * *

"That will be all," said Lothair, dismissing the three young chevaliers, his hand hovering over his mouth and nostrils.

Perhaps he should have insisted they wash before they responded to his summons. He had, after all, given the young chevaliers cesspit duty for their role in Ulrik Voclain's escape. He strode to the window, banged open the shutters and breathed in sweet, fresh air. It could take weeks to get the stench from his chambers.

"Mon Seigneur Comte." The capitaine of his guard entered the room. His nose twitched and his eyes watered a little. "You wished to see me, Mon Seigneur?"

"Yes. How goes the hunt for Voclain?"

The capitaine paled and pursed his lips. "There has been no sight of him, Mon Seigneur. I had men tracking him from the postern gate. He headed north, but we lost his tracks when he entered a creek. We are combing the creek bank now, trying to pick up his trail, but the storm has hampered our progress. I suspect he is heading for Blois."

"Then you would suspect wrong."

For all his impulsiveness, Ulrik was one smart chevalier, and he was loyal to his alpha. He would not abandon Gaharet. If Lothair was right, he would turn up where he least expected him to and, most likely, right under his nose. It was what *he* would do. No, Ulrik had not headed for Blois.

"I have a new target for you, Capitaine. A woman."

Clement, and the young chevaliers who had manned the postern gate the night Ulrik had escaped, all concurred. The woman was unusual. She would stand out. Find her and they would find Ulrik. If he was anything like Gaharet, or Aimon—and Lothair suspected all werewolves would be—he would do almost anything to protect her. Renaud, it seemed, did have the occasional good idea.

"A woman, Mon Seigneur Comte?"

"A woman. With green streaks in her hair, skin markings on her arms, and silver in her ears and nose.

Concentrate to the west of the keep, as far west as the d'Louncrais estate. Find her and bring her to me."

The capitaine bowed. "I will see it done, Mon Seigneur Comte."

With a wave, Lothair dismissed him. He rubbed the back of his neck. Perhaps he should abandon his plan. It had flaws. For all their strengths, werewolves had weaknesses. Wolfsbane and silver they could avoid, and once he had dispatched Renaud, none would know of them but the werewolves themselves. But this weakness for women, this possessiveness and protectiveness they each displayed for *one* woman, that he could not bear. It was something he could use to control any werewolf he turned, but if he were to become one, if he were to follow his plan through to its ultimate objective, then his enemies could use it against him, too.

Chapter Twenty-Nine

With the cool waters lapping around their bodies, Bek lay snuggled against Ulrik at the edge of the pond. Lazily, he traced the tribal pattern of a tattoo that snaked around her arm in a band.

"That's my first tattoo."

"Mmm. Tat too. Tat too. A strange word. It does not begin to describe your skin markings." He traced the black ink as it twisted and swirled. "Do they serve a purpose? Is there some meaning you attribute to them?"

She chuckled. "That one? No. I didn't think too much about the design. I just wanted a tattoo like my brothers. This one"—she pointed to a large red and black goth butterfly that covered the top of her right arm—"I got as a symbol of my emancipation from my god-awful family."

Ulrik brushed his fingers over the butterfly's deep red wings, sending shivers through her, reminding her they were still naked, his thigh between hers and pressed against her core.

Lord, Bek. The man gave you four mind-blowing orgasms. Isn't that enough?

No. The sudden realization hit her, stealing her breath. It wasn't enough. Her fingers curled through his chest hair as her mind stuttered away from the implication.

Shit.

"And this one?"

His raspy voice snapped her from her thoughts. He slid his fingers over her collarbone to the string of flowers inked into her skin and her nipples pebbled all over again.

"Uhm. Sunflowers. My favorite flower. My gran had sunflowers in her garden." Bek pushed her worrying thoughts aside and focused on the conversation. "Gran didn't approve of the life my parents chose." Sweet, good, big-hearted Gran. "She tried so hard to get us kids to follow a different, more honest path. My brothers were a lost cause. Too hooked on that life. The quick return for no real effort. They wanted the good life and the good stuff, but like my parents, working for it the old-fashioned way wasn't part of their agenda. They'd rather steal it or con it from someone else who had worked for it. For me, my gran was the only one who understood me."

When her gran had died, and her sunflowers with her, Bek no longer had a reason to stay.

"And the phoenix on your shoulder?"

Bek looked away, staring out over the moonlit pond. She could make something up, give him some story to satisfy his curiosity, but that didn't seem right. Not after he'd opened up to her about his scars. Not after the intimacy they'd shared. Not now that she... *What? How far did she want to take this?*

"I was dating...in a relationship..." *God, how do I explain modern dating to a tenth-century knight?* "I was living with my lover."

A growl rumbled in his chest and he pulled her tighter. *Is he...jealous?* A thrill skipped through her.

"I'd been living with my lover for a few years. Spider—"

"His name was *Spider*? Is that a common name in the future?"

Bek snorted. "His real name was Dwight, but he belonged to a gang of...outlaws, so they gave him the nickname Spider." She followed the path of her finger drawing circles across Ulrik's chest, twirling it in his chest hair. Anything rather than look him in the eye. "He wasn't a good man. He often broke the law, and he did some terrible things that could have seen him locked up for a very long time."

"Your lover was an outlaw?"

Bek flushed and halted her exploration, curling her fingers into a fist. "It's not exactly something I'm proud of. I've made a lot of mistakes in my life, Spider being one of them."

She shifted against him, sending ripples out across the pond.

He stroked a hand across her shoulder and down her arm, rubbing gently. "We all make mistakes in life, Rebekah. Lord knows, I have made plenty in mine."

She couldn't bring herself to look at him. He had no idea of the mistakes she'd made or the things she'd done. She should've known better, chosen better. Spider was no different from the brothers, the family, she'd fled from.

How did I not see that from the beginning?

"Spider liked to use a forbidden substance," she continued. *More than use.* Selling drugs had brought in a good income for his club. She'd traded her con artist, thieving family for drug dealers. In hindsight, it'd been a stupid move. "Getting caught with it in your possession is a criminal offense."

For all that she'd moved on, turned her back on Spider, the crew and that lifestyle, her ex-lover's betrayal still burned fiercely.

"One day, to avoid getting caught with this substance, he slipped it into *my* bag and claimed I was the one who'd had the stuff all along. I paid the price for his wrongdoing." Her throat tightened and her chest burned. That he'd never paid for that, or any other crime he'd committed, and had willfully let her and others take the rap for him, made her blood boil. "They locked me up for eighteen months and he didn't even look back when he walked away."

Bek blinked away the unshed tears in her eyes, certain Ulrik would see them.

"Ah, baby." He cradled her face.

She leaned into his hand. "When I got out, I was determined that I would never go back to him or that life. That, like a phoenix rising from the ashes, I would get my life back on track and make something of myself. Every day I spent in that prison, I promised myself never again would I make that mistake. Never again would I put myself in the hands of a man who'd allow someone else to suffer for something he'd done."

Ulrik stiffened and pulled back, his hand dropping from her face. She reached for him, but he rolled away from her in a splash of water. Bek sat up, the night air suddenly cold against her skin now the warmth of his body was gone. She stared after him as he strode toward the bank and snatched up his shirt.

What the fuck?

"Hey!" She followed him, stomping through the water, coming to a halt right in front of him, naked and dripping. "What's your problem? No, gee Rebekah, I'm sorry you got stiffed by your lover? Or, man, that sucks? What an asshole?"

He picked up her clothes and thrust them into her arms, leaving her no choice but to take them.

She gaped at him. "Surely a little sympathy is in order? It's not like I was the one who did the wrong thing. I just have lousy taste in men."

He stilled, a muscle ticking in his jaw. With a snarl, he shoved his arms into the sleeves. "Get dressed, Rebekah. It is late in the eve and we must get back."

She swallowed, shoving down the hurt that had blossomed at his retreat. "Fine."

She turned her back on him and threw her dress over her head. It clung to her wet body, but she was too angry, too stung by his rejection to give a damn. Her jeans, she rolled up into a ball, contemplating pegging them at his head. *Why waste the effort?*

Instead, she concentrated on getting her boots on and laced up. "Now who's being the asshole?" she mumbled under her breath.

"Come."

He took her by the arm and led her back down the path to the cottage, the intimacy of a few moments ago shattered. For a second, she'd considered staying in the tenth century. Imagined it wouldn't be all that bad. Erin seemed happy. Clearly, *she* wasn't going to get an invitation anytime soon. Typical, now that she'd just begun to wish for one.

They reached the cottage and Ulrik wrested open the door and hurried her inside. Neither of them had said a word since they'd left the pond, but each of Bek's footsteps had fallen harder than the last. So what if she'd spent time in prison? Even if the coke had been hers, it would've been her first offense. Notwithstanding the shit her family had dragged her into when she'd been too young to know better. None of that had resulted in a record, thank God. She'd never claimed to be an angel.

Bek glared at his profile. First Spider, and now Ulrik. *I'm an idiot. My man barometer is truly broken.*

Ulrik released her arm. "Stay here, Rebekah." He turned on his heel. "I need... I will take first watch."

He stormed out of the cottage and slammed the door behind him.

Erin was on her feet. "What's going on?"

Bek threw her jeans onto the seat. "When I first met him, they had him chained to a wall in a dungeon. Now *he's* upset because he found out I've been in prison? For something I didn't even do?" She clasped her hands in her hair. "Argh! Infuriating man."

Erin came around the table and gave her a hug as Gaharet slipped out of the door after Ulrik. "Oh, honey. We'll sort this out."

Bek pulled away from Erin and plopped down onto a stool.

Erin patted her shoulder. "Here, let me get you something to eat. You've had a long day and..." She glanced at the door. "I'm sure Ulrik will cool off and you can talk it out with him." She set a bowl of stew in front of Bek and handed her a large chunk of bread. She inclined her head to the door. "What exactly happened out there between you two?"

Bek didn't think she could eat right now, but she nodded at Erin and gave her a half-hearted smile of thanks.

She tore at the bread, breaking it up. "I don't get it. Everything was fine. We had sex. *Good* sex, *great* sex. More than once. Hell, the man knows his way around a woman's body. We were lying in the shallows, post coital bliss and all that, and he asks me about my tattoos. He wanted to know what they meant and why I'd got them. I was telling him about the phoenix on my shoulder blade—"

"A phoenix? Doesn't he have a—"

"Yeah, yeah. I know." Bek waved her hands at Erin. "It's Ulrik's family crest. And before you say it's kismet, or fate or something equally ridiculous, it's not. It's just a coincidence."

An amused gleam entered Erin's eyes. "A coincidence? Maybe. What made you choose a phoenix, may I ask?"

Bek sighed. There was no point keeping her shady past a secret now.

"I ended up in prison for something my partner did. I paid for his crime. Now, I'm trying to get my life back on track and put my past behind me. I got the phoenix as a reminder of that, and the promise I made to myself to never again fall for a man like Spider. To never put myself in the hands of a man who'd allow another person to take the blame for something he'd done."

Erin's eyes widened. "Oh, dear."

"What? What did I say?"

Erin chewed on her bottom lip. "I don't know *exactly* what happened to Ulrik. Gaharet hasn't told me the full story, but Ulrik did something that angered Comte Lothair. To keep him safe from retribution, his parents sent him away to Bretaigne. While he was gone" — Erin cringed — "Lothair imprisoned his family and had them condemned to death as punishment for Ulrik's crime."

Bek stared at the other woman, the food forgotten. "Are you serious?"

Erin nodded.

"Oh, *bollocks*."

He'd worshipped her body more fervently than a teenager with his first ever *Playboy* magazine, and what had she done? Told him he'd never have a chance with her. Not intentionally, but still...

She stared down at her bowl. "I didn't know. He never told me. When I said that, I didn't mean *him*." She closed her eyes. *Fuck.* "It was all going so well, too." She made to rise. "I should talk to him."

Erin's hand on her shoulder halted her. "Let Gaharet talk to him. Give Ulrik some time. He'll figure it out once he's cooled down." Understanding glimmered in her eyes. "I was right. You really like him."

"I didn't want to," Bek mumbled, settling back into her seat. "He's everything I've avoided since...well... since I got sent to prison."

Erin chortled. "Don't I know that feeling."

Bek rolled her eyes. "Been to prison, have we?"

Highly doubtful. As if a woman who'd lived a far better life than she could hope to understand.

Erin, unperturbed by her sarcasm, stared her down. "No. But Gaharet wasn't my idea of a perfect match either. Wealthy, arrogant and used to getting his own way, I thought he was everything I loathed in a man. I busted my ass trying to find the reverse spell for the amulet and get back to the twenty-first century. Now look at me." She raised her hands in a shrug. "I'm a werewolf. I'm mated to the man I thought I loathed and" — she rubbed her hand across her belly — "I'm carrying his — our — baby."

She locked on Bek with a stare every bit as intense as her husband's. Bek had to give her credit. The woman was no pushover.

"Any regrets?"

Erin chewed on her bottom lip. "No. Not really."

Could Bek stay here? *If* she could patch things up with Ulrik. Give up her life in the twenty-first century, as Erin had. Not much of a sacrifice. Not like Erin.

"You were an archeologist. What's that, like four years of study? And a decent career. And you, what? Gave it all up for him? For love?"

Erin's expression softened, and a smile crept across her lips. "I did." Her smile slipped, and two little frown lines appeared between her eyebrows. "I won't lie to you and tell you it was easy. It wasn't. It took me almost dying to change my mind. Right until the moment I made my decision, my thinking was more aligned with your reaction than you might think. All I could think about was modern conveniences and clothes and what I had achieved. What I was still to achieve in my career. All the things I would have to give up, not what I would gain."

Erin slid onto the seat next to her. "Do I miss things? Hell, yes. I had some good friends and great colleagues. My mom and I...well...our relationship wasn't the best." She frowned. "The bra and knickers I'm wearing won't last forever. I'll miss those. And coffee — God — waking up without coffee every morning is the pits. But I have Gaharet. I can make new friends." Her hand slipped to her belly. "And I'll soon have my own family."

"Yeah, but...what about your career?"

"Look around you, Rebekah. I'm living in the very thing I spent years studying. I'm seeing things firsthand. Wait until you see Gaharet's keep, his library, and oh, my lord, his *armory*."

Bek arched an eyebrow. The woman looked as though she'd give herself an orgasm just thinking about a building, some old books and a bunch of swords. *Whatever floats her boat.*

"Hey." Erin held up her hands. "I'm not saying my decision would work for everyone, but it worked for me. How about you, Rebekah? What do you have to leave behind?"

Bek focused on a piece of bread, tearing pieces off it and dropping them into her stew. What *did* she have to leave behind? Nothing. Well, nothing she cared about losing. A crappy apartment, a criminal record, a dick of a parole officer and dead-end job at Charlie's, avoiding his grabby hands and disgusting propositions. Nothing worth shedding a tear over.

Like Erin, she'd miss coffee. And flushing toilets and hot showers. She looked down at her boobs. Lack of bras could be a problem. Unless she got some regular support, they'd lose their lift quicker than a helium balloon on a hot day. Not a good look. But wine appeared plentiful. *Happy days.* And if, eventually, she ended up living in some sort of castle or keep, chances were, she'd eat better here, too. No more two-minute noodles. Even living in this little cottage didn't look so bad. Erin was surviving here just fine.

Then there was Ulrik. She stared at the stubbornly closed door. But Ulrik had made no promises beyond sex, and now...

"You don't have to make your decision in a hurry, Rebekah. I don't know if Ulrik told you, but there's no reverse spell for the amulet."

"What?" The bread fell from her nerveless fingers.

Erin held up her hands. "Don't panic. There could be. We'd have to make one, that's all. To do that, we need a full coven of witches. That's thirteen witches." Erin gave her an apologetic smile. "Right now, we know of only one. Constance."

So she'd been right about Constance. And about Ulrik keeping information from her. What else had she missed? What else was he keeping from her? What crime had he really committed against the count?

"As you can imagine," said Erin, "we can't just put out a classified ad to find witches. With the current religious climate, they won't be shouting their presence from street corners or in the town square."

Well, shit.

"Gaharet will help you, and so will I. If that *is* what you really want." Her voice betrayed her doubt.

Erin had a point. Who threw over a hot medieval knight for a single life working in a sleazy bar? To what? Live in a flat with peeling linoleum, a druggie neighbor and a landlord that would terrify Attila the Hun? Nobody. That's who. And she'd be a right bloody idiot if she did.

From the moment she'd laid eyes on Ulrik and heard his raspy voice, her body had been all in, even if her mind had missed the all-points bulletin. It was getting it *now*. When perhaps it was too late.

Bek swallowed, the memory of her words ringing in her ears.

'Never again will I put myself in the hands of a man who'd allow someone else to suffer for something he'd done.'

Fuck. She cradled her head in her hands. She hadn't known. Given the way he'd lost his family, it was easy to see *now* why he'd reacted the way he did.

'Family is precious.'

He'd told her that. As she'd sat by the fire while he cooked the hares he'd caught. The man had saved her from the keep guard, fed her, brought her to the one person who could understand her predicament and perhaps help her and she'd hurt him. Rejected him. Stabbed him in his heart with his own dagger. She pushed away her bowl of food.

Bek, as usual, you've completely screwed things up.

Chapter Thirty

Ulrik stared out into the gloom of the forest, unseeing.

'Never again will I put myself in the hands of a man who would allow someone else to suffer for something he had done.'

Lying there with her in his arms, the cool water of the pond lapping at their bodies, her words had sliced through him with more steel than the blade of a battle-ax. One bad decision. Was he forever to pay for it? Had he not suffered enough? Lost enough?

The door of the cottage opened, and his alpha's familiar scent surrounded him.

Gaharet stopped beside him, matching his stance. "Your mate is upset."

Ulrik ground his teeth. "She is not my —"

Gaharet snorted. "Is she not? Rebekah is perfect for you."

He opened his mouth to refute it, but no words came out. Smart, stubborn and not afraid to speak her mind, she challenged him in every way. *Merde,* his cock was already thickening at the mere mention of her name. He tossed his head back and stared at the sky, picking out stars and tracing patterns between them. Anything to shift his focus from his need for the woman he had not so long ago been inside of.

"Your wolf knows."

As if to confirm Gaharet's words, his wolf prowled to the forefront of his mind.

A numbness seeped into his chest. "It does not matter, for she will not have a man like me."

Gaharet scoffed. "What do you mean, a man like you? A man who would sacrifice himself to save the life of his friend and his friend's mate? A man who would rescue a woman from a danger she had no understanding of, though the lesser risk would have been to leave her behind? Any woman should feel honored to have a man like you."

Warmth swelled in his chest at Gaharet's words, but it could not overwhelm the certainty, the fatalistic acceptance, settling in his gut. "That may be, but it does not erase my past."

"No," Gaharet agreed, "but it need not define your future. Have you told her what happened? That your intentions were good?"

Ulrik barked out a laugh. As if that would make things better. No. Not after the betrayal of her previous lover, Spider. That he had had a reason for doing what he had done, that he had not known of Lothair's reaction in his absence until it was too late, would not matter.

"My family died because of me. My sisters' lives cut short, never to know the joy of being mated. It is only right that pleasure be denied me as well."

"Ulrik…"

Ulrik turned away from Gaharet and stripped off his tunic and breeches. "Go back to your mate, Gaharet."

He shifted before Gaharet could argue. Though Gaharet's current circumstances could not have been worse, his alpha had found his mate. Erin now carried his unborn child. With Aimon mated, too, it was natural for Gaharet to wish that for all his pack. Fate, it seemed, had other plans for him. Right now, staying in that cottage, watching what could not be, was beyond his forbearance. With one last glance at the door, he loped off into the forest.

* * * *

Bek stood expectantly as the cottage door opened, but only Gaharet entered. "Where's Ulrik?"

Gaharet shook his head. She headed for the door, but Gaharet blocked her way.

"Stay here, Rebekah. Ulrik has gone for a run, and it is not safe for you out there alone."

She stared up at him, jutting out her chin. "I need to talk to him. Explain…"

She rubbed her hand against her chest. It hurt that she'd hurt him.

"Sit."

The command in his voice rolled over her, a wave of physical force threatening to knock her down. Her knees shaking, she held her ground. "But…"

"He will return soon."

From the set of his jaw, she figured he'd stand there, guarding the door all damn night if he had to. She thrust her shoulders back and locked her knees. He wasn't *her* alpha. If he thought —

"Oh dear," Erin moaned. "I think I'm going to be sick."

She jumped up from her seat, grabbed a bucket from beside the fire and clutched it to her chest. With her hair shrouding her face, she leaned over it and retched violently. Gaharet was by her side in an instant.

Bek glanced at the door. Could she leave them when Erin was clearly unwell?

Erin groaned and leaned over the bucket again. "Someone should have warned me morning sickness doesn't just happen in the morning."

Gaharet hovered over Erin. "Can I get you anything?" His hands flexed at his side, as if he held himself back from trying to grasp hold of Erin's illness and rip it from her. "Tell me what will help you?"

The commanding, in control alpha of moments ago was gone, reduced to an anxious mate.

"A cool, damp cloth would be good," came the mumbled reply, muffled by the bucket and Erin's hair.

Gaharet rushed to grab a cloth, soaking it in a bowl of cool water. As he turned his back to them, Erin lifted her head and winked.

"*Go*," she mouthed and made a shooing motion with her hand.

She dropped her head and gave another pitiful moan as Gaharet brought her the cloth.

Erin pressed the damp cloth to her forehead. "Thanks, honey. You're so sweet."

Bek covered her mouth with her hand, hiding her smile. Yeah, he was sweet. And gullible. Especially when it came to his mate. It worked for her, though. With Gaharet's back turned, his attention on Erin, Bek scooped up her jeans and quietly slipped out of the cottage and into the night. She had to find Ulrik. She had to make this right.

A few steps into the forest, Bek paused. No movement from the cottage. No Gaharet barreling out the door to drag her back. Good. She hurriedly threw on her jeans. How the women of this century gallivanted around the forests all day in dresses and no knickers was beyond her. Not Bek. She'd take all the protection she could get.

Now, where would Ulrik have gone? He'd said he'd take the first watch. A patrol? He'd do a sweep around the cottage first, wouldn't he? She had to hurry. Despite Erin's theatrics, Gaharet would soon notice her gone and come after her. Bek wasn't going back to the cottage to wait like a good little female. No way, no how. She'd go back once she'd found Ulrik. Once she'd got it into his thick head that she hadn't meant him.

She did a loop around the cottage, keeping within the cover of the forest. Not that it'd hide her from Gaharet for long, but it'd buy her time. No Ulrik. She glanced about the clearing. Would he scope out the pond? A reasonable presumption. The path to the pond beckoned, disappearing beneath the darkened canopy of leaves and limbs.

Seriously, Bek. You're scared of the dark and a few trees?

She'd dealt with some of the worst people in London. Served them beer. She'd lived the life of a biker's girlfriend. The only wolf out here was Ulrik. Bek plunged into the forest. Filtered moonlight shining the way, she strode down the path with purpose. She wasn't going to let a forest at night deter her.

She emerged from the trees to stand on the edge of the pond, the water a silvery sheen broken only by the gentle splash of the waterfall. A rush of images — her on her knees before Ulrik, Ulrik behind her pounding into her, Ulrik devouring her breasts, — brought a flush of heat to her body. But no Ulrik.

With her hands on her hips, she surveyed her surroundings. If he'd gone for a random run in the forest, she'd have no hope of finding him. She had to believe he'd stay close. Bek eyed the opposite bank. A faint path disappeared away from the pond. Only this afternoon, she and Ulrik had emerged from there to be confronted by a red and a white wolf — Kathryn and Aimon — standing on the spot she stood now. On patrol, Ulrik would likely traverse the pond and follow that path for a way, ensuring no one else was finding their way toward them. Wouldn't he?

She glanced back over her shoulder, down the path she'd come. *What if I get lost?*

She snorted. The pond wasn't that big. She could keep it in her sight and follow it around, no problem. And if she still didn't find him? She huffed out a breath, the air condensing into a smoky vapor. Then she'd admit defeat and head back to the cottage. She'd sit by the damn door and wait for him if she had to. Gaharet would be pissed at her for leaving. He could just deal. Her lips set in a stubborn line, Bek set off around the pond.

* * * *

Ulrik paused, the cool earth damp beneath his paws and the breeze ruffling his fur. He had meant only to circle the hut and clear his thoughts, but his roiling emotions were too much, and too big to contain. With a glare at the flickering light and muted voices streaming out from beneath the door, he stretched himself out into a run. His normal pursuits when such emotions bested him — indulging in his two favorite pastimes — were not an option. A run through the forest, scouting out the area as he went, was his only choice to ease his mind.

He avoided the pond. Memories of Rebekah's sassy mouth wrapped around his cock taunted him as he ran. *L'enfer*, he had never had a woman leave him as satiated and yet have him in such turmoil as Rebekah. Never had he wanted to lie basking in the afterglow of their lovemaking and hold a woman close and talk, discovering every little detail about her. Never before had he thought of any intimate relations he had had with a woman as *lovemaking*. It had always been sex — healthy, simple, lustful fucking.

Bold and demanding in ways he had never seen in a woman, Rebekah had matched him passion for passion, as he had known she would, and he wanted more. *Merde*, he wanted everything she could give. Listening to her talk — hearing her tell of this man, this *lover* who had betrayed her, allowed her to suffer the punishment for *his* crime — Ulrik had wanted to wrap her in his arms and vow to her she would never face such a thing again. Make promises to her that he would protect her from the pain and anguish that had shimmered in her eyes.

He shook his big, furry head. She would never accept such things from a man like him. She had made that clearer than the stars on a moonless night. Ulrik huffed, his warm breath fogging in the cool night air. He may not have paid for his actions as his family had, but they were not without consequences. They were his penance, no less than he deserved, and he would bear them as stoically as he could. Already he had been blessed with forgiveness from Gaharet, something only days ago he had believed nigh on impossible. He should content himself with that.

His ears pricked at a sound in the distance. *Voices.* He halted, raised his nose to the air and sniffed. Men. And horses, too. He sniffed again and caught the unmistakable scent of steel, the stench of unwashed bodies and the lingering foul miasma of Langeais Keep. He bared his teeth. Keep guards. On the d'Louncrais estate. Their presence would be no accident.

Ulrik spun on his heel and raced back to the cottage. He charged into the clearing, shifted and burst into the cottage with naught a care for his nakedness.

"We need to move. Now. The keep guards are here."

Gaharet exploded to his feet and Erin sprung up from her prone position on the cot, the cloth on her forehead dropping into her lap.

Ulrik took in the room. "Where is Rebekah?"

Gaharet's eyes widened. "*Merde.*"

Ulrik snarled, his wolf pushing forth and his hackles rising. "How long has she been gone?"

Erin clasped her hand over her mouth. "Oh, shit. This is my fault. I thought she'd be fine. Ulrik was out there, and I didn't expect the keep guards to turn up. She hasn't been gone long, I swear."

Gaharet turned to his mate, his expression stormy. "Erin?"

Erin tucked her hands beneath her arms, her expression contrite in the face of her mate's thunderous expression. "I'm not really sick, okay? I distracted you so she could leave." She turned to Ulrik, her eyes full of concern. "She just wanted to find you and talk to you." Her gaze flicked between them. "I'm sorry. I really am. I didn't think there'd be any harm. I was just trying to help her patch things up with Ulrik. She can't have gone far."

Gaharet's nostrils flared, and his lips thinned. "We will talk about this later, Erin. Ulrik, go find her. We will wait for you."

Ulrik gritted his teeth and held his temper. His alpha's mate was pregnant. They should not linger here. Not with the keep guard close by. It was too great a risk. Rebekah was wily and stubborn. She may have gotten further than any of them would expect.

"No. I will find her. Gaharet, take your mate and find somewhere safe."

Gaharet hesitated, then nodded. "We will go to my keep. With Aimon and Kathryn there, we will have the benefit of greater numbers."

Ulrik frowned. *Aimon and Kathryn? At the d'Louncrais keep?* When, how had that happened?

"Yes. Aimon and Kathryn now reside at the d'Louncrais keep. Much has changed, my friend, since Renaud entrapped you." Gaharet slid his hauberk over his head. "I will explain it all once we are all safe. Go. Find Rebekah. Bring her to my keep." He buckled his sword to his side, and Erin helped him lace his leather vambraces to his arms. "We will await you there and make plans for our next move. If Lothair has sent the guard here, anywhere on my estate will not be safe for long."

Gaharet wrapped Erin in a cloak, securing it at her throat. "Stay safe, Ulrik."

Ulrik swept out of the door and shifted. Nose to the ground, he picked up Rebekah's scent. It called him in two directions. One skirting the clearing inside the tree line. The other heading for the pond. The path to the pond beckoned him. He did a quick loop around the hut, just to be certain, then set off at a run. The guards were coming from the opposite direction. If luck was with him, he would find her quickly and they would be long gone before the keep guard discovered the cottage or Rebekah.

As he reached the pond, it took him only a moment to realize luck was not with him, and neither was Rebekah. With ever-increasing frustration and dread, he followed her scent to where she had paced on the bank. He tracked where she had rounded the pond and taken the path deeper into the forest, before backtracking and climbing the rocky ledge to stand above the waterfall. She had changed direction again, crossing the creek and attempting to skirt the pond. He paused where a fallen tree had diverted her from her path. There she had taken a wrong turn. Ulrik's blood froze. Toward the keep guard.

Merde.

He raced along the game trail, his claws digging into the soft earth and his heart thudding in his chest. Please God, let him find her first.

A woman's scream split the night. Ulrik put on a burst of speed. Rebekah's curses, loud violent words, spewed into the still air. A soft thud and a man's muffled groan had Ulrik grinning. She was fighting them.

That is my girl. Hold on, Rebekah. I am coming.

A loud slap, a hand meeting flesh, and a cry from Rebekah had a snarl ripping from his lips. They had his Rebekah. They were hurting her. He gnashed his teeth. They would pay for laying a hand on her. He would rend them, limb from limb. Tear out their throats.

He made no effort to conceal his approach now, crashing through the forest. A horse whinnied.

"Give her to me." A guttural voice, a scuffle, and Rebekah's denials guided him toward them. "Keep still, woman."

"Ulrik!"

The fear in that one word screeched into the night, squeezed his heart and nearly took his legs out from under him. *Hold on, baby.* He glimpsed a horse's rump through the trees. *I am here. I am coming.*

The terrified whinnies of the horses echoed through the forest. They sensed his presence, a predator closing in on them. A guard yelled, and hoof beats pounded away from him.

No!

He had lost his family to Lothair. He could not lose Rebekah, too. Ulrik dug deep, calling on every bit of speed his wolf could give him, but with the terror of the horses giving the keep guards speed in their escape and his body tiring, he fell behind. Ulrik gritted his teeth and plowed on, pushing his body to its limits, but the gap between him and the horses widened until all he had were the sounds of their retreat.

Ulrik slowed to a stop and howled his anguish to the moon. He shifted, slumping to his knees, his lungs heaving and his head in his hands as his wolf continued to howl in his head. His chest burned as though he had ripped out his own heart. He could not lose his *petite cracheuse de feu.* He did not think he could survive it. Not Rebekah. Not his... He stared at the forest floor.

Mon Dieu. Gaharet is right. She is my mate.

He staggered to his feet, staring after them as the thudding of hooves and the jingle of the horses' bridles faded. They would take her to Langeais Keep. He could follow them, slip in through the postern gate and into the storeroom through the secret tunnel. And then what? Face Lothair's army by himself? He had lived a decade regretting the impetuousness of his youth. He was no longer a pup. Racing off after them alone would not serve Rebekah.

He straightened, his jaw set. Though it pained him to do so, he turned his back on the distant sounds of the keep guard's retreat, shifted once more and headed back toward the d'Louncrais estate. He would seek the aid of Gaharet and Aimon. They would come up with a plan that would have a better chance of success. Ulrik would not allow another person to suffer because of him. Lothair had targeted Rebekah, like he had targeted his family. She might not want to be his mate, but his wolf did not care. She was his to protect, and he would save her from Lothair's clutches. No matter what it cost him.

Chapter Thirty-One

Crushed in the burly arms of her captor, the pounding of hooves beneath her reverberating along her spine and the forest flashing by, Bek struggled to free herself. The way they'd scrutinized her hair, her piercings, pulled up her sleeves to reveal her tattoos — it all pointed to the keep guard. They'd come for Ulrik and they'd found her. Now they were taking her back. Back to the keep, to the count and, most likely, to that dungeon. The last place she wanted to go.

Her captor cursed at her in French, his hold around her ribs tightening, making it hard for her to breathe. The sour stench of his body odor mingled with the metallic scent of steel stung her nostrils and made her eyes water. If he squeezed any harder, he'd cut off her air and she'd pass out.

Be smart, Bek. Think.

She stopped struggling and willed herself to relax against him. If she could remain calm and bide her time, an opportunity to escape might present itself.

The tight band of his arm around her eased a little and she sucked in deep lungfuls of air. Behind them, the sounds of pursuit faded, her captor's laugh cut off by the mournful howl of a wolf. *Ulrik?* Did she imagine the anguish in the long notes as the howl trailed away? Or had the wolf pursuing them been Gaharet? She hadn't seen it, only heard its snarls, the crashing through the forest undergrowth and the panicked squealing of the horses as it closed in on them.

She'd tried to fight, to free herself and run toward it, but her captor had been too strong. Her cheek burned from his brutal backhanded slap, and her arm throbbed from where she'd tried to elbow him in the ribs, only to be met with the steel links of his armor. Now the wolf had fallen behind. Or given up?

Gaharet had a pregnant wife to think of. Would he risk his own life to save her? And Ulrik... Would he come after her, mount a rescue attempt? Bek swallowed the feelings that threatened to overwhelm her. She couldn't blame him if he didn't. She'd given him a damn good reason to walk away. The risk of him returning to the keep would have to outweigh any responsibility he might feel toward her. Especially after what she'd said. A few rounds of awesome sex didn't a connection make. She couldn't pin her hopes on something that might not happen.

You're on your own now, Bek.

Déjà vu slapped her in the face. Again she was being marched toward prison, on a horse this time, instead of in the back of a police van. Again, her reason for apprehension was a man. But as she'd come to realize during time in prison, the blame did not solely rest with them. Nobody had forced her to be a biker Vice President's old lady. To throw her lot in with a bunch of criminals. Just as no one had forced her to leave the cottage to find Ulrik. That was all on her. Gaharet and Ulrik had both insisted she stay. That the danger was too great to risk her going out alone. She'd ignored them.

Will I ever learn? Am I doomed to make poor decisions for the rest of my life? Which could be rather short, if Erin's talk of Count Lothair was anything to go by. Bek needed a plan.

Her captor reined in the horse, and they settled into a jolting trot, the pommel of the saddle jarring against her ass. She was going to have more than a bruised face and elbow by the time they reached the keep. She supposed she should be thankful they'd not slung her face down over the saddle. The horse slowed further, to a walk. Thank the lord for small mercies. It still wasn't the most comfortable thing, but it was better.

The guard said something, and the other guy looked over his shoulder and laughed. Ulrik had been helping her with her French, but the guard spoke too fast for her to make out more than the odd word. As the two men bantered, Bek took stock of her situation. Would the horse tire carrying two people? Would they stop to rest? Maybe. It was a big horse, a warhorse, bred for carrying armored men with weapons and shields. But if they *did* stop, what chance would she have of escaping them? Both men were armed, armored and bigger than her. She'd no hope of overpowering even one of them. The dark forest offered no help. If she did manage to slip away, they'd be on her in a flash. Two men on horseback versus a woman on foot could only end one way.

She could wait until they rode through a village—*if* they rode through a village—and beg the villagers to help her. That hadn't worked for her before, and if these men were keep guard, villagers wouldn't dare come to her aid. She shifted, angling for a better look at their surroundings and a more comfortable position, and something dug into her hip. Something in her pocket. *The amulet?* She traced the round object and a trickle of hope blossomed. She peeked up at her captor. Though his arm still caged her against him, his conversation with his fellow guard held all his attention. The other guard had his back to them, occasionally looking over his shoulder at them to comment or to laugh.

In the filtered moonlight beneath the canopy of the forest, she could barely make out their features. Good. Their vision was no better than hers. If she could get her hands on the amulet, if she could remember the spell and if she could cut herself somehow, she could get back to Ulrik. There were a lot of ifs, but what other option did she have?

Careful to make her movements slow and subtle, Bek inched the hem of her dress higher. Already bunched up around her knees, she needed only to raise it another foot to reach into her pocket. Watching the guard in front of them, she moved her hand only when he had his back to them.

The conversation paused and Bek stilled, her breath catching in her throat. Then the other guard chuckled, and the talk resumed. She eased out her breath and continued to edge up her dress until she could slip her hand in her pocket. Her fingers closed around the amulet. *Yes.* Careful not to make any sudden moves, she drew it out. Now to make herself bleed.

The guard had his sword sheathed. No chance of getting hold of that without him noticing. The knife strapped to his calf was out of her reach, and in the dim light, nothing sharp on the saddle caught her eye. She could bite her tongue, but she'd have to bite it damn hard to make it bleed. There had to be something.

A piercing?

She had one in her nose, and four in each ear. Three through the lobe and one through the cartilage at the top. She winced at the thought of ripping one out. It would hurt like a bitch, but it *would* make her bleed. She reached up, pretending to scratch her ear, and finding the silver loop in the first hole. Perfect. She could hook her finger in it and pull.

The men talked on around her. The horse kept its plodding pace. Bek slipped her pinky finger through the small loop, gritted her teeth and pulled.

Ah, fuck!

It took everything she had not to make a sound, to not cradle her ear in her palm. She breathed in deep breaths, struggling to hold her body still. It *burned*. Worse than when she'd had it pierced, but the sudden wetness made it worth it. Had the guards noticed? She glanced up. He was watching her. Bek gripped her fist tight around the amulet and dropped her hand from her ear.

The other guard edged his horse closer. Bek tried her best not to react, letting her gaze wander away, but she kept them in the periphery of her vision. The horses walked on and she waited, not daring to make another move. Not until their attention shifted away from her.

Come on, come on.

Her captor relaxed, and the guards' banter resumed. *Finally.* Slow and steady, she raised her hand and gingerly touched her ear. Her fingers slick with her blood, she rubbed the amulet, smearing her blood into the grooves of the script.

God, I hope this works.

In her head, she recited the words of the spell and waited.

Nothing. No sudden darkness. No sensation of falling. She remained confined in a keep guard's arms on the back of a horse, riding inexorably away from Ulrik, Gaharet and Erin.

Did I get the words wrong? She didn't think so.

Her mind raced back to that night in her flat — the taste of cheap red wine on her tongue, the pounding beat of Black Sabbath seeping through the thin walls. Maybe she needed to say the words out loud.

Bollocks.

The guards were already wary of her. She'd have to whisper.

Bek clenched her fist around the amulet and drew in a shaky breath. "*Vanish from all human sight, those who favor moonlit —* "

The guard's arm tightened around her ribs.

" *— night. To bloodstone shall they return —* "

He reined the horse in. A shaft of moonlight settled on them, like the beam of a spaceship spotlighting them, her bloodied hand clenched around the amulet clearly visible. The other guard edged in, his horse bumping against her knees, and he grabbed her wrist. Bek struggled. He unclenched her fingers and snatched the amulet from her grasp.

"No!"

Bek reached for it as he held it up, the gold glinting in the pale light. Should she keep reciting? He held the amulet in one hand and her wrist in the other. Would it, *could* it, transport the three of them, horses and all, to Ulrik? It was worth a shot.

" *— so no man —* "

The guard laughed. He held it up, grinning and released his grip on her wrist.

Bek stopped reciting. *Fuck.*

She slumped against the guard and raised her fingers to her throbbing earlobe. She'd been so close. With the amulet in the guard's possession, she had no other option than to wait and hope another opportunity presented itself. *Before* they locked her in that dungeon. Once there, on her own, the chances of her escaping were almost nonexistent.

Chapter Thirty-Two

Ulrik burst into the d'Louncrais keep to be met by a waiting Gascon.

"Monsieur Ulrik, some clothes." The thin, balding servant pressed a tunic and breeches into his arms. "Mes Dames Kathryn and Erin are not yet as comfortable with your kind's nakedness as what you are."

Ulrik chaffed at the delay, but he slipped on the clothes before hurrying barefooted down the corridor toward the voices in the hall. Flames flickered in the center pit, and shadows danced across the large wall hangings, giving the impression the embroidered figures were in motion, riding across the fabric. Ulrik spared them only a glance, striding across the large room toward Gaharet, Erin, Kathryn, Aimon and Kathryn's father, Farren, who were seated at the large oak table.

Anne stood by them, one hand on her ample hip, the other wagging a finger at Gaharet. "Now, do not speak to your mate like that, lad." Anne's disapproving voice echoed about the hall. "Especially with her in the condition she is, or I will box your ears."

"I'm pregnant, Anne, not dying." Erin leaned her elbows on the table. "Gaharet has every right to be angry. This is my fault. I *deliberately* deceived him so Rebekah could go after Ulrik."

"Be that as it may, I will not have him talking to you like that."

Erin patted the old cook's arm. "It's all right, Anne. I can take care of myself."

Ulrik did not have time to discuss who was to blame. Not now. Not with his mate soon to be in the hands of the man who had killed his family.

"Ulrik!" Her face beaming, Anne waddled over, intercepting him and enfolding him in a hug. "It is good to see you again, young man. And to see you none the worse for your stay in Lothair's keep."

Ulrik met Gaharet's questioning look over her head. His alpha peered past him.

Ulrik shook his head. "They got to her first, Gaharet. They have taken her to Langeais." He released Anne and strode over, slapping his palms on the table. "We need to get her back. *I* need to get her back. I cannot, I will not, leave her in Lothair's clutches. Lothair cannot win. Not this time. He has taken too much…"

He hung his head and closed his eyes, collecting himself. He did not wish to face off against his alpha. Not again, but…

He raised his head and met Gaharet's gaze. "I cannot do this on my own. I need your help. Please." He rubbed his hand against his chest. "You were right, Gaharet. She is my mate."

Gaharet stood, placing a steadying hand on his shoulder. "I know, and I have felt the terror you now feel, wondering if you are going to lose her. I will not let that happen, Ulrik. That I promise you. We will find a way to get her back. You did the right thing by coming to us for help."

Some of the tension eased from Ulrik's body. "Thank you."

Gaharet turned to Gascon. "Have Henri saddle the horses for us. Anne, can you organize armor and boots for Ulrik, please?" He looked to Aimon. "I will not ask you to leave your mate, but we could use your help."

"Gaharet, no," Ulrik protested. "It is no wiser for the pack to confront Lothair in these circumstances than it was when he killed my family." In his anger and his grief, he had not understood that then, but he did now. "Lend me some of your men. That is all I ask."

Gaharet's dark stare bored into him, his jaw set, and the aura of command settled over his alpha like a shroud. "I am coming with you, Ulrik. Confronting Lothair may not be necessary."

Ulrik shook his head. "You cannot leave your pregnant mate, Gaharet. Nor can I ask Aimon to leave Kathryn unprotected. It is not safe."

"Erin will not be unprotected, and Lothair does not know she is here."

"But they found Rebekah. Lothair will suspect you and Erin were close by. With me."

Gaharet shrugged. "Perhaps, but would he assume I have come here, or that I have fled?"

Aimon skirted the table to join them. "I will come, too." Aimon smiled at his mate. "Kathryn is more than capable of protecting herself."

Kathryn straightened in her seat. The young she-wolf's eyes almost glowed at her mate's praise.

"Farren is here." Aimon nodded at Kathryn's father. "And there is always the training room."

The training room, able to lock from the inside, would give the women added protection. That would give Gaharet and Aimon time so they could return to the women's aid if need be, but still…

"I shall double the gate guards and have men patrolling the walls," said Farren.

Gascon shared a look with Anne. "Anne and I will alert the villagers. They will waylay any keep guards that should come that way and give us warning."

Ulrik stared at his pack mates, a tightness squeezing in his chest. After all he had done, the way he had behaved, they would come to his aid? Would risk all *they* held dear?

"Thank you." He clasped his hand over his heart. "This means…"

Gaharet's expression softened. "We are pack, Ulrik. We are friends. No. More than friends. We are brothers. We will not let you face this alone. Let us help you."

For so long he had sat on the periphery of the pack — shunned, a pariah. Now, both Gaharet and Aimon were willing to risk their lives, and the lives of their mates, to help him. The enormity of it choked him.

"I would be honored if you would accompany me."

Gaharet gripped his shoulder. "Welcome back, Ulrik." He turned to Farren. "Lower the portcullis after we leave. Gascon, send a man to the herbalist in the woods. Due east of Langeais Keep, no more than five leagues. The woman's name is Constance. Tell her I sent you. Tell her we will need the same brew she gave to Erin during her turning."

Ulrik raked his hands through his hair, a bitter taste souring the back of his throat. "Rebekah does not wish—"

"She is your mate, Ulrik. Can you tell me you would let her walk away?" There was no judgment in Gaharet's eyes, only the knowledge of a lived experience. "Let us have the brew now, so we are prepared for any eventuality." He strode toward the door. "Come, Ulrik. It is a half-day ride to Langeais Keep. Let us go rescue your mate and bring her home."

Chapter Thirty-Three

The early rays of dawn streaked across the sky as Bek and her captors cantered into a village. Little mud huts gave way to more substantial buildings the closer they came to a tower atop a hill. The Keep. Home to the notorious Count Lothair. Bek had only seen it once. Beneath a red moon. Tainted by her shock at its existence and colored by her experience within its walls, it had appeared monstrous and forbidding. Here, now, it loomed over the village, a menacing presence no less sinister in the cold half-light of the early morning.

Bek shivered, her weary body bruised and her earlobe throbbing dully. She'd forced herself to stay awake, seeking opportunities to escape. Nothing had presented itself. She was right back where she'd started this... *Adventure? Nightmare?* This time, she had no Ulrik to help her escape.

How she'd feared him in those initial moments. When he'd stalked her in the pitch-black dungeon.

How she'd railed at him when he'd thrown her over his shoulder, unwilling to go wherever he'd planned to take her. Now, she'd give her right arm to see his face, to have him come riding up behind them, rescuing her like some fairytale knight in his shining armor.

She choked on a laugh. Ulrik was more rogue than gallant knight. His armor more scarred with use than polished. She liked him like that. Better a battle-experienced warrior than some fancy show-pony. Fairytale knight be damned. Bek wanted Ulrik. But he wasn't here, and chances were, he wasn't coming.

You can do this, Bek. You survived Bronzefield Prison. You can survive this.

But Bronzefield had had rules, regular mealtimes and standards that the staff were legally bound to. Sure, it had been no picnic, and things had gone on that weren't supposed to, but it was a far cry from that hole in the ground. That dark dungeon she was most likely destined for. The keep had no oversight committee, no OHS, no medical and no parole board. Just a count and his whims.

The gate swung open as they approached, and guards rushed over and pulled her from the horse with their rough hands. Despite the early hour, the keep was bustling with activity. Stable hands scurried by and guards strode about with purpose. Some stopped to look at her, their curious stares unnerving. Others ignored her, hurrying about their business.

They dragged her up the hill to the stone fortress, her legs heavy and refusing to cooperate. Her ears rang, her vision blurred and memories assaulted her. The hard stares of the prison officers, the sense of dread as she faced the unknown, the open curiosity, and in some cases, malice that emanated from the other detainees. It all came flooding back. The numbness that had settled over her as they'd fingerprinted her and taken her mugshot threatened to descend. She shook her head and fought it. The guards had not brought her here to serve out a predetermined amount of time. She had to keep her wits about her. She had to get herself out of this. Somehow.

They halted in front of another guard. Words were exchanged, few of which she understood. The new guard ran his fingers through her hair, tilted her chin and turned her face from side to side, as her captors had done. He pushed up her sleeve to reveal her tattoos. He exchanged more words with her guards, then her captors led her into the tower.

She barely had time to take in the stone walls of the dimly lit corridors as they whisked her past servants, along corridors and down several sets of stairs to the bowels of the keep. They stopped in a room she had been in before. A room with a table, a few chairs and the familiar grate covering the hole in the floor.

God, I hate it when I'm right.

More guards joined them and as they settled about the table, someone produced a pair of dice, another a wineskin, and yet another threw a few coins onto the table. One of her captors dipped beneath his armor and held up an item. The amulet glinted gold in the candlelight. He said something, his grin wide and boastful, and tossed it on the table amongst the silver coins. Bek lunged for it, only to be dragged back against her captor and hauled over to the grate.

With a screech of hinges, a guard flung the grate open and shoved her into the hole. It clanged shut, and a key turned in a lock. What little light penetrated from the room above revealed the narrow stairs chiseled out of the rock, disappearing into the dark. This time, she did not have her phone to light up the room. This time, there was no Ulrik to save her.

Bek slumped against the wall. The guard's laughter filtered down to her, and she eyed the steps as she inched away from the grate. She paused. Had they moved the dead guard? Or had they left him there to rot? She gagged. *Nope. Not going down there if I don't have to.*

She settled herself on the steps at the very edge of the darkness and leaned her head against the rough stone wall. Once again, she was on her own. Dependent on no one and free to make her own decisions. Something she'd been *so* determined about and fiercely protective of from the moment she'd stepped out of Bronzefield. Except now, instead of feeling empowered, a hollow emptiness settled behind her sternum and gripped her tight.

She stared down the darkened stairs. Her future had never seemed so bleak.

* * * *

Bek started from her restless doze at the sudden lack of raucous laughter and the scraping of chairs. She eased herself closer to the grate, peering between its bars at the dusty boots surrounding the table. The game of dice had stopped. *Why?* A voice, deep and authoritative, cut through the silence and a pair of boots scurried toward her. Bek retreated down the steps and into the pitch-black room, her hands following the rough stone to the farthermost wall. All she could smell was damp and mold. Fingers crossed, that meant she wasn't sharing this space with a corpse. Her pulse racing, she pressed herself into the corner.

Hinges screeched, then soft footfalls descended the stairs, the flickering light of a candle preceding whomever had come to see her. The captain of the guard? The count? As the cheers, the belching, the clatter of dice and the clink of coins had not resumed, she doubted it was someone as mundane as a servant bringing her food and water.

She had a moment to appreciate the confirmation there was no decaying body in the dungeon with her, before polished black boots appeared, followed by muscular calves in fitted black trousers. Her gaze traveled up a knee-length black tunic shot through with gold thread to a jeweled belt cinched across lean hips holding in place a sword. Further still to the embroidered gold dragon spewing fire that flowed across broad shoulders and up around the collar. Bek tensed. *The count it is.*

Would he be as bad as Erin had made him out to be? Could she eke out some measure of empathy for a woman stranded out of her time? Her hopes died with one look at his face. If this man had ever had a benevolent bone in his body, it was long gone. Handsome in a sharp-edged kind of way, there was a hardness to his face, to the thin line of his lips, the set of his jaw, and the dark gaze that raked over her, stripping her bare and flaying her soul.

She swallowed—her mouth drier than the Sahara Desert in the middle of a drought. He prowled toward her with the grace and menace of a predator. If Erin hadn't told her otherwise, Bek would have taken him for a shifter, a werewolf. An alpha at that. Power, confidence and menace rolled off him in waves. He was the type of man she wouldn't have wanted to meet in a twenty-first century dark alley, let alone in a dark dungeon. *His* dark dungeon. He made Spider look like a toothless tiger. Even Mrs. Wu would cower before this man.

He stopped in front of her, holding the candle aloft, his eyes taking in every inch of her. There was no sexual heat to his gaze, no leer advertising lecherous intent, but Bek shivered all the same. He reached out. Bek flinched, then locked her knees to prevent herself from shrinking away. She'd not let him see her fear.

He ran his hand through her hair before grasping her jaw and turning her head from left to right, his eyes narrowing at the blood on her ear. She searched his expression for a hint of compassion, regret, anything that might suggest her injury concerned him. Nothing. Not even a flicker. *Soulless bastard.*

Though her insides quivered, she raised her chin. A foolishly defiant act, perhaps, but she would not cower before him.

"*Mon, mon, tu es courageuse. Ou stupide.*"

Bek snarled. Had he called her stupid?

He smirked. "*Fougueuse.*"

When Ulrik spoke to her in French, even when he was angry with her, the words were like a caress across her skin, his accent sending shivers down her spine. Not so with the count. It made her skin crawl. "I don't speak a lot of French."

His eyebrows shot up. "From Bretaigne?"

Bretaigne? Britain? "So what if I am? Are you going to help me get back home?"

Was she stupid, as he'd suggested, poking the beast? Probably, but she'd never been good at playing the damsel in distress.

He chuckled, and genuine amusement shone in his eyes. "*Non.*" His eyes glittered with a shrewdness that had the hair on the back of her neck standing on end. "But *you* will help *me* get back something I have lost."

"Something you've lost? I don't..."

How could she help *him*? And get back what?

"Ulrik Voclain."

Bek sucked in a breath. *Of course.* Like with the detectives assigned to her case, she was but a pawn for a much bigger prize. Though things were different this time around. She wouldn't cover for Ulrik like she had for Spider, hoping he would come for her. Believing she'd get a warning, a slap on the wrist. Not this time. She had to be smart. The stakes were too high. Ulrik had proved he could take care of himself. He was a shifter. She, a mere human. One with few choices left available to her.

"How?"

"You are already playing your part. By being here."

She forced out a laugh, a little high-pitched. If she couldn't convince the count Ulrik wasn't coming, she would die in this cell.

"He'll not come for me, but... Perhaps I could lead you to him."

She'd no more be able to find Ulrik again, especially if he did not want to be found, than she could will herself back to the twenty-first century.

His smile chilled her more than the damp stone at her back. "Oh, he will come for you. Of that I have no doubt."

She huffed out a breath. "I wish. But you're wrong. He won't. We parted on...unfriendly terms. I said some things..." She looked away. "He stormed off and left me. That's how your men found me."

The count shrugged, and the embroidered dragon rippled across his shoulder as though taking flight. "Do you know what he is? What he can turn into?"

She nodded, still not meeting his eyes. "Yeah."

Keeping Ulrik's secret wouldn't help her now.

He stepped closer. "Do you know what their weaknesses are?"

Bek pressed her tongue against the roof of her mouth, the unfamiliar absence of her tongue ring swamping her with memories. Her face flushed and her body heated. In for a penny, in for a pound. "Yeah. Silver and wolfsbane."

"And their women."

What? Her head snapped up. The count's mocking smile taunted her.

"Yes. Their women." His lip curled. "For all their strengths, their savagery and their cunning, all it takes to bring one of them to heel is to threaten their women. Gaharet risked my displeasure by taking Erin as his betrothed. Aimon was willing to defy me for Kathryn. Oh, Ulrik *will* come for you. Of that I am certain."

With a final sardonic twist of his lips, he left her, taking the limited light of the candle with him. Bek slid down the wall to the floor, the clang of the grate as it slammed shut above echoing in the darkened room. She hugged her arms about her and closed her eyes. There was only one problem with the count's theory. As much as she wanted to be, she was not, and probably never would be, Ulrik's woman.

* * * *

It could've been hours, maybe an entire day — Bek did not know how long she'd sat in darkness before the grate hinges screeched again. After the count's visit, neither sitting so close to the grate and the guards, nor sitting alone in the dark, had appealed. She'd found a happy medium near the bottom of the steps, the light spilling through the grate still giving her some comfort.

She got to her feet, her body stiff from the cold, and slunk back into the soul-sucking darkness of the dungeon. Who would it be this time? The count again? Someone bringing her food? Her stomach rumbled, and despite the dampness of the dungeon, her throat was parched.

Bek eyed the descending light warily. A man in a black cassock, a cross around his neck and a magenta skull cap stepped into the small space, his candle held aloft. A priest. Not a bog-standard one either. One with rank, if the silver thread woven through his robe was anything to go by. The archbishop Erin had spoken of?

The flickering candlelight cast eerie shadows over the priest's face, making his cheeks seem sunken and his eyes deeper set, as though his skin stretched tight over his features to reveal the skull beneath. A chill ran up her spine. She'd tolerated the well-meaning priests who'd come to Bronzefield. If she'd had any connection with religion, she might have found comfort in their visits, in their quiet words from the bible, or their prayers for her forgiveness. But if this guy had come to offer her solace, then she was the Queen of England.

She bore the coldness of his calculating scrutiny in silence. Who posed the greater threat? The count or the priest?

He held something out in his palm, something gold. *Could it be?* She leaned forward. It glittered in the candlelight. *Yes. The amulet.* She reached for it. The archbishop curled his fingers around it and snatched it back.

He let out a dry and dusty cackle that would have made the Wicked Witch of the West proud. "You know what this is?"

Her eyebrows shot up, and she took a step back. He'd spoken in English. Was he tag-teaming with the count? Bad cop, worse cop?

"I found your piece of parchment." He held up the amulet again. "Four lines of script. Four lines of Latin, and four lines of a rather strange version of the language of Bretaigne. Is that where you have come from? Bretaigne?"

Would Bek have a better chance of manipulating him into getting her out of here? Better success than she'd had with the count?

He stepped closer, the amulet clasped firmly in his bony hand. "I want to know where it takes you. If you say the words. If you recite the spell."

He didn't know how it worked. He didn't know about the binding stone. Hope, tentative and fragile, fluttered in her chest. She did. Ulrik had the binding stone. He was most likely with Gaharet. Neither would want to be found by the archbishop, but they were both more than capable of taking care of one man. She'd missed her opportunity in the forest. She wasn't going to waste this one.

The priest's eyes glowed with an almost demonic fervor. "Tell me what I want to know, and I will see you released."

Bek's eyes narrowed. He might be a priest, but Rebekah didn't trust a word that came out of his mouth. *He* shouldn't trust *her*, either.

"I..."

He sidled closer. "You want to be free of this horrible place, do you not?" he asked, his voice deceptively gentle.

Bek nodded. That was the truth.

"Then, my dear, tell me how this amulet works."

She nodded again and gave him what she hoped was a tremulous smile. "Okay. Um... I...don't know where it takes you." A complete lie. "Um... I've never used it."

The archbishop scowled.

"But I do know how to make it work."

Truth. A truth she would use to her benefit.

His cold eyes blazed, and his thin, bloodless lips turned up in a semblance of a smile. "Go on."

"You have to hold the amulet and recite the words." She captured her bottom lip between her teeth and fluttered her eyelashes. *Too much?* She was so bad at this shit. Hapless female was *not* her scene, but he was gobbling up the morsels she threw him quicker than a stray dog in a sausage factory. "You have to say the words out loud."

There was that awful cackle again.

Bek repressed a shudder and leaned in. "And you need blood to make it work. On the amulet. Your blood."

His beaming smile, all teeth and jutting cheekbones, made for a caricature of a corpse. This dude was scary. Creepy in a way the count was not.

"Thank you." He turned away and made for the stairs.

"What about me?" she called after him. "Are you going to get me out of here?".

He huffed and cast a look at her over his shoulder that oozed derision, any hint of his smile gone. "So gullible. Your trust is sadly misplaced. You, my dear, are going nowhere."

Bek hid her smile as the archbishop retreated up the stairs. She might not be going anywhere, but he certainly was. Chances were, he wouldn't like his destination.

Chapter Thirty-Four

Ulrik paced the clearing, unable to sit still any longer. The sun had reached its zenith, though it penetrated little through the heavy tree canopy. Nearby, the horses grazed, resting from their hard ride from the d'Louncrais Keep. Gaharet and Aimon sat on a fallen tree, silently regarding him, a small fire and the remains of a roasted hare carcass at their feet.

The coolness of the surrounding forest and the company of his friends could not calm him. "We are but half a league from Langeais Keep. Why must we wait here? Why must we wait at all?"

A sense of urgency tugged at him. His Rebekah needed him.

"It is the middle of the day, Ulrik." Gaharet tossed a leg bone in the fire. "It is too risky. We must wait for nightfall."

Ulrik ground his teeth. "You think I am going to wait here, while Lothair has Rebekah in his horrid underground chamber, doing who knows what to her?

That I would leave her alone to fend for herself for a full day?" He glared at Gaharet. "Would you wait? If it was Erin instead of Rebekah confined to that godforsaken hole?" He shook his head. "No. I will not wait."

He strode toward his horse.

"Ulrik. Stop."

The alpha command rolled over him, and he paused, his hands on his saddle.

"Think, Ulrik." Gaharet rose and blocked his horse, gathering the reins. "Lothair does not want Rebekah. He wants you. Rebekah is but the lure. Do not fear. He will do naught to her, save for keeping her prisoner. We have time."

"Argh." Ulrik raked his hand through his hair and turned away from his horse. He hung his head and stared at his boots. "You are right." Gaharet was always right. He was a far wiser alpha than Ulrik would ever have been. "It is just..." He pinched the bridge of his nose. "The thought of her, alone, in the dark and at the mercy of Lothair, the guards..."

Gaharet sighed. "I know, but rushing in is not the answer. We need —"

Pounding hooves of an approaching horse stilled all conversation and Ulrik reached for his sword. He sniffed the air. Over the smoke of the fire and the scent of roasted hare, he caught something familiar.

"One of your horses, Gaharet?"

"Yes. And Gascon. As ever, he is resourceful. It must be of some importance for him to track us down."

Horse and rider appeared through the trees, and Gascon reined in and dismounted. "Mon Seigneur Gaharet, Mon Seigneur Ulrik, Monsieur Aimon." He thrust a sealed parchment at Aimon. "This arrived for you this morning, Monsieur. I thought it best to bring it to you immediately."

Ulrik's gut clenched as he caught sight of the wax seal. "It is from Lothair."

Aimon took the parchment. "Most likely, it is to inform me he has Rebekah. He knows I have contact with Gaharet." Aimon broke the seal. "*Merde.*"

Ulrik's heart dropped. "What is it? What does it say?"

Aimon handed the parchment to Gaharet. "He is commanding all of us—Lance, Godfrey, the twins and I—to present ourselves in the hall. Today." Aimon sighed. "We are to kneel before him again. Repeat our vows. It is something he called for after your capture, Ulrik."

Ulrik's shoulders sagged. The missive did not bring news of Rebekah. "This does not affect our plans. You go, Aimon. Do Lothair's bidding. Tonight, we will enter the keep and rescue Rebekah."

Aimon would not meet his gaze. Gaharet handed the parchment to him, and Ulrik read the message, his attention catching on the last line.

"I have Ulrik's woman. Guilty of aiding his escape, I will pass sentence on her today."

"*Merde.*" Ulrik balled up the message and threw it into the fire. The parchment darkened, flames curling at its edges, but the vellum didn't catch. "He is going to sentence her to death. He is going to kill her."

"We will not let that happen, Ulrik," said Gaharet. "*I* will not let that happen. We will—"

"Gaharet!" Aimon pointed to Gaharet's chest, his eyes wide. "The bloodstone. It glows."

Ulrik stared at Gaharet's chest. Aimon spoke true. The binding stone glowed.

Could it be… "Rebekah?"

Did she still have the amulet? Or was it another fallen werewolf?

Gaharet drew his sword. "Maybe."

Ulrik slid his sword from his scabbard. "Maybe not."

Aimon also drew his sword, and he moved with Ulrik to flank Gaharet. United they stood, and waited.

A figure in black, his robes shot through with silver thread, appeared, grunting as he landed on his hands and knees. In his bleeding hand, he clutched an amulet.

Ulrik gaped at the figure. "Renaud?"

The man who had trapped and killed so many of their kind. Had turned Comte Lothair against them. How the hell had he gotten his hands on an amulet?

The archeveque looked up, and he blanched. "D'Louncrais. You are supposed to be—" Renaud pressed his thin lips together and got to his feet.

Ulrik raised his sword. "*Now* will you let me kill him?" At Gaharet's raised hand, Ulrik stilled. "You cannot mean to let him walk away?"

Gaharet's jaw clenched. "No. We cannot."

Renaud backed away a step.

"You are not going to suggest we simply tie him and leave him, are you?" Ulrik stared at Gaharet, incredulous. "We risk him escaping. Or Lothair's guard's finding him."

"Kill me"—Renaud's face twisted in a vicious snarl—"and you will burn in *hell*."

"Oh, I will not have Ulrik kill you, Renaud, but you may well wish for death." Determination glittered in Gaharet's eyes. "Thanks to you, Lothair wants an enhanced army. I plan to show him what is involved in that, and you are going to help us."

Ulrik's eyes narrowed on Renaud. The archeveque, eyes wide and his heartbeat loud and racing in Ulrik's ears, shuffled backward. A slow smile spread across Ulrik's face, and his canines punched through his gums.

"Get some rope, Aimon." Ulrik sent Gaharet a questioning look. "May I?"

"You are the one who Renaud trapped with wolfsbane and bound in silver." Gaharet held out his hands, offering up the archeveque. "The pleasure is all yours."

Ulrik sheathed his sword, unbuckled it from around his waist and handed it to Gaharet. As he prowled toward a retreating Renaud, he removed his vambraces, greaves and boots.

Renaud's face paled, and his steps quickened. In his haste, he tripped over his robes. He scrambled to his feet. "Call off your dog, d'Louncrais."

Ulrik ignored Renaud's high-pitched command, the scent of the archeveque's fear sweeter than any fine wine. He pressed forward, shucking his hauberk and gambeson, and pulling his tunic over his head.

"I can tell you who my informant was!" Renaud's voice rose to a screech. "Who betrayed you!"

Ulrik paused. This was important information. Would Gaharet stop him?

His alpha shrugged. "Soon he will be in so much agony he will tell us whatever we want to know."

Ulrik grinned and slipped out of his breeches, the change rippling through him the moment he stepped free of them. Sandy-colored fur sprouted across his shifting body, his snout elongating and his spine contorting. With a shriek, Renaud turned and fled.

Ulrik laughed, the sound distorted by his changing vocal cords. Renaud could not run fast enough or far enough to escape him. He slunk down on all fours, his transformation complete, and ran after his prey. Renaud ducked and wove through the trees, pushing aside branches and plowing through shrubs. Ulrik, vengeance in his heart, nipped at his heels.

"Stop toying with him, Ulrik," yelled Gaharet.

Ulrik whined but increased his pace. Renaud was an agile man for his age, but he was no match for a wolf. Especially not a werewolf. Ulrik bore down on him. All his pain and rage, all his suffering in that chamber, the lack of control forced on him by the cursed wolfsbane, and the bite of the silver against his skin that had bound his wolf, he directed at Renaud. He leaped on the archeveque, hitting him hard and bringing him to the ground. His two front paws held Renaud in place as he leaned in, putting his muzzle next to Renaud's face. He bared his teeth.

Renaud's eyes widened, and his body trembled. "No, no, no. You cannot. I am an archeveque." His voice pitched higher. "You cannot make me...I can*not* be one of you." His words tumbled out of his mouth, his face deathly pale and sweat beading on his upper lip. "I am going to be a cardinal!" he shrieked.

Not anymore.

Ulrik lunged and sunk his teeth deep into Renaud's neck, the metallic taste of blood filling his mouth. Renaud screamed, and he beat his fists on the ground. Ulrik tightened his hold as his saliva entered his victim's veins. Renaud's body shuddered. A spasm ripped through the prone archeveque and his back arched, his mouth open in a silent scream.

Gaharet came up behind him. "It is done."

Ulrik released his grip, the distinct and unpleasant scent of urine filling his nostrils. Renaud had voided his bladder. Ulrik backed away and shifted as Aimon and Gaharet bound Renaud in rope and gagged him with a strip of cloth. He took the offered wineskin from Gascon and washed the blood from his mouth, spitting it at Renaud. He wanted no reminder of Renaud on him when they rescued Rebekah.

Ulrik took his clothes and armor from Gascon and quickly dressed. "What now?"

Gaharet nudged Renaud with his boot. "Now we go to the keep and rescue your mate. We can no longer afford to wait until nightfall, lest someone come looking for Renaud." He jerked his chin at Aimon. "You will answer Lothair's summons. We still have a traitor, and he will be there along with the others. Ulrik, Gascon and I will take Renaud through the postern gate and enter the keep via the secret passageway. We will free Rebekah and leave Renaud in her place. We may have to kill a few guards, but that cannot be helped."

Yes. Ulrik fist-punched the air. *Hold on, Rebekah. I am coming for you, baby.*

"Gascon," said Gaharet, "fetch the horses." Gascon retreated through the forest. "We will get your mate back, Ulrik. I vow it to you."

Ulrik gripped Gaharet's arm. "Thank you. I do not think I could…"

"You have suffered enough loss in this lifetime, my friend. We all have. Come." He pointed to the writhing archeveque, his moans muffled by the gag. "Help me get this weasel onto my horse."

Together, they lifted Renaud and slung him across Gaharet's stallion.

Ulrik tossed Gaharet a rope. "Have we made a mistake, do you think, in turning him? Not that I did not derive great pleasure from biting Renaud."

"At his age" —Gaharet shook his head—"it will surprise me if he survives the turning. Three days of agony should be enough to stop his heart."

"And the evidence of our existence?"

"Do you think Lothair would like it known he had a werewolf confined in his keep?" Gaharet wound the rope around Renaud and secured him to his saddle, pulling the knots tight. "Besides, the church would not view favorably his chaining up of an archeveque in his underground chamber."

Ulrik took his horse's reins from Gascon and swung himself into his saddle. "And the information we need about the traitor?"

Gaharet mounted his horse. "Once in that chamber, we can confine him in silver and get the answers we need." Gaharet set his jaw. "Then we leave him there to die."

A smile hovered on his lips. Leaving Renaud to die in the chamber that had once confined him... A fitting end, and it pleased him well. He would see it done.

Chapter Thirty-Five

The grate clanged open and Rebekah picked herself off the cold, damp step. Perhaps they were bringing her more food. Another lump of stale bread and more water of questionable cleanliness? But she'd eat the bread and drink the water. She had no idea how long she'd be here, and she wasn't in a rush to die of dehydration or starvation. One thing at a time.

Flickering candlelight preceded boots down the stairs. Then one, no, two guards stepped into the room. She eyed them warily, her hands clenched into fists, ready for anything. There'd not been a repeat of her first visit to the dungeon. No smarmy guard looking to rape her. *Yet.* Bek searched their expressions, looking for a hint of their intent. They stared at her dispassionately. She'd rejoice at a breath of compassion, but she'd settle for this. It beat the alternative.

One guard said a few words and held something up. Not food. Shackles. Metal manacles linked with a thick chain. They approached, and Bek held her hands out. There was no point in fighting them. They were taking her out of here — *a plus* — and she wasn't about to give them a reason to get handsy.

The cuffs enclosed her wrists, frigid metal against her cold skin, and the guard locked them into place. Taking an arm each, they led her up the stairs. She squinted against the bright light of the room. Had Ulrik come for her? Is that why they were taking her from the dungeon?

A thread of hope tugged at her heart. How long had she waited for Spider, expecting the lawyer the Devil's had in their pocket to be engaged for her defense? He'd never shown. But if Ulrik had come...

How long have I been here? Half a day? A day?

She wanted to rejoice, but the cold cynicism of past experience weighed her down like a pair of cement shoes. *Don't get your hopes up, Bek.* More likely, the count tired of waiting.

The guards propelled her past the game of dice on the table and out into the corridor. A set of stairs, more stairs and endless corridors. She tried to get her bearings, should an opportunity to escape present itself, but the guards kept her moving and it all looked the same. Down a long corridor, they stopped at a small door. She could hear voices. Lots of them. At a knock from a guard, the door swung open and they dragged her through.

The noise, the smell of sweating bodies, the sheer size of the room hit her and Bek stumbled, the guards' grip on her arms the only thing preventing her from falling. She closed her eyes, drew in a deep breath, and gagged. The air in the dungeon had been stale and dank. Here, beneath a sickly sweet herbal smell, was the odor of rotting garbage and raw sewerage. The council bin at the back of The Spicy Dragon hadn't smelled this bad. Her eyes watering, she lifted her head.

The immense room was filled with people milling about in groups and hugging the walls. There had to be over a hundred people in the room. Lording it over all of them, on a raised platform, sat the count. The dragon on his shirt spewed fire at her, and his dark eyes promised nothing good. Her stomach clenched, and she swallowed the nausea that rose in her throat.

Lined up in front of him, their faces stern and unforgiving, were four men. Four knights. None of them were Ulrik. One man she recognized, with his white-blond hair and eyes as blue as his coat. Aimon. A flash of concern flickered across his face. What did it mean that he was here? That all four men were here? Lined up in front of the count like naughty schoolchildren in front of a headmaster. Were they all shifters like Aimon?

She sized up the man next to Aimon. Large and muscled, there was a hint of gray at his temples and in his beard. His coat, a dirty orange-red, covered his armor. His crest, some sort of weird bird — part dragon, part rooster — in deep red. Like Aimon he wore chain mail, but neither he nor Aimon had a sword belted at his waist.

She skipped to the next man. *Fuck, he's huge.* He wore a coat of green with a brown bear as his crest — *fitting* — and his face he'd twisted into a scowl. Not at her, but at the count. A possible friend? Someone who would come to her aid?

Her attention lit on the third man. *Twins?* Just as big and wild, though not quite so fierce, he wore the same colored coat, with the same crest. Neither had a sword either.

Wait. Twins. Hadn't Erin said two of Gaharet's men were twins?

'Gaharet, Ulrik, Aimon, who you've met. Twins Edmond and Aubert. Godfrey and, the oldest, Lance.' That's what Erin had said. Her gaze settled on the one familiar man in the blue coat with the white dove crest. Aimon. The twins. Then the other guy, the one with the touch of gray at his temples. Lance, the oldest? These had to be Gaharet's men. Had they come for her?

"Bring her to me," commanded the count, beckoning her forward.

Unlike the other men, the count was wearing a sword. As were the guards who surrounded him. And her. They dragged her forward, depositing her next to the count. He grasped her arm and spoke to the crowd, his deep voice ringing out. A proclamation? Some sort of decree?

Silence fell. A hundred eager eyes stared at her, and a ripple of excitement ran through their ranks. Aimon blanched. The scowly twin's expression darkened. The count stared up at her with a sardonic tilt to his lips. Bek trembled. What the hell had he said? Lord Almighty, was she to be the guest of honor at a public hanging?

Fuck. Why the hell didn't I pay more attention in French?

Chapter Thirty-Six

Ulrik eyed the bodies of the four guards, their game of dice interrupted and scattered across the bloodied floor. He and Gaharet had killed two more guards at the postern gate. A regretful circumstance, but one Ulrik would commit to again to free Rebekah.

"I have found the keys." Gascon tossed them to Ulrik.

Ignoring the burning of the silver key, he inserted it, unlocked the grate and swung it open. He paused at the top of the stairs. The dank, stale smell wafted up from the hole, and he shuddered. Memories skittered along his skin. The emptiness of his mind, his wolf bound and silent, the silver burning his skin... A familiar scent broke through his thoughts. *Rebekah.*

Ulrik plunged down the stairs. He exploded into the dark space and skidded to a halt. He spun around, searching for her, the darkness no barrier to his enhanced vision, eager to get to her and wrap her in his arms.

Empty.

His heart all but stopped beating. The chamber was empty. Her scent lingered, but Rebekah was gone. But the scent was fresh. They had missed her by moments, not hours.

He beat a hasty retreat up the stairs. "She is gone. Lothair must have her in the hall." He roared at the ceiling and kicked a chair across the room. It slammed into the wall and fell to the floor, broken. "We came too late."

"Maybe not." Gaharet's voice of reason cut through his despair. "Aimon will be there. He will allow nothing to happen to her."

Ulrik threw out his arms. "What can he do? He is no match for Lothair. He will not risk his life for Rebekah. Not when his mate sits unprotected back at your keep. And I would not ask it of him." He paced the room, heedless of the carnage on the floor. "I cannot leave Rebekah to her fate." He thumped his chest with his fist. "She is there because of me."

He raked his hands through his hair. She could not lose her life because of him. Not like his parents.

Ulrik closed his eyes and an eerie calm settled over him. His family had suffered fate's punishment for his crimes, but he could not, would not allow another to take his place again. Not while he still had breath in his body. Not when he could prevent it. Perhaps it should have come to this years ago. Maybe this was always the end destined for him. He opened his eyes, taking in the dead guards, the open grate, his alpha. He knew what he must do. "I must go to her."

"Ulrik—"

"We cannot defeat all Lothair's guards, Gaharet. It is suicide to attempt it. I must give Lothair what he wants.

Me." He stood before his alpha, his mind decided. "Take care of Rebekah for me. Find her a way home, if that is what she truly wishes. Please."

Gaharet snarled. "We will find another way, Ulrik. It should not come to this."

"It will and it must." He stared his alpha down. "You know I am right, Gaharet. You know this is the only way. It is time for me to take responsibility. No one else should risk their life or die because of me."

Renaud moaned and thrashed about on the floor.

"Gascon will help you get Renaud into the underground chamber. Then you must leave. If Renaud does not die because of the turning, I will ensure he does. And I vow to you, I will not turn Lothair, nor anyone else at his bidding." He clasped Gaharet's shoulder. "Farewell, my friend. I have missed our friendship in these long years past. I am glad we reconciled before we came to this."

He straightened his shoulders, firmed his resolve and headed for the door.

"Ulrik…"

He turned to Gaharet, his alpha, his friend. "Do not stop me. I *must* do this."

Gaharet clasped his hand over his heart and bowed his head. With a nod, Ulrik left the room. He hurried down the corridors, racing up the flights of stairs until he stood at the double doors of the hall. The guards eyed him warily. He raised his sword, expecting the guards to draw theirs, to deny him entry, but they opened the doors for him and let him through.

Ulrik stood inside the hall as the doors closed behind him. Nobles, ladies-in-waiting, guards and chevaliers. They filled the hall, their backs to him, focused on the dais at the other end.

"Lothair!" he roared.

Startled gasps echoed around the room, and the crowd parted. Curious whispers buzzed in his ears. The onlookers, the voyeurs ever eager for a spectacle, closed in behind him as he walked the length of the hall. Standing before the dais, before Lothair, were his fellow wolves—Aimon, Lance and the twins—their eyes wide. Aimon nodded. Good. He could trust the young wolf to have his back. Shock rolled off Edmond and Aubert, tinged with anger. He could not fault them for that. They believed him to have killed Gaharet. From Lance, strangely, he sensed nothing.

He might have given Godfrey's absence more thought had his gaze not fallen on a figure, straining against two guards beside Lothair. Rebekah. To be standing there, shackled, and understand few words that were spoken, must be terrifying for her, though she did not show it.

Her dark eyes misted over, and she stared at him with such longing for a moment he considered, had circumstances been different, she might have come to accept him as her mate. He brushed the thought aside. It was not to be.

Aimon squeezed his shoulder as he passed. Edmond frowned, casting a glance at Rebekah, then back at him, sudden understanding flickering in his eyes. The twins shared a look and Aubert's furrowed brow rose. They both stepped aside. Then he was standing before Lothair, his sword in his hand and his fellow wolves at his back.

Keep guards stepped forward, but Lothair raised a hand, halting them, a triumphant smile hovering on his lips. "Ulrik. So good of you to join us."

Ulrik stared at his comte. The man who had taken so much from him. His family, and for a time, his freedom. His gut clenched with the strength of his rage. He would not let him take Rebekah.

He threw down his sword, and it clattered at Lothair's feet. Ulrik dropped to his knees. "My life for hers," he said in the language of Bretaigne. For her. "My life, for hers."

A collective gasp rose from the crowd, and mutterings swept through the hall. A rumble came from Aubert, a snarl from Aimon. Ulrik ignored everything but Rebekah.

She closed her eyes and two tears tracked down her face. "You came for me," she whispered.

Had she thought he would not come? Had she believed he would abandon her like her previous lover? *Never.*

Lothair got to his feet and moved toward him. Ulrik held his stance. He was on his knees, but he would not prostrate himself, nor bow his head. Lothair kicked his discarded sword beyond his reach, giving him some satisfaction. Lothair still viewed him as a threat.

"Your life for hers? Hmm." Lothair tapped his chin. "What is there to stop me from taking both?"

A growl rumbled from behind him. Aimon again. The young pup was growing teeth. Then another and another. The twins. His heart thudded to life, sweeping aside old resentments. Though they believed he had killed Gaharet, they would protect his mate.

Ulrik gritted his teeth. "It is me you want, not her. *My* life, for *hers.*"

"Well, well, well. The most wayward of Gaharet's men finally stepping up to assume his responsibilities. Who knew it would only take a woman?"

Lothair inclined his head toward the guards holding Rebekah and they dragged her to him.

She spat at Lothair. "Bastard, mother-fu—" The guards shoved her to her knees, and Ulrik pulled her into his arms. She struggled against him and lunged at Lothair.

He grasped her shoulders and spun her around. "Rebekah, stop. I need you to stop. Please."

She ceased struggling and put her palms on his chest. "You came, and God, I love that you did. After what I said. I'm so sorry, Ulrik. I didn't know, but…"

"Yes, Rebekah. For you." He brushed his knuckles across her cheek. "Always."

She leaned into him, her forehead resting against his chin. "But you shouldn't have." She gripped his surcoat. "Now he's going to kill you."

"You would have me leave you here? Risk *your* life for mine?" He set her back and cupped her face in his hands. "I would give my life a thousand times to know you are safe." He touched his forehead to hers, their breaths mingling. "If this is my end, I go to it having met you, having loved you. I do this for you, Rebekah." His grip tightened on her face. "You promise me something, Rebekah. Promise me you will go with Aimon. That you will survive. I need you to do this for me."

"I—"

Lothair clapped his hands, once, twice, three times. "How *very* touching." He gestured for the guards. "Take him."

The guards grabbed his arms and dragged him to his feet.

Rebekah clung to him. "No. No. You can't—" She grabbed one guard's arm and tried pulling him away from Ulrik. He shoved her. She fell to the floor.

Ulrik roared and struggled against the guards. "Do not touch her!"

Aimon stepped forward, grasped Rebekah by the arm and pulled her to her feet. She lunged at the guard again, but Aimon held her firm and dragged her away.

"Aimon," Ulrik beseeched him.

Aimon nodded, encircling Rebekah's waist with his arm. Though it burned to see another male, even a mated one, with his arms around his mate, he repressed his need to go to her. To rip her out of Aimon's arms. He had to let her go.

Certain Aimon had Rebekah safe, her foul curses ringing in his ears, he stopped struggling. He had made his choice.

Lothair raised an eyebrow at a particularly foul shriek from Rebekah involving a man's anatomy. "She is feisty." Lothair crossed his arms over his chest. "Perhaps I will—"

Ulrik brought the beast as close to the surface as he could without shifting. "You will never touch her. She leaves with Aimon."

Lothair studied him, his eyes narrowed. "And you will give me what I want?"

Ulrik snarled at Lothair, revealing a canine sliding into place. Lothair held his ground. His comte must have pure steel flowing through his veins.

"I always get what I want, Ulrik." Lothair's smile was smug. "One way or another."

A door slammed behind them. The crowd gasped, and the guards drew their swords.

"Gaharet? You are...alive?"

The choked words had come from behind him. From Lance.

With studied calm, Lothair faced the intrusion. "Gaharet, what a surprise."

The slide of steel against his scabbard rang loud in the sudden silence as Lothair drew his weapon.

Gaharet, his bloodied sword held nonchalantly by his side, prowled into the hall. "You wanted to talk, Lothair. Here I am."

Ulrik tensed. What was Gaharet doing?

Lothair eyed the packed hall. "Then we shall talk." Lothair motioned to his guards. "Get them all out. And once you are done, leave."

"But Mon Seigneur—" Lothair's snarl cut off the capitaine and he gulped. "Of course, Mon Seigneur Comte. As you command."

With a wary eye on Gaharet, he began issuing orders to clear the hall. The guards started to drag Ulrik away.

"Not him. He stays." Lothair waved his sword at Rebekah. "And so does she."

Ulrik struggled against the guards. "No. She leaves with Aimon."

Lothair gave him a look that could have cowed an army. "You are in no position to make demands, Voclain. She. Stays."

As soon as the two guards released him, he had Rebekah in his arms. He rested his cheek on her head, breathing in her scent. He had thought he would never have this again. And while it may only be for this moment, he would take it.

A sword pointed at his throat snapped his head up. Lothair. His comte grabbed a startled Rebekah by the arm, and Ulrik had no choice but to let her go.

"The rest of you"—Lothair swung his gaze to Aimon, Edmond, Aubert and Lance—"leave. Now."

They stood their ground.

Lothair glared at them. "You would dare defy me?"

They stood resolute, looking to Gaharet.

Lothair's jaw tightened and the cords on his neck stood out. "Do not look to him. I am your comte. You obey *me*!"

Gaharet inclined his head. "Go."

The twins turned and followed the crowd. Lance hesitated, the older chevalier's lips pinched and white, concern etched across his weary face. Then he, too, slunk away. Aimon, his shoulders slumped, was the last to leave. He had done his best. It was Ulrik who had failed to keep Rebekah safe, not Aimon.

The last of the guards filed out of the hall, and the large double doors swung shut, leaving the large room empty but for the four of them. Ulrik hoped his alpha knew what he was doing.

Chapter Thirty-Seven

Ulrik kept his arms fisted at his side as he let Lothair drag Rebekah away from him. For once, she was silent. It seemed his little fire breather had run out of insults. If their situation were not so precarious, he might have found that amusing.

Lothair kicked Ulrik's sword further away. "Is this what it has come to, Gaharet?"

"You forced my hand, Lothair," said Gaharet, stepping down from the dais. "But I did not come here to fight you."

"Your bloodied sword suggests otherwise."

"I could have killed you many times over the years, Lothair, but I did not. You are as safe with me as you have ever been."

As Gaharet kept Lothair talking, Ulrik edged himself to the left, closer to his sword.

"Your keep is by far more secure than the last time I was here," said Gaharet. "As once your adviser and commander of your troops, I commend this improvement, but it has meant there were unfortunate casualties."

Lothair's attention snapped to Ulrik, and he pressed his sword against Rebekah's stomach. She sucked in a breath and Ulrik halted. It had been a bold move for Lothair to send all his guards away. Even with only the two of them, they far outmatched him. Either Lothair was delusional about his chances against two werewolves, shifted or human, or he had the fortitude of a wild boar. Perhaps it was a little of both. That he held Rebekah complicated matters, but Ulrik would give his all to ensure his mate walked away from this confrontation.

"Ulrik has brought you a gift," said Gaharet, drawing Lothair's attention again.

"A gift?" Lothair cocked his head. "Am I going to like it?"

"I liked it," rasped Ulrik, but Lothair ignored him.

He took another step toward his sword.

Gaharet shrugged. "Perhaps you will like it. Perhaps not. But it is something you need."

"Something I need?" The disdain in Lothair's voice was unmistakable.

Careful, Gaharet. Ulrik eased two more steps to the left.

"The gift of understanding."

Lothair shifted slightly, keeping both him and Gaharet in his sights. Lothair was an experienced and fearless warrior. Taking him down, even with their advantages, would not be easy.

"And where is this…*gift*?"

"In your underground chamber. Bound in silver." Ulrik grinned, letting his canines show. "We thought you might like someone to replace me."

Lothair's eyes narrowed, his gaze shifting between the two of them. "You put Godfrey in there? Is *he* Renaud's informant?"

Godfrey? Was it possible? Could Renaud have uncovered Godfrey's secret and used it against him?

"It is not Godfrey," said Gaharet. "But I think you will appreciate our choice."

"You let Ulrik *bite* someone?"

Gaharet chuckled. "Oh, I gave him my blessing."

Lothair's eyes blazed with an unwholesome longing. Ulrik suppressed a shudder. He hoped Gaharet was right. That the turning would kill Renaud. They needed information from the archeveque — the name of his informant — but they would forgo it to keep their abilities, their advantages, out of Lothair's hands.

"Who have you put in my underground chamber, Ulrik?" asked Lothair.

Gaharet inclined his head toward the door behind the dais. "Come and see for yourself."

Lothair considered them both, his dark eyes restless and wary. "Very well. Lead the way." Lothair pointed his sword at Ulrik, halting him. "Not you. Gaharet." He dipped his head at Rebekah. "And her."

Ulrik's wolf reared up, and he almost shifted on the spot. It was only the presence of his alpha, strong and sure, that stopped him. "No." His wolf hovered close — a tingle of awareness along his spine. The trust reflected in Rebekah's eyes warmed him. He hoped he could live up to her belief. "Where she goes, I go."

"You think your greatest weakness is wolfsbane? Or silver?" Lothair tugged Rebekah closer, moving the edge of his sword flush against Rebekah's throat. Rebekah paled and Ulrik took a step forward until Lothair pressed the blade in firmer, halting him. "You could not be more wrong. Your greatest weakness is your women."

"Or our greatest strength," said Gaharet. "Never underestimate the lengths one of our kind will go to, to protect his woman. It is an unwise man who would turn his back on a wolf when you have threatened his mate." Gaharet backed toward the door. "Your choice, Lothair."

The prickle of a shift hovered below the surface of Ulrik's skin, and his musky scent grew stronger.

"Go, then," Lothair snarled. "After Gaharet."

Ulrik met Lothair's snarl with one of his own, but he pushed his wolf down. If he were to shift now, his clothes would shred, but his armor would entangle him. He would be of no help to Rebekah. Though the hackles on his neck rose at having an armed Lothair at his back, he would suffer it. He liked the idea of Rebekah being taken from him even less.

He followed Gaharet's lead, and they trooped along corridors and down two flights of stairs until they were standing in the room with the grate. Ulrik eyed the bloodied bodies of the four guards. Would this savagery alarm Rebekah? Offend her? As grateful as she was he had come to her aid, would she view him the same knowing him capable of this?

He stepped over a body as he moved into the room. In the periphery of his vision, Rebekah's lips twitched and a grim satisfaction played across her face. She *liked* the justice he had meted out to those who had captured her. His lungs filled and his chest puffed out. His woman was strong and resilient.

Gaharet opened the grate with a screech of hinges, lit a candle and they descended the stairs. Ulrik did not need the light to discern the moaning shape of a man curled on the floor. Renaud, his arms and neck red and blistered from the silver shackles chaining him to the wall, twitched, then his back bowed as a spasm hit him hard.

Ulrik had sat by Aimon as he had gone through his turning. Listened to his agonized screams for days. His inability to do little but hold Aimon down, wash his burning brow with cool water and cover him with blankets when he shivered like a newborn left out in the snow, had tormented him. He had no such sympathy for Renaud. Archeveque Renaud had trapped and killed many of his kind — men, women and children. Friends. All so that he could... What? Rise through the ranks of the church and become a cardinal? The man deserved every twitch, every spasm, every slice of agony the turning would bring him.

Gaharet held the candle aloft, lighting up the space and the figure on the ground.

"Renaud?" Lothair's face twisted in grotesque fury. He spun on Ulrik, dragging Rebekah with him. "You bit *Renaud*? I wanted an army of werewolves, not some decrepit werewolf priest!"

Ulrik stood his ground, conscious of the sword against Rebekah's quivering throat. "You wanted me to bite someone. I wanted to bite Renaud."

Renaud struggled to his feet with a clinking of chains, panting, his blood-tinged lips peeled back in a snarl. He must have bitten his tongue. Renaud opened his mouth to speak, but another spasm hit. He strained against his chains and let out a bloodcurdling shriek that bounced off the walls and pierced Ulrik's sensitive ears. Renaud dropped to his knees, his chest heaving.

Feel it all, you miserable old cretin. You deserve every bit and more.

"Be grateful I did not bite you," Ulrik rasped. "That is what Renaud wanted. You turned and bound in silver. So he could present you to Rome, no doubt. He had plans to rise in the church ranks. He had eyes on a cardinal's robes."

"And what, pray tell," spat Lothair, tension rippling through his body, "am I supposed to do with him *now*?"

His grip tightened on Rebekah, and she whimpered. Ulrik clenched his fists, fighting the urge to lunge at him.

"If I hand him over to the church as a werewolf, they will descend on my county in droves. If I kill him — the same. I cannot have him wandering my county, free. I would not trust Renaud as a werewolf any more than I do as a man."

"Look at him, Lothair." Ulrik stabbed his finger toward the archeveque. "Look at what being turned means."

Another spasm hit Renaud, and his teeth snapped at the air. His eyes rolled back in his head, revealing only the whites of his eyes, and his veins stood out blue against his pallid, sweaty forehead. He tipped his head toward the ceiling and howled. Lothair recoiled.

"Three days of this. He will be lucky to survive. If he does, he could well have lost all sense and be nothing more than the ravaging monster the myths proclaim us to be. Is that what you want for yourself? For your men? Is that a risk you want to take?"

Lothair stared at the groaning shape on the floor. Renaud reached out and his blood-shot eyes pleaded. Lothair pulled back, dragging Rebekah with him. Ulrik edged closer. Her face was pale and her eyes were wide as the horror of a turning unfolded in front of her. With

Lothair so distracted, could he pull her free of his grasp? He reached for her, and she slipped her hand into his.

Renaud staggered to his feet, his bony hands clutching at the wispy strands of his gray hair. The silver prevented him from shifting, but there was nothing human about him. His eyes bulged, and he bared his teeth, gnashing at the air. He pulled against his chains, straining them to their limits.

Ulrik's grip tightened around Rebekah's hand. Aimon had snapped his bindings in the throes of his turning. It had taken everything both he *and* Gaharet had to restrain him. Aimon's straps had been leather. Iron chains held Renaud fast to the wall, but would they hold?

Renaud shuddered and shrank back, the chains slackening as he leaned against the wall, panting. He wrapped his arms around himself, hissing as fresh welts appeared on his wrists and fixed a malevolent stare on Lothair.

No hint of Renaud remained in his blood-shot eyes, only pain and rage. He roared and lunged, hitting the end of the chains hard and, as Ulrik had feared, the iron chain snapped. Renaud fell to his hands and knees. Lothair stumbled back and raised his sword, and Ulrik took his chance, pulling Rebekah from him. He shoved her behind him, shielding her with his body.

Renaud held up his hands, the broken chains dangling from his wrists. He lurched to his feet and roared his triumph. Then something happened Ulrik had never thought possible. Still bound by the silver shackles, Renaud part shifted.

Merde.

Ulrik pushed Rebekah toward the safety of the stairs. He had no weapon other than himself, and he had no time to remove his armor. Renaud's head, fully wolf, swiveled to follow Rebekah's retreat and his lips peeled back, revealing slavering jaws.

"Gaharet." Lothair's voice had an alarmed edge to it that Ulrik had never experienced. Not even on the battlefield. "I thought silver would contain your kind."

Renaud's gaze snapped to the comte.

Gaharet gaped, his shock writ large across his face. "So did I."

Ulrik eyed the monstrosity that had once been Renaud, his body tense and preparing for anything. How much of Renaud had shifted, he could not be certain, with his black robes hiding his body. He stood on two feet like a man, but his head was all wolf, and coarse gray fur covered his hands. The silver had to be preventing the full shift. There was no way Renaud had the mental control to *part* shift. That required rigorous training. That he could even shift at all...

A shudder rippled through the archeveque's body, and he hunched over. Renaud had to die. Now. Ulrik looked to Gaharet for confirmation, but Gaharet stared past him, alarm stamped across his face.

Rebekah? *No! She had run up the steps, had she not?*

Ulrik could not risk turning to check, but he did not have to look to know she was there. He scented her fear and her determination. *Why* had she not run up the stairs as he had told her to? Locked the grate? She would be safe. He *needed* her to be safe.

She thrust something into his hand, and his fingers closed around the familiar grip of a sword. His brave mate had come back to arm him. His heart swelled, then all but lodged in his throat as she moved to stand beside him. With both hands, she gripped a sword of her own and held it in front of her. If they got out of this alive, he would show her how much he loved her courage and her determination. Then he would spank her perfect, lush ass for risking her life.

The thing that was Renaud lifted its head. It straightened, eyes bereft of anything but rage as it stared at them. Then it lunged.

Ulrik swung his sword in a wide arc toward the beast, and with a single stroke he lopped off its head. Renaud dropped with a thud and a rattle of broken chain. The wolf's head fell with a sickening squelch, rolling away from the black-robed body.

The underground chamber was suddenly bereft of sound, save for heavy breathing.

Ulrik dared not move or say a word. Lothair no longer had a werewolf in chains. How long would it take before the comte forced him to take Renaud's place? He could take Rebekah and flee, though he doubted they would get far. And Lothair would forever hunt them. No. He had made a vow. His life for hers, and he would stand by it to see her safe.

Visibly shaken, Lothair was the first to move, stepping forward and toeing the body. "Are you certain he is dead?"

Ulrik forced out a laugh. "It would take more than werewolf blood to reattach a man's head."

"Good to know. Though we had it wrong about the silver." He eyed both Gaharet and Ulrik. "This goes no further than this room. I will have your vow on that."

"You have it," said Gaharet.

"Ulrik?"

Ulrik nodded. Having the church find out about their existence would not be good for their pack, any more than it would for Lothair.

"I will have a few of my most trusted men fill this room in, bury it"—he nudged the body again, as though to be truly certain Renaud would not suddenly rise again—"and him with rubble. I do not need to tell you the consequences if the church were to find I have a dead archeveque in my keep, werewolf or no." He sheathed his bloodied sword and strode to the stairwell.

At the base of the stairs, he halted. "You have given me much to consider, but this is not the end of things. I expect every one of you werewolves"—he looked pointedly at Ulrik—"in my hall within the week, kneeling before me."

Ulrik stared, lost for words, as Lothair climbed the stairs. That was it? He was *free*? He had killed Renaud. Was his life not forfeit? He clutched Rebekah to his side, waiting for Lothair to change his mind. To remember the efforts he had gone to, to have Ulrik in his clutches.

"And, Gaharet?" Lothair's voice floated down the stairwell. "I expect to see *all* of your men, so you had best find Godfrey."

Chapter Thirty-Eight

In the room above, Ulrik searched the bodies of the guards until he found what he was looking for. A ring of keys. "Give me your hands."

Rebekah lifted them and he tried three times before he found one that unlocked the iron bolts. He dropped the shackles to the floor.

Rebekah rubbed her wrists, the skin marked and a little bruised, but not broken. "Am I glad to get those things off."

He tilted her chin so he could get a better look at her face.

"Yeah, he got me a good one. A back hander." She rubbed her cheek. "I could've done with some ice or a bag of frozen peas."

Frozen peas? He spotted dried blood and turned her face for a better look, his puzzlement at her need for frozen food forgotten. "What happened to your ear?"

Had Lothair or one of the guards cut her? A canine punched through his gum.

She raised her hand to her bloodied ear. "Oh, I'd forgotten about that. I had the amulet in my pocket when those keep guards found me, and I tried to use it to get back to you. I had to rip one of my piercings out to make myself bleed. Hurt like a bitch. Turned out, it was all for nothing. The guard took the amulet from me. Then somehow that priest got hold of it."

Renaud had *Rebekah's* amulet? Ulrik scrutinized his mate. "You told him how to use it."

She scrunched up her nose. "Yeah, about that. I kind of didn't have a lot of options. I'm sorry. Are you mad? That I gave away some of your secrets? I figured —"

He cupped her chin and dropped a kiss on her lips. This woman... She surprised him at every turn. He should have known she would have tried something.

"No need for apologies. You did the right thing. You did the smart thing." He took her hand. "Let us leave here before Lothair decides letting me go free was a mistake. We will get your injuries tended to when we get to..."

Where would he take her? Where would they go?

"D'Louncrais Keep," said Gaharet, coming up behind them. "After we have met with the others, we will go to my keep."

Ulrik led Rebekah from the room and they made their way out into the bailey. "Are you not concerned, Gaharet, that Lothair will come for us if we go to your keep?"

They crossed the bailey to where Gascon waited at the gate, holding their horses. Gaharet took his horse's reins. "Where would we go if not there? Another county? With no wealth, no reputation, no power base, we would have to start from nothing. Lothair knows we will stay. He would not have let you go had he not believed we would. He wants us, *needs* us, on his side. As long as we kneel before him in a sennight, he will not come for us. My keep is more than big enough for all of us, and Rebekah will have Erin and Kathryn for company." Lapsing into Franceis, he added, "It will be good for Rebekah to have them close through her turning and training."

The turning. One of the many things Ulrik had yet to discuss with Rebekah.

Ulrik tossed his horse's reins over its neck and moved to mount up.

Rebekah groaned. "Not another horse ride." She rubbed her ass. "I'm still sore from the last one. Saddles just aren't meant for two people."

Ulrik cursed himself for his lack of foresight and unbuckled the saddle from his horse. He dropped it to the ground, leaving the padded saddle blanket across the horse's back.

"There," he said, lifting Rebekah onto the horse. "Now both we and the horse will be more comfortable this way." The last thing he wanted was to remind Rebekah of her journey here.

She hitched her dress and swung her leg over, straddling the horse. "Much better."

Relieved she still wore her breeches, Ulrik hoisted himself onto his horse behind her. She settled back against him, and he took small comfort from her trust in him. It might not last. Once she had had time to think things through. Once he had told her everything.

Gascon handed him a small bundle and a wineskin. "Anne sent this. Food and water for Rebekah."

God bless Anne.

Rebekah seized the wineskin, removed the stopper and drank down large gulps of water. Trickles flowed down her chin and dripped on her dress, but she did not stop.

"Easy there." Ulrik took the wineskin, forcing her to take a breath. True to his nature, Lothair had treated Rebekah no better than he had Ulrik whilst in that dark hole.

"So thirsty," she muttered, snatching it back.

"I know, baby, but you do not want to make yourself sick." He opened the bundle and set it in her lap. Bread, cheese and fruit. "Eat. We must meet with the others, then we have a long ride ahead of us."

"The others?" she mumbled, as she chewed on a chunk of bread. "You mean Aimon and those other three guys that were in the hall? Aubert, Edmond and…Lance?"

He took the wineskin from her, sealed it and looped it over his shoulder. "Yes. They are Gaharet's men." He nudged his horse forward, and they set off through the village.

She twirled an apple stem in her fingers. "Wasn't there supposed to be another guy? Godfrey?"

Ulrik chuffed. She did not miss a thing, his mate. "Yes, Godfrey should have been there. Lothair had summoned him, too."

"So why didn't he show?" She took a bite from the apple, staring up at him expectantly.

Good question. "I do not know. Perhaps the others do."

Ulrik secured an arm around her waist, and she clutched at the food bundle as he urged his horse into a trot. Where *was* Godfrey? Both Godfrey and Lance had tracked them in the forest until the storm had helped them slip away. Had Lance been the only one to return?

* * * *

Aimon, Edmond, Aubert and Lance were waiting for them at the crossroads beyond Langeais village. Their smiles and the scent of their relief greeted him as they rode up to meet them.

Edmond nudged his horse forward. "Welcome back, Gaharet. It is good to see you alive."

A chorus of agreement rumbled through the men.

"Ulrik…" The big man looked uncomfortable, pained even. "We have done you a disservice. We doubted you. *I* doubted you. Hell, I wanted to kill you for what I thought you had done." He lifted his bearded chin. "I was wrong."

"As was I," rumbled Aubert.

Ulrik took them all in. Aimon's relieved smile, Edmond's and Aubert's honest and repentant expressions. Lance's uncomfortable silence.

"We meant for you to think I had killed Gaharet, but I am glad we have this settled." He gave them a cocky grin. "I would not have wanted to embarrass you both by beating in you in a sword fight."

Aubert scowled.

Edmond raised an eyebrow, then threw back his head and laughed. "Any time you want to test that theory, you let us know. We will fight you one at a time. I might even give you an advantage and wear a blindfold. That is the only way you would beat either of us."

Ulrik made a show of considering Edmond's offer. "Maybe not today."

Their laughter was strained, but the tension eased somewhat.

"You should all know, I have returned the binding amulet to its rightful owner." He pursed his lips. That it needed to be said was not in question, and he had long known it to be true, but that did not make his admission any easier. "Gaharet is, and always was, the alpha. It is not a role I want. Nor am I meant to have." He looked away and rested his chin on top of Rebekah's head. "I was wrong to challenge Gaharet all those years ago. My only excuse…" The weight of the pack's expectant stares had him floundering.

Edmond shifted his horse closer and clasped his shoulder. "We know, Ulrik. We forgave you a long time ago."

They had? When? He searched for any hint that Edmond lied, but all he saw was the truth of it. They had forgiven him? Ulrik's grip on Rebekah tightened. Perhaps she sensed his torment, for she reached out and placed her hand over his.

"Thank you." He heaved in a shaky breath, his voice raspier than usual. "All of you."

Edmond leaned back in his saddle. "The only person who is yet to forgive you, Ulrik, is you. Perhaps now is the time to let go of your regrets. Put aside your old ways."

Ulrik let Edmond's words sink in. What was the big chevalier saying? That it was not his lust for revenge on Lothair, nor his challenge to Gaharet that had threatened his place in the pack? Was he the only one still holding himself to account?

Edmond inclined his head at Rebekah. "You have found your mate, yes?"

He glanced down at the women nestled in his arms. He had found his mate, but… "She has not agreed to be mine, and I have yet to tell her everything."

Wary looks all round.

"She is from...Bretaigne." He slid a quick glance at Gaharet. "Like Erin, but she speaks little Franceis."

How much of their conversation did she understand? She was a canny one, his Rebekah, and she had picked up much when he had begun teaching her. Though she busied herself with the bundle of food in her lap, she watched and she listened.

"Two women from Bretaigne?" Edmond's eyebrows rose. "Two mates." He shared a glance with his twin. "Perhaps it is time for us to visit Victor of the Ludenwic wolves and see if we can find some more Bretaigne women."

Ulrik dared not look at Gaharet, lest he reveal more than he should.

"Has anyone heard from Godfrey?" asked Gaharet, turning the conversation away.

"I have. He came to see me." Lance shifted uneasily in his saddle. "He had something on his mind and was not at all himself when we last met."

Was this the day he had seen Godfrey riding through the village on the Vautour estate? "What did he have to say?"

Lance shook his head. "He never had the chance to tell me. One of my farmers informed me of a strange woman in the village wearing your surcoat. He reported seeing her in the company of someone looking remarkably similar to you. We went to investigate and tracked you through the forest. A storm hit and I lost both your scent and Godfrey in that storm."

Aubert and Edmond shared a glance.

Gaharet leaned forward in this saddle. "You know something?"

Edmond's expression darkened. "Perhaps." Another troubled glance between the twins. "We have been spying on Renaud. There is a new eveque in the village. Eveque Faucher."

Ulrik's blood chilled. "Faucher? The priest who hunts for witches and demons?"

"The very one. He arrived a sennight ago, and Renaud was none too pleased with his arrival. Yesterday, he had a change of heart. He gave Faucher a name. Whose name?" Edmond shrugged a muscled shoulder. "We do not know, but Renaud told Faucher he had been working with a chevalier who claimed to be a werewolf."

Lance stiffened. "I have known Godfrey longer than any of you. I find it difficult to believe he was so desperate for power he would murder so many of us."

"Then who did? You?" Aubert pointed his finger at the older chevalier. "Or Edmond?" He tapped his chest. "Or maybe you think I did. That *priest* Faucher," he spat, "is a curse. To us, to everyone. He hunts for those suspected of entertaining the evil arts. He has tortured women accused of witchcraft—their only true crime being herbalists, outcasts, or being the brunt of someone's jealousy or gossip. Renaud gave Faucher a name. Now Godfrey has not responded to a summons from Lothair." A mountain of a man, few would not cower from, Aubert stared Lance down. "Or perhaps you are accusing us of lying."

Ulrik had never heard Aubert utter so many words at once. He usually let his twin speak for him. He had never doubted his intelligence, but Ulrik—all of them, judging by the astonished looks on everyone's faces— now had a new insight into the silent depths that were Aubert. Though, Ulrik noted, neither his twin, nor

Gaharet, looked at all surprised. Gaharet truly was the best man to be alpha.

"Let us not rush to any conclusions. Godfrey's whereabouts is unknown. Given what Aubert and Edmond have learned, it is suspicious, but let us do due diligence first." Gaharet turned to Lance. "Go to the Lagarde estate. See if you can find any trace, any word of him. Perhaps his servants may have some information. Aubert and Edmond—find Faucher. Follow him, spy on him, but be discreet. The last thing we need is for him to discover there is more than one werewolf in Langeais."

"What about Renaud?" asked Edmond.

Ulrik sniggered. "Renaud lost his head over recent events."

Gaharet rolled his eyes.

Ulrik sighed. "Gaharet let me bite him," he explained. "We chained him in silver and let him suffer through the turning, but then..." He shared a glance with Gaharet. "He snapped the chains and part shifted *despite* the silver."

"What?"

"That cannot be."

They all stared, blinking at him owlishly.

Lance gasped. "He part shifted? How is that possible? Bound in silver, he should not have been able to shift at all."

Before tonight, Ulrik would have agreed. "I would not have believed it either, had I not seen it with my own eyes."

"Could you shift, Ulrik, when you were bound?" queried Lance.

"No. I could not feel my wolf at all." Other than when he had first learned of his family's fate, he had never felt more empty. "It is a sight I never wish to see again. He was so strong he snapped his chains. I had no choice but to lop off his head."

Lance shrugged. "I, for one, will not mourn Renaud's passing."

"Nor I," agreed Edmond. "We have suffered enough at his hand. It is only fitting one of us brought him down."

Aubert grunted his agreement. It seemed he had used up his quota of words for now.

"Perhaps," said Gaharet, tugging on his beard, "it is the power of the turning. Aimon broke free of his restraints during his transition. It took both Ulrik and I to bring him down." Gaharet turned to Lance. "When you go to the Lagarde estate, see if you can find anything in Godfrey's library. His father kept a good collection of tomes. I will search mine and see if we can find any answers." He gathered his reins. "We will meet here again in a sennight. Lothair has ordered we re-affirm our vows."

Aubert grumbled something unintelligible, its meaning muffled and lost in his beard.

Lance grimaced, then shrugged. "It is not unexpected." He turned his horse toward the Lagarde estate.

"Stay safe, Lance. All of you." Gaharet placed his hand on his chest. "Remember, I have the binding stone back. If you need to, use the amulet."

Ulrik sat on his horse, Aimon on one side of him, Gaharet on the other, watching as Lance and the twins rode off. "Why did you not tell them the traitor killed your father, Gaharet? And D'Artagnon?"

Gaharet stared after the men. "For the same reason I did not tell them we never suspected the twins."

Ulrik's eyebrows shot up. "You do not believe Godfrey is the traitor? You still suspect Lance?"

Gaharet rested his hands on the pommel of his saddle and chewed on his bottom lip. After a long pause, he said, "Given what the twins have learned about Renaud and Faucher, Godfrey's disappearance implies he is the traitor, but I will not condemn a man so quickly. Lance has proven he will hide the truth when it suits him. He is not above suspicion." Gaharet gathered his reins. "Come. We have a long ride to the keep, and your mate is weary and in need of care."

Ulrik nudged his horse forward, and Rebekah leaned into him, nestling her head against his chest. He had saved her from Lothair and survived the experience, but where did they go from here? Would she accept him as her mate? Would she choose to stay in his century as Erin had? And if she did, after all she had seen in that dank chamber beneath Langeais Keep, would he be able to convince her to undertake the turning? To become one of them?

* * * *

Lothair sat in his chambers staring at an elaborate wall hanging. A beautiful piece he had taken from a monastery as the spoils of war. A battle raged across it—armored chevaliers on horseback, bowmen and pikemen—all engaged in fighting their foe. But it was not them that held his attention. He stared at the single figure in the bottom corner, different from all the others, sword raised and roaring out a challenge. He was no ordinary warrior. Seated on his horse, he had the armor and body of a man, but the head of a wolf. A werewolf. Like Gaharet. Like Ulrik. Like all of Gaharet's men.

He had once thought it a fanciful figure, added at the whimsy of the monk who had created the piece. Now he knew differently. When Renaud had approached him with his strange tale of a beast hidden within a man, Lothair had immediately thought of this figure — this half-man, half-wolf. As Renaud had talked, outlining their abilities and their strengths, Lothair's desire to have it for himself had simmered within his breast.

He wiped his hand across his brow. Now, having witnessed a turning, did he still want it? Was it worth the agony? Should he take the risk? With the knives of his enemies always sharp, and poisons readily available, how long would he survive if he did not?

* * * *

The scared wolf lay low on his belly in the forest, staring at the postern gate of the human building they called Langeais Keep. He had lost the scent of his enemy in the storm and he had yet to find it again. He had retraced his steps, scouted the estate he had tracked him to, but could not find fresh scent. Perhaps he had come here.

He blinked his one good eye at the gate, the stench of blood and death strong. The black wolf had come this way recently. With the yellow wolf. The one who had fled to the little cottage in the woods in the company of the strange woman with green in her hair and silver in her ears. The cottage with the pretty woman with the unusual eyes who he could not get out of his mind. He shook his big, furry head. He could not waste time thinking about her. Not when his attacker remained alive and undetected by the pack.

The need to find his quarry, to exact his vengeance, burned as strong as it had since the day he'd struck him down. Where had he gone? If he was inside this Langeais Keep, he was beyond his reach for now. Too many humans here for him. He would wait. His enemy would come for the black wolf, the alpha. Eventually. Like the enemy had come for him.

Movement at the postern gate caught his eye. Not the man he sought, merely the changing of the guard. Perhaps it was time he made his presence known. Joined forces with the black wolf and fought beside him, as he had once done. With one last look at the walled fortress, he turned and slunk into the forest and headed west. To the d'Louncrais estate. To reunite with his brother.

Chapter Thirty-Nine

Bek woke as they rode beneath a castle gate. Secure and warm in Ulrik's arms, she'd succumbed to sleep not long after they'd left the other knights.

"Not far now, Rebekah," rasped Ulrik into her hair. "We are almost there."

Almost where? Did she care? The heat from his body soaked through her dress, and his muscular arms and thighs bracketed her. He'd come for her. With his head held high and his sword drawn and bloody, he'd strode through the crowd, streaks of red splashed across his coat and droplets of it clinging to his beard. He'd been every bit the medieval Thor she'd first encountered in that cell. *What a man.* Her heart had pounded in rhythm with her clit.

Then he'd thrown down his sword and fallen to his knees. '*My life for hers,*' he'd said, and her heart had cracked wide open.

How could I ever have thought he was like Spider?

Yes, he gave off bad-boy biker vibes. *He's a medieval knight. What did I expect?* He could be violent, savage even, and he had a problem with authority, but that was where the similarities ended. Where Spider was callous and self-serving, Ulrik had a streak of honor flowing through his veins wider than the Thames. He wasn't perfect. He'd made his mistakes in the past. As had she. But within that muscular chest of his, beneath all that overt sexual arrogance, beat a good heart. And, God help her, she wanted to believe it beat for her.

She rubbed the sleep from her eyes as they cantered past a row of mud huts. Tendrils of smoke floated from the pitched straw roofs, and flickering light escaped around the edges of closed shutters. Perched at the top of the hill, backlit by the rising moon, loomed another castle, a keep, dominating the surrounding landscape. A stronghold against this archaic world.

There was so much she still didn't know. Things she didn't understand. She might not have understood all their words, but she'd understood enough. And she could read body language and tone of voice. There was trouble brewing. Back at Langeais Keep, listening to Ulrik talk with the other knights, she'd gotten the gist of it. This Godfrey guy was missing. Probably the one who'd betrayed them. She wouldn't like to be him when they caught up with him. Not with the way the big, growly twin had gotten all up in Lance's face.

Ulrik reined in at the keep and dismounted, and men appeared to lead the horses away. He tucked her hand in his and led her inside the forbidding building, into an immense room with a crackling fire and an enormous table. She barely had a moment to acknowledge Kathryn, rushing to greet Aimon. Or Erin's relief at seeing Gaharet. An older woman, in a flour-dusted apron with the most enormous bosom, whisked her and Ulrik away, up a flight of stairs, along a corridor and into a bedroom.

The door clicked behind them, and they were alone. *Finally.* She ignored the room, all her attention fixed on the big warrior. The man who'd been willing to die for her.

Ulrik stood unmoving by the door, watching her, his fists clenching and unclenching, uncertainty simmering in his eyes. They'd been through a lot since their time at the pond, and there was still a lot that needed to be said. She opened her mouth to speak, then closed it again. Right now, with the memory of her gallant knight storming to her rescue, the last thing she wanted to do was talk.

Bek took a hesitant step toward him. He sucked in a breath, then he was on her, smashing his mouth to hers. His big hands roamed her body, seeking access to her skin. He wasn't the only impatient one.

"Fuck, why do you knights have to wear so much bloody armor?" Bek pulled at his wrist braces, struggling with the buckles as he fumbled with the laces of her dress. "Damn it." She slapped his hands away. "You do you. I'll do me."

He grunted his agreement and tore at his clothes and armor. By the time she had her jeans in a crumpled pile, he'd stripped his tunic over his head and had his breeches around his ankles.

She paused, her hands on the hemline of her dress. God, the man was a work of art. Chiseled abs, slim hips, muscular thighs and... A sound lodged in her throat, part moan, part purr. She wanted her hands on him.

Ulrik kicked his legs free of his breeches and reached for the neckline of her dress. She glimpsed an extended claw as, with a brutal swipe, he tore the material from neck to knee. Her dress slipped off her shoulders and pooled at her feet, leaving her breathless and naked.

He reached for her and, laughing, she threw herself at him. He caught her and she wrapped her legs around his hips, crushing her breasts against his chest.

Hell, yeah.

Bek curled her fingers through his hair, yanking his face to hers and kissed him, desperate, needy and oh so hungry. The crack and the sting of his palm against her ass cheek broke the kiss and made her squeal. She clenched her legs tighter, crushing his hot, hard cock between them. She opened her mouth to protest and he slapped her other cheek.

"The first one," he said, before she could utter a word, "is for not staying in the cottage like I told you to."

She pouted. "And the second one?"

"For not staying in the cottage like Gaharet told you to."

She huffed. "You know I don't take orders well."

"That I do know, and that is what this one is for." He slapped her ass a third time.

"Hey!" Her ass was burning, but the effect of his slaps was not limited to her cheeks. She squirmed, her slickness coating the length of his cock.

His nostrils flared, and a rumble started up in his chest. "You like it when I smack you?"

"No, I—"

He slapped her again, and she couldn't prevent the moan that slipped out.

He rasped out a chuckle. "You can't lie to me, Rebekah. I can *scent* you."

Her face flushed, but not from embarrassment. With heavy-lidded eyes, she met his gaze. "Do it again."

Dark shapes twisted within his irises, and he took her mouth in his with a brutal kiss that spoke of more than passion, more than lust. It staked a claim, declared ownership. And he did own her—her body, her mind and her bruised and distrustful heart. He slapped her again, then he spun them around and pushed her back to the door, entering her with a single, deep thrust. He buried his face in her shoulder, his hot breath teasing her sensitized skin and she bared her neck, giving him greater access.

He went deathly still, his breath stuttering. A heavy, musky scent surrounded her, and the muscles in his shoulders went taut beneath her hands. A deep growl rumbled in his chest, full of longing and a primal hunger that—sank into her bones and had her digging her nails into his firm flesh. She shuddered, her body tightening around his cock, and she could not stop the cry that ripped from her lips. God, this man would be the death of her.

Her cry snapped Ulrik from his stupor. He lowered his nose into the crook of her neck, his chest heaving as he centered himself and got his wolf firmly under control.

Merde, I almost bit her.

Instead, he rasped his tongue over her skin, then licked and nipped his way down the column of her throat and across her collarbone. His gums throbbed with the effort to keep his canines at bay, to use only his blunt human teeth. *Soon, but only with her permission.*

"Ulrik." She clenched her body around him. "Move."

He chuckled. "So demanding," he teased, but he withdrew, then thrust again.

She clung to him, locking her ankles behind his back, digging her heels into the cheeks of his ass. He pressed his mouth to hers, avoiding the temptation, the craving, and his wolf's call to bite her. He plunged his tongue into her mouth, and she met him with a swipe of her own, fighting him for control. Ulrik answered her challenge, refusing to secede. A shiver ran through her and she melted against him.

Ulrik lost himself in her mouth, in the softness of her body. There was nothing in this world like the feeling of *her* channel stretching around his shaft. *Her* body softening against him, as she ceded to his dominance. And, *merde*, he loved it. Loved her. Rebekah. His mate. He tossed his head back and howled, giving voice to his feelings in the only way he knew how.

She clenched around him, her whole body vibrating her pleasure. "Ulrik," she pleaded with a little catch in her voice, and he had never heard a sweeter sound.

He called on his werewolf strength, shifting her weight, and slipped one hand free to cup her breast. He flicked his fingers over the engorged nipple, tweaking it with a pinch. She arched into his hand, thrusting him deeper inside her. His hold over his control almost slipped again, his need for release sizzling through his testicles. But to watch her squirm, hear her panting breaths and to have her beg him to fuck her hard would be worth it.

He pinched her nipple again, harder this time, and paired it with a thrust of his hips. She chased after the sensation and he clenched his jaw. *Not yet.*

"Ulri—" His named faded off into a whimper, as he gave another pump of his hips.

"Yes, Rebekah? Something you need?"

His words came out through gritted teeth, the rasp of his voice a mere whisper of sound.

"I need…"

Another slow grind of his hips, and he plumped her breast in his hand.

"Fuck me. Now. Hard." Her breath hitched. "Please."

Her words hit him, a pulse of heat to his cock, and he released his restraint and gave her what she wanted. What he wanted. He pounded into her, rutting her deep and hard against the door, like the animal he was, his guttural groans mixing with her cries for more. If the occupants of the keep had not guessed what was happening with his earlier howl, they would know now. He cared not. Rebekah was no silent, indiscreet liaison with a married woman, or a hurried coupling with a servant girl in the dark corners of Langeais Keep. She was his, and he wanted the world to know it.

Her climax hit and her pussy spasmed around his cock, her hoarse cry bouncing off the stone walls of the room. Sensation ripped up his spine, and he stiffened, plunging deep one last time, roaring his release as she milked him of his seed.

He collapsed, spent, his chest heaving. She flopped her head on his shoulder, her pussy still fluttering around his semi-hard cock. He would never get enough of her, not in his lifetime. Ulrik wrapped his arms around her waist and planted a kiss on her sweaty brow.

He had to tell her the truth about his past. After all she had been through because of him, he owed it to her. But with what they had just shared, and Rebekah beginning to trust him, would the truth be the one thing sure to drive her away?

Chapter Forty

Ulrik walked her limp and sated body to the bed and laid her down. She sank into the downy softness of the mattress with a groan. A bed. Such a simple pleasure, but one she'd sorely missed. She stretched, a languid arching of her body, her gaze catching on the rounded globes of Ulrik's firm naked ass as he strode to a table. Her own ass cheeks still tingled from the spanking he'd given her, and the thought of it brought a fresh flood of heat to her body.

He threw a glance over his shoulder at her, a wicked smirk teasing at the corner of his mouth. She sucked in her breath. Was that...a hint of *fang*? Her pussy clamped down on a throbbing emptiness and another flush of heat washed over her. More dampness pooled between her thighs. God, if he made her any hotter, she'd spontaneously combust.

His nostrils flared and heat simmered in his eyes, but he turned away, tipping a jug of water into a bowl, and soaking a cloth. He returned to the bed, and with more care than she'd thought a big warrior capable of, he tenderly washed her from head to toe. Like she was something precious, someone special. A princess or a duchess. Someone other than the parolee barmaid from Deptford.

Bek looked away, a lump forming in her throat. Such gentleness, such devotion to her needs, had her choking back emotion. A girl could get used to this. She wanted to get used to this. Any appeal, slight as it was, to return to her less-than-perfect life in the twenty-first century, died at the thought of living it without this. Without Ulrik. If that meant she had to give up coffee, go without a bra and never get another tattoo…well… Bek could live with that.

The bed dipped as he lay beside her, curling on his side to face her, darker shades dancing in the depths of his eyes. Her nipples pebbled and her heart thudded in her chest. He brushed his hand across her cheek so tenderly her eyes burned with the sting of tears. Without breaking their connection, she captured his hand, brought it to her lips and kissed his palm.

He shifted uneasily and broke her stare, dropping his hand to caress her shoulder. "I need to explain why I reacted the way I did at the pond."

His voice was raspier than normal and thick with emotion.

"Okay." Nothing he said would change the way she felt about him. Lord knew she'd done some monumentally stupid things in her life. She'd paid a price for them, too, though not one as hefty as Ulrik.

His Adam's apple bobbed in his throat. "Comte Lothair had been in power for but a few years. We had yet to see the ruler he would become, the one we would all come to fear. I was young and" — he sucked on his bottom lip—"idealistic, and truth be told, a little arrogant." A half-smile, half-grimace settled on his lips. "I was a score and two years old. Impetuous, hotheaded and I believed in my own importance a little too much than was good for me. My father was a viscount, and one day I would take up that mantle."

He was silent for a moment, staring at his hand as his fingers stroked over her shoulder and down her arm.

"Lothair was waging a war against another count, fighting for territory. He needed funds to support his army." His lips thinned and his brow creased into a frown. "He declared an increase in taxes. Not uncommon, but this was a substantial increase. My family could well afford the extra tax, but there were many who could not. People who barely had enough food to feed their children. Winter was coming. Already, autumn had been harsh—raining for weeks on end, flooding the rivers and creeks. Livestock had drowned and crops had failed. Almost every day we were seeing more and more peasants at our gate begging for food."

He flopped onto his back and stared up at the ceiling. "These people, farmers, servants, some merchants, could ill afford this tax and they had neither the money nor the power to fight it."

She rolled onto her side, facing him. This wasn't what she'd been expecting, this tale of injustice. "But you did."

He grimaced. "I *thought* I did. I believed my family's wealth and power, our title, made me immune to any punishment."

Bek reached for his hand, clasping it in hers.

His loaded sigh carried all his regret. "Other nobles, like Gaharet's father and mine, tried to reason with Lothair to get him to reduce the size of the increase, but Lothair refused to be swayed. I believed we could do more. We *should* do more."

His grip on her hand tightened.

"When the people revolted, I was amongst them, adding my voice to theirs. I thought it would help, and I thought…" He blinked his eyes shut and shook his head. "I do not know what I was thinking. A member of the noble class supporting the disenfranchised peasants…"

He opened his eyes, leveling a look at her so filled with pain it broke her heart. "I *sorely* underestimated the impact it would have."

Yeah, Rebekah could imagine. It would have gone over about as well as Megxit had with royals. "What did Lothair do?"

Ulrik rested the back of his hand on his forehead. "Gaharet's father got word that Lothair was sending the keep guard for me. So, my parents arranged for me to go to Bretaigne. There is a pack there, in Ludenwic. They thought if I were not here, Lothair's wrath would cool and he would soon forget my role in the uprising."

"But Lothair didn't forget." No, the man she'd met in that dungeon wasn't the forgetting type. Especially not with a challenge like that to his authority. "He couldn't get to you, so he took it out on your family."

His bearded face crumpled. "My parents begged the pack to keep my family's imprisonment a secret from me. They thought it best if I… If I did not know. They feared I would have returned." His voice cracked. "I would have. I would *never* have left my parents, my sisters, to suffer the fate they did had I known. *Never.*"

He forced the words out through his clenched jaw, his grip crushing her hand. Bek kept silent, despite the pain in her fingers.

"Because I did not return, Lothair condemned them to death. I lost my whole family because of my ignorance, my hubris."

Bek pulled her hand free and straddled Ulrik's thighs, and he wrapped his arms around her, drawing her close.

She leaned her forehead against his. "You would have come for them. Like you came for me. I *know* you would have, and I'm sure they knew it, too. You are nothing, *nothing*, like the man who betrayed me. You stood up for those less fortunate than you and tried to right a wrong. It is not you who is to blame for your family's deaths. That sin rests with Lothair."

She took his face in her hands, her heart breaking for him. "You are a good man, Ulrik Voclain, and don't you *dare* think otherwise. Without you, I would never have survived in this world of yours." She leaned down and pressed her lips to his.

He pulled away. "I wish... That is not all. I... I learned nothing from my mistake. When I returned and heard of my family's fate, I wanted vengeance. Nothing short of Lothair's death would satisfy me. I wanted the pack to turn on Lothair. To take him down and destroy him as he had destroyed my family."

Bek touched a hand to his scars, tracing the raised edges of skin. "Gaharet wouldn't do it, would he? He was the friend you challenged and lost."

"Yes. One of many decisions I have lived to regret. Rebekah, I know I have done little to deserve you..."

Bek sat up. "Ulrik, no one is perfect. Least of all me. My family are a bunch of crooks. *I* was an outlaw gang member's girlfriend. No one could accuse me of being sweet and innocent." She poked him in the chest. "You saved me from that awful guard that was going to rape me." She poked him again. "You rescued me from Langeais Keep." Another poke. "Twice." And another poke and this time she kept her finger there. "You *do* deserve me, and maybe... Maybe we deserve each other."

"You do not wish to return—"

"I'm staying." She frowned, catching her bottom lip between her teeth. "If you'll have me."

"If I will have—" He pulled her to him and rolled them over, caging her with his arms and settling his thighs between hers. "Baby, if you stay, then I am never letting you go."

She couldn't help the grin that spread across her face.

"But...um..." His forehead crinkled in a frown. "There is something I must tell you first."

"Oh?" She had a sinking feeling in her chest and a lump formed in her throat. "You're not...already married, are you?"

"What? No!" He huffed out a breath. "I do not wish to frighten you, after..."

Whatever it was, was it that bad? "Tell me."

"To stay with me, you will need to become like me. A werewolf."

An unexpected thrill skipped up her spine. Why did the prospect of becoming a werewolf not frighten her? It should, but she couldn't dredge up an ounce of fear.

"I have to become a werewolf? Like...you'll have to bite me?"

He eyed her warily. "Mmhmm."

"Okay, I'll…bite." *Pun intended.* "Why?" *Can I not summon an emotion other than curiosity?*

"For one, we are far longer lived than humans, and…" He stroked a hand down her face and her pulse did a little hop, skip and a jump. "Werewolves can only procreate with other werewolves, remember."

"Oh." Right. He'd told her that at the pond.

She stared at his bearded chin as she processed what he was saying. Was this the werewolf equivalent of the 'do you want kids' conversation? Was he…proposing? Kind of? Bek rubbed her hands across his chest, enjoying the tactile feel of his hair against her palms, her mind racing. There was a lot more involved than 'putting a ring on it'. A lot, *lot* more. It should have her running for the hills.

"I'll be able to turn into a wolf, like you? Like Aimon and Kathryn? And Erin?"

He nodded.

"And I'll get an extra strong sense of smell, enhanced hearing, perfect eyesight and increased strength?"

He considered her list, then nodded. "Yes. And more. There are many benefits to becoming a werewolf. A longer lifespan, protection from disease and our ability to heal most wounds, even those that would kill a human. And there is nothing like the feel of running free in the forest as a wolf."

And she would be with Ulrik. Bek wasn't seeing a downside here. "What's the catch? I mean, I get it. You'll have to bite me, but it not like my tatts didn't come without pain."

"I…"

"Oh." Her eyes widened. "That priest. In the dungeon. That's what was wrong with him, wasn't it? You'd bitten him."

"Yes, but it need not be that way," he rushed out. "Renaud was a despicable, scheming excuse for a priest who deserved every bit of the agony of a turning. We *could* have eased his transition, but we chose not to. I would never put you through the pain Renaud suffered."

She tracked his line of sight toward the table. Beside the bowl and pitcher sat a goblet. "What's in that?"

"A herbal mixture."

Bek eyed the goblet. "Mm, okay, and it does…what, exactly?"

"It will take away your pain, and you will sleep through the worst of the turning."

"Huh." Who'd have thought. A medieval anesthetic. "It probably tastes like crap, right?"

"Uh." He tilted his head to the side. "I guess. I do not actually know as I have never… I was born…" He regarded her, confusion simmering his eyes. "You…are not afraid?"

Bek shrugged, and Ulrik's gaze dipped to her breasts at the movement.

He's such a boob man.

"I thought Erin was brave, but you… I have yet to meet a more courageous woman than you. You are…an amazing woman, Rebekah Clarke. *The* most amazing woman, even if you do have the foulest, most defiant mouth of any woman I have ever met."

Ulrik chuckled, dropping a kiss on her nose, then her lips. He licked the seam of her mouth and she opened for him. He dipped his tongue in briefly, withdrawing far too soon for Bek's liking.

Bek grinned. "I like you, too. In fact…" She ducked her chin. "I think I more than like you. Maybe, I think, I might have…fallen in love with you."

Ulrik stilled above her, and Bek waited, anxious she'd said too much, too soon. She'd been with Spider for a year, and she'd never dared mention the 'L' word. She'd known Ulrik for…how long? Two weeks?

He stared at her for long moments. Had she ever felt this self-conscious before? Then he swooped in and took her mouth in his and for a moment Bek lost her train of thought, her concerns.

He pulled back with a final suck of her bottom lip. "I love you, too, Rebekah. And that mouth of yours very, very much."

He *loved* her? The truth burned bright in his eyes. He loved her.

"So, um…" She trailed a finger down his chest. "Does that mean I'm your mate, given that you're a wolf shifter? Is that how it works?"

Her shifter romance read hadn't gotten everything wrong.

"Oh, yes. Rebekah Clarke, you are unequivocally, undeniably and forever my mate."

He took her mouth in his, his arms bracketing her, surrounding her with his body, his scent. His cock announced its presence, hot and hard against her pussy. It was all she could do to think straight, but she still had questions. She wrested her mouth from his, her breath coming out in little pants.

"What do I have to do? Do I just…drink the stuff, lie down, and you bite me?"

"That is one way." He ground himself against her and his heated gaze dipped to her breasts. "There is another. Do you trust me, Rebekah?"

Chapter Forty-One

"Do you trust me, Rebekah?"

An image slid into Bek's mind. Of them in a sweaty mess of tangled limbs, thrusting, panting and moaning as he buried his large canines in her neck. There had to be something wrong with her. Some faulty wiring in her brain. Some dodgy hormone or synapse that fired up her lust, making her throb with it, instead of kicking in her survival instinct and urging her to flee.

Did she trust him? *Hell, yeah.* She wasn't running. She was all in.

"Bring it on, wolfman."

He did that growling thing again, and she all but orgasmed as it rumbled through her. Then he dipped his head, his large hands cupping and plumping her breasts, as his mouth licked and sucked, his teeth scraping over her taut nipple. With the sting of a nip and the rasp of his tongue, he devoured her. First one breast, then the other. Never had a man worshiped her breasts as he did now. It undid her, had her writhing beneath him and clutching her fingers in his hair to hold him in place. She never wanted him to stop.

Ulrik untangled her hands from his hair and held them above her head. He pinned her with his gaze as much as he did with his hands, and she could not look away. She could not breathe.

He pressed her hands to the bed. "Do not move them."

She nodded, trapped in his orbit, incapable and unwilling to break free. He slid down her body, a wicked smile curling up the corners of his mouth. His tongue flicked out to lick his lips as he slipped an arm beneath her thigh and lifted her leg over his shoulder.

With only his gaze holding her prisoner, he swiped his tongue along the length of her seam. Bek flung her head back, her mouth dropping open in a silent gasp, and she all but bowed off the bed. He took another swipe, swirling his tongue around her clit, and this time she did cry out.

She'd wondered, back in the forest, if he'd be as good with his tongue as he was with his fingers. Now she knew. He was better. He raised his head and grinned, his lips glistening with her juices. It took everything she had to keep her hands where he'd put them, wanting desperately to press his mouth back to her throbbing flesh.

He shifted her other leg over his shoulder, opening her up and baring her for his perusal. "So pretty," he murmured. He teased her folds open with his fingers. "So pink and so wet. And all mine."

He set about licking and sucking her pussy until she was a mindless mess, whimpering and begging, hovering on the very edge, but never quite tipping over.

"Do you want to come, baby?" The murmur of his words, his hot breath against her core, had her clenching on air.

"Yes. Yes. *Yes.*"

Then his tongue replaced the emptiness, slipping inside her, and with a flick of his thumb across her clit, Bek exploded. Her hands flew to her sides, clutching at the blankets. Bek squeezed her thighs on his face, keeping him in place as his tongue stroked inside her, wringing every last shiver and moan until she collapsed on the bed, panting.

Through hooded lids, she watched him. He gave her one last lick, a self-satisfied smirk on his face, then slipped her limp legs from his shoulders and got to his knees. He wrapped his hand around his cock and gave it a long stroke. Then another, rubbing his pre-cum down over the crown. He wasn't finished with her yet.

He flipped her over, dragged her ass in the air and pressed her shoulders to the down-filled mattress. Gripping her hips with those long fingers of his, he rubbed himself through her slick and swollen folds.

"Are you ready, Rebekah?"

She had the presence of mind to moan a response, nothing more. He lined himself up at her entrance, and slowly, inexorably slid inside her, stretching and filling her as she quivered around him.

"*Merde.* You feel like…" He moaned. "Bliss."

He ground his hips against her ass in a circular press that pushed deep, touching places and stroking previously unknown nerve endings into life.

He groaned again. "Rebekah, you ruin me. I cannot hold back much longer."

Bek moaned into the bedding. "Then don't."

He howled, and the sound reverberated around the room. With a thrust of his knees, he spread her legs further and impaled her on his cock with a savagery she had only ever dreamed of. With her face pressed into the bed, she had no option but to take all that he had to give. He pounded into her, laying waste to her desire and challenging her to new heights that threatened to break down her walls and leave her crumbling. She encouraged him, goaded him to push her higher, gasping and moaning her need. He did not leave her wanting.

Then he dropped his body over hers, bringing him into full body contact and his hand slipped around to pinch her nub. Pleasure streaked through her and her orgasm hit with blinding force. She screamed, and he pinched her clit again and again as her core spasmed around him. He stiffened and thrust deep once more. He roared out his release and struck, sinking his teeth into the flesh of her shoulder. Pain, sharp and deep, sparked her orgasm higher, rolling over her like a freight train on steroids until she thought she would pass out from the ecstasy. She collapsed beneath him, trembling. A trickle of blood dribbled down her shoulder.

He rolled his weight to the side and pulled her with him, spooning her from behind, the rasp of his tongue across the wound sending shivers through her body. She floated, her body tingling and her mind lost in a post-orgasmic bliss even the throbbing of her shoulder couldn't deflate.

It started with a tingle, her skin beneath his lips becoming oversensitive and the slide of his tongue annoying. She pulled away. The tingle became a burn, like a scald from coffee too hot to drink. The burn spread. Down her arm and across her chest, its fiery trail sped. Fingers of fire had found her blood and raced through her arteries and veins. A spasm gripped her body, and she cried out, her back arching as pain ripped through her.

Ulrik's comforting presence left her and she whimpered, curling herself into a ball. The pain, the fire, reached her stomach and her lungs seized at the strength of it. Giving birth would be less painful.

Ulrik appeared before her, the goblet in his hand. He cupped the back of her head and pressed the rim of the goblet to her lips. "Drink."

She took a sip and nearly gagged. The burning continued to spread, reaching her thighs and calves. No wonder that priest had been out of his mind. She grabbed the goblet from Ulrik, steeled herself, and threw it back like a shot of alcohol. Just in time. Another spasm ripped through her.

Ulrik took the goblet from her shaking hands and tossed it aside, then climbed on the bed and pulled her into his embrace. He said nothing, holding her, and it wasn't long before her eyelids drooped.

"Shhsrong sstuff," she mumbled, her head flopping back against his shoulder.

"Sleep now, baby. I will watch over you. I will take good care of you."

Her head swam, and she could no longer feel her limbs. A heaviness settled over her body and the fire in her veins lessened, mere sparks from embers as her vision clouded.

"When next you wake," he murmured, a whisper of breath on her forehead, "you will be one of us."

The love in his eyes was the last thing she saw before darkness claimed her and she slipped into a deep sleep.

Epilogue

Ulrik slipped from the bed and eased the covers over Rebekah, tucking her in. Her eyelids fluttered and she moaned in her sleep, but she did not wake. He brushed a strand of dark hair off her forehead and dropped a kiss on her nose. How had he been lucky enough to come across a woman so perfect for him? And so forgiving? She had said he *did* deserve her. That they deserved each other. He would spend the rest of his life proving it to her.

With one last look at Rebekah sleeping peacefully, Ulrik slipped from their bedchamber. Three days he had stayed by her side, spooning more of Constance's ghastly concoction between her lips, feeding her slices of raw and bloody meat, washing her down with a damp cloth and holding her in his arms as her body transformed. She had awoken, a fully transitioned werewolf, and they had spent three more days in bed wrapped in each other's arms, only leaving it to eat

He grinned. If he'd been worried about how his mate would handle her new body, he should have known better. Rebekah had wanted to test her newfound abilities straight away. He had convinced her a bath and rest were more important, and soon fatigue had pulled at her. After he had assured her this was normal, that Aimon had spent the first week mostly sleeping, she had returned to bed. Soon, he would begin her training. His cock surged, pushing at his breeches. Training between mates, he had heard, often led to sex. Sex with Rebekah was something he would never get enough of.

He stood in the doorway watching her — the steady rise and fall of her chest, the smile tugging at her lips as she dreamed. He had never felt so blessed, and yet the situation he was bringing his newly turned mate into concerned him. For all that three of the pack had found their mates, they had never been more at risk than they were now. Never had their kind, their very existence, been more vulnerable or faced so many threats.

Renaud was dead and they had appeased Lothair — for now — but the fact remained, they still had a traitor amongst them. Did Godfrey's absence speak to his guilt? Or was Gaharet right to be cautious of Lance? And what of this new threat? Eveque Faucher? *The witch hunter.* For what reason had he come? From what Edmond had said, it was unlikely Renaud had sent for him. So who had?

He took the stairs down to the hall, following the echo of voices. Anne, Gaharet, Erin and Farren stood around the central fire pit. Erin's shoulders drooped and her face was pale beneath her the veil of her blonde hair. She rubbed her hand over her stomach. Gaharet paced, agitated steps backward and forward as he tugged at his beard. Anne, her expression darker than an autumn thundercloud, glared at Gaharet. Farren cupped his hand over his mouth, amusement twinkling in his hazel eyes.

"I had a colleague who had morning sickness for nine months. Morning, noon and night," said Erin, swallowing hard, as though just the thought of being sick churned her stomach. "So, *excuse me*, if I'm not feeling super excited about being pregnant right now."

Gaharet halted in his pacing. "Nine months!" He shot a concerned look at Anne. "Surely werewolf blood would cure this?"

Anne snorted. "Pregnancy is not a wound or a disease to be cured, Gaharet. It is a natural bodily function. A woman's body, whether human or werewolf, goes through many changes during a pregnancy. If I remember correctly, your mother was ill for a time when she carried both you and D'Artagnon."

"How long was my mother ill for?"

Anne levied a flat look at Gaharet. "Three months or so."

"Three months!"

The look Anne sent Gaharet had Ulrik backing away. His friend was on his own.

"I am beginning to understand Erin's less than enthusiastic response," Gaharet muttered.

Ulrik pursed his lips and tried to quell his amusement. The old cook's whole body vibrated with her displeasure. Gaharet was a wise alpha, and usually an astute one. Clearly his instincts were failing him now.

Anne fisted her hands on her ample hips and arched an eyebrow. "Now I am sure your concern is for your mate, not for the lack of what is happening in the bedchamber."

Gaharet's face flushed and Anne's eyebrows descended into a frown.

"I taught you better than that, boy. You will be looking after this lovely mate of yours properly, or you will answer to Old Anne. Now, dear," she put her hand on Erin's shoulder, "ginger brew will help with the queasiness."

"Ginger brew, Anne," agreed Gaharet. "Lots of it. As much as Erin can bear."

She grunted at him. "Just like your father."

Gaharet glared at him. "Do not laugh, Ulrik. It will be your turn soon enough."

Ulrik looked away, stifling his mirth, and spotted Gascon standing in the doorway. Gascon blinked, blinked again and opened his mouth to speak, then closed it again.

Ulrik stepped toward him, a familiar scent tickling his nose. He called his wolf to the surface, the hackles on his neck rising. "Gascon? Is there a problem?"

"Forgive the intrusion, Mon Seigneur Ulrik, but there is someone here I think you should all see."

Gascon stepped aside.

A big black wolf, heavily scarred, padded through the doorway. Long thought dead, staring at them with his one good eye, stood D'Artagnon. Gaharet's younger brother was alive.

Want to see more from this author?
Here's a taster for you to enjoy!

The Descendants:
The Wolf and His Witch
K.E Turner

Coming Summer 2025

Excerpt

Paris, France

Beep. Beep. Beep.

Balls deep in the woman of his dreams, Gabriel paused.

Beep. Beep. Beep.

The woman beneath him blurred then disappeared altogether as his eyes fluttered open to find himself exactly as he'd gone to bed. Alone. Gabriel groaned and rolled over, seeking the red numerals of his alarm clock. 2.45 am. He flopped over on his back, his unsatisfied cock tenting the blanket. *Putain.* He'd dreamed of her again.

He scrubbed his hand across his face, trying to banish her from his thoughts. Blue eyes and a sexy smile goaded him.

Beep. Beep. Beep.

Gabriel frowned. What the hell *was* that? It wasn't loud like a car alarm, nor the *whoop whoop* of a fire alarm, but to his sensitive hearing, it might as well have been.

Beep. Beep. Beep.

Putain. He threw back the covers. One thing was for certain — it wouldn't stop until he figured out what it was and shut it the fuck off.

Grumbling, he dragged himself and his throbbing balls from his bed and padded out into his living area. Christmas lights winked on and off on the over-decorated Christmas tree — courtesy of his twin brothers — washing his living area in green, red and blue. Had the flashing lights tripped an alarm? No. The annoying as fuck beeping was coming from his office.

He turned his back on the Christmas monstrosity, padded across his living area and nudged open his office door. Numerous computer screens stared back at him as he pushed into the room. Black, silent, the only thing he saw in them was his own naked reflection. Except for one.

Beep. Beep. Beep.

A green curser flashed in time with the beeping. An alarm he'd set. For what? His fingers raced over the keyboard, calling up the data. He stilled, staring at the screen.

Fuck me.

Someone was mining the internet for information on Eveque Faucher. Someone in San Francisco, California. It was her. It had to be. The witch sent back in time to target Faucher — the tenth century witch hunter and his ancestor's arch nemesis. Sent back to prevent the slaughter of thousands of woman — witches — and change the course of history.

Bella Rodriguez. The witch. Gabriel and his brothers wouldn't be born if she didn't go. She'd stayed and mated his ancestor. She would become his paternal-many-times great grandmother.

Gabriel snatched up his phone, the ache in his balls momentarily forgotten. It was time for him to go to California.

About the Author

K.E. Turner can't remember a time when she wasn't writing stories or reading books — as a teenager in class instead of doing math, in her lunch break at work, or at home when there's housework to be done. With a love of history, mystery, suspense, paranormal, and romance, she likes combining more than one element in her stories.

An award winning author, she writes spicy paranormal romances and romantic suspense, with strong but good hearted heroes, smart, sassy heroines and an often unexpected villain or two, to shake things up.

A Western Australian based author, she lives with her husband, two dogs, two cats and a menagerie of farm animals on their property in the southern region of the state. A hopeless romantic, she enjoys beach sunsets, sitting by the wood fire with a good book, a nice shiraz and good food.

K.E. Turner loves to hear from readers. You can find her contact information, website details and author profile page at https://www.firstforromance.com

ENTWINED PUBLISHING